George Green was born in Dublin and brought up in Tipperary, where he lived in a house built on an ancient burial mound. After university he embarked on a career in sport and leisure in the hope that it would not be too difficult and help him meet girls. Ten years later he realized his mistake, took an MA in Creative Writing, began teaching and now works for the Department of English and Creative Writing at Lancaster University. *Hawk* is his second novel, his first being the highly acclaimed *Hound*.

For more information see <u>www.george-green.co.uk</u>

Also by George Green

Hound

and published by Bantam Books

Hawk

GEORGE GREEN

BANTAM BOOKS

LONDON • TORONTO • SYDNEY • AUCKLAND • JOHANNESBURG

HAWK
A BANTAM BOOK : 0 553815385
9780553815382

Originally published in Great Britain by Bantam Press,
a division of Transworld Publishers

PRINTING HISTORY
Bantam Press edition published 2005
Bantam edition published 2006

1 3 5 7 9 10 8 6 4 2

Set in 10.5/13pt Times by
Falcon Oast Graphic Art Ltd.

Bantam Books are published by Transworld Publishers,
61–63 Uxbridge Road, London W5 5SA,
a division of The Random House Group Ltd,
in Australia by Random House Australia (Pty) Ltd,
20 Alfred Street, Milsons Point, Sydney, NSW 2061, Australia,
in New Zealand by Random House New Zealand Ltd,
18 Poland Road, Glenfield, Auckland 10, New Zealand
and in South Africa by Random House (Pty) Ltd,
Isle of Houghton, Corner of Boundary Road & Carse O'Gowrie,
Houghton 2198, South Africa

Printed and bound in Germany by
GGP Media, Pössneck.

Papers used by Transworld Publishers are natural, recyclable
products made from wood grown in sustainable forests. The
manufacturing processes conform to the environmental
regulations of the country of origin.

*For Adrienne, without whom nothing
really happens*

ACKNOWLEDGEMENTS

When I first started writing novels they told me that I'd be spending a lot of time in an attic on my own. They were right about that. But what they didn't tell me about was the astonishing number of people it takes to get a book written. I must thank Lizzy Kremer for her energy and encouragement, Simon Taylor for his careful editing and understanding, and both of them for an insight into what I was trying to do that often exceeded my own. Amongst others who helped, lent books, made useful comments and smiled encouragingly were: Saleel Nurbhai and Kathy Flann who gave tireless and generous criticism of the early chapters; Steve Miller and Anthony Jones who gave ideas, talked comics and kept me honest; the nice person who emailed me from Belgium about writing chariot races; Linda Anderson for her support from way back; Harry Whitehead for reminding me why writing is important; Rory, Tyrone and Charles for taking an interest; and finally Graham Mort, Paul Farley, Jayne Steel and any number of blameless students for not complaining too much when my thoughts were in the first century AD instead of where they probably should have been.

1

General Varus was not feeling well. The night before he was due to march east from Gaul to begin his subjugation of the rebellious German tribes, he ate an oyster that disagreed with him. Varus had actually eaten several dozen oysters, but his doctors thought probably only one of them had made him ill. The result left him prostrate, retching and helpless. He was certainly unable to get on a horse for a full day's march. Varus refused to lead his army in a litter or carriage. He wanted to march out of the camp at the head of his men, on horseback, like a latter-day Alexander.

His officers reported that everything was ready for the march to begin.

His doctors advised him to delay the start of the march, as he was not yet well.

His officers told him that delaying the march would be damaging to morale.

His doctors mused on the probable effect on morale if, as was likely to happen, two hundred paces into the march the General had to jump off his horse and sprint for the bushes while tugging frantically at his underwear. Not so much like the incomparable and warlike Alexander, more like a fat old man with bad guts.

Varus thought about that prospect, and then agreed to let the army march out of the camp without him. He lay in bed in a pool of oily sweat for three days in the grip of stomach cramps that bent his body like a grasshopper's leg.

On the third morning he woke, feeling a little better. His doctors gave him some of the truly revolting lentil porridge that the soldiers lived on and which was regarded as a sovereign remedy for a rebellious stomach. If you were well it made you feel ill, but if you were ill it made you well. Varus had never been a legionary and so hadn't eaten it before. To his amazement the bowl of greasy pulses stayed down, though the General now knew why most officers regarded legionary's porridge as the greatest spur to the desire for promotion in the whole army.

The next day, still fragile but somewhat restored, and determined that fighting berserk Germans was preferable to eating even one more bowl of lentil porridge, Varus carefully mounted his horse and, wincing and shifting from side to side in his saddle, trotted briskly at the head of his personal guard to catch up with the three legions marching into Germany.

In the General's saddle-bag was the Emperor Augustus' most recent letter. Varus had it by heart.

Identify the German tribes in revolt with all possible

speed, subjugate and punish them and then withdraw to your winter quarters. On no account commit all your men at one time to one endeavour. Better to lose a battle and withdraw with the army intact than lose the war. This is not an expedition to extend the Empire, and even if we wished it to be so you do not have sufficient troops or resources for such a venture. Your mission is to consolidate and pacify our northern border. I repeat, General Varus, for emphasis: quell the rebellious Germans severely and quickly, fill them with regret for their foolishness, ensure that they will not rise lightly again, then leave. I rely on you to keep our Northern Command an effective fighting force.

It was addressed to 'Varus, Commander, Imperial Army of the Rhine', and signed 'Augustus, Emperor'. No salute, no recognition of his achievements or even his rank, none of the warmth he deserved. Varus was, he thought, a distant cousin of the Emperor, but this relationship had never been officially acknowledged. Augustus didn't like him, had always treated him as a slightly dim-witted servant. He had made Varus a general because there was no one else available, and hadn't taken the trouble to hide his unwillingness to entrust the expedition to him. Varus smiled as his black stallion trotted swiftly towards the rearguard of the huge Roman army in front of him. The Emperor was an old man and had an old man's fear of adventure. He, Varus, would finish the German problem once and for all. Augustus would curse him for disobeying orders, but Old Butter-No-Parsnips would smile as he did so. The Empire would be larger, stronger and more secure, and Varus would have a Triumph, would march through Rome at the head of his victorious army, the envy of every man and the desire of every woman. Augustus would welcome his return home, flatter him, shower him with honours. The Emperor might even admit he had misjudged him. Well, on reflection, probably not that, but he would know it in his heart.

The General smiled to himself and kicked his horse forward. He could live without the apology. He'd settle for the Triumph.

The Seventeenth, Eighteenth and Nineteenth legions had set out to join Varus' garrison command from Rome a month before, swelling it to eight times its normal size. They marched ten abreast in legionary style, a stride strict enough to be military but natural enough to allow a man to walk all day for weeks on end without breaking down. There was pride in their marching; they were the legions whose pace was so consistently precise that the army used them to measure distance when it had to be exact. When these legions marched two thousand paces, it was a mile, no more nor less.

When Varus and his guard caught up with the vanguard of the army, deep within the Teutoburg Forest, the General knew immediately that he had problems he hadn't foreseen.

The legions were stretched in a thin column, moving slowly through the dense centre of the huge forest. The officers reported that for the last four days the legionaries had not marched ten abreast, or any number abreast at all, and their step had been anything but precise. They had trickled across the ground like water, scrambling, tripping and cursing their way through the forest. There were no roads or paths, no straight lines, no space between the trees wider than a man. Much of the time they could not see their way in front of them. On every side a dark wall of leaves and wood rose up and joined above them in a thick mat that allowed only the most occasional shaft of light through. The day was eternal twilight, the night an absolute dark which moonlight – if it even existed in Germany – could not penetrate. Young trees spread their branches at head height so that the soldiers had to duck and sway to avoid them; mature trees stood a hundred feet high and six feet wide across the soldiers' way, and between the growing and mature trees were every size and shape of fallen trunk and branch, laid across each other at random angles and in haphazard directions and crumbling with slick dark rot and pungent fungus. Everywhere around the fallen trees were thick bushes, fierce with thorns and slippery with mildew, that tugged and snagged at the hessian puttees the legionaries wore to protect their calves. A sheen of damp and mould covered everything, like grease in an ill-tended kitchen. It rained constantly: sometimes a thin haze that crystallized on men's tunics and then sank silently into their bones until the legionaries ground their teeth with the ache of it, sometimes a curtain of water that splashed audibly when it hit the ground, made every handhold treacherous and turned the ground into a swamp.

And reports were coming in of a different type of danger. There were shadows in the forest, wraiths that the nervous soldiers saw out of the corners of their eyes but that slipped away as soon as they looked directly at them. The Romans were in a foreign land and far from home, and the gods they had brought with them – so virile in the bright warmth of Italy – seemed old and cowed and timorous in the cold shadows of the silent forest.

The men pushed and hacked their way forward, slipping between the obstacles any way they could. Within an hour of entering the forest the officers had given up trying to maintain any sort of recognizable formation. The soldiers initially pushed forward briskly enough, but the baggage wagons behind them could not cross the fallen trees. The officers then ordered the trees to be cleared and straight roads driven through them, but the men were soon exhausted, and so they gave up on straight roads and began to look for the lines of least resistance. This meant winding and circling along narrow paths that might lead away from their direction of march, and often the carts would stutter along the track for a mile only to emerge almost where they had begun. The forward column of men would march for an hour and then see the middle of the army appear in front of them, and there was total confusion.

At the end of the first day after his arrival, General Varus came up from the rear of the army and held a meeting of his officers. He demanded to know why the army was moving so slowly, why there was so much noise, why the men were complaining. The officers were good soldiers, professionals, and their reply was unanimous and unsparing. A huge African captain called 'Bull' by his men spoke for them all. In short, brutal sentences he told of an army on the verge of chaos, moving cramped and blind over impossible terrain towards an enemy who must surely know it was coming. Once he had finished, he paused, then sat down slowly.

The situation was the exact opposite of the conditions that any Roman veteran liked. There was silence as the officers waited for Varus to speak. He looked around the tent. Every man met the General's gaze, nodded agreement to what had been said. They waited for him to make up his mind.

Varus looked around and understood the situation. He was aware they thought him many kinds of fool, but he knew what they wanted him to say, and he knew that there are times when a leader has to appear to listen, even if he has no intention of committing himself to what he hears. He gestured in a way that gave them the floor.

'What do you suggest?'

The leaders of the great army leant forward and talked into the night.

It was agreed that a series of groups of lightly armed sappers would go in front of the army to cut a trail as best they could. The soldiers would cut and hack and trample themselves into exhaustion for an hour, then another group would relieve them. They would work around the clock. At night they would make progress while the army rested and reorganized, and the army would gradually catch up during the day.

On the fifth day Varus rode up to just behind the vanguard of the army and smiled. It was raining, the usual bone-chilling German drizzle that made him yearn for the warm dry slopes of Tuscany. The rain-clouds made the gloom even deeper under the trees, but Varus was content. The path-clearing idea was working. The way was rough and the wagons would find it heavy going, but the soldiers were getting better at clearing the undergrowth and the way was passable.

Varus rode around a sharp bend in the trail and was forced to halt. The vanguard were no longer moving forward. The narrow path was completely blocked by a tight press of soldiers, standing in a confused group and being shouted at by centurions. Varus stood in his stirrups to see what was holding the march up.

An officer shouldered his way slowly back through the group and saluted.

'Centurion Morius, Tenth Legion.'

Varus nodded. 'What's wrong? Why have the men stopped?'

'Sir, I . . .' The centurion's eyes looked sideways. The men around him were listening with interest.

Varus could feel his control slipping away. 'Why have the men stopped moving? Answer me!'

Morius hesitated, then straightened himself to attention. He pointed to the front of the column. 'Would you come with me, sir?'

The trail was narrow. Soldiers climbed up earth banks and disappeared into bushes to make room enough to permit Varus' horse to pass up the line. It took a long time to travel the hundred paces to where the path ended. A wall of trees and matted vegetation rose up in front of them.

Varus looked around uncomprehendingly. He opened his mouth to shout at Morius, then paused and gestured the centurion to come closer. He leant forward, and said, 'Centurion, where are the men supposed to be cutting the path? Why aren't they working?'

The centurion swallowed, and looked over Varus' shoulder as he replied in an undertone similar to the General's. 'We don't know, sir. When we arrived this morning to relieve them, this was as far as they had got. None of them were here.'

Varus sat straight on his horse and tipped his head back so that his chin pointed straight out in front of him, a habit much imitated by his soldiers. 'What do you mean, not here? Deserted?'

There was a snort of derision from one of the soldiers behind him. 'No bloody chance of deserting here. Where the fuck would they go to in this midden of a place?' The men around him laughed and murmured their agreement.

Morius snapped a glance sideways and the soldiers were silent. He knelt down and pointed to a spot just in front of him. 'I don't think so, sir.'

Varus looked at the ground. The darkness made the muddy grass almost black, but he could see that the ground was darker where the centurion was pointing. Varus swung his leg across the horse's back and dismounted. He knelt and put his hand on the grass, then lifted it close to his face. His palm was dark and slippery. There was a smell, a sweet, sickly odour, animal. Varus looked around. Nearby, a gap in the foliage allowed a thin stream of weak sunlight to filter through. He walked across and let the light illuminate his hand.

It was covered in blood.

He turned to the centurion. 'All gone?'

Morius nodded. 'No sign of them, sir. No bodies, no weapons, just blood on the ground.'

Varus lifted his head again. He had been faintly aware of a distant sound beyond the hundred clashings and murmurings that a marching army makes. He realized that the sound was becoming louder.

'What's that noise?' he said.

When Alraic was almost a man but still a boy, it was the greatest story they had, so they all heard it often. Everyone who sat around the camp fires knew by heart how the Great Chief Armin led their leaders to where all the German tribes had agreed to meet in council. They knew the story of how Armin spoke and how the tribes buried their differences, and made plans to wipe out the Romans and ensure they never came to trouble the Germans again. The bards told about the incredulity that filled the tribes when they heard how the Romans were advancing into the Teutoburg, and how that disbelief became a fierce joy when it became clear that their prayers had been answered and the god Wodan had delivered the Romans into their hands.

Alraic heard the stories too, and his heart rose as he remembered how he had walked with his brothers that day, moving silently beside the advancing Roman column, often close enough to reach out and touch the miserable soaking legionaries as they hacked their way forward, and yet the alarm was not given once. The Romans slipped and fell and cursed and got up and pushed on, ever deeper and deeper into the forest. The Germans' natural inclination had been to meet the invaders at the earliest opportunity and protect their homeland at its frontier, but Armin had made them see that letting them advance well into the forest made the Roman defeat more certain by stretching both their supply lines and their defences, as well as making sure that the column was not the bait in a trap. The tribes let the legions slide and curse and struggle their way deep into the forest until there were thousands of warriors and many tens of leagues between the Romans and safety, until even the most cautious chief agreed that the fear of a trick or an ambush was an illusion.

Then they struck at the invaders like a clenched fist, all Germans together, harder and more united than ever before.

The Romans were stretched into a thin spine of disorganization, without formation or lines of communication. The main body of soldiers travelled by day and rested at night, but the vanguard worked constantly to clear a path. It was hard, slow work, and when the army stopped for the night there was no distance between the vanguard and the main body. However, they worked on through the night, and by the morning they were a good distance in front of the army. They were lightly armed and exhausted from the work. They were killed easily with arrows, and their bodies dragged away. Silent men filled the trees and bushes to wait for the Roman chief to arrive, to see him realize his men had vanished, that he was not alone in the forest.

The expression on his face was worth the wait.

Meanwhile, the encircling warriors attacked the back of the column, partly because it was the weakest part of the line, partly to prevent any possibility of a retreat. The forest was so dense that legionaries in the rearguard were dying while their comrades a bow-shot away were unaware that anything was happening. The Roman line lay across the forest floor like a carelessly dropped rope. They could not form their squares, could not co-ordinate their movements. There was no possibility of taking up a defensive formation, no chance of doing anything but fighting the man who rose up out of the ground in front of them. The attackers worked their way up the line like tidal water moving up around a sandbar, some of them punching up through the line, killing every Roman they met, while others moved silently and unseen up both sides of the column. As the next section became aware of the attack behind them they would turn to face it, and then the encircling Germans struck from the front and both sides. There was added confusion caused by the Roman habit of positioning their food wagons and other supplies near the back of the column. When the soldiers guarding them were killed, the horses panicked and ran forward, dragging the broken wagons through the ragged lines the legionaries were forming to meet the German attacks and wrecking what little order their officers managed to create.

Word spread up the column. The warriors in the trees watched as the camp followers, women and slaves who had been deliberately spared from the massacre as being militarily useless but a reliable source of panic, ran up the line, screaming that every man at the rear was murdered and that a hundred thousand Germans were coming at a run, every one invisible and seven feet tall and covered in Roman blood. Soldiers near the centre of the column who had thought themselves relatively safe now realized every man behind them was dead and that they were now the rearguard. A few of them – the auxiliaries, Gauls mostly, not legionaries – threw away their weapons and ran blindly into the forest, where the Germans killed most of them instantly. A few of the fleeing auxiliaries were Germans. These men who fought for money against their own people were captured and spared for later, a treat for the women.

Those who stood firm did their best to make a fight of it. Some found small clearings between the trees and were able to form defence lines and small squares. The German tribes knew from long experience that many of them would die without profit if they attacked the squares directly, so they stood back and broke the Roman formations with arrows and then attacked them from all sides when there were too few men left to form an unbroken front. Where the trail was narrower and the legionaries could do nothing but stand with their backs to a comrade, the attackers threw spears out of the dark forest into them, jumped from the trees onto them, ran out from the bushes and killed them where they stood. The huge column dissolved into a maul of desperately struggling bodies. The legionaries fought well, but the Germans were too many and the invaders were far from their own country, surrounded by a foreign forest, standing on the cold earth of Germany.

By the afternoon the fight was almost over. Both sides

paused for breath. All the remaining Romans were gathered around their Chief in a clearing on a slight hill. Men in the trees overlooked them on all sides, and they were entirely surrounded. Had they been Germans they would have charged, tried to break through the encircling line and died honourably, but they were Romans with a different sense of what is proper. They had the high ground, such as it was. They formed their defensive square, interlocked their shields and waited.

Armin made the tribesmen stand in a great circle around the Roman position. Already several individual groups of Germans had tired of doing what they were told, had disobeyed orders and attacked the Romans in the traditional way, head-on and screaming defiance. They were beaten off with heavy losses, and had unwittingly demonstrated the need for the tribes to obey the commands of the Chief. Now Armin had control of the army again, and the Germans waited. The legionaries' destiny was written clearly, both attackers and defenders knew it, but the manner of it was still to be decided. The warriors approached carefully. They knew that a wounded bear is still a bear. They were not in a hurry.

Armin's only concern was the possibility of reinforcements arriving. He waited until all his scouts had returned. They all told him the same thing. Every Roman on the German side of the Rhine was either trapped in front of him or lying dead on the forest trail. Armin was a cautious man. Some called him a coward for it, but he achieved victories against Rome like no German before or since. He knew the invaders would come again eventually, and it might be soon. He did not wish to lose any more men unnecessarily, but nor did he have the time or inclination to sit and wait for Varus and his men in their square to starve to death.

Armin had the German warriors collect branches and wood. They grumbled about doing work they regarded as fit only for slaves, but they did it, and they piled everything that would burn into a wall around the Roman square on three sides, everywhere taller than a man. The sacred fire was brought, oil and tar were thrown onto the wood, and the pyre was lit. The wood was wet, and at first there was little in the way of flames, but dense clouds of smoke poured out and completely obscured the square. Then, as the wood dried in the heat, hot flames emerged and reared across the ground towards the line of shields. The legionaries suffered it with courage, and although the tribesmen could hear coughing, shouts and curses, none broke formation. From the other side of the three-sided fire, the women threw new wood and branches over the flaming barrier, which then caught fire in turn, and the clear space between the square and the fire grew smaller and smaller. The Romans tried to throw the burning branches back, and they had some little success before arrows from high in the trees pinned them back, but there were too many branches and the burning wall closed inexorably in on the men trapped inside it.

The tribesmen waited for them at the open end of the square. The smoke billowed over the shields, and the Germans watched as the Romans' uniforms began to smoulder. The story-tellers spoke admiringly of how, when their shields grew too hot to hold and turned each man's forearm into one long blister, the Romans still held their line. Finally, when the fire was close enough to set hair alight, they gave up any hope and, with a desperate shout, ran at their tormentors, howling their last. Every man of them knew he was about to die, and every one of them fought with a frenzy that no one had seen possess Romans before. Almost like Germans. Many of the tribesmen died with them.

When it was over and the flames had died down, they found the Chief of the Romans on the ground, dead by his own hand rather than be taken prisoner. Our women had made plans for him if he was taken alive, and any-one who has seen our women go to work on an enemy would say that Varus made the right choice. Denied the pleasure of feeding lightly toasted bits of the General's anatomy to him on a stick, the women waited until the few captured legionaries had been interrogated and the madness of their march into the Teutoburg Forest understood, then practised on them instead. Once they had perfected their skills, they went off in search of the Germans who had been captured fighting for the Romans. For those men no one had any sympathy, but their screams would have made a stone wince.

When the fight was over, the eagle standards that every legion carried were brought to Armin. They were sent away to be kept by the druids in three separate hiding places at the centre of the forest, and for seven years no Roman ventured into the Teutoburg Forest again.

Alraic saw the standards taken away. He saw the Romans die, saw the fires, heard the screams, smelt them burn. He saw the celebration that lasted for days after-wards. He was sixteen years old.

2

The crowd shouted and shoved at each other in anticipation when they saw the huge iron-studded doors at
both ends of the arena being closed and sealed.
Thousands of excited voices combined in a deep roar of
approval as the sluice-gates opened wide and cold green
water poured into the arena from all sides. The water
came from the sluices under such pressure that it
fountained up and over the sand until it came down
almost at the arena centre, and then, where the opposing
jets collided, it flew upwards and tumbled backwards on
itself like huge waves hitting a cliff. Those exposed to
the sun in the seats nearest the arena side shrieked their
delight as a cool spray fell on them.

Behind the closed doors sweating men worked desperately to make things ready. Today the crowd was even
more than usually impatient. Even before the arena was
properly ready, while the foaming water still poured in to
mix with the sand from the arena floor, they were already
stamping their feet and shouting for the action to begin.

Several dozen hurled seat-cushions were floating on the water's surface like giant lilies, and a group of young men near the Senator's box, already drunk on the Senator's wine, were yelling cheerful abuse at him for keeping them waiting.

Senator Catullus Appius smiled and waved, acknowledging their presence and pretending that he couldn't hear what they were saying. Nearby stood Marcus Otho, the Master of Games, with lines of strain showing on his face. The small cane which hung from the Senator's fingers had been tapping irritably against the side of his chair for some time. The old man was paying for the games, and he wasn't enjoying laying out a fortune just to be kept waiting and have insults shouted at him from the cheap seats. Otho knew that the Senator would shortly be looking for someone to blame, and he had a shrewd idea who that someone would be.

The Senator glowered at Otho with pursed lips and rapped the cane sharply against the leg of his chair. Otho knew from long experience what was going on in the old man's mind.

The process was simple. Whenever a games went according to plan, the man paying for it would accept the plaudits of the crowd and his peers as no more than his due; he had, after all, come up with the idea personally, and had followed it through, backing his judgement with hard cash, ignoring the misguided – and perhaps self-seeking – counsel of those more timorous than he, and was reaping no more than his just reward. However, when a games threatened to go badly, the man whose money and reputation were at stake invariably had little difficulty in persuading himself that he had been gulled into holding a games wholly against his better judgement, seduced by – probably mendacious – appeals to his generosity and good nature, and that the foolishness, bad faith and inefficiency of those around him were entirely to blame.

Otho knew that, in the latter case, this blame was, primarily for reasons of proximity, most commonly vested in him, the Master of Games. He moved his weight uneasily from one foot to the other and prayed that the games would start before the Senator's patience ran out. It was going to be a close race.

In theory the games were intended to honour the goddess Diana and give thanks for the successful return of one of the Senator's treasure ships. In practice, as everyone knew, including, presumably, the goddess herself, who might have been expected to have an opinion, the games were designed to make the Senator's son, Claudius Appius, noticed and popular. If the day went well, Claudius Appius would probably be elected tribune in the next election and he and his father could look forward to a prosperous future. On the other hand, if the day went badly, Claudius Appius would never be heard of again, his father would have crippled himself financially for the next five years for nothing, and Otho would get the blame. The Master of Games felt a worm of sweat run down between his shoulder-blades. Neither the Senator nor the crowd were in a forgiving mood. Otho concentrated on looking like a man with absolute confidence in his subordinates and the imminence of great events.

The Senator stopped beating his chair with the cane and, with a feeling of immense and increasing dissatisfaction with everything in his world, looked balefully at Claudius Appius. His only son was standing at the front of the box with a fold of his pristine toga held languidly over one arm. He was striking a pose that he no doubt thought looked patrician, but which reminded the Senator of an overfed lapdog sniffing the wind for interesting scents it would never bother to chase. He shook his head ruefully. The Senator had trained himself to think of the differences between himself and his son as merely the gods having their little joke, but there were times when he looked at Claudius Appius and his suspicions broke through his determination like a bull through a picket fence. He would wonder for the hundredth time if his wife's shrill protestations and the midwife's assurances that a fully grown baby could be born a mere seven months after his wedding day were to be trusted. It was not a possibility he enjoyed considering.

At such times, and this was one, the Senator found that a little wine soothed both his nerves and his fears.

The jewelled cup next to the Senator's right hand had already been refilled several times both discreetly and speedily by a tall slave carrying a jug of wine who stood silently at the back of the viewing box. Claudius looked disapprovingly at his father every time the slave stepped forward, and the Senator looked back at his son defiantly. The Master of Games, standing to one side of the box with his apprentice by his side, saw the glances, counted the cups of wine, and winced at the clouds gathering on his master's brow. Otho felt that he was surrounded, as always, by impatience and incomprehension. He sighed silently and looked around critically at his empire.

The arena was by now almost full of water, foaming and browned with the arena sand. To obtain such an enormous amount so quickly the engineers had fitted a series of valves to the three main aqueducts that supplied the city from the rivers to the north. In a few moments these valves could divert almost the entire contents of all three aqueducts into the pipes that fed the arena. Every time the pipes were opened – six huge troughs large enough for a man to stand up in with a child on his shoulders, aided by thirty smaller pipes the diameter of a man's thigh – the whole of Rome, every tap and every fountain, every sewer and every drain, even the Imperial baths, ran dry, until the thirst of the arena was satisfied and the valves could be switched back to normal again. The sluices were so big and so numerous that the crowd could leave their seats to relieve themselves and know that the arena would be a lake by the time they returned.

Otho leaned over the edge of the box with an irritable expression. Lucius, his apprentice, a dark-haired boy with the eyebrows of a startled nymph, leant over at the same time in the same way and with the same expression. The Master of Games was both flattered and annoyed by this. Every time it happened Otho felt he should say something about it to the boy, but never knew quite what.

Below him, immediately behind the studded leather-sealed gate that led to the arena, a mass of swearing, sweating men were failing to provoke a huge spindle lever into movement. From almost immediately above them, Otho could see that there was a problem with the launching equipment. The foreman, a short barrel-chested man called Cornelius who always wore a heavy black leather jerkin and a length of dark cloth rolled up into a rope and tied around his head to keep the sweat from his eyes, looked up at the Master of Games and held up both hands. He needed more time. Otho shook his head abruptly and, keeping his own hand down where the Senator could not see it, cut him off with a sharp gesture. Then he turned back to the Senator with a smile laced with what he hoped was an appropriate mixture of the willing and the unctuous.

'Where are the ships? What is the delay?' growled the Senator, the returning beat of his stick accelerating to a rhythm that not even the feet of an Egyptian dancer in a pit of scorpions could have kept up with.

'We are almost ready, Excellency,' murmured Otho. He cursed the fact that his employer had specified that he wanted the arena flooded, which meant that the tactics usually open to Otho in the case of delay – the use of nearly naked young women dancing a bacchanalian ritual was known to be highly effective – could not be employed. Unless the show began as soon as the arena was full of water, the crowd suspected that something was wrong and immediately became restless. Otho thought of the great days, when masters of games were emperors of the arena, creating spectacular works for the public. Mountains were built, piled high with men, and then collapsed as if in an earthquake, pitching the men

30

into a vast cage of wild beasts underneath. Otho smiled to himself. The pinnacle of his career. Appreciated, lavished with gifts, feted even. And now it had come to this: dealing with idiots possessed of the sensibility of a wild boar's backside.

An apple core hit the parapet in front of Claudius Appius and dropped down onto his foot. He looked at it for a disbelieving moment before kicking it away irritably. 'See?' the Senator said, a note of self-pity entering his voice. 'It's apples now. They'll be throwing vegetables in a minute. If my luck holds.' He raised his voice and called to his son. 'Claudius, for Jupiter's sake come away from there.'

Claudius turned, an expression of irritation on his face. 'My friends are watching. How do you think it makes me look if you order me about?'

There was something about his son's voice that made it easy for the old man to imagine himself running forward and pushing him over the edge of the box with a glad cry. Instead he forced himself, as so often before, to explain.

'The crowd are not admiring you, they are using you for target practice. If a piece of fruit hits you it could lose us a thousand votes. If your so-called friends see a suggestively shaped vegetable come within ten feet of you then we can kiss goodbye to the election, and how you look won't matter a handful of lentils.'

Claudius retreated unwillingly back into the box. He pushed his lower lip out and stood with a fist on his hip, like a child whose new toy has been confiscated. 'The people need to see me, surely? Isn't that the point of this farrago?' The whining note was still in his voice. The Senator shifted irritably in his curved chair and pointed to a spot beside him. Claudius trudged over and stood nearby. The Senator sighed and reached for his cup with the air of a man nursing a dozen deeply held grievances. He looked at Otho with red-rimmed eyes. Claudius stood glowering behind his father. Otho braced himself. Both men were looking for someone to blame and Otho knew for certain that the someone they would find would be him. The Senator poked holes in the air around Otho with a finger.

'How the hell are we supposed to convince people that Claudius has the dignity suitable to a tribune if those braying idiots down there are permitted to yell insults at him while turning the place into a market fruit stall?' The finger stabbed again. 'You told me, assured me, that you had men planted in the crowd to make sure that this sort of thing didn't happen.'

'There are, Excellency, my men are . . .' Otho's voice tailed off as, to the accompaniment of much laughter from the young blades below, a long pole with a cross-piece was held up in front of the Senator's box and waved drunkenly from side to side. A woman's dress was hung on the cross-piece and two melons had been stuffed into the front of it.

'Well, if, and I say if, your men are in the crowd then they aren't doing their fucking job,' growled the Senator. A turnip hit the column to Otho's left and rolled across the floor towards Claudius Appius. The Senator looked at Otho maliciously and again pointed a plump finger at the face of the Master of Games. 'I want to see men's heads on spikes after this is over, either those of the drunken peasants down below turning this place into a grocery stall, or else those of the cretins who should be stopping them.' His cheeks were flushed a dull red and a sheen of sweat covered his face. 'Come to think of it, I want to see both.' He gestured towards the toiling men below them and wine slopped onto the ground. He thumped the cup down on the armrest and the slave stepped forward smoothly to refill it. 'I am approached every day by informers clamouring to tell me about how their brother-in-law showed disrespect by being so drunk that they couldn't raise a toast to the Emperor when one was called.' A large cabbage came bowling up and over the parapet and would have landed in the Senator's lap if Otho had not leapt forward to catch it. The Senator looked at him with almost closed eyes. 'Could not some of those informers be employed to tell me who the market traders below are who seem so eager to share their produce with us so generously?'

'I'll see to it,' stammered Otho, hastily putting the cabbage behind his back. Lucius took it from him silently and dropped it over the edge of the box, enabling Otho to clasp his hands in front of himself again. The Senator beckoned him forward. As the Master of Games came within arm's length, the old man reached out and grasped his cloak at his throat. He jerked Otho down until their faces were level and a hand's length apart.

'Start the fucking games,' snarled the Senator, his spittle landing on Otho's cheek. 'Now.'

'But . . .'

Claudius Appius suddenly leant forward, pushing his

face almost against the other side of Otho's face. His voice was a malevolent hiss. 'My father has spoken. Tell those morons down there that the show starts right now, or else tell them that they will be the highlight of the main event in a colourful demonstration of synchronized slow bleeding to death, and I can assure you that you will be leading them by vivid example. Clear?'

Otho swallowed with difficulty and nodded once. 'It is done, Excellency.' He leaned back again and looked down at the toiling men. Cornelius looked up at him with an anxious face. Otho held up one finger and then drew it sharply across his neck in a universally understood movement. Cornelius raised his hands in a gesture of frantic resignation and began yelling orders. Otho didn't catch his words, but resolved to ask him later what he had said, for it had the effect of a burning torch thrown into a drain full of rats soaked in fresh pitch. All around the foreman men stopped what they were doing. Dozens of others appeared at a hard run from the passages nearby. At the foreman's screamed command every one of them threw himself with grim enthusiasm at the jammed equipment. The giant lever moved slightly. Cornelius bawled encouragement, so loudly that Otho could hear him above the shouts of the crowd, offering rewards for success and promising – at much greater length and with far more vehemence – an imminent and hideous end for all of them in the event of failure. The sweating men heaved frantically. Yet more men arrived and added their weight to the effort. There was a paralysed moment of immobility, and then the lever moved, slowly and then a little faster, and it kept moving.

The foreman looked up at Otho and signalled success. Otho smiled and turned back to the Senator.

'We are ready, Excellency. With your permission . . . ?' Catullus agreed with a peremptory gesture, as a large hunk of the bread that his slaves had distributed earlier to the crowd came careering over the balcony edge and bounced off the breastplate of one of the Senator's guards. Otho kicked it quickly to one side and moved to the front of the box overlooking the arena. He raised his arms. An ironic cheer started immediately below him and spread quickly around the arena. People stopped drinking, fighting, arguing and throwing food and cushions as they realized that at last something was about to happen. The water now reached to just a few feet below the first rows of seats. The front three or four rows tended to be occupied by those just below the first – businessmen who had yet to buy rank and their families and mistresses, and groups of the younger sons of the senators and knights a few rows behind them. These rows tended to be the most drunk and the most hysterical of all. Now hands reached down towards the water to help those who had been pushed in – or had fallen – to get out. Otho waited while a couple of very drunk young men dived in and retrieved one of their number who had become so overcome that he was now floating motionless and face down in the turbid water. There was a loud cheer as the rescued man came back to at least some of his senses as he was dragged back over the edge of the lake. He stood up on the edge to take an unsteady bow. Otho waited patiently until the drama was played out, and then spoke in his best rhetorical cadences.

'By the grace of my master Senator Catullus Appius, and his son Claudius Appius,' Otho turned and indicated them both with a flourish, 'by your gracious favour the next Tribune of the People, we offer you, the good citizens of Rome, a spectacle that even yourselves, the most sophisticated audience in the world, will appreciate for its magnificence and attention to historic detail.'

'Very good, but no one can hear you,' slurred the Senator from behind him. 'Let's get on with the killing and be done. I want to go home.' Claudius didn't speak, as, now that people were no longer throwing vegetables at him, he had stepped forward next to Otho and had struck another patrician pose at the front of the box.

The Master of Games looked around the arena. Catullus had a point. The people on the other side of the arena could not have heard him even if the place had been empty and silent, whereas there were thousands of screaming men and women everywhere he looked.

'The Battle of Actium, then,' he said in a conversational tone. 'For all you care about it.'

He raised his arms high, paused, then brought them down dramatically. The crowd howled their approval. They couldn't hear him, but everyone knew what his gesture meant.

At intervals around the arena, soldiers carrying long bows with arrows already notched took up their positions. Otho watched approvingly, then spun on his heel and went to the back of the box to check on progress. Below him perhaps fifty men were holding the door closed with all their strength. The foreman was standing with an enormous axe, looking upwards with an expression that mixed desperation and resignation. Otho signalled with a downward gesture. The foreman brought the axe down on the jammed mechanism with all his strength.

Whatever the remaining problem with the launching apparatus was, the axe solved it. As fast as the men had flung themselves onto the machinery earlier they now scrambled frantically to get off it as ropes flew around wheels, cogs ground, gears creaked. With a lurch and a scream of tortured wood and metal, the top of the gate opened and the ship behind it slid down a ramp into the water-filled arena. A few moments later, an identical ship appeared on the other side of the lake.

The crowd stood and pressed forward with excitement, craning forward to get a good view. The two ships were half-size near-replicas of the sort of galleys in which Antony and Octavius had opposed each other a few decades before. Long rams protruded forward from the bow at the water line. In order to allow them to float in the shallow water of the arena lake the galleys had been built without masts or keels, and so were wider-bottomed in order to prevent capsizing. Apart from that, they were the same design as the originals. Or at least, as the head carpenter had replied to an amateur historian who had pointed out a list of inaccuracies, the design was 'Near enough to the real thing for a lot of drunken illiterate city-dwellers who wouldn't know a Republican war-galley if they woke up to find one fucking them.'

Octavius had always favoured the colour red, and so one of the ships flew a red flag from its stern and was completely painted in that colour too. Mark Antony's ship flew a green flag and was painted green, for no reason Otho knew other than that it was different to red. Each ship was crammed with naked men, also painted with either green or red dye. There were nearly as many men aboard as there would have been on the original full-size ship, and so they were closely packed on the rough-cut planks of the decking. Each man was equipped with either a sword or a spear, but had no armour. The Senator looked down at the ships incuriously and then leant forward with sudden interest. He curled a languid finger. Otho bent to hear him. The heavy odour of unwatered wine surrounded the Master of Games as the Senator pointed at the boats and spoke unsteadily.

'Otho, does my memory fail me, or did our gallant soldiers at Actium really go into battle without any armour?'

Otho smiled. 'Your memory is excellent, Excellency. However, I am reliably informed that, while as a general rule the crowd does appreciate some attention to historical detail, when it comes to watching men kill each other they are firmly of the opinion that armour – and indeed clothing of any sort – is an unnecessary hindrance.'

The Senator raised an eyebrow. 'Indeed? One might have thought that they would prefer some armour, make the soldiers take a bit longer about it, put up a bit more of a show?'

Otho continued to smile, ignoring the impending cramp in his jaw muscles, and shook his head. 'Once that was undoubtedly true, Excellency, at a time when the crowd was more knowledgeable and, shall we say, more appreciative of quality than quantity. However, for better or worse, nowadays the crowd like to get to the point as quickly as possible.' He leant close to the Senator's ear. 'And there was the cost to consider, too.'

The Senator nodded. 'Indeed, a very good point. The people have spoken, in their wisdom, as always. Naked it is then.' He lifted an arm and waved to the crowd. There were a few cat-calls. The rest of the audience was too busy laying bets on the outcome of the fight in front of them to pay attention to their benefactor.

'Fuck 'em,' muttered the Senator, and raised the cup to his lips again.

The two ships rowed straight across the arena and collided almost head on. Both rams splintered and shattered. The red ship managed to gain a slightly favourable angle as the ships collided and was almost undamaged. The green ship was badly holed in the bow on the side nearest the Senator. The crowd roared with excitement as it began to list and take on water.

The men inside the green ship were presented with an unenviable choice. In front of them, the men on the red ship stood on their gunwales, yelling defiance, jabbing at them with their spears, their swords held out, daring the green men to jump across. The green men knew that to jump into the water and swim away was not an option. At the first sign of a prisoner leaving the battle the archers around the arena would fire at them. The prisoners knew anyway that, without a good fight to sate their appetites, the crowd would throw them back in or even tear them to pieces rather than let them escape.

And their situation was about to get worse.

There was a loud creak of wooden sluice-doors, and after another moment the crowd let out a howl that defeated all their previous choruses. Antony's men on the sinking green boat unenthusiastically eyed the jeering men on the red boat opposite, and the waiting archers above them, and then, hearing the noise of the crowd change and knowing that, whatever the new factor in the equation was, it was almost certainly not going to make their lives simpler or more pleasant, glanced back and knew that their minds had been made up for them. Triangular waves were closing in from every side.

'Crocodiles!' shouted the crowd gleefully to each other.

The men on the green ship now knew that their only hope was to take over the red ship; their red opponents were determined not to surrender it for the same reason. The sinking ship was a poor platform from which to launch an attack, and the red men were prepared and determined to resist. Nevertheless, encouraged and organized by some of their number who had been soldiers, the green men mounted a concerted assault. Many of them died immediately on the red men's swords but some broke through and the defenders had to turn to fight them. Suddenly there were gaps in the line of swords, and the remaining green-painted men poured across the gap between the two boats just ahead of the arrival of the crocodiles below them.

In moments men were everywhere screaming, dying, falling from the boats. The crocodiles thrashed their great tails and stirred up the sand as they tossed the bodies of dead and half-dead men around in the water.

The crowd watched the pitched battle on the deck of the red ship with a mixture of fascination and ribaldry. There was little technique to admire or skill involved in the fight; the two sides hacked and chopped at each other like drunken woodcutters competing to demolish a forest. Only strength and speed counted for anything. The desperation of the attack by the green men carried the fight before them, and for a time it seemed that the day was won. Then a huge red-stained man with the long fair plaits of a Gaul hanging around his shoulders yelled 'Octavius!' in a voice which carried all around the arena. He rallied the remaining red fighters around him and, placing himself at their front and carrying an axe in one hand and a long sword in the other, led them in a purposeful attack across the length of the ship. The deck was slippery with blood and humped with corpses, hindering both sides, and none of the fighters wanted to get too close to the edge for fear that they would get knocked overboard. The crocodiles circled menacingly below. The red soldiers fanned out in a spearhead formation behind the Gaul and picked off their enemy individually. The crowd soon saw the way that the fight was going and a roar of support began to build up. By the time the steady march of the red phalanx was half-way up the length of the ship the green men's cause was lost and the crowd was baying hysterically. The green men could only try and stay alive until the fight was finished, and hope that the crowd would spare them. To this end each man fought desperately, so that from the seats in the top tiers of the arena far above them the group of advancing red men resembled a hedgehog attacked by green wasps. The green men fought well, but eventually every one of them was either dead or lying helpless on the deck.

The Gaul walked wearily to the prow of the boat and faced the Senator. The red ochre covering his naked body was streaked with darker patches of blood. He raised his arms in the gesture of victory and the sun overhead caught his pale hair and surrounded his head in light. The crowd stood up at this sign of divine favour and howled its own approval.

Standing behind the Senator, Otho bent slightly to whisper, 'They honour you, sir.'

The Senator's eyes were nearly closed. He did his best to smile, almost managed to sit up, and made a gesture something like a salute of recognition. 'Of course. Well done. Very good.' He slumped back in his chair again, took a large mouthful of wine and rested the cup on his chest.

The red-painted Gaul pointed with his sword at the dozen or so opponents still left alive.

Otho leant forward again. 'They ask for the lives of the survivors, sir.'

The Senator belched loudly and looked at Otho through narrow red-veined eyes. 'Oh? Shall I . . . oh, do what you think best.'

Otho walked to the edge of the box. The crowd cheered, and as always Otho allowed himself a few moments of silent satisfaction on a successful event. He pointed down towards the shivering men in the boat and raised his other arm in an enquiring gesture. The noise increased in volume. Otho's thumb was parallel to the ground. The crowd cheered and booed in equal measure. Otho waited for a few moments, then looked back at the Senator. His master was comatose in his chair, out of sight of most of the crowd. A thin trickle of wine-coloured saliva was running from one corner of his mouth onto his toga. Otho hesitated briefly, then nodded as if he had received an instruction. He turned back to the crowd, waited for a few more moments to allow the tension to build, and then turned his thumb slowly in the symbol for death. The roar of the crowd became deafening. Otho saw the Gaul nod, then reach down and take the first captive by the hair. He pulled the man's head back to bare his throat and drew the serrated edge of his sword across it in one smooth movement. The death was too quick for some of the crowd, who screamed for Antony's soldiers to be thrown overboard to the crocodiles, but the red men despatched their prisoners quickly and efficiently. In a few moments it was done.

They were, after all, merely prisoners. Had they been gladiators, professionals, then Otho would have spared them. Gladiators were expensive to buy and ruinous to train. It was rare to see one killed. Prisoners, on the other hand, would be freely available as long as there were border wars. And there were always border wars.

The green ship was by now sitting on the sand at the bottom of the arena. The red ship was now also sinking, but more slowly, the water reddening as it lapped over the gunwales onto the blood-soaked deck. At a signal from Otho the drains were opened, and with a sucking rush the water flooded to the sewers. While the water drained away the archers amused the crowd by shooting at the crocodiles. Otho watched the spectacle with disapproval.

'Criminal waste. They took months to bring back.'

The trumpets blew. The crocodiles lay immobile on the sand, arrows spining their hides. The corpses of dozens of men lay around them. The crowd stood up, grumbling cheerfully. They knew that it would take an hour or so to drain the water, lay fresh sand and get the arena in a fit condition for the races in the afternoon. They had plenty of time for more of the Senator's food and drink, and the opportunity to stretch their legs before the main event. The great market held every ninth day was in full swing outside, surrounding the arena and spilling over into the side streets, providing every imaginable type of item for sale. They left their cushions and a slave behind to guard their seats, and for a while the whole arena was almost quiet. The sun reached its highest point and steam rose in clouds from the wet sand as the boys dressed as Mercury dragged the last of the bodies away and the markers were put into place in readiness for the afternoon's races.

Deep below the feet of the Mercury boys, underneath tons of stone supported by the vast columns of the arena, a dark warren of tunnels boiled with activity. Otho had finished yelling at the foreman about the delayed start and had started worrying about how it probably meant another delay after lunch. The foreman, in his turn, was screaming abuse at his carpenters about the faulty launching mechanism of the boat, and later on the carpenters would no doubt be taking it out on their apprentices.

Nearby, in the stables, chariot axles were being greased and wheels polished. The horses were groomed and their hooves inspected. Slaves checked the harness and fixings of the chariots belonging to the amateur racers, the young men who raced for prestige and the admiration of the crowd. Beside them, silent professionals saw to their own equipment with stern faces and absolute concentration. Once they had inspected everything, they did not leave or take their eyes off the chariot. If they were called away for some reason, when they returned the checks were carried out again in their entirety. They were men who knew that their lives hung by a thin leather strap, and that there were others nearby who might have thousands, even millions of shining reasons to wish them ill.

3

The line of men and wagons rattled slowly through another of a seemingly endless series of narrow ravines.

It was nearly evening and the birds were settling for the night. A small copse of high thin trees nearby was dark with raucous crows. The noise they made dropped gradually as the light began to fade and the heat went out of the air and their dispute.

Then one bird let out a harsh cry of warning and in a second black shapes exploded out from every part of the copse, for a moment dragging the outline of the trees into the sky with them, then wheeling away like a cloud of dark rags thrown up into the breeze.

Serpicus was almost asleep in his saddle.

'Keep your eyes open,' murmured the rider immediately in front of him.

Serpicus woke with a start. He looked around uneasily and put his fingers around the handle of his sword. The big German was seldom mistaken about trouble. He signalled to a much younger man riding behind him.

'Decius,' Serpicus said in a quiet voice. 'Brutus heard something. Pass the word back. Keep alert.'

Decius turned his horse in its own length and, with a pleased expression, trotted back along the line. Serpicus watched him go and smiled to himself. It was the young man's first trip. He had somehow managed not to get himself killed; he was good with the animals and the men liked him, although they never stopped teasing him. Serpicus hadn't been sure if the lad would cope – or even survive – but he was glad he'd taken a chance on him.

Decius went back along the line of tired men whispering, 'Keep alert.'

'Why?' asked the first one.

'Serpicus says that Brutus says that he heard something.'

'Oh.' He looked at the man nearest him with a grin. 'Well, whatever it was, if Brutus heard it then it wasn't someone else making a suggestion.'

Several people nearby chuckled, and then the rumble and clack of falling rocks from above made them all wince and look up. The sides of the ravine were steep. There was nowhere to run and there wasn't room to turn around quickly, even if there had been time to give the order. Boulders were falling along the length of the ravine. The men ducked and cursed as sharp shards of rock bounced down onto their heads. The horses twisted and fretted under them as they tried to untie their shields one-handed. Several men at the front of the column spurred their horses forward in reflex, and then pulled them up as it became clear that the main fall was fifty paces distant. Serpicus watched as dozens of huge boulders crashed down in front of the column, rolling up the other side of the ravine and then settling back to form a wall higher than a man.

A fist-sized stone passed above Brutus' head, close enough to graze the ancient leather cap he wore over his red hair, and crashed against the side of the cage beside him. A howling went up from inside the cage accompanied by a frantic scratching of claws against the wooden sides.

The rocks finished falling with a surprising abruptness. There was silence apart from the distant cawing of crows and the beach-sound of pebbles making small rushes down the slope. The rock-dust settled quickly around them, still damp from the morning's brief rain. Brutus stood high on the wooden foot-pegs attached to his saddle, stretching his thigh muscles, and then settled back heavily with a thump that made his horse jerk its head in tired surprise.

'Well,' he said, in a voice loud enough to be heard at the top of the ravine, 'if anyone is planning on ambushing us I can't think of a better opportunity.' He sounded like an indulgent parent letting concealed children nearby know where he was.

The first two arrows struck simultaneously. The first sank deep into the pommel of Brutus' saddle and stuck there quivering. The second went clean through the throat of the man riding next to him. The man gave a soft gasp of pain, then his life bubbled up from his mouth and he fell sideways off his horse. Decius let out a yelp of surprise.

Serpicus pointed at several figures at the top of the ravine. 'Ambush!' he shouted.

Brutus looked at the arrow in his saddle and then down on the final thrashings of the man on the ground. He raised his head to look at Serpicus with an amused expression. 'Never short of a statement of the obvious,' he said mildly.

Brutus stood up in the saddle again and looked back along the line of men trying to control their horses while working out where the danger was coming from. 'Tomas!' he yelled, waving an arm and pointing back the way they had come. 'Up there. Quickly.' The men at the rear of the column were already turning their horses in anticipation of the order. More rocks began tumbling down the slope, but the attackers hadn't co-ordinated their efforts well enough. Stones fell near Tomas and his men, but too late to do any damage and too few to block off their retreat.

Brutus watched Tomas' men until they rounded a corner and were no longer visible, then gestured to the remaining men behind him. 'Get those bloody horses in closer to the rock!' he shouted. 'Leave the cages, it's the animals they want, they won't shoot at them.'

An arrow hissed past Serpicus' head. He ducked and kicked his horse towards the side of the ravine, where a narrow shelf protruded the width of a man's shoulders about half-way up the rock-face and offered just enough to hide them from the attackers above.

'You, you and you, get out there and shoot at anything you see.' Brutus was pointing at the three best archers. They scowled sullenly, then grabbed their bows and ran back out, finding what cover they could. Any attacker at the top of the ravine who wanted to fire at those below had to lean over the edge, exposing himself to their shafts. They knelt and waited with arrows notched. One of them suddenly brought his bow up, loosed the arrow and brought it down again, all in one fluid movement. There was a sharp cry from above them and a moment later a body landed with a dull thud on the ground nearby and lay still. The marksman grinned and turned to call to one of his comrades, then fell silent. He looked down with a surprised expression to see an arrow growing silently from his own chest. His eyes closed, as if he had dozed off, and he slid sideways and fell gracelessly to the ground. The other archers hunched closer to the rocks.

Brutus waited until every man apart from the archers was pressed against the side of the ravine before he took cover himself. Then he ran until he crashed into the wall beside Decius.

'Serpicus?'

Serpicus' dark face looked sideways. Decius was next to him, separating him from Brutus. The young man looked frightened. Brutus looked something more like amused. Not frightened anyway. Serpicus wondered what his own expression betrayed. 'What?' he said.

'How many do you think?'

Serpicus was breathing deeply but just about under control. 'I saw five, maybe six.'

There was a deep chuckle and Brutus leant out to peer around Decius to get a look at him. 'Lucky you, getting the six who can't shoot straight.'

An arrow from above careened off the rock beside Serpicus' face, its force mostly spent but spattering him with sharp splinters of stone. 'Then why don't you go out there and see if they have any better luck shooting at you?' he growled, wiping his face and seeing bright blood against the white rock-dust on his hand. 'No matter how bad their shooting is, they couldn't possibly miss your great fat arse.'

Brutus laughed again and his white teeth showed through the shadows. 'I might just do that.' He sniffed loudly and looked up. 'They aren't hitting anything. I bet these ambushing bastards are Spaniards. Spaniards can't shoot for shit.'

Serpicus raised an eyebrow and indicated the dead men lying on the ground nearby. 'Those two might disagree.'

Brutus shrugged. 'If enough arrows get shot, even Spaniards will hit something once in a while.'

There was a pause. Decius looked at Serpicus and then at Brutus. 'Do you think Tomas will be there yet?' he asked diffidently.

'Should be, near enough,' Serpicus said.

Brutus extended his arm and lifted his sword slowly until it was level with his face, then rotated his wrist to look along both edges. He nodded with satisfaction. Sharp enough for what he had in mind. 'If these bastards up there think that I'm going to just hand over my beautiful animals after six weeks of breaking my bloody back to catch them, they can think again,' he murmured.

Serpicus looked at him with a studied expression. 'It's been a privilege to help you in your endeavours,' he growled. Brutus just grinned.

'So,' he said to Serpicus. 'Six or so of them up top we know about, assume maybe six more who you didn't see because you were too busy running for cover.'

'I'd have run a damn sight faster if I hadn't been stuck behind you,' Serpicus said.

'And Tomas has just four men plus himself,' Brutus said cheerfully. 'Even if he catches those bandits dismounted he's going to have problems. We're going to have to help him.' Serpicus sighed and nodded agreement.

Decius looked bewildered. 'How can we help him? He's up there and we're down here.'

Serpicus looked along the ravine both ways. Each direction was as bad as the other. 'You and me, left?' he said to Brutus. The big man nodded once and leant out, looked up swiftly and then jerked himself back under cover again. An arrow smacked into the flat rock next to him and ricocheted sideways, slicing across the skin of his foot. A thin line of blood oozed out between the leather straps of his sandal and mixed with the thick second skin of brown dust on his instep. He looked at it and then glanced up. 'This lot are starting to annoy me.' He tapped the two men next to him on the shoulder and gestured to the end of the ravine. 'We'll go left. You two go right.' They nodded agreement. 'Take off everything that you don't need, you'll want to be moving as fast as you can.'

They stripped off most of their light armour. Serpicus took several deep breaths. The idea of trading protection for speed struck him as one that suited someone who could run very fast. Faster than him. Serpicus didn't have anything on his arms or legs anyway, and arrows bristled from the ground like spiteful weeds around them. He decided that he was keeping his body armour even if it did slow him down.

'What shall I do?' asked Decius. Serpicus didn't get the feeling that Decius much wanted to get shot at, but nor did he want to be left behind. Serpicus preferred Decius' state of youthful ignorance, which was likely to keep him alive, to his own clear adult recognition of what needed to be done and how it was going to get him shot at and probably killed.

'Stay here, keep everyone under the shelf, don't move,' growled Brutus and then cuffed Decius heavily round the head. Serpicus grinned at the young man, who tried to smile. They both knew that the ringing in Decius' ears was Brutus' way of saying 'Look after yourself'.

With what was intended to be a roar of defiance but which Serpicus suspected probably sounded more like a howl of fright, he broke cover with Brutus close behind him and ran to the left, heading back towards the rear of the column. The two other men went right, forward towards the wall of fallen boulders. They were shielded by an intermittent overhang for a spear's throw, but then they would be exposed and moving slowly as they climbed. With luck, neither pair should get hit too soon or too often. In theory, the ambushers would be pre-occupied with shooting at the four running men, which would give Tomas time to get to the top of the hill and attack them. However, if the archers saw Tomas early enough, by the time the horses reached them there wouldn't be anyone on the horses' backs.

So they raced across the floor of the ravine, offering themselves as targets, jinking from left to right, their shields held across their backs and over their shoulders like old men holding up their togas to protect them from a sudden shower of rain. Serpicus heard metal shriek off a rock nearby, and another shaft pinned a scuttling lizard to the ground just beside him. Then he felt a dull thud as an arrow struck his shield.

'Thought you said they weren't any good,' he snarled.

Brutus instinctively dodged sideways from an arrow that landed just in front of him. 'I may, after all, be wrong about the Spaniards' shooting ability,' he gasped. 'Or perhaps even wrong about them being Spaniards at all.' Brutus turned to Serpicus for a moment and Serpicus could see that Brutus' shield was no longer fully covering his head. Serpicus opened his mouth to shout a warning but he was too slow. An arrow hissed over Brutus' shoulder and sliced through the flap of his ear, ripping most of it off and knocking the leather cap sideways. A second tore at the muscle at the top of his shoulder as it passed. Brutus slapped a hand to his ear and saw dark blood.

'Definitely not fucking Spaniards,' he said, smearing the leather cap more firmly onto his head with his blood-stained hand. 'Run like Hades or we're dead.'

Two more arrows hit a large rock nearby, and then the barrage suddenly stopped. Either the two men were out of range or Tomas had arrived on the hill top. Brutus ducked behind the rock and ripped a strip of cloth from his shirt. Serpicus slowed down and then turned and knelt, holding his shield in front of his body.

The attackers were silhouetted against the sky. Some had their hands raised, a few were fighting desperately against the horsemen who rode amongst them, using the horses to knock the archers off balance and then hacking down at them. The crest on Tomas' helmet was clearly visible. Serpicus saw one man jump at him, trying to drag him off his horse. Tomas swung his sword in a back-handed arc. The attacker clutched at his face and fell backwards into the ravine with a sharp cry.

It only lasted a few more moments. The horsemen rounded up those ambushers who were left alive and pushed them back down towards where Serpicus and Brutus were standing. Serpicus noticed that Decius had appeared nearby.

'Are you all right?' Decius nodded. Serpicus realized that it was probably his first fight. He reached out and put a hand on Decius' shoulder. The flesh trembled against his palm.

'Take a look at the animals,' Serpicus said. 'Make sure none of them were hurt.'

Decius nodded and trotted back to the cages. Brutus watched him move away, and raised an eyebrow at Serpicus. Serpicus nodded assent.

'He'll be fine,' he said.

4

When they arrived at the collection pens that afternoon, Galba was waiting for them. His fat arms were folded and he rested his weight on his good leg as always. Brutus looked at the Thracian and let out a low growl as he slid down painfully from his horse. A thick dark carapace of dried blood crusted one side of his neck like bark on a tree and the bandage around his head was stiff with bloodstains. A similar cloth covered the wound in his shoulder. His ancient leather cap was filthy with blood and sweat and covered in dust, and so merged seamlessly with his face.

Galba looked up at Brutus in the same way that one might look at a complete stranger who has just claimed in all seriousness, but without any evidence, that he is about to burst suddenly into flames.

'So,' he said carefully, 'how did it go?'

Serpicus got wearily off his horse. 'No real problems,' he said. Brutus let out another growl and Serpicus moved smartly away from him. 'Well, nothing serious anyway.'

He stepped behind a pillar as Brutus reached for an earthenware jug. 'Nothing you'd really feel pressed to mention.' The jug crashed into shards against the pillar.

Galba shook his almost hairless head at Brutus. 'You're a mess,' he said. 'Come on, I'll get the doctor to clean it up for you.'

Brutus coughed and spat. 'Later.' He glanced at the tired men unloading equipment around him. 'I've got to sort this lot out first.'

'Go on, take him,' Serpicus said to Galba. 'We'll see to things here.' Decius nodded enthusiastically at the idea on behalf of the rest of the men. Unloading was never easy, and Brutus in his present mood could make it twice as hard. Brutus looked unsure. Serpicus gestured him away. 'Go on. You can always come back and check on our progress when the quack has finished sewing you up. And while he's doing it you can tell Galba all about how you saved us from the bandits.'

Brutus hesitated and looked at the men. 'Tell them I'll be back.'

'I've no doubt they'll be waiting eagerly. Now go.'

Galba limped after Brutus. Serpicus went over and helped start to unload the cages with the feeling that nothing was ever really simple.

The collection pens were a huge complex of barns and stables, a short ride to the north of Rome. All the animals for the arena that had been caught by trappers without their own stables to keep them in – which was most of them – were delivered there. The animals were kept, fed and rested, and then taken to Rome when they were needed. It meant that the animals were properly counted and the hunters paid correctly. It also meant that convoys of wild animals were not brought through the streets of Rome unsupervised.

The pens had grown steadily over the previous decades, and a small town had grown up around them, mostly taverns offering facilities designed to relieve the newly rich trappers of their cash.

Serpicus and Galba set about unloading the animals. The cage-wagons opened into holding pens, which were shaped so that as the animals went forwards they were funnelled into narrow passages. The wolves were watchful and shivering, their hind quarters poised low on the earth, and seemed glad to disappear from the cage into the dark in front of them. The wild boar were less willing, and stood at bay, legs braced, breath coming hard, their tails stiff and twitching. Serpicus had to climb on top of the cage and use a long pole to get them to move. When they suddenly broke and ran the noise was like a lance in the ear. The rest of the animals were easy. Tired and hungry, the sight of food in front of them was enough to decoy them out of the door.

A system of trap-doors and gates allowed the handlers to direct each animal to the appropriate stable without needing to come into contact with them. In theory the handlers did all the work and counted the animals into the stables. In practice the trappers worked with them, partly so that they would not have to bribe the handlers as much, partly because the handlers were notoriously prone to inaccuracy when adding up the number of animals received.

The stables at the collection area were well-aired,

quiet and reasonably clean, in contrast to those under the arena, which were crowded, noisy and dark. The air there was fetid with the sharp stink of wild animal, a heavy pungent dampness that clung to the clothes. Every kind of intractable beast was kept almost within reach of each other, predators and prey mixed together, snapping and clawing through the bars if a foot or head came close. The authorities justified it blithely, said that the close proximity made the animals wilder, that it made for a better spectacle in the arena, but the truth was that there was no other way of keeping them. The number of animals consumed every day by the huge mouth above them was too large to allow the handlers to keep them properly.

The trained animals were privileged and caged separately, kept deep below the arena in the dark and quiet, out of sight of each other, in order to keep them calm. When training or exercise was required they were brought up to another quiet area to the side of the race track. It was necessary. Lions don't much like being screamed at by eighty thousand people, and it's hard for a trainer to get them to do what he wants, even if it's something that comes naturally to them, like eating perfectly innocent people who have upset an emperor.

Serpicus and one of the handlers, an old slave that he knew well called Calligus, did most of the unloading. Serpicus liked the old man. He worked without fuss, and the animals trusted him. There were others there who could have helped, but Serpicus preferred not to use them. They shouted and hit the bars with sticks to make the animals move. It was quieter and quicker in the long run if he did it his way. Serpicus saw Decius watching intently how the work was done, and gave him a few jobs to do. The youngster was a quick learner.

The work was almost done by the time Galba returned. There were several comments about his timing. Galba ignored them. He could afford to: Serpicus and Decius were covered with stinking sweat, whereas Galba's clothes were clean and smelt only of the herbs he hung with them at night to keep them fresh. Serpicus dismissed Calligus with a substantial tip, sent Decius off on an errand and sat down on a box beside Galba. He wiped his hands on a reeking cloth.

'Is he all right now?' he asked.

Galba laughed gently. 'He'll live. The doctor had to dig around in his shoulder a bit and so we fed him a big skin of wine first to take his mind off it, and now he's just getting his breath back.' He took Serpicus by an arm. Serpicus looked at the Thracian and realized how glad he was to see him. As always Galba's head was freshly shaved, and his small pink ears stood out in a way that made Serpicus think of a kindly weasel.

'Come on,' Galba said, 'I'll buy you a drink and you can tell me what the hell happened to you.'

'Didn't Brutus tell you the story himself?'

'Of course. He told me all about how he fought them off single-handed while you lot quaked and pissed yourselves under the wagons. I thought you might like the opportunity to put the record straight.'

Serpicus hesitated and then allowed Galba to lead him away and up the street.

'Just the one,' he said. 'I have a family who haven't seen me for a month.'

Galba put a manicured hand on his shoulder and patted it in a way that Serpicus knew meant he had something to tell him.

'What is it?'

'Sure you don't want a drink first?'

Serpicus stopped and faced him. 'No, now.'

Galba hesitated and then sighed. 'Metellus is dead.'

Serpicus was ready for almost any news, but not this. 'What? How can he be dead? He's only . . .' Metellus was a few years younger than himself, not much more than twenty, with the sort of healthy good looks that made Serpicus silently promise to take better care of himself every time he saw him. Metellus had been well when they left Rome. If he was dead now then there could only be one reason for it. Serpicus dropped his voice, kept the tone of his question neutral. 'Does anyone know how it happened?'

Galba shrugged and looked around casually. No one was nearby. 'The usual thing,' he said softly. 'He's rich, he's got a nice villa and some good vineyards around it, in Rhodes I think. Someone noticed. His friends stood by him, but Someone was more powerful than them. So Metellus lost his villa and his lands, and, when he protested, Someone called it treason and the poor bastard lost his head too.' Galba spat. 'And now his family are in exile in Crete, living on charity and anyone who was their friend is wondering who's next.'

Serpicus sighed, a sound that came all the way up from the soles of his feet. He had liked Metellus. And he was their sponsor and main buyer. 'So, we've got a cargo of animals and no one to pay us for them.'

Galba looked at a manicured fingernail. 'The news isn't quite all bad. Well, for Metellus I suppose it is. But there's some hope for us.'

Serpicus grabbed his arm. 'You found another buyer?'

'Yes, but don't get too excited.'

Serpicus hesitated. 'How much?' Galba pulled at a tiny fragment of cuticle with great concentration. 'Come on.'

'Two thousand.' Galba narrowed his eyes and winced as he spoke.

Serpicus let go of Galba's arm in disbelief. 'Two? That's half what Metellus was going to pay. We'll be lucky to cover our costs.' He leant back against the nearby wall. He felt as if he had just completed a long and exhausting race and had then been told to go out and do it again. The business was under enough pressure already. All the established firms of animal trackers were suffering because a plague of amateurs, mostly veterans with no income, were coming into the trade in the hope of quick profits. The amateurs were incompetent. They killed as many animals as they brought home and scared off most of the others. Catching the beasts was getting harder, costs were going up while prices were being driven down. The demand for suitable animals was enormous but it surely wasn't infinite, and even if it was the supply of easily obtainable beasts wasn't. Eventually, and probably sooner rather than later, it would start to get difficult to find the animals that were still left and then the amateurs would move on and the people who knew what they were doing would get their business back again. But for now, the market was flooded with beasts and the buyers had the upper hand. Metellus had been a shrewd businessman, but a fair one. He had driven a hard bargain with Serpicus, but it was reasonable and they could have survived on what he would have paid them. The money would have settled their debts and allowed them to take a rest, and there would still have been just about enough left over to re-equip for the next expedition. For the first time in ages they would not have been in debt before the expedition even set off. They might just have made a profit.

But now Metellus was dead, and the deal died with him.

Galba kicked a stone across the street. 'It was the best offer around, and believe me I have spent a month grovelling to people I wouldn't normally even nod to in the street. There are just too many animals around.' He raised and then dropped his arms again so that they slapped against his sides. 'We're too early. The big games aren't for another six weeks. Once the Ludi Plebi have taken place, the Masters of Games will have slaughtered everything they've got bigger than a sewer rat and the price will rise again, but for the moment no one is buying seriously. If we had storage space we could . . .'

'But we don't,' Serpicus said. He put a hand on Galba's shoulder. 'I'm sorry, I blamed you and that's unfair. I know you've done everything you could.'

Galba waited. When Serpicus didn't say anything, he said, 'So, what now?'

'We'll just have to go straight back out again.' There was no choice. Serpicus didn't say the obvious: that they had no capital to pay themselves with, that they would be living on credit at ruinous rates of interest, and that every last penny they could raise would have to be ploughed into the next expedition. Still, they both knew that life was suddenly very simple. If the next trip wasn't a success, they were bankrupt.

Galba managed a weak smile. 'So, I suppose no drink then?'

Serpicus smiled back and offered him his hand. 'No. We'll talk tomorrow.' As he reached the corner he turned to see Galba was heading for the tavern. Brutus and the others would be there soon. Serpicus suddenly wanted a drink very much, but he wanted to see his family more.

He went back to the pens and chose the horse that looked least tired. The road was quiet and he made good time to Rome. He stabled his horse and walked the short distance to his house. It was getting dark when he pushed the front door open and walked into the atrium of his house. A single taper burned on the wall. It was warm inside, and he smelt new bread. Two cups and a jug with condensation on the sides were on the table.

Antonia looked around the corner of the alcove where the oven was built into the wall. She smiled and as always he was sure that the room got brighter.

'Not long,' she said and turned back to the table.

He stood behind her and put his hands on her hips. She didn't speak or turn round, just pointed to the back door with one slim arm. He didn't argue. A man who works all day smeared with the sweat and shit of dozens of frightened wild animals could perhaps hope that his wife might still love him when he got home, but not that she would immediately want to kiss him.

He went out into the tiny yard. There was a shallow stone trough and two wooden buckets filled with water, and a clean robe hanging from a nail. He pulled his tunic off and stood naked in the trough. He soaped and washed himself from the first bucket then poured the remains over his head, gasping with the cold of it. The second bucket he poured more slowly, sluicing himself carefully. As he put it down she called to him and a soft cloth flew out through the door. He caught it and dried himself, enjoying the warm night air.

He wrapped the robe around himself and went back indoors, clean and dry. Antonia was putting olives and bread on the table. He poured two cups of wine and passed one to her. She pressed her lips gently against his and then pulled away and smiled again. 'That's a lot better,' she said, and raised her hand. The two cups touched. They drank.

'Hungry?'

He nodded, and walked to the tiny room where the children slept. He pulled back the curtain. They were curled up together like puppies. Serpicus let go of the curtain and the two of them sat down and ate together. For a long while they didn't speak. When people live in a small house and they have children, sometimes an uninterrupted silence feels like the most profound communication they can achieve.

Which of course it isn't, as they proved after supper. Lying next to her afterwards, face to face, thigh to thigh, slick with sweat, he knew there was no better place for him to be. He ran a finger down the soft line of her mouth and then pulled her silently against him, as if to imprint the memory of her on his skin. She winced and pulled away. With a smile she took hold of the leather thong around his neck and held what hung from it in her hand.

'No doubt,' she said.

He smiled. 'Always.'

She frowned at it. 'This thing gets in the way.'

As always he took her hand in his, and as always he remembered the day they were married.

When the priest had pronounced them one, Artemidorus, her father, stepped forward and held out his hand. In it was a pale circle of what looked like polished bone, with two small holes drilled into it.

'Ivory,' he said.

He took it in both hands and pushed gently. The circle snapped in two. He produced two thin leather thongs, threaded them through the holes and tied the ivory around their necks. They could see that the circle had not broken evenly, but with a jagged point around the middle.

Antonia was pleased, but still complained to her father. 'Couldn't you have broken it evenly? The edge presses into me.'

Artemidorus looked at her seriously. 'It is meant to. I prepared it so earlier, drew a knife point down the centre of the bone until there was a groove along which it would break.'

She laughed with surprise. 'You wanted it to be jagged? Why?'

He paused. 'Two reasons. To make it impossible to duplicate, so that there would only be one man who could ever wear the other half that matches your own, and to make it snag on your clothes sometimes, and so remind you of this day.'

And so it did. And they complained and joked about the ivory amulets, and sometimes they cursed him, but they never took them off, and any time one of them took the other's token in their hand, they would hold the two halves so that the two jagged sides matched, and they would remember.

And every time Antonia held it she said 'No doubt', and every time she did so he replied 'Always', because of the agreement they made the night they were married, standing together in front of the statue of Apollo. They swore they would never doubt each other, and he never had doubted her; nor had he given her cause to doubt him.

She fell asleep almost at once, but Serpicus lay awake for a long time, watching her in his arms, feeling her warm breath on his chest. He had not yet told her that, having just returned, he was going to turn around and go straight back out again. Or that there was no money, and that soon he might not even have a job. There would be time enough for talking and worrying tomorrow.

5

To Aelius Sejanus, from his Servant:

As you have commanded, the search for the two Germans has commenced. We know that they are of the Treveri tribe, and it is believed that they are still within the city walls. Enquiries are proceeding with the utmost circumspection; your command that they should not be aware that we are searching for them is being heeded by every one of our agents. Were it not for this necessity I believe we would already have run them to ground. Nevertheless, I am confident that you will have them within a few days.

To Aelius Sejanus, from his Servant:

The two Germans have now, as I assured you, been located. The one called Sigmund now calls himself Decius, although it is understood that most of those around him call him 'the German boy', so the change in name from German to Roman is at best academic. The other barbarian Alraic calls himself Serpicus, as our previous intelligence indicated.

Enquiries have been made as to their circumstances, as per your instructions. Both men are employed – as many of their race are – in the stables attached to the Circus. It is understood that the barbarian Serpicus used to race chariots there, but has retired from that occupation for reasons unspecified. The boy Decius has raced a few times and, although lacking physical and mental maturity, is believed to show promise.

The income from stable work is insufficient to support a man all year round, and so a number of the Germans have gone into business as animal trappers. They work the stables for the summer and autumn, when the races are frequent, and use the off-season to travel to Africa, Asia Minor or the north to collect animals for the arena. I understand that business has not been good for the last two years, for a variety of reasons. The death of Metellus has, it is rumoured, left them in a difficult position. There is every reason, therefore, to anticipate that they will be receptive to your proposals.

To Aelius Sejanus, from his Servant:

Please be assured that my only concern is to facilitate your wishes, and that if I have overstepped the bounds of my responsibilities in seeking to offer advice or conclusions, it is only in that spirit and no other that it

*was done. I took your instruction to omit no detail too
literally. I will confine myself to the facts in future.*

*The Germans will be approached today, as you
instruct.*

6

The next morning, Serpicus walked to the arena with a lot on his mind. When he came around the final corner he looked up, as always, and even though he had seen it a thousand times, unfailingly he stopped to admire the sheer scale of the building. Those who knew it intimately, as he did, often said that it was just as well that the scale was breathtaking as there was little else to commend it.

The design of the arena was praised by architects and politicians alike. The public too thought it was wonderful. It was admired and pointed to with pride by almost everyone. The only ones who hated it were people like the charioteers and animal handlers, those who actually had to use it. For some reason the stables for the racing horses were placed close to the pit where the dead and dying animals were thrown by the arena slaves, and the smell and noise were atrocious. Panic and fear flowed from the doomed animals and swirled around the racing horses like steam, making them skittish and fretful.

Everyone who worked in the arena complained about it, everyone knew it was wrong, but nothing was ever done.

Like everyone who worked under the arena, Serpicus had to protect his animals against the problems posed by it. No chariot driver who cared anything about his horses wanted to leave them there longer than was absolutely necessary, but the crush in the streets each evening after the games usually made it impossible to leave until well after dark. Some charioteers left their teams to the tender mercies of the track animal handlers, who were surrounded by every kind of animal slaughtered every day and saw no reason to spend time or effort on a particular team of horses. Not without a stupendous bribe anyway, and even a bribe only meant that, all other things being equal, they probably wouldn't actively mistreat the horses. When he was a driver Serpicus had preferred to stay with the horses himself until the streets cleared enough to allow them to leave. Other drivers, those who could afford it and who had orgies to go to that couldn't be put off until later, employed trusted men to look after their teams. Serpicus was married, he didn't get many invitations to orgies and he couldn't have afforded to employ a groom anyway, so he always did his own work. He knew that the horses were calmer and easier to lead from the stable if he stayed with them, not to mention being a lot less difficult to handle when coming back in again. More than once a horse being led into the arena to compete in a race had turned and bolted at the sight of one of the track handlers.

Between trips most of the trappers worked under the

arena looking after the animals. The smell was stupefying and the pay little better than slavery, but it was better than starving and it allowed them to keep an eye on what animals were popular and which weren't. The popularity of different types of animals went in waves. For a while every games would feature hordes of wild boar, and the audience would scream and not be able to get enough of them. Then, suddenly, they would tire of boar and yell for lions, and anyone who put a boar into the arena would find themselves booed out of the city. More than one group of trappers had returned with a good catch of animals and discovered that what they had caught was last month's fashion and was now worthless. It paid to move fast and keep your ear to the ground. Most trappers paid people to do their listening for them. Serpicus and his partners couldn't afford to do that so they went one better: they did it themselves.

They were attending to the horses. Galba and Brutus were grooming the horses' shaggy coats, pulling a thick-toothed comb through the rough hair with long measured strokes. The wound to Brutus's head was covered by the rag he wore around it, and if any blood was still left on him it was covered by a thick film of sweat and dirt. Decius was fetching water and talking at length about a slave girl he'd seen that afternoon who he thought might have looked at him. Serpicus was showing a slack-mouthed stable-lad the correct way to use a grooming brush – 'the side with the bristles goes onto the horse, the side without the bristles goes in your hand' – when he heard the door behind him open. An educated drawl came through it.

'I am Calcas. I am looking for some Germans. I seek Serpicus, and the one named Decius whom some call Sigmund.'

Brutus looked up. He was standing on the other side of Serpicus' horse and so could see who was talking. He leant on the horse's rump and looked over Serpicus' shoulder at the man who had come in.

'Lots of Germans in these parts,' he said lightly. 'Who wants them?'

There was a wary silence. 'I seek the Germans called Serpicus and Decius only.'

'Who wants them?' Brutus repeated, still amiably but without interest.

'As I have said, I am Calcas.' The voice came closer behind Serpicus. 'Are you Serpicus?' Serpicus heard the sound of a bucket being put down nearby. Decius was listening but wasn't going to show himself just yet. Galba came out of a shadow and stood beside Brutus. Both of them folded their arms on the horse's back and rested their chins on their arms. They looked like boys peering over a wall at adults who think they aren't being watched.

'Who's this?' asked Galba.

'Says he's Calcas,' said Brutus. 'Looking for Germans, apparently.'

'Plenty of those about,' said Galba. Brutus made a grunt of agreement.

The voice behind Serpicus became slightly strained. 'I don't have time to play games. I have an important message to deliver.'

Brutus chewed on a piece of straw and looked at the

messenger with a yokel expression that he used whenever anyone was annoying him. 'Let's suppose I'm Decius or Serpicus, then, and you can deliver the message to me.' Brutus stopped leaning on the horse and unfolded his arms. The horse let out a sigh of relief. Slapping the horse on the backside, he walked away to the other side of the stable. 'Just so you can get some practice in message delivering.' Brutus was now on the other side of the room, and presumably the messenger behind Serpicus would be watching him. Serpicus turned round.

The man in front of him was about sixty, tall and thin, well dressed for a servant, and with a face like a greyhound drinking vinegar. Serpicus got the feeling that life and everything about it was a perpetual disappointment to him, and that meeting people like Brutus merely confirmed him in this opinion. He didn't trouble to hide his distaste at his surroundings. A taller, thinner man with dark skin stood a spear's length behind him, his head bowed like a servant's, unmoving in the shadows. Serpicus squinted to see the man's face and, as if he had somehow felt Serpicus' eyes upon him, the man withdrew silently further into the darkness.

'So, what's it all about?' asked Brutus.

'The Partner's uncle wishes to discuss the possibility of employing the Germans.'

'Ah. So you are here to . . . ?'

'I am come to request their presence tomorrow night at the Palace.'

'What palace is that, exactly? There are so many these days.'

Calcas made a sort of hissing sound and spoke with a reverent emphasis. 'The Palace of the Partner of His Labours.'

Brutus and Galba exchanged indifferent glances. 'No, never heard of it,' they said together.

Serpicus leant forward. It was suddenly no longer funny. 'Sejanus' palace?' he said. Calcas looked at him with the expression of slight hope and almost certain disappointment with which a teacher in charge of an extremely slow group of students looks at an unusually dim-looking boy who has suddenly spoken for the very first time.

'The same,' he said, with a slight movement of his head towards Serpicus and then a more exaggerated one at Brutus. 'Although the actual invitation is from Blaesus, the Partner's uncle, whom I have the honour to serve. Perhaps you could impress on your . . . your friend here, the honour – the singular honour – that is bestowed on him by this invitation.' He looked at Brutus with a sour expression, and got a cheerful grin in reply. 'If, that is, your friend is indeed the man I seek.'

Brutus pointed with his stalk of straw at the messenger. 'So, just to be clear. You are Calcas?'

'Correct.'

'From Blaesus?'

'As I have said.'

'This message is for Decius, yes?'

'Yes.'

'Previously Sigmund.'

'Yes.'

'And Serpicus?'

'Yes.'

'The German.'

'Yes, him too.'

'Just Decius and Serpicus invited to dinner then?' asked Galba with a winning smile.

'Yes.'

'Not, say, Decius and Serpicus and their particular and most loyal friends?' The messenger hesitated and looked at him with renewed dislike.

'The invitation was for Decius and Serpicus alone.'

Galba shrugged. 'I'll pass the message on.'

'Thank you.'

'From . . . who was it again?'

The messenger sighed deeply and looked directly at Serpicus, as if perhaps he might be a dim torch of sense in the darkness that Brutus and Galba were surrounding them all with. 'Is it possible perhaps to talk to someone who speaks a known language?'

The dark man in the deep shadow behind him lifted his head slightly and Serpicus thought his thin lips curved slightly into a smile. The man somehow didn't look like a servant. Serpicus didn't know what he was.

Brutus was enjoying himself. He pushed his leather cap further back on his head. 'And you've come here to do what, again, exactly?'

'Request his presence. Their presence.'

Brutus pulled a face. 'Ah. "Request", eh? Not, for example, "require"?'

Calcas made the same noise that an old dog makes when it is tired of children pulling its tail. 'Indeed. It is an invitation, not an order.' He gathered his dignity as an elderly woman pulls her skirts around her after falling down in the street. 'The honour of such an invitation is such that the idea of compulsion would be as ridiculous as it would be unnecessary.' He sniffed loudly. 'As any man of breeding would know.'

The insult was wholly wasted. Brutus looked thoughtful. 'I see,' he said seriously, tapping his chin with his straw. 'Then this must be a very great honour indeed.' The messenger looked slightly mollified, but remained suspicious. Serpicus felt he was probably right to be so. Brutus walked slowly up to him and stopped a hand's breadth away from his chest. The other man in the shadows behind him stepped back slightly, as if Brutus had pushed him even though he was nowhere near him. Calcas stood his ground but looked uneasy. Brutus had that effect on people. Not only was he taller and wider than most people, he had an air of danger about him, like the sort of tail-up mongrel dog that doesn't care one bit what you do to it so long as it can get a bite at your throat while you're doing it. For anyone with any normal sense of self-preservation, the idea of someone of Brutus' size who genuinely doesn't care what happens to them was highly unnerving.

Brutus tapped the old man's chest with the straw and put it back in his mouth. 'Consider it done.'

Calcas appeared about to say something more, then thought better of it. He left the room with a haughty expression that looked a bit frayed at the edges. The man who had followed him in and listened without speaking left too. Serpicus wondered again for a moment who he was – not a slave, not a servant, but not a master either.

Galba grinned at Brutus. 'Your gift for making friends remains undimmed.'

Brutus spat cheerfully. 'You see people like that, there's just something about them. Makes me want to stick a thistle up their arse.'

Serpicus was silent and looked thoughtful. 'I heard all that,' he said, 'but I didn't understand it. What was it all about?'

'The usual thing,' said Galba. 'Dinner invitation to a rich man's house, to be followed by much drinking and an orgy. Most likely, anyway.' He scratched himself absently. 'Of course, if it was me, I probably wouldn't bother going.' Serpicus chuckled.

'Don't be an arsehole,' Brutus said, jerking a thumb at Serpicus and Decius. 'Why would the uncle of the most powerful man in Rome be inviting a couple of no-name German animal catchers like these two to his house?'

'No offence,' Serpicus said mildly.

'To give his beautiful young wife a damn good servicing, I imagine, as prescribed in the animal catcher's instruction manual,' said Galba. 'At least, whenever I get an invitation from someone like Sejanus, I usually find that's what it's really about.'

Brutus looked at Galba as if he was seeing him for the first time, and shook his head slowly. Galba gave him his holiday-best smile and then gestured to Serpicus. 'Come on,' he said. 'I need a drink.'

'No, I promised . . .' Serpicus said, but Galba was already almost out the door. Brutus and Serpicus looked at each other, shrugged and set off after him. Decius hastily put down his broom and turned to follow them.

There was a crash as he fell headlong over the bucket he had just placed on the floor. A few moments later he was trotting beside them in a way that suggested that his leg hurt but he was pretending it didn't.

'Sejanus? Sejanus wants to see us?' he asked carelessly.

Serpicus nodded. 'That's what the man said.'

'I thought . . . I thought he said something about the Partner of His Labours?'

'He did.' Serpicus turned to face Decius as they walked. 'Tiberius once called Sejanus that, and Sejanus has never let anyone forget it. Remember, if we do see him, he likes to be called the Partner.'

'Less of a partner, more of a tapeworm,' muttered Galba, and Serpicus and Brutus looked around nervously.

'If you want my company in the street, don't say such things out loud,' Brutus said in a low voice. 'The whole city is full of people who earn a good living reporting things a lot less insulting than that.'

'I've met a few,' said Galba to himself. 'Leeches. They hang on your lips until they are full and then they drop off.'

Brutus stared at him for a moment. 'Have you been doing more of that reading thing again?'

'Go screw yourself,' Galba said.

Brutus grinned. 'That's my boy.'

They walked past a street vendor packing up his stall. A smell of roast pork and herbs surrounded them.

'Anything left?' asked Brutus hopefully.

The vendor looked up with a morose expression on his

thin face. He didn't give the impression that selling scraps of burnt pork on thin sticks was much of a business even on a good day, and Brutus' arrival clearly didn't represent any sort of improvement. Serpicus could understand his lack of enthusiasm. Pork was the only meat that the poor of Rome could afford, and the meat sold in the street was the bits that the butchers couldn't sell, and now Brutus was hoping for free samples.

'Three for the price of one,' the vendor said gloomily. Brutus smiled happily and reached into his pocket.

They came to a street corner and Serpicus turned left.

'Going home?' asked Galba.

'Yes.'

Brutus was worrying with a blunt finger at a morsel of stringy pork caught between his back teeth. 'Not coming for a drink?' he asked.

Serpicus shook his head seriously. 'I'll see you tomorrow.'

That night after the children were asleep Serpicus told Antonia about what had happened to Metellus, and that he was going out on another expedition in a few days. Her face became serious.

'I thought . . .' She stopped talking and bit her lip.

'I know,' he said. 'So did I.'

She looked at the floor. 'I hate what you do.'

He tried to smile. 'So do I. I must try and get a job that smells a bit better.'

She looked at him in a way she had never done before, partly angry, partly asking for something. 'No, not that. I don't mind when you work at the arena, I don't mind the smell or that you work every public holiday or the lousy money, I don't even mind that it's sometimes dangerous.'

He wanted to smile but recognized that silence and the slightest movement of an eyebrow was probably sufficient. Sometimes there is no right thing to say.

She leant forward and held his hand. 'Because you're here, don't you see? You come home to me every evening, and I see you every morning before you leave and I know you'll return that day. You're there when I wake up in the night, that's all that matters.'

Serpicus pressed her hand in confusion. This was new; she had never spoken like this before.

A tear ran slowly down her cheek and she gestured at the room around them. 'I don't mind being poor, I don't mind living here, I don't mind any of it.' Her voice became urgent. 'I don't mind any of it so long as you're here. It's the going away that I mind, the not seeing you. I can't stand that. I don't care about money. I'd rather you were here and we had nothing than see you go away, no matter how much we might have when you get back.' She wiped her cheeks on her sleeve. 'I'm sorry, this isn't helping.'

They sat silent for a while, and then Serpicus came to a decision. He didn't know how he was going to do it, but he knew what he had to do. He took both her hands in his.

'This is the last time, I promise,' he said. 'I don't know what it'll take or how we'll manage, but whatever happens, whatever I have to do, I will never leave you again.'

She lifted her head and looked into his eyes. Serpicus knew that was the right thing to say.

But he wondered why he hadn't told her about Blaesus' invitation to supper.

7

To Aelius Sejanus, from his Servant:

Your invitation to the barbarians Serpicus and Decius has been delivered. We had been told that they could be found with the animal hunter Brutus and his confederates at their lair under the arena. It is a dark and pungent place, with noisome air thick with sweat and the scent of animals. The stench is enough to make a civilized man choke in his handkerchief at the time and breathe with difficulty for three days afterwards. Perhaps unsurprisingly, the barbarians who spend the day there appear to thrive on it.

We came upon the German in the stables, grooming a horse. Brutus – or the man I took to be him, for, like all those present, he found it amusing to refuse to identify himself – is a tall unkempt man with the coarse red hair that only another German could find pleasing. His associate, whose name I did not ascertain, is also

German and dark. Both men have long moustaches and affect strips of coloured ribbon in their hair. Another man was with them, a Greek whose baldness suggested Thracian origin. There was also a boy present, perhaps seventeen years old, who may have been Decius, or may have been some form of relative of the other three judging by the deference with which he regarded them. The boy is also red-headed, and I thought I marked a resemblance between Brutus and him – whether racial or familial I do not know.

The German addressed Calcas your servant disrespectfully, in the usual manner of their race. The Germans delight in mockery and rough talk, and I saw every other man in the stable smiling and laughing as the Germans traduced your servant. The Thracian took his cue from this lack of appropriate deference. Several times I intervened, to inform them as to who they were speaking to, and to warn them that their rudeness to the servant of the Partner would not go unremarked, but their insults continued. If it were not that I understand that these people may be able to render some service to you, I would already have had them arrested for their treasonous remarks.

Having delivered the invitation as commanded, we withdrew with our dignity intact, and I fancy that the Germans were – despite themselves – impressed with our demeanour. But they are a rough and uncivilized people and it will surely be many years before the influence of Rome changes their manners in all but the surface. The Greek does not even have the excuse of barbarism.

The details would be tedious. Suffice to relate that the man who spoke assured us that both Serpicus and Decius would be present at your house tomorrow night.

8

The Palace of the Partner of His Labours, as it had been known for several years, was heavily but discreetly guarded. It had been built by Augustus as a home for part of his burgeoning family. Tiberius gave it to Sejanus when the Partner became head of the Praetorian Guard, shortly before Tiberius left for Capri never to return. The Palace was a spear-throw from the Praetorians' sprawling barracks on the Viminal Hill, and although relatively small was luxurious and expensively appointed. Sejanus, as the Emperor's Regent and right hand, now spent most of his time in the Imperial dwellings on the Palatine Hill directly opposite the Viminal. Thus Blaesus, Sejanus' uncle, had come to use the Partner's Palace as his base. Both palaces overlooked the Senate House. Not only was this symbolic in a way that both Sejanus and the Senate recognized, the buildings were also convenient for the court houses where the treason trials were held. Sejanus did not have time to attend every day, so at his suggestion Blaesus went in his stead. Sejanus found that the presence of a member of his family tended to concentrate the judges' minds on punishment rather than leniency. And there could be no leniency for treason. Tiberius was many miles away, but his spies reported to him every day. Sejanus had no intention of allowing the Emperor to wonder if his Regent was becoming soft in his absence.

Serpicus and Decius appeared on time and freshly scrubbed for dinner. The captain of the guard at the imposing outside gate was expecting them, but searched them efficiently anyway before escorting them to the main door, a heavy and heavily decorated oak slab, where a household slave took over.

'Come this way, please,' the slave said. Serpicus heard the familiar accent and lifted an eyebrow.

'Thank you,' Decius replied, using the language of the Treveri, and the slave looked back at him with a startled expression. He opened his mouth to speak as they entered the outer atrium and then he dropped his head and said nothing. Serpicus saw that two men were walking towards them. The older man was in his late thirties, with weather-beaten skin covering wiry muscle, and a long scar on his right cheek. He wore a plain toga and walked like a soldier. The other was a few years younger, heavy-set like a boxer but with the angles of his face beginning to soften with dissipation. He wore a jerkin edged with colour and the careless air of a blade-about-town. His hair was thick and dark blond, almost the gold of fresh straw.

At the sight of them the younger man held out an arm to stop his companion. 'Look, Marcus,' he said in a high voice. His face split with a vicious child's smile as he looked at them intently. 'These must be the Partner's Germans.' He sniffed the air. 'At least, they smell like Germans.'

The man he called Marcus glanced quickly at him as if he'd said something he shouldn't, then looked at Serpicus with the expression that Roman patricians used to remind others of their respective status. 'Certainly Germans,' Marcus said, staring at Serpicus steadily.

Serpicus swallowed a retort and glanced at Decius, shaking his head slightly but emphatically. They were in the heavily guarded house of the favoured uncle of the most powerful man in Rome, being insulted by men who seemed to be related to him. It was not a time for standing on dignity. He tried to look just respectful enough and hoped they would soon tire of goading him. Decius took the hint and stepped back out of the way.

The blond man sidled up beside Serpicus. 'I leave for Germany soon. Perhaps you'd like to come with me?' Serpicus couldn't help showing his surprise. The young man grinned again. His eyes were unnaturally wide and bright under the pale hair. 'You see? He wants me to take him home.'

Marcus' face relaxed into the thinnest of smiles. 'Better not,' he said. 'He might not like what you're going to do to his people when you get there.'

Something inside Serpicus spilled over. 'Be careful,' he said softly. 'They may do it to you first.'

The smile vanished and the dark man's face was an implacable mask. 'You suppose so?' he said in tones colder than a glacier stream.

'Varus thought as you do,' Serpicus said, meeting his

gaze. 'He had to change his mind when they lit a fire around him in the forest.'

The younger man let out a noise that was almost a scream, and leapt towards Serpicus with his arm upraised.

'Consilius!'

At the sound of Marcus' voice the blond man stopped as if he'd hit a wall, though the expression of excited malevolence on his face didn't alter. Serpicus knew that, if Marcus had not snapped the order, a moment later they would have been rolling on the floor like boys in a playground. Consilius lowered his arm and leant his face close to Serpicus.

'This is not the place,' he hissed. 'We will meet again, and then there will be a reckoning.'

Serpicus said nothing, knowing he had said far too much already. The two Romans swept past him and through the door.

The household slave, who had evidently acquired the invaluable knack of melting into a wall when necessary, rematerialized by his side with Decius immediately behind him.

Serpicus gestured to the door. 'Who were they?'

The slave looked surprised at his ignorance. 'Marcus and Consilius,' he said. 'The sons of Blaesus, cousins to Sejanus.' He switched from Latin to his own tongue, speaking rapidly and quietly. 'You have made a bad enemy in Consilius. He and Marcus leave in a few days with the Seventh Legion to put down the revolt in Germany. I would advise staying out of their way until they depart.'

'Revolt? What revolt?'

Serpicus wanted to ask the German slave more but they were at the open door leading into the main apartments, and through it he could see their host rising to meet them. The slave did his disappearing-into-walls trick again as Blaesus came forward.

'Serpicus, so glad you were able to come tonight. And Decius, welcome. Come in, come in. I am Blaesus, the Partner's uncle. You may have heard of me.'

There was only a hint of a question at the end of the sentence. Blaesus was a general, a senator, and Sejanus' uncle. He looked like a man who enjoyed the benefits of all three positions. His voice was deep and sonorous. As the Senator came across the cool marble flagstones that lay at precise geometric angles across the atrium of his house to meet his guests, Serpicus felt something stir in his memory. Perhaps he'd seen Blaesus in the Forum or at the games without knowing who he was. There were a lot of rich men in Rome and they all looked a lot like Blaesus. No doubt, to him, poor men all looked a lot like Serpicus.

'Come, sit. We'll have some wine.'

They slipped off their shoes and reclined on low couches, Blaesus facing the two Germans.

Serpicus had never liked the fashion of lying down rather than sitting, not when talking and especially not when eating, but reclining was plainly what was expected and to do anything else would have been the mark of a bumpkin. Decius perched silently on his couch with the air of a man who had been told that at any moment it might suddenly fall through the floor.

Blaesus said nothing, letting his guests absorb their surroundings. There were coloured silks thrown carelessly over the couches. Serpicus was used to seeing cloth from Tarentum dyed by being soaked in water containing the powdered shells of the local mussels. He had a feeling that Blaesus' cloth and colours came from rather further away. It was intended to impress.

He looked around and saw a shadow move in a distant corner of the room. They were being spied upon. He wondered if Blaesus knew. Perhaps Blaesus took it for granted that a man in his position should assume that he was never alone.

They were separated from the Senator by a long narrow table. The legs and frame were made of a dark wood Serpicus did not recognize, decorated with finely detailed gold leaf. The surface of the table was made from a single sheet of startlingly white polished marble with thin veins of the faintest grey running through it. A large gold bowl of fruit sat in the centre. The bowl overflowed with russet apples, smooth-skinned oranges, black sticky dates, and several armfuls of tiny yellow grapes, all resting on a bed of ice chips that made clear runnels of cold sweat run down the outside of the bowl to pool on the pale stone underneath.

Blaesus plucked a sprig of grapes and motioned to them to do the same. The grapes were very sweet. The three men chewed slowly and in silence as they waited for a slave to pour three cups of wine from a heavy stone jug. Once the slave was finished and had stepped back out of sight but not out of hearing, Blaesus cleared his throat noisily and unselfconsciously. Serpicus hesitated.

Blaesus leant across the table and handed a cup to each of them.

'Your health,' he said with a smile.

There was a moment during which Serpicus felt that Blaesus was waiting to see what he would do with it. In Rome, above a certain social station, the normal rules of hospitality had become reversed. A poor man in the country entertaining a guest will delay drinking, waiting for the guest to sample the wine first. A rich Roman's guest, however, would far rather see his host drink before he tried it himself. Serpicus knew enough to be aware that poison had been changing history since Romulus and even before, but in the recent past too many people for comfort had died of mysterious stomach ailments after dinner parties. The problem had become worse since the Blessed Julius' legions marched him into Egypt and into Cleopatra's bed. The Romans brought aqueducts to Egypt, and in return a wealth of knowledge in the theory and practice of using narcotics flooded back into Rome, spreading like the Nile spilling onto the desert sands. Poison expanded from the exclusive use of the upper classes to the wider population, and moved from the social to the political arena. Before Egypt became part of the Empire, most cases of deliberate poisoning were carried out by amateurs motivated by passion, lovers getting rid of rivals or wives removing inconvenient husbands, but increasingly the poisoner's art was becoming a tool of political debate. It was easier – and far cheaper – to engage a professional poisoner to deal with a political rival than it was to spend the fortune necessary to beat him in an election. The problem now was to ensure that your own personal poisoner knew more than your rival's.

This development meant changes in dining etiquette. At business meetings between rivals, the host sometimes drank first from every cup on the table, just to show good faith. A few of those hosts fell foul of guests with a sense of irony, who paid a servant to lace the master's cup.

Serpicus swallowed the wine and examined the flavour without knowing what he was looking for. There was nothing unusual about it that he could discern, except that it tasted a good deal better than that which he was used to, but he reasoned that the mark of a good poisoner is presumably that the victim doesn't know he is dying until he is actually dead. He waited for whatever was in the wine to reach out inside his chest and squeeze his heart till it stopped. His heart continued to beat and he felt only a pleasant warmth. Perhaps he would survive the night after all. He tipped the goblet slightly towards Blaesus in tribute. 'Excellent. Cretan?'

The Senator looked mildly impressed. 'Close enough, and the same vines,' he said. 'Rhodes. My own vineyards.'

'My compliments.' Serpicus wondered which poor bastard had owned the vineyards before Sejanus raised Blaesus to his present position, and what type of treason had been conjured up against him in order that he could be relieved of his possessions. Serpicus took another sip. The manner of its getting hadn't affected the quality of the wine. He waited without speaking.

Decius was looking at his cup like a man staring at a letter that might just possibly contain news of a legacy and a promotion but might equally well contain his death warrant. Then he took a hurried gulp.

Serpicus remembered his father saying that when the wolf has fed well, he walks past the deer with hardly a glance. The deer sees the wolf's full belly and knows that he is safe for a time, but the deer still doesn't take its eye off the wolf. So do rich men move slowly past poor men, and the poor men watch them always, more carefully than the rich men watch them, for they never know how quickly the wolves may become hungry again.

Which was fine common sense, but it didn't stop Serpicus feeling annoyed and contrary when it happened.

Serpicus heard Decius shift uneasily on his couch. He watched as Blaesus ate the last grape left in his hand. He then picked up an apple the colour of the finest Tuscan wine and began to peel it in precise movements using a tiny fruit knife with a carved ivory handle. Serpicus waited. Blaesus put a thin shaving of fruit between his thin lips, then he pointed at both of them with two languid flicks of his forefinger.

'You were both born in Germany.'

Serpicus nodded. 'As the Senator knows.'

Blaesus looked at the apple as if it were of great interest. 'You, in Gelbheim, Decius in Praunberg, and your rumbustious friend in Glaudern. All villages in the lands of the Treveri.'

Decius smothered a startled cough. Serpicus said nothing, though he too was surprised. Not many Romans would even know the Treveri existed, let alone be able to name three villages there. Blaesus had done his research.

'And, as any man of the Treveri no doubt knows, I fought with Germanicus against the Germans. Against the Treveri. And others.' His gaze flicked up at Serpicus, and he let a pause fall. Serpicus kept his eyes on Blaesus.

'The war is long finished,' he said carefully. 'The past is over, what is done is done. Germany is a loyal part of the Pax Romana. There is peace between the peoples of Germany and Rome along the length of the Rhine.'

Blaesus pulled a flake of apple off the knife blade, extending his top lip like a horse. 'Actually,' he said in a way that was carefully offhand, 'there isn't, not just at the moment. Several tribes revolted just a few weeks ago. Others are very likely to join them.'

Decius sat silently, listening. Even though the Treveri slave had already let the news slip, Serpicus was careful to look startled. 'I had not heard.'

Blaesus looked at Serpicus carefully and then gave a little shrug. Either he decided to believe him or he didn't want to pursue it just then. 'Not many know, yet,' he said, 'but the news is travelling towards Rome. The Senate will be told officially tomorrow.'

'Do we know why the tribes are in revolt?'

Blaesus gave another shrug and put a tiny grape in his mouth. 'Between ourselves, it has been coming for some time. Romans and Germans aren't designed to sit well together. Rome knows that the price of empire is a war every so often, and Germany is one of the places where it will always happen.' Another grape vanished. 'The official reason is that a temple was desecrated and a Roman soldier's knife was found there afterwards. Ergo, it was Roman soldiers who did the desecrating, and the next day twenty thousand outraged Germans are attacking garrisons all along the Rhine.' He sighed. 'If I were Emperor, religion would be banned.'

Serpicus took a breath. 'Are the Treveri among the rebel tribes?'

Blaesus shook his head. 'I understand not, yet.' He paused for a moment. 'Presumably you have relatives, friends still in Germany?'

Serpicus saw the danger in front of him. 'Of course. But I cannot believe that they will be involved in any rebellion against Rome.'

The Senator smiled, and looked at Decius. 'Of course not. Tell me, are there not hostages still in Rome since the . . .' He paused momentarily, as if chewing over the word to extract every subtle flavour – 'the pacification of your tribe?'

Serpicus looked blank. 'I would not know about that. I understood that hostages are normally exchanged after five years.'

'Normally, yes. But not always. It depends on . . . so many things.' Serpicus winced. The Senator knew his history.

'So,' Blaesus said cheerfully, looking at his two guests. 'Your tribe is likely to be at war with Rome soon. You have lived here for some time, and will not be unaware of the privileges you enjoy as a result. Is there any way the two of you would wish to serve Rome at this time?' His eyes narrowed very slightly. Serpicus took the hint.

'If the Senator would tell us any way in which we can serve Rome, it would be a privilege and an honour to carry out his wishes.' The words felt like grit in soft bread in his mouth. Decius was still sitting immobile.

Blaesus tapped thoughtfully at a very white front tooth with the blade of the fruit knife. The sound was high and clear. 'Very well,' he said, putting the knife down. His voice was different, decisive. 'I want the two of you to do something for me.' Serpicus waited. Of course he did.

'We are your servants.'

'I want you to take a journey.'

'We enjoy travel.'

'I want you to go back to Germany, to your village. Specifically, to Gelbheim.'

Serpicus hesitated. 'Did you not say that there was a revolt in progress there?'

Blaesus frowned slightly. 'No. I said that the Treveri are at peace. Even if they are rebels, that need be no concern of yours. Unless, that is, you choose to make it so.'

'Why me – why us?' Serpicus asked. Blaesus paused and gave him a shallow smile.

'It's actually very simple,' he said.

Serpicus was prepared to wager that it wasn't anything of the kind.

'I want you and your colleagues to go to Gelbheim and bring an animal back to Rome for me.' Serpicus blinked with surprise but said nothing. 'You will need to go by sea at first, to Genoa.'

'Sea?' Serpicus said.

'Yes. The roads will be busy and progress would be too slow. There will be military reinforcements going north to Germany, messengers and petitioners heading south to Rome, and a lot of hysterical civilians in the middle going around in circles and getting in everybody's way. It'll be a lot quicker by boat.'

'Boat?' Serpicus said. Blaesus nodded.

'Boat to Genoa. Then ride north to Gelbheim. You'll have to go a slightly longer route than the one the legions take or you'll get caught up in whatever is going on, although I suspect it'll all be over by the time you get there. Secure my animal, bring it back to Genoa where the boat will be waiting, then back to Rome and the job is finished.'

He sat back, looking entirely satisfied with the plan he had outlined. There was a long silence. Serpicus heard Decius clear his throat. He glanced at the young man and followed his gaze downward. Serpicus had loosened his grip on his cup and the contents were spilling slowly onto his sandals. He put the cup carefully onto the table and sat back.

'May I speak freely?' he said.

'Of course.'

'You are hiring men and sending an expedition to the farthest reaches of the Empire during a border rebellion to collect a single animal, and you want me to believe there is nothing unusual going on?'

Blaesus made a small fly-swatting gesture. 'It need make no difference to you. All you have to do is collect the animal and bring it back.'

Serpicus smiled and shook his head. 'You want me to plan this trip, I have to know what I'm preparing for. You want a professional, you have to treat me like one.'

Immediately he knew he had gone too far. Blaesus'

expression lost the urbane good humour it had contained since their entrance, and it was as if the sun had gone behind a cloud and a north wind sprung up in its stead. His eyes narrowed and he raised an admonitory finger, like a teacher warning an unruly child. There was a brief pause while Serpicus wondered what the price of dignity was, then he began a rapid retreat.

'I apologize, my tongue sometimes runs away with me, it is a fault others have often told me of.' Serpicus made the traditional open-hand gesture that poor men make to rich men when they are offering the rich man something that, in every meaningful sense, he already possesses. 'I will, of course, serve the Senator in any capacity that my small abilities will permit. Please forgive my rudeness, caused by my surprise at the honour of being chosen in this way.'

Serpicus waited. Blaesus took a drink and appeared to relax a little. He seemed to be waiting for Serpicus to speak. Just a little more flattery and they might survive the night.

'May I ask the Senator a question?'

It was the first time Decius had spoken. Blaesus turned to him and looked benevolent.

'Of course.'

'May I ask how you found us?'

Blaesus looked pleased with himself. 'No real difficulty,' he said. 'Simple logic and asking the right questions to the right people. Slave traders tend to deal in slaves from a specific area, and they keep good records. I sent my housekeeper down to talk to the traders in German slaves. He found a man from your tribe who was about your age. The barbarian didn't need much persuasion to identify you. He gave me the answers to a few simple questions, and then I knew who I was looking for.'

Serpicus acknowledged the Senator's perspicacity with an inclination of the head. 'Why us?' he asked.

Blaesus picked up his cup and looked carefully into it. He might have been looking for mosquitoes, or he might have been taking his time in replying.

'You have experience in catching and transporting animals. You are from the tribe which is selling the animal to me. You know the country, and you speak the language of some of the tribes on the way. You have a reputation for honesty and efficiency. I understand also that you are in something of a financial quandary at present. I need someone who knows what they are doing, you need the work. We can help each other, no?'

Serpicus looked at him. Blaesus knew all about them, knew their business, knew that the deal with Metellus had fallen through. Serpicus suddenly flinched inwardly. Metellus, with his easy ways and his villa with its good vineyards in Rhodes. Serpicus looked into his cup with a sense of queasiness and wondered if Blaesus had arranged to get himself some nice vines and an impoverished animal catcher in the same movement.

'You trust me to come back again?'

Blaesus paused while he poked at a grape with the tip of the knife. 'You will have guessed that I have made enquiries, and I have it on good authority you are a sensible man.' He stared at his fingernail with great interest. 'Trust is not really the issue. Your family lives here in Rome.'

Serpicus felt as though he had been punched in the stomach. 'You intend to hold them hostage?'

Blaesus smiled in a way that should have been avuncular but wasn't. 'Hostage is a cruel word. Let us just say that, during your absence they will be under my personal protection, and naturally I shall make their welfare my especial concern.' He sat back and concentrated on peeling a small orange. Serpicus was working hard at not crossing the table between them to kill him there and then. Blaesus smiled thinly at the effect of his veiled threat. 'As long as you do as I have suggested, you may be sure that I shall look after them well.'

Serpicus managed not to tell him how much better that made him feel.

'All right,' he said. 'I accept.' He knew that he had no choice.

'Good. You will have three months.'

Serpicus shook his head. 'Impossible. There are no roads once we get past the frontier.'

'Indeed. There is nothing that a Roman would recognize as a road. Southern Germany has not been part of the Empire long enough. There are plans, but . . .' He smiled. 'Mind you, the Germans seem to manage all right without them.'

'Is the area pacified?'

'There is a revolt, as I said.'

'I mean are the tribes between here and the revolt peaceful?'

Blaesus replied a little too quickly, as if he'd been anticipating the question and wanted to avoid a revealing hesitation. 'You may meet some . . . hostility.'

A carefully chosen word, thought Serpicus. 'Hostile to Romans? Or hostile to the Treveri?'

'Neither, specifically. Just hostile.'

'Can they be bought off?'

Blaesus shrugged. 'I imagine it's like any barbarian land.' He looked from Serpicus to Decius and back again. 'Some barbarians you can buy, some you can't. No consistency.' He smiled condescendingly. 'You would know more about that than I would.'

Serpicus ignored the insult. 'So, if we can't bribe them then we'll probably have to fight them.'

Blaesus nodded. 'Some fighting is probably inevitable.' Serpicus decided that he preferred it when the Roman was trying to cover things up. His honesty was all bad news. 'I will give you thirty-six men. Twenty-four of them fully trained ex-legionaries, experienced men who enjoy a fight.'

'By which you mean retired soldiers who've drunk away their severance money, or who were invalided out and can't walk more than a mile without having to lie down to recover.'

'All citizen heroes,' said Blaesus imperturbably, 'brave fighting men who have served Rome well in the past and will again. Plus twelve barbarian auxiliaries, each one useful with a bow, a knife or a garrotte.'

'By auxiliaries you mean criminals.'

Blaesus made a slight gesture of demurral. 'Too harsh. Ex-criminals. Men who have paid for their crimes. They have served their sentences and discharged their debts, and they now wish to put their . . . shall we say, unusual skills to honest use.'

Serpicus changed tack. 'This is not an ordinary animal, is it?' Something wasn't right. The games were consuming thousands of wild creatures a week, it was true. The more exotic beasts were becoming difficult to obtain and prices were rising, but you still didn't have to go five hundred leagues across the Empire to get one.

The Senator didn't reply immediately. He was a politician, the sort of man who could make a hesitation look like a judicious pause by putting a grave face on it, but this was definitely a hesitation.

'Before I tell you, understand what it means,' Blaesus said. 'I am not an ungrateful man. If you succeed in this endeavour, my favour means that you will never need to look for a commission again.' He paused for emphasis. 'But know this. If you fail, you will watch your family die first in the arena, and then you will die as slowly as can be arranged, and you will scream with pain every moment of that time.' He paused again. There was no need, Serpicus was already terrified. Blaesus took a breath, as if readying himself for a shock. 'This information is a secret,' he said. 'If it becomes known outside this room then the animal becomes worthless to me.' He looked enquiringly at both of them. Serpicus nodded. Decius was listening carefully in silence.

'I understand.'

Blaesus hesitated, then plunged.

'And in answer to your question, no, it isn't just any animal. It's unique. It is a white bear. Completely white.'

'Ah, I see.' Serpicus obviously didn't.

'The official historians assure me that, in all the games that have ever been since records began, there has never been a pure white bear seen in the arena.' Blaesus visibly swelled with pride, and a faraway look entered his eyes. 'People sometimes talk of them, but they are a myth, like centaurs and flying horses, and sober Celts.' He looked up at the ceiling with a rapt expression. 'When my white bear is brought through the gates, I will have made the myth real. How many men can say that? The White Bear Games will never be forgotten, and my name will be remembered with them.'

Serpicus didn't care about Blaesus' animal or his games, nor was he taken in by his fine words about posterity when the whole thing was probably just a politician's trick to get his candidate elected to office. And he didn't like threats against his family.

'I'll need fifty legionaries at least,' Serpicus said. 'All with recent battle experience and army fit, fully equipped, none over forty years old or with a bad injury, and at least two of them have to be officers who know what they are doing. Plus at least twenty auxiliaries. I don't care where they come from but they must all speak serviceable Latin. I'm not having men getting away with insubordination by pretending they misunderstood their orders. Better make sure at least some of them are Germans. I can't get a large group of men across Germany and persuade people we're friendly if none of them speak the language. And I will see all the men in training before we leave, and we will not leave until they are fit and ready.'

Blaesus was silent for a moment, and then spoke. The

mystic and his games for posterity were gone, and the businessman was back in his place. 'Thirty legionaries, all fit veterans. One of them was a full centurion, and I gather two of the others were Optios at some point.'

Optios. Kids playing at being officers. True, most officers had been Optios to start with, but the idea that Blaesus' men had not progressed beyond that stage didn't inspire confidence.

Blaesus smiled slightly at Serpicus' expression. 'Several of the others were, I understand, officers at some point in their careers, though they may not still have been so when they actually left the army.'

Which meant that they were officers who had been dishonourably discharged for drunkenness, cowardice or stealing, which would lose them their rank, their pension, everything. Would leave them, in fact, in need of a job very much like this one. Serpicus didn't fancy adding drunken insubordinates to his list of problems.

'And the auxiliaries?'

Blaesus paused, and then raised his hands in surrender. 'Very well, very well. I can probably manage twenty auxiliaries, and you may see them all train with their weapons before you go. If it will put your mind at rest.'

'A boat, obviously, converted to my specification.'

'My best ship is in the harbour. You are welcome to inspect it and – within reason – I will authorize changes.'

'I'll need special equipment.'

Blaesus bridled just enough for Serpicus to see it. 'I think you'll find that everything you need is already stowed on the boat or is being made ready for collection when you arrive in Genoa. You will travel faster with less equipment.'

'Good men to sail and row it, obviously.'

'You'll have enough sailors to keep the sails furled and the boat off the rocks, and they'll row when necessary. The auxiliaries will row, obviously, and the soldiers will too when you need them.'

'The soldiers won't like it.'

'It'll keep them fit and stave off boredom. Anyway, do you care what the soldiers like? I don't.'

Serpicus wasn't going to get any further with that one. He moved on.

'Men who know animals and how to trap them.'

Blaesus looked complacent. 'My bestarii are the finest in Rome.'

'No they aren't. I don't want your men unless I can keep them under control. I want Galba as animal master.'

'Take him if you wish.' The businessman in the Senator woke up at last. 'You will also capture and bring back any worthwhile animals you encounter on the way. I will accept the bear with other animals or on its own, but I will not accept anything at all without the bear. If you bring the bear, any additional animals will be paid for at the market rate.'

'And what happens if the ship is lost in a storm or we fail to return in time for the games? If we are delayed for reasons beyond our control?'

The Senator shook his head. 'That is not possible, it cannot happen,' he said softly. For a moment he was an older man advising a younger man in his care. 'You know how these things work. It is a secret, but word will have spread. Something special will be expected at the games. It will appear, it must. Put any other thought out of your mind.'

There was a long silence.

Blaesus gestured to the slave to refill the wine cups, and sat back with a cheerful smile. 'So,' he said. 'How is it you've not raced for two years?'

That was one question that Serpicus wasn't expecting. The years peeled back.

9

The sound of the crowd surrounds him, dull and monolithic, as if he hears it while swimming underwater.

Above the din, he hears a high-pitched voice chanting his name repeatedly, as if repetition will ensure his victory.

'Serpi-cus! Serpi-cus!'

So, at least one person is betting on him.

He stands in the racing chariot with slightly bent knees – as any charioteer will do automatically if he knows what he is about – narrows his eyes against the sun and looks down the long side of the course.

The oval arena course is a good bow-shot long and a spear-throw wide. At even intervals of roughly ten paces, three-sided spear-shaped stone pillars stand in a tighter circle that mirrors the shape of the arena. The stones only come up as high as the horses' heads, but are firmly embedded deep in the arena sand and sharply angled at the base. If a chariot strikes one then a wheel will be ripped off or smashed.

A race is usually ten circuits, although he has competed in challenge races reduced to a single sprint around the arena. A team of good horses could, in theory, get around the course in about thirty heartbeats if yoked to a well-made chariot and if driven by someone who knew his job and was left to drive without distractions. However, the horses, the chariots and the drivers are all of variable quality, and there are always distractions. Other chariots will always get in the way, sometimes legally, sometimes illegally. The crowd sets up a constant howl of encouragement and imprecation, and can be counted upon to throw cushions, fruit, coins and anything else that comes to hand at a driver who is beating their own choice. Some spectators take it even more seriously than that. Every driver knew the story of the woman (though she had no name) who sat every day in the front row (at a games that no one could name precisely), betting enormous but unspecified amounts, and every driver, even if they hadn't actually been there themselves, at least knew someone who knew someone who had been sitting close to her on the very day that she pushed her husband over the balcony and under the hooves of a chariot which was beating her favourite.

Perhaps she was the same woman who threw a small dog at Serpicus as he rounded the final corner of the last race on the last day of a particularly fevered games, on which it was said that houses, futures, entire fortunes had been bet. Serpicus supposed that if he himself had a house and a fortune, and if he'd bet it all on a particular charioteer, he'd probably be hurling everything that came to hand including his children at the other charioteers' heads too. Throwing them a damn sight more accurately than the dog that had been thrown at him.

He shades his eyes with fingers deeply scarred by years of the pull of the reins and looks down the track. The start of the course, a third of the way along one of the long walls, is just wide enough for all ten chariots to stand abreast, their wheels almost touching. A cluster of knee-high buttresses protrude into the track from the marker stone, making the turns at the top and bottom narrower than the rest of the track by about ten paces. If all the chariots arrive there together, or if the angles of approach are less than absolutely perfect, or if one of the drivers wants to win too much and tries to cut inside, then wood and stone and metal and flesh will collide.

Serpicus looks sideways across the line of chariots. Brutus smiles back. Serpicus then looks up at the crowd. He sees a man standing close to a betting man's slave raise an arm, and Brutus waves back and points at him so that Serpicus will see him. He knows what it means. All charioteers have their superstitions, their ways of placating and encouraging the gods. Brutus hasn't been racing long enough yet to have developed anything complicated – some drivers have a sequence of actions that have to be followed absolutely the same way every time like a religious ritual, and similarly have to be begun again if they make a mistake, and so could take half a day – but Serpicus knows that Brutus already carries a clay model of Hermes next to his breast, and that he spits on the right wheel before every race. Serpicus' own ritual is simpler than most. He always commissions the man who is waving from the crowd to bet two sesterces on him to win. If he wins, he uses his winnings to make a sacrifice to Mercury. If he loses he does nothing. If the gods weren't looking after him that day then he sees no reason to pay any attention to them either. However, he always bets. If he didn't, then the gods might think he didn't care what they did either way.

He hears the bookmakers' voices filtering through the cauldron of noise.

'The race is about to begin. Final bets please. Cassius even money, Serpicus and Brutus two to one, Galba five to two, Arragus and Decius seven to one, ten to one the rest. Last bets please.'

'Good luck,' says a voice Serpicus doesn't know to his left.

A young man, barely more than a boy, stands next to him. His face is split with an enormous smile. Serpicus can't help but smile back. 'Good luck to you too. Your first race?'

The young man nods and strikes a pose. 'First of many!' He laughs, taking the arrogance out of his words. 'Arragus, at your service. We'll drink a wineskin together later.' He reaches across and punches the shoulder of the red-haired young man in the chariot next to him. 'Which this useless pudding will be paying for, once I've beaten him to the finish.'

The youngster rubs his shoulder ruefully. 'Yes, in your dreams,' he says. He nods to Serpicus. 'Decius, at your service.' A German, by his speech. Serpicus wonders how he has become mixed up with a Roman rich boy like Arragus. Serpicus is about to warn them to hang back and get the measure of the race first, but at that moment a woman leans out over the edge of the wall so that her dress opens and she hurls a flower which hits Decius on the cheek. He turns to see her and blushes. If the boy is still in one piece at the end of the race then he has a promise for the night in his pocket. Serpicus hopes that the sour-looking man beside her isn't her husband, for all three of their sakes. Both Decius and Arragus are too young. Too young to race and perhaps get killed doing it. Too young to be propositioned by women old enough to know better. Except that the women, and there are many such women, it seems, didn't know better at all, and their age didn't seem to be an issue. The men who fought and raced and died in the arena had their every move watched and the details exchanged like coins amongst those who followed them. Their lives, their bodies, everything about them seemed to be public property. There was even a group of women who waited outside the public baths at the end of every day to claim the sweat that had been scraped off their favourite gladiators' bodies by the masseur. Sometimes there were fights in the street over it. Jupiter perhaps knew what they did with the sweat once they got it home; Serpicus didn't want to think about it.

The moment before a race starts is always greeted with silence. Serpicus uses that silence to close his eyes and take a breath. There is no danger of missing the beginning; the starter always waits, drawing out the tension. As the moments pass Serpicus feels as though he is pulling in the scattered parts of himself, like a harassed stallkeeper gathering together his remaining goods off his tables and shelves at the end of a busy day.

When his eyes reopen, he looks up at the seven eggs and seven dolphins which are reversed to indicate the passing of each of the seven laps. He looks at the statue of Rameses the Second, taken from Egypt and placed at the exact centre of the Circus by Augustus, so that the Emperor could sit in the Royal Enclosure on the Palatine side and compare his own glory to the Pharaoh's. Then he looks down the race track. He is ready.

He gathers the reins carefully, placing them between his fingers in a slow and deliberate order that he repeats before every race. The horses lift their heads. Serpicus sees their ears point forward and their nostrils flare. He glances sideways. Cassius, the favourite to win the race and drawn on the very inside, looks back at him coldly and bares his teeth as he adjusts his hold on a long whip. He is a wiry, intense-looking man. They have never spoken nor competed before, though Serpicus has seen him race and knows his reputation. He is what the betting men call a hare, a man who always races from the front, a driver who holds his line regardless of what anyone else does. It takes courage, perhaps even arrogance. Certainly it requires a lack of imagination: Serpicus has seen too many charioteers fly from the starter's flag and wrap themselves around the first corner-marker to contemplate trying it himself.

Brutus has the outside lane. He is tall and red-haired, easy for his supporters to spot in the mayhem of the race even under the soiled leather cap he always wears. He looks across at him with a serious expression that Serpicus knows means that he has withdrawn into his own mind ready for the competition. He is a friend and can be trusted not to do anything stupid. He will beat Serpicus if he can and he is good enough to do it if his friend makes a mistake, but he won't kill him to win.

Serpicus sighs. To his right a friend; to his left a man dedicated to winning at all costs, and two other race virgins mixed in with them who could ruin it for everyone.

Just another day at the race track.

A thin haze of dust from the previous race hangs in the air over the course and the sun shines through it like a veil. The silence is like the silence that surrounds a lion before it makes its attack.

The starter looks up at the patron's box. The Master of Games leans towards Senator Catullus Appius, who is slumped in his chair and makes no move. The Master of Games waits a moment and then nods, as if the comatose old man has spoken graciously. He signals to the starter, who draws himself up importantly. He waits a few moments, then opens his hand. The silk rope stretched between the two marble Hermes at the front of each starting gate falls in slow motion.

As the rope touches the sand the arena opens its mouth and roars.

The horses know the signal of old; they are already moving by the time the end of Serpicus' long whip lightly touches their flanks. Arragus lashes at his horses, forcing them forwards. The animals rear in their harness, taken by surprise. Amateurs, Serpicus thinks, rich boys out for a day's sport. A professional trains his horses to know when the race is about to begin.

There is a growl of metal and wood as the wheels clash. Serpicus hears a shrill voice above them scream 'Jupiter be on my side, two white bulls if the German fails!', and then it is lost in an animal howl of excitement from every side as the horses bound forward.

Cassius gets the best start and is slightly in front of Serpicus and two others as they near the first bend, with the rest in a clump just behind. They tuck in behind him and wait for an opportunity. The spectators' faces at the edge of the arena blur into a featureless white streak as they lean forward to scream encouragement and curses at them. Out of the corner of his eye Serpicus sees one of the rich boys – red hair, so Decius – come up beside him, his arm pumping, the whip cracking across his horses' backs. The professional in Serpicus wants to take the boy quietly to one side and tell him that it is pointless, the horses are already going as fast as they can, but the other part of him remembers, knows, still feels and has learned to channel the excitement that once filled him like boiling wine. If it is a man's first time and he does not know what to expect, the start of a race is like a dam breaking, the thunder calls him and a river of light floods through his body. Serpicus can see that the boy is intoxicated and blinded by it. He is going too fast, trying to make up for his bad start. Serpicus shouts a warning that the boy has no chance of hearing. They all swing left for the first time and the youngster overshoots the corner. His horses keep galloping, which at least saves them from getting the chariot up their backs. The chariot skids sideways until it smashes into the wall on the far side. The noise is almost drowned by the roar of the crowd. The chariot holds together somehow, but a shower of sparks fountain from the axle as he wrenches the horses around and back into the race.

As they bowl out of the corner and speed down the long straight, the other youngster, Arragus, overtakes Serpicus. He lets the boy go and concentrates on staying close to Cassius. Decius' chariot is damaged and he is far behind and not going to win, but the rest of them are in a tight bunch. Serpicus knows without looking that the head of Brutus' near-side horse is level with his hip. Cassius is just ahead of him, and Arragus is between them. A brave – and exceedingly foolish – man could have run across the horse's backs from the leading chariot to the last without touching the ground.

Cassius is racing like a hare in front of hounds. Serpicus can see that Brutus and he have the same strategy. Let the boys charge ahead if they want to, stay out of their way when they crash, as they must, and keep up a good pace while you're waiting. Meanwhile make sure that Cassius doesn't break away, and if all that means a race spent chewing the dense acrid cloud of dust that the hotheads threw up behind them as they charged towards disaster, so be it. Better to be alive and coughing up the harsh orange earth for three days after the race, than to have lungs as clean as the shining coins they will press on your eyes.

Arragus draws level with Cassius. Serpicus sees him lean to the left as he bores into the leader, pulling his horses across his line in an attempt to force Cassius to slow down and surrender the inside track. The wheel-hubs touch and there is a high grinding scream as the tortured metal around the hubs buckles and cracks and smoke pours from them. Serpicus has seen races where sheets of flame shot up from the wooden wheels as they ground against each other. Arragus inches ahead and for a moment it looks as if his ploy has worked. Serpicus sees Cassius glance momentarily down at the clashing wheels and then his arm swings and cracks the whip over his horses' heads. They jump forward, and suddenly the two chariots are level as the next corner approaches. The boy has a second to make up his mind. He can slow down and tuck in behind Cassius, forcing Serpicus to give way, and try to come out of the corner fast to take Cassius on the next straight, or he can speed up again and cut across Cassius as he did before, only this time Cassius will be ready for him and an instant later the corner will be upon them. If Cassius doesn't give him way then Arragus will have to swing out quickly and take the corner wide, avoiding Cassius' chariot as best he can as it skids round the corner. This will leave Arragus at a disadvantage coming out of the other side of the corner. He will be in the outside lane and behind. He may even lose his place to Brutus or Serpicus, pounding after him in the centre of a cloud of Cassius' dust.

Arragus lashes his whip wildly at his horses.

Serpicus glances across at Brutus and shakes his head. The boy doesn't lack courage. His whip waves again and the reins slap down on the horses' necks. The animals make a desperate effort and Arragus' chariot pulls ahead by the length of a spear. Cassius looks down again at the wheels. Serpicus knows that Cassius has to make an immediate decision, and suddenly, with an absolute clarity, he knows what Cassius is going to do. Serpicus opens his mouth to shout a warning to Arragus, but it is too late.

Through the sun-goldened dust Serpicus sees the favourite's arm rise and fall. The end of his whip flicks forward and coils around Arragus' wrist, above the hand that holds the young man's reins. In skilled hands the lash of the whip rips skin and flesh like a sword blow, numbing muscle and paralysing nerves. Cassius is a master with a whip.

Arragus' frozen hand drops the reins. The horses, suddenly free, slow down and pull sideways, away from the looming confrontation. Cassius' chariot leaps ahead as the youngster makes a wild grab for the reins with his other hand. It is too late. The reins are already on the ground amongst his horses' feet.

Dropped reins are an occupational hazard during races, and chariot racers have a choice as to how to prepare for when it happens. Some tie their reins around their wrists or their waist in order to make sure that if they lose their grip then the reins don't fall to the ground. They carry a short-bladed knife in their belt sharp enough to cut themselves free with one movement if the need arises. Both waist and wrist are good ideas in their ways, and each has its adherents. However, both are bad ideas if you are thrown from the chariot. Unless you get the knife to the reins before you hit the ground you will have the flesh flayed from your body by the time the horses stop running. Alternatively, you can hold the reins in your hand in the same way that a horse-rider would do, lacing them loosely through your fingers, which means that you won't get dragged along the ground if you fall out of the chariot, but you accept that if you drop the reins you are out of the race as there is no way of getting them back. Professionals tend to do the latter. Arragus had copied the professionals. The chariot slows.

Then the gods desert him.

As the chariot slows, momentum carries Arragus forward, pressing him against the front edge. As he begins to straighten up again, one of the cantering horses treads on the trailing reins. The horse's head dips suddenly as it stumbles and tries to stay on its feet. The other horse holds its companion up but the beast's falling weight wrenches the chariot sideways and half-halts it. The boy is taken by surprise and is thrown against the side of the chariot. His weight pivots on his hip and he falls over the side and sprawls in the dust. He lies in the dust for a moment, coughing and dazed. Then his wits clear and he sees his friend's pale face high above him.

His arm comes up as he throws himself sideways.

Even above the excited screams of the crowd Serpicus thinks he hears a sharp crack like a dry branch breaking as the frantic horses pull Decius' chariot over Arragus' prone body.

Serpicus pulls his protesting horses to a halt and slaps a palm against the side of his chariot. 'Did you see what that bastard did?'

Brutus shrugs. 'If the judges didn't see it then he'll get away with it.' Brutus sees something in Serpicus' face and his eyes open wider. 'You'll report him?'

Serpicus hesitates, anger running hot and bitter through him like cheap wine, then he comes back to reality. His shoulders relax. 'No, I suppose not. If the judges haven't said anything by now then either they didn't see it and he'll just deny it, or they didn't want to see it, in which case he won't need to deny it. I doubt any of the spectators could have seen anything even if we'd been going slowly, and the speed we were going gave them no chance.' He coughs and spits arena dust from a mouth dry with disgust.

'There would be a mark on his arm.' Decius is sitting on his own in a corner of the room. His head is thrown back, resting against the wall, and his eyes are un-naturally wide. He has killed his friend in their first race. The drivers all know it wasn't his fault, they know that he knows it wasn't his fault, and they know that know-ing it won't make any difference. The boy has been shocked into becoming a man, but the soft edges of his face still look as if they could crumple into tears in a moment.

Brutus puts a hand on Serpicus' shoulder. 'The gods will see justice done.'

Serpicus frowns. Brutus has a deep faith that things have a way of working themselves out in the end, that the gods – and therefore life – are just, even if sometimes hard to understand. Serpicus can happily agree that they are hard to understand. He hasn't seen much in the way of justice in this life.

Serpicus sees Brutus look over his shoulder and his eyes flicker a warning. Serpicus knows who it must be and doesn't turn round. Brutus speaks slightly louder, wanting Cassius to hear him. 'The boy had bad luck. If Decius' chariot hadn't been right behind him when he fell he would have walked away.'

Serpicus hesitates before turning to face Cassius. Cassius looks at him with mild curiosity. 'I was in front of him when he fell. Did you see what happened?' His voice is thin and nasal.

'After your wheels clashed, one of Arragus' horses stumbled and he was thrown out. Decius went straight into him. He hadn't a chance.'

Cassius gives a tiny shrug. 'Bad luck. He was brave.' He walks away. Serpicus slowly unclenches his fists. Brutus looks into his face.

'You're in the wrong business if a boy's death bothers you.'

'It isn't the death, it's the manner of it. It was murder.'

'Yes. And it's part of what we do.'

Time stops. Serpicus feels as though iron bands are closing around his chest. Then he takes a deep breath and quits the racing business for ever.

10

To Aelius Sejanus, from his Servant:

The two Germans Serpicus and Decius came to the Palace of the Partner tonight and agreed to go to their homeland and bring back the bear for the games. As planned, I shall accompany them, and carry out your wishes.

Further to our earlier enquiries, our sources confirm that the younger German Decius is of the Treveri tribe, given as a hostage for the Praunberg district. When the time came for hostages to be returned he elected to stay on in Rome. He had become friends with Arragus Pollo, son of Septimus Pollo who, you will no doubt remember, was convicted for treason last year. The two boys trained together to be chariot racers. Arragus was killed in his first race, some say through his friend's incompetence. Serpicus was a competitor in the same race. As Septimus Pollo naturally wanted nothing to do with the boy who had killed his son, and he had no other means of support, Serpicus took him on as an apprentice working with the horses in the arena.

I understand your instructions that all messages are to come directly to yourself rather than to your uncle. It will be done as you wish.

11

It had been a long day, and Serpicus was glad to be home.

As he pushed the door open, the two small siege-catapults at the other side of the room were activated. The missiles hurtled across the room, one striking him on the thigh and the other in his midriff. He doubled over with a whooshing sound and fell backwards. The missiles frothed around him, letting out delighted shrieks.

'Mummy, Daddy's home!'

'I would never have known.' Antonia came through from the kitchen with a bowl of fruit and put it on the table. 'Priscus, Diana. Stop killing your father and go and wash before supper.'

The children looked down at him and he made a face at them behind their mother's back. They ran howling from the room, pretending to be wolves.

'Yes,' she said with a smile, 'they have indeed been like that all day, and where were you when I needed you?'

He put an arm around her waist, sat down and pulled her onto his lap. She put an arm around his neck and looked at him with eyes that could see anywhere inside him that they wanted to. 'So,' he said, 'you don't ever want to have any more then?'

'Do I want more children?' Her face turned serious, as he had known it would. She always took questions seriously even when they were entirely frivolous. She pulled at her bottom lip with a slim thumb and forefinger. He would have teased her about the habit but was afraid that if he ever mentioned it she'd stop doing it. 'I'm not exactly in a hurry, but I suppose if they came along I wouldn't mind.'

He pushed his face into the soft cleft between her shoulder and neck. She pulled his head back by the hair so that she could see his face. 'You're the one who is supposed to be working, why aren't you tired?'

'I am.'

'But you think you're up to it?'

'Keep up with you anyway.'

'Think so?'

'Know so.'

'Want to bet?'

He looked around. 'Everything we own belongs to me. That's what being married means. What would you bet with?'

She gave him a hard look and then reached out to pick up a small pewter flask from a shelf. 'See this?'

'Yes.'

'It's full of oil.'

'Oil and flask both belong to me.'

126

'True. But irrelevant. You can keep the flask. Winners get the oil rubbed into them until there's none left. Losers get to do the rubbing.'

'Good bet,' he said. 'I might even lose deliberately.'

She smiled. 'I was rather counting on that.'

The children came back into the room. They were like puppies, with only two speeds: flat out and sound asleep. They ate polenta and fruit, usually simultaneously, stuffing it into their mouths between and during excited reports of the day's activity. Their parents had a system. Serpicus looked interested while Antonia kept pushing their hands towards their mouths. It was efficient, if noisy and messy.

An hour later the children were in bed. They sat down to eat. Serpicus poured them both wine and told her about Blaesus and his proposal. He didn't mention that Blaesus was effectively keeping them hostage. She knew what the situation was. She listened carefully and let him finish before speaking.

'How long would you be away?'

He shrugged. 'Assuming no hold-ups beyond the usual, it'll take two weeks to get the men together. Three days to Genoa, five more to the mountains, a week to cross them, then maybe three weeks' march. Four days to rest and resupply, then return. We'll be pulling a heavy cart on the way home, so maybe twice as long to get back to Genoa.'

She was silent for a few moments, and with her fingers she dipped between her breasts and pulled out the jagged-edged amulet that hung there on a thin silver chain. She rubbed it thoughtfully between forefinger and thumb. 'Say about ten weeks?'

'Assuming no hold-ups. Three months might be closer.'

Serpicus knew that Antonia was the only woman he had ever been with who not only said she didn't want him ever to lie to her, but meant it. Everyone says it, of course, but they don't really mean it. Antonia meant it. There are worse reasons for marrying someone.

She pondered for a while. He let her do it. Then she put a finger on the back of his hand. 'Do you have a choice?'

Another shrug. 'Perhaps, in theory. But a lot of men have died recently testing that theory.'

She nodded and looked at the wall, pursing her lips slightly. 'I thought so. And might it be advantageous?'

'We'll probably get paid. I suppose it can't do much harm to my prospects if I please the uncle of the most powerful man in Rome.'

The same nod. He put a finger against her chin and turned her head back to look at him.

'Do you mind?'

'What? Being married to a rich and favoured businessman?'

'Being alone. Saying goodbye.'

'I'm working on not minding. A number of very expensive presents on your return will undoubtedly speed up the process.'

She took his hand and stood up. He looked at her enquiringly.

'You know you said there would be just one more trip?'

'Yes.'

'This is it?'

'This is it.' He hoped it was true.

'Come on then,' she said.

'Where to?'

She looked at him as if he was being stupid, which he supposed he was.

'You've been away for weeks, and you're going away again. How much explanation do you need?'

Later, when he was lying awake, looking at the ceiling, his thoughts a whirlpool, she pushed herself up on one elbow and looked down at him.

'Are we in danger?'

He opened his mouth to reassure her, and then shut it again on the lie.

'I thought so,' she said. Her finger drew a slow thoughtful circle on his chest. 'He made you do it by threatening the children.'

Serpicus looked at her directly. 'Not quite as bad as that. It's a business deal. You only came into the discussion when I asked him why he trusted me to deliver.'

'Ah,' she said. 'You mean we're a sort of insurance. Hostages.' She tapped his chest with a fingernail. 'So then I suppose, if you fail, for whatever reason, so long as Blaesus knows that you did your best, we needn't worry.'

'I . . .' He didn't know what to say. She put a finger on his lips.

'I understand. You would travel to Hell if it protected the children, as I would. You will succeed, all will be well. But I still think we should make some

129

arrangements, don't you? Just in case. Then, if things don't go according to plan, you can send us a message and we'll leave the city before Blaesus finds out what's happened.'

Serpicus took her in his arms and held her close to him.

'I could not bear the thought of anything happening to you,' he said.

She smiled. 'Then make sure you bring that damned animal back.'

That night Serpicus lay awake until the shouts of the returning night-fishermen told him that dawn was close, and then rose without having slept at all.

As he left the house he saw someone – a man by his height and dress – standing in a doorway some distance down the street. When he saw Serpicus he dropped his gaze to the ground and swung slowly out of sight. Serpicus walked briskly to the street corner, waited for five heartbeats and then looked back around it again. The man was in the same place, but he was visible and relaxed. Serpicus waited a short time. He saw the shutters on his house creak open and Antonia's hands pushing them wide. The man faded into the doorway again.

The house was being watched. The man hadn't followed Serpicus, so it was his family, not him, that they wanted to keep under surveillance. He wasn't going to be able to arrange for them to leave Rome easily.

He spent most of the day talking to sailors, those who would pause to speak with him. The docks were a warren of furious activity. Serpicus asked about the revolt in the north, about which most of them appeared both ignorant and indifferent. They didn't seem to think that a few uppity Germans would make much difference to someone travelling to Genoa. The one person Serpicus spoke to who professed to know what he was talking about, a captain of a large fishing boat, told him that prices were about to rise, the pirates were returning and no one knew how to sail a boat properly any more.

Late in the afternoon Serpicus went despondently to meet his partners. Blaesus had advanced him a small amount of money for expenses to keep them going while they planned the trip. So Brutus, Galba, Decius and Serpicus sat down with the expenses and split a jug of wine and tried to puzzle out how to do it. That didn't work, so they wondered if the wine wasn't strong enough for the job, and so they had another. That didn't work very well either, but the ideas were coming faster, so they had another, sure that this time they'd find out what they wanted.

The third jug was obviously a bad one. The ideas suddenly dried up, the sensible ones anyway, and all Brutus and Galba could think of was going to look for women. Decius was slumped with his mouth open, staring at the far wall as if trying to read something written in tiny letters.

'No,' Serpicus said, standing up and stabbing at the table with a forefinger in a fit of seriousness. 'No women, not yet. This is business, not pleasure.'

'But it might be just the sort of thing that, how shall I put it, releases the creative mind?' said Galba.

131

'Exactly,' said Brutus. 'I've always found it helps me concentrate better.'

'Nonsense,' Serpicus said, still standing up but wondering how much authority he would forfeit by sitting down again, and wondering who the sensible person was who had apparently taken up residence inside him and was even now using his voice. 'Women, yes, of course, always, eventually, soon. Just not yet. Tell me what to do to get this expedition off the ground and I'll put enough of Blaesus' ill-earned sesterces on this table to make sure that none of you can walk straight for a week afterwards. But until that's settled, until we know what we're going to do, no one is going anywhere.'

'There's an incentive,' said Galba to Brutus without a trace of mockery.

'True,' said Brutus, equally seriously. Serpicus had their attention. They all sat down.

'So,' Serpicus said, filling up the cups. 'Who do we know who would be good at putting an expedition together? We need someone who can train soldiers, and it'd help if he knows how to get those useless bastards on the dockside to do something other than scratch themselves and rob us blind.'

Brutus scratched his chin. 'He'd have to be a good organizer.'

Galba nodded. 'And we'd have to be able to trust him.'

'He'd have to be available.'

'Not much use to us if he's not.'

'Good at making people do what he wants.'

'Good at fighting.'

'Good at making decisions.'

'Good at giving orders.'

Serpicus put up an unsteady finger. 'Good at taking orders too. He's organizing everything but I'm still in charge.'

'Right,' said Brutus, looking at Galba while jerking a thumb at Serpicus. 'He'll have to be good at pretending to do what Alexander the Great here thinks should be done, while actually doing the opposite or we'll be in serious trouble.'

'And he needs to be available right now.'

There was a slight pause, then Galba and Brutus looked at each other, nodded in unison, stood up, lifted their cups in a toast and drained them in a swallow each.

'Obvious, really,' said Brutus.

'Don't know why it took us so long to think of him,' said Galba.

They both stood up.

'Come on then.' Brutus patted Serpicus cheerfully on the head like an idiot child. 'The girls will be getting bored waiting for us.'

Serpicus shook his head in annoyance. 'Not yet, I told you. We have to find someone to organize things first.'

'Done,' said Galba with a grin.

Serpicus knew he had missed something. 'Who?'

They each put a hand under an armpit and lifted him off the chair. 'You already know,' said Brutus. 'It's obvious.' They put him on his feet and brushed down his clothes with their hands. 'Now, hold all your money tight in your hand and let's go see if Ox has any lucky girls on his pay-roll that we haven't made the acquaintance of yet.'

Serpicus felt the sensible person who had been using his body shrug his shoulders and leave him to look for a better companion.

'Who is it?' he said, allowing himself to be propelled along the pavement. They patted him on the back in a reassuring fashion.

'We'll tell you in the morning. Everything will be fine, you'll see.'

They had said everything would be fine. He had trusted them. They had lied to him. His head hurt, so everything wasn't fine at all. And then they told him who they had in mind and things got much worse.

'Severus?' he said, sitting up. A wave of pain flooded through his eyes and into his head. 'Are you both completely insane?'

'Think about it,' said Galba, kneeling on the floor at the end of the narrow trestle bed in the tiny courtyard that Serpicus used when he came home the worse for wear. Antonia didn't mind him getting drunk once in a while, indeed it was almost expected on returning from a long trip, but had, long before and with her sweetest smile, made it plain that she wasn't going to share her bed with an 'odious grunting drooling farting belching lecherous pig'. Which, Serpicus had to admit, seemed fair enough.

'I have thought,' he said, carefully lying down flat on the mattress again. 'It's a terrible idea. The man's a monster, a slave-driver.'

Brutus leant forward, his face a parody of encouragement, the sort of face you'd use while persuading the village idiot to hand over the sharp-pointed knife before he hurts himself. 'That's the point. If we're going to make a success of this we need a monster. And he's only a slave-driver if he's the centurion and you're a legionary under him.'

'Which we won't be.' Galba folded his arms on the bed and rested his chin on them. 'Remember how they wanted to transfer him to the Seventeenth Legion? And how Lucius refused to let him go?' He had his serious face on. 'I know we all hated him, but he was the best centurion in the legion. And he could fight just about anyone and beat them.'

They weren't going to give up or go away. Serpicus sat up. 'Isn't this all rather a moot point? He's in the army. He's a lifer. He'll die there.'

They both shook their heads vigorously. Looking at them made Serpicus profoundly queasy. He couldn't take any more. He held up his hands in defeat.

'All right. He isn't in the army. He's perfect. You know everything. Fine. Get him, let's talk to him.'

Brutus stood up and went back to the doorway. He leant out and made a jerking movement with his head and then came back into the courtyard. Decius came in slowly after them, paler than ever and looking as if his eye-sockets were too small for his eyes.

Followed by Severus.

Serpicus sat up to attention in the bed, he couldn't help it. Severus walked forward and saluted him. 'Serpicus.' The old man looked him up and down and Serpicus resisted the urge to pull the blanket over his stomach. 'Good to see you again. I hear you have some men who need licking into shape.'

Severus looked much the same – he was a bit more grizzled, his hair was thinner and what was left was a greyed silver, and there was a deep scar across his left forearm that Serpicus didn't remember, but his body was every bit as rigid with authority as it had been. And whether he was still in the army or not he hadn't put on weight or lost muscle. He was still a wall of a man, and he wanted to join them.

Serpicus knew that Brutus and Galba were right. If anyone could get Blaesus' men ready on time, Severus could.

The old soldier looked around. 'So. Who do I have to fuck to get a drink round here?'

Antonia appeared at the door out to the courtyard. 'Me, actually.'

Serpicus groaned and pulled the blanket over his head.

12

Later that day, after Serpicus had sweated his head clear at the baths, he and Severus went to the local training ground to meet Blaesus' soldiers.

The soldiers were the mixed bag Serpicus had anticipated, although to be fair Blaesus had sent more men than he promised. Serpicus watched as Severus got them into a ragged line and inspected them. Severus came over and stood beside him.

'We need more men,' he said quietly.

Serpicus shrugged. 'I agree, but we haven't got any. How many of these can we use?'

'I see how it is. We take any man who can walk without assistance.' Severus shook his head in resignation, and went back to his inspection. It was plain that some of the men were long past their best days, and others had injuries that slowed them almost to uselessness. One man had scars on both hamstrings, the mark of a captive of the Parthians who had tried to escape. This suggested a good attitude, but he would never run again. Several of the other men looked surprisingly athletic. The army only got rid of fit men if they were cowards or criminals. That wasn't necessarily a drawback. Serpicus had no problem with cowards. He was usually one himself. Animal trappers generally had a fairly relaxed attitude to criminality. It came with the trade.

Severus walked up and down the line without changing expression. Serpicus wondered how many of the men knew him already.

Over the next few days Severus put them to the test. He had a simple method for finding their suitability. He drilled the men until they were so tired that their limbs trembled with exhaustion and they could barely stand. Then he made them fight each other. With real swords – blunted ones admittedly, but proper metal, not the wooden gladius that legionaries used to train with. The only difference was that the swords had additional metal guards that covered the back of the hand, to protect the inexperienced swordsman from getting his fingers pulped before he had learnt to defend himself. The other advantage of a wooden gladius from a training point of view, apart from being difficult to kill someone with, was that the wood was hollowed out and filled with lead. After a few weeks of training with one of those, fighting with a real gladius felt like stabbing with a toothpick. Severus recognized the worth of that, so he had the armourer put an extra weight in the handle of each sword. Apart from that, the fight was for real. The clash of metal rang around the training ground.

'D'you think perhaps they should use the training swords?' Serpicus asked tentatively, stepping aside as a soldier swung his arm through a half-circle, cutting the air a hand's breadth above his ducking opponent's skull. Serpicus was starting to worry that Severus' methods might lose half of the men before they'd even made a decision as to which ones were suitable.

The centurion looked at Serpicus and read his thoughts. 'You think I'm too direct?' He was a short man, but the words rumbled all the way up from his feet.

'Not exactly, but . . .'

'Your instructions were clear,' he said, the irony bubbling through his voice. 'I understood that we were in a hurry.'

'We are, but . . .'

'I'd rather have ten good men than thirty useless ones, wouldn't you?'

'Of course, but . . .'

'The last ten men still standing will be our core force. We can add a few more who have performed well if we need extra.'

'I see.' Serpicus had given up using sentences over two words long with him, they weren't getting him anywhere. Severus watched the perspiring men battering at each other. For a moment he seemed to relent.

'Don't worry,' he said quietly to Serpicus. 'I'll get you enough soldiers for what you need.' He looked back at the men and frowned. His voice rose. 'And if any of these useless donkeys aren't up to scratch then there will be time on the voyage to lick them into shape, as well as providing us with the cleanest latrines you've ever seen.'

At that, the two nearest men redoubled their efforts, glancing at Severus as they fought, like boys showing off some new skill to their teacher. They fought in the training manual fashion, one advancing a few steps while the other retreated, then swapping. Severus watched them for a few moments then raised a hand and walked towards them. They stopped fighting and took a step back from him. The old man stood with a scarred fist on each hip.

'Want to come with us, do you?'

They both nodded eagerly. Severus held out his hands for their swords. They both reversed their weapons in the approved military manner and handed them to him. He looked carefully along the edges of each weapon, and then dropped his arms to his sides.

'Piece of advice,' he said. His tone was confiding. They leant in to hear him.

'When you are fighting,' he said quietly, 'even if it is only poncing about for show like we're doing here, don't just pat each other.' He dropped his voice and leant slightly forward. The two soldiers bent forward to hear him. 'If you want to be part of my army,' Severus said, 'you'll need a bit of this.'

As he said the last word, both his arms came up like pistons, fast and hard, and the hand guards on the pommels of the two swords smashed into their owners' faces. Serpicus heard the crunch of broken bone. The two men reeled away backwards and fell to their knees.

Severus waited for them to recover. It took a little time. Eventually both men stood up. They swayed with tiredness and pain, blood streamed down their faces and they looked at him murderously. Severus nodded contentedly.

'Like that,' he said mildly. 'All right?' They both growled at him and he tossed them their swords. He stood there, with his arms behind his back, not stepping away, watching them with a benign and slightly expectant expression on his face.

Serpicus tensed, ready to jump forward. Their fingers opened and closed on the handles of the swords. Severus stood there, as if waiting for children to do a trick to earn a treat.

Serpicus felt the air stop moving around him.

Then the moment passed, and the two soldiers hurled themselves at each other with a new vigour.

Severus looked around. Every man on the training ground was now belabouring his opponent for all he was worth. The reek of fresh sweat mixing with stale surrounded them. Severus gave Serpicus a small look of satisfaction.

Serpicus gestured to the men he had hit. 'I suppose those two won't be coming?' he said.

Severus shook his head. 'First on my list,' he said proudly. 'Both with broken noses and just look at them going at each other now.'

He let the men fight on with the heavy swords until their arms were too tired to lift and their nerveless fingers couldn't hold onto them any longer. Then he formed them up into ranks and invited anyone who wanted to leave to do so. Ten men picked up their gear and walked away. Then he got the remainder wrestling in pairs until they lay on the ground gasping for air. He gave them a too-short moment to catch their breath and then they were on parade once more. Again he offered them a chance to leave. Two more men staggered away, and Severus told another who had fallen awkwardly and broken his right arm to step out to the side.

'You can't fight, you can't row, you can't carry. Sorry, son. You're no good to us.'

The soldier held the useless arm across his chest and looked hard at Severus. They moved away from the men and stood near Serpicus.

'I am Soldi,' he said quietly. 'You were my centurion when I was stationed in Germany. It was my first year as a soldier. When the Marcomanni came over the wall, hundreds of them, screaming like devils, I was about to jump back off the rampart to run and save myself. Then I saw you leap forward and strike down the leading barbarian. I was ashamed of myself, and I stayed and fought beside you with every other man in the garrison. We beat them off. You saved us all that day, and you saved my honour. If you are on this expedition I want to be on it as well.' He looked at his useless arm and shrugged. 'Besides, I'm left-handed.'

Severus looked at the man carefully, then paused for a moment. He looked at the man's arm as one might look at the teeth of a horse one was thinking seriously of buying. 'Tell you what,' he said gruffly. 'We'll let the doctor do his worst with that arm. If you don't make a sound while he's mauling you, and if he says the break isn't too bad, then maybe we'll find something for you to do while it's mending. No promises, mind.'

Soldi nodded his thanks and stepped back into the ranks. Severus stood beside Serpicus.

'Didn't look too bad,' Serpicus said. The centurion

rocked slowly on his heels and said nothing. 'Probably just a dislocation. It'll be mended by the time we need him to use a sword.'

'That's what I thought,' said Severus gruffly, as if he was thinking about something else more serious.

'And he's been to Germany before. He might be of help with the terrain, even the language.'

'Useful,' said Severus, pursing his lips and nodding.

'We need someone to keep count of supplies, that sort of thing,' Serpicus said. 'We could keep him busy doing that.'

'Good idea,' Severus said.

'After all, someone's got to do it.'

Severus nodded abruptly, as if it was of little consequence. 'Might as well be him then, eh?'

'Might as well.'

Serpicus smiled to himself and said nothing more, lest he should think that he was suggesting for even a moment that the old man was anything less than Severus the bastard, the hardest bastard centurion in the whole bastard Roman army.

13

To Aelius Sejanus, from his Servant:

*I have placed myself in a position to join the expedition
without arousing suspicion. I have every confidence that
I will be included in their number and will thus be able
to carry out your instructions. It may be necessary to be
out of communication for short periods, but I will
endeavour to report regularly.*

Brutus and Serpicus had gone to the docks at Ostia, ten
miles from Rome, to look for the ship. Their ship.

It was moored exactly where Blaesus said it would be.
A large pile of provisions was on the dockside. One man
was standing beside it, with an attitude of relaxed con-
templation. As they approached he picked up a small
bundle and walked slowly towards the ship. Some other
men were playing dice nearby. They looked comfortable.
If they had been loading supplies onto the ship, it was
plainly some time since they started their break.

The man who looked most like a ship's captain stood on the bow, eating a ripe fig with slow enjoyment. He was tall, deeply tanned and appeared sober. He looked at them suspiciously as they approached. Serpicus called up to him.

'You must be Cinna.'

The look of suspicion deepened. 'Who's asking?'

'Serpicus and Brutus. From the Senator.'

'From the Senator?'

'Yes.'

'Ah, I see,' said Cinna, pausing to pick at a seed in his teeth with a fingernail. 'Which one?'

'We don't have time for this sort of bollocks,' said Brutus, loud enough to be heard on the ship.

Serpicus agreed and ignored the captain's question. 'We need to look around the ship.'

'Ah. You need to look around my ship,' Cinna repeated, only more slowly. His tone suggested that, while he was a tolerant and experienced man, he found it difficult to believe that they knew what a ship was, or that, in the unlikely event of them successfully identifying one, they could look around it without hurting themselves or falling overboard and drowning. He leant back against a rigging rope in a way that managed to imply that if they were lucky enough to survive climbing the gangplank then they'd probably get lost trying to find the mast. Serpicus heard a growl from Brutus just behind him.

'Yes, the ship,' Serpicus said, in what he hoped sounded like an authoritative tone. 'There are things we need to know.' He waited. The captain didn't move. 'But don't you trouble yourself to show us around, we'll just find our own way.'

'Good,' Cinna said. 'I'm busy.' He gestured to the man on the dockside. 'Hey! Carry that more carefully or I'll throw you into the bay!'

The man looked back at him and grinned cheerfully. 'Up your arse, my Captain.'

'My kind of discipline,' muttered Brutus, shaking his head in disbelief.

They walked carefully up the steep gangplank. The ship rolled gently as they stepped onto the deck. Brutus put a hand on the mast. He looked uneasy. Serpicus wondered if he was ill.

'Did I mention that I hate boats?' Brutus said.

'You'll be all right,' Serpicus said. 'You can swim better than I can.'

Brutus shook his head and glowered at the mast. 'I said I hate boats, not the sea. The sea and I have no quarrel at all. I'll swim all day quite happily in the sea, spend all day looking at it with a smile on my face. The sea is fine. I just don't like boats, and as of this morning I don't like the sort of men who sail in them much either.'

Serpicus glanced back at Cinna, who was yelling at another sailor perched high in the rigging. 'He's a charmer, all right.'

'They're all like that,' growled Brutus. 'Never met a civil sailor in my life.'

'Come on. We need to check what Blaesus has lumbered us with.'

* * *

146

That evening they went for a drink, to plan the expedition. Serpicus was still feeling fragile from the previous evening and had promised he'd be home early, and so swore he would only have one drink. Galba promptly announced that he was buying, partly to take advantage of Serpicus' temperance, partly because he had won a bet with several of Severus' soldiers. He had bet them that he could get a straw out of a man's outstretched hand with a racing whip without hitting the man. Galba didn't look much like a chariot racer, and no one told them any different. When he managed it once they said it was a fluke and bet him again, and lost. Then they doubled the bet when he claimed he could do it left-handed. They stopped betting after that, but by then Galba's party trick had earned him a pocket full of silver. Now he was in the mood to spend it.

The place was almost empty. The landlord was named Ox, a Parthian, well known to all the animal trappers. He was called Ox because he was big. Very big, in every sense. He was an unusual man in ways other than his size. Most Parthian businessmen in Serpicus' experience owned one flea-ridden hovel which charged the earth for half a cup of rancid vinegar and a lump of gristle on a dirty plate, and then wanted a month's salary to go with a surly slave girl who had to be beaten between customers in order to stop her catching lice from her clothes and flicking them into the face of anyone who came anywhere near her. Ox's establishment was a pleasant exception. He had three well-run wine shops, which charged fair prices for good food and drink; in them he kept a string of good-looking women, and while he kept them busy, he paid well and allowed them to make their own choices about who they went with. Serpicus had been a regular customer until he got married, but he'd hardly seen Ox since then.

The big man turned round as they walked in. His face split into a smile below his heroic moustache and he roared his delight at the sight of them.

'Germans, in my house!' He clapped his hands and jugs of wine appeared on the table faster than seemed possible. Brutus and Serpicus sat on one side, Galba and Decius on the other. Severus sat at the head. They had wine in one hand and were working on persuading some of the women into the other. Ox smiled generously and put a hand on Brutus' shoulder. 'Life is good, no?'

Brutus raised his cup in salute. 'In your house, life is indeed good.'

Ox beamed his pleasure and stroked his moustache. The wine-roses in his cheeks were more livid, but apart from that he'd hardly changed since the last time Serpicus had seen him. 'It does my old heart good to see healthy smiling German boys in my house, fondling my women and handing over their money to me.' He fussed over them for a few moments and then went to attend to something in the kitchens.

They had been there perhaps an hour and were well on the way to thinking themselves very fine fellows when Serpicus became aware of half a dozen men who had come in not long after them and were sat in the far corner of the wine shop. He couldn't quite work out why he was suspicious, but something was wrong. He leant over towards Brutus, who had persuaded a pretty Egyptian woman onto his lap and was investigating the fastenings on her robe, which were plainly wholly inadequate for the function they might have been expected to perform. Brutus was telling outrageous lies about the sexual prowess of German men, something to do with druidical potions. Serpicus doubted that she believed a word, but she seemed to be enjoying him telling her about it. Serpicus tapped him on the arm. Brutus turned and smiled, and then put an arm around his shoulder.

'What's up, my friend?' he asked. His voice was slurred. Serpicus hoped he wasn't as drunk as he sounded. Brutus kept smiling and looking at the girl as Serpicus spoke.

'The men at the table in the corner, who you aren't going to look at just yet. Have a glance in a minute, tell me what you see.'

Brutus smiled broadly at him and then grabbed the woman, pulling her off balance. She shrieked as he caught her before she hit the floor, and the two of them turned sideways as he wrestled with her before returning to their original position.

'Nothing,' he said. 'They aren't interested in us. Didn't even look at me.'

Serpicus looked straight at him and kept the smile in place. 'Exactly,' he said. 'I've been watching them and they haven't looked at us once, not even the ones facing us. Why is that, do you think?'

Brutus was having trouble concentrating, as his new friend was sliding her hand down the front of his tunic. Serpicus looked at him intensely, willing him to pay attention. Brutus sighed deeply and held the girl's wrist firmly. 'All right,' he said. 'What's your point?'

Serpicus kept his voice down and spoke quickly. 'We've been making a spectacle of ourselves ever since they came in.' He indicated a group of men at a nearby table. 'That lot think we're funny and keep trying to join us and share the joke.' Brutus nodded and looked around the room without moving his head. 'They are here for a drink and a laugh, and they are enjoying our company. Everyone else is here just for a quiet drink, and they wish we'd shut up and go away. They become tense and look up resentfully so that we can see how irritating we are to them, especially when you start singing.' Serpicus looked at Brutus steadily and indicated the remaining table with the merest flicker of his eyes. 'Everywhere you look, no one is ignoring us except them. Even if they were indifferent to what you call singing – and like it or not, they'd be in a minority of themselves if they could ignore it – most of your very attractive friend's very attractive chest is plainly visible. Now, given all that, don't you think it's slightly odd they are so assiduously not catching our eye?'

Brutus threw his head back in song. Several other tables joined in, laughing at the cacophony, and the rest hunched their backs and growled to each other over their cups. After a couple of verses Brutus stopped, took a mouthful of wine and leant across to Serpicus, putting a hand on his shoulder in a drunkenly over-friendly way. His face was almost comically inebriated, but his voice was unslurred.

'You're right,' he said. 'The bastards are ignoring us,

and that's something I won't tolerate.' He lifted the cup to his lips but Serpicus saw he didn't drink. 'Ever seen any of them before?' Serpicus shook his head.

The Egyptian woman on Brutus' lap tapped with a fingernail on his chest. She spoke casually towards her hand, without looking up.

'I have,' she said. 'Two of them were in here yesterday. They asked about legionaries. They talked to Ox for a while, seemed very interested to know where he came from. The dark one sitting at the back asked if there were many other Germans in the legions posted here.'

'Did he now?' asked Brutus casually. He slapped the woman on the backside and lifted her off him as he stood. She protested, more at his leaving than at the slap, but he pointed at the privy and held up one finger, then used it to point upstairs. She smiled and let him go. There was a broken stool nearby. Serpicus reached out as casually as he could and pulled it towards him. He gathered his legs under his seat, shifting his weight onto the balls of his feet.

Galba leant across the table. 'What's up?' he said. Decius was looking at one of the women in a glazed sort of way, and plainly wasn't going to be much use, but Galba's eyes were still bright. Serpicus leant forward to meet him.

'Brutus may need some help in a minute,' he said quietly.

Galba smiled widely.

'That should be fun,' he said. He looked without interest across the room. 'That lot over there?' Serpicus nodded. Galba sniffed dismissively and grinned.

151

'Miserable lot of bastards. I'd say they deserve whatever lands on them.'

Brutus moved slowly towards the privy, doing the walk that drunk people use which is not quite a stride and not quite a stagger. It took him past the table where the men were sitting. They didn't look up at him as he approached. If Serpicus still had any doubt about whether they were behaving strangely or not, it vanished then. If Brutus was drunk and walking towards someone and they were to ignore him, it would be like standing at the bottom of a cliff and hearing a landslide starting overhead and not looking up. It would be automatic. The only sort of man who would not look at a drunk Brutus lumbering straight at him would be a man who didn't want to catch his eye under any circumstances.

As Brutus came level with their table he seemed to lose his balance slightly. He put a foot out to one side and lurched towards them, then stopped, getting his bearings. The man nearest him seemed to flinch but didn't look up. Brutus put a hand out as if in apology, and he rocked back on his heels. There was a suspended moment. Serpicus saw the nearest man gather his legs under him, and open his mouth to shout.

Then Brutus moved.

He seized the two nearest heads by their hair, one in each hand. The heads came together like cymbals once and were thrown backwards away from him. He grabbed the table edge and threw the table up and towards the men on the far side, knocking them off their stools and pinning them against the wall. The two men at the sides of the table struggled to stand up. The one on the left hardly managed to straighten himself before a huge fist swung into his face. He dropped without a sound. The remaining man reached under his cloak as if for a knife and then hesitated. Serpicus wasn't surprised, he would have hesitated to take Brutus on alone too. Brutus was close to him, and flight was not an option. The man's hand came up from under his cloak and there was a flash of metal. Brutus' arm swung up and away from his body. The metal disappeared as the man's hand was thrown sideways. Brutus grabbed his shirt and threw him onto the upended table. The two struggling figures still under the table were knocked back down again by the knifeman's weight. His head struck the table with a loud dull sound and he stayed down, moaning softly. Brutus stood straight, breathing slightly hard and steady as an oak.

Serpicus and Galba hadn't even made it across the room to help him before it was all over. Galba shrugged and sat down again, enjoying the expression on the other customers' faces.

Ox came out of the kitchen, wiping his hands on a cloth. He took a bronze cup with an ox-head etched into the side off the bar and sipped from it. He nodded appreciatively and replaced the cup on the bar. He picked up the jug beside it.

'Anything of mine broken?' he asked, narrowing his eyes and giving the room an appraising look.

'No furniture, just heads,' said Brutus, smiling at him like a slightly naughty favourite son.

Ox gave him a satisfied smile. 'You are fortunate,' he said. 'My tables come expensive.' He stepped over the nearest prone figure and held out the wine jug to Brutus. 'But for men's heads, there is no charge.'

Galba lifted his cup and looked at Serpicus with a thoughtful expression.

'We haven't even left Rome yet and people are following us for no apparent reason.' He took a drink. 'Things could get complicated before this is over.'

14

Within two days and a night Severus had chosen his cohort of soldiers, and an additional half-dozen others who had no legion experience but who had useful talents. They would be used as auxiliaries. Those rejected had walked away in disgust, or been carried off unconscious, or had staggered off shaking their heads in pain and bewilderment. Usually, when men were recruited for this sort of work, they were chosen on the basis of their experience, their reputation and their testimonials. Severus paid scant attention to anyone's claimed experience, none at all to their reputation and the first soldier who made the mistake of presenting a tablet of written references was invited to put them in a dark and painful place. No one else tried it.

Serpicus was watching carefully and could see what Severus was up to. Those he chose all had certain things in common. They had all answered him back at some point. In fact, most of the men had answered him back at some point, but Serpicus thought he saw a difference. The majority of them had sounded angry, petulant, mutinous. These were rejected. The men Severus chose were different. They stood up to him, told him what they thought, but carried on doing what he had told them to do. Beyond that, they had borne everything he had thrown at them. Naturally, they were all handy with their weapons. All of them had a good deal of combat experience, and it showed.

Then there were the six auxiliaries. Roman commanders liked having auxiliaries, as they swelled numbers and were regarded as expendable. The problem was getting Roman soldiers to accept them. No Roman legionary would ever admit that any man other than another legionary was his equal, and often he would only admit it about men from some legions and not others. He certainly wasn't going to admit it about auxiliaries, particularly in light of the fact that most of them had been defeated by Roman legions in order to bring them into the Empire in the first place. Officers were usually careful to deploy auxiliaries in such a way that the legions could see that they were in a support role, not part of the main body of troops. Each man Severus had chosen exhibited at least one unusual skill that might be useful to the expedition. There was a small man from Rhodes, dark-skinned almost like a Nubian, who could swing a rope with a noose and throw it thirty paces and land it over a man's head four times out of five. There were two Persians, both expert archers. There was a German – not from the Treveri, but from the far north – and a huge red-haired Gaul. They were both veterans of the legions with experience of having been officers. They had been cashiered for reasons they didn't wish to discuss, but neither of them gave the impression that the cause of their disgrace was cowardice.

The sixth man was a knife fighter from Crete. They called him Snake. He owned a collection of blades which he carried in a flat leather wallet strapped to his chest.

'An impressive collection of cutlery,' said Severus. Snake looked at him impassively.

'I eat with my hands,' he said.

Severus stood back, pointed at a soldier, and indicated to Snake that the space was his for a demonstration.

Snake held a knife in each hand, wickedly sharp double-bladed things, shaped like the horns of a bull with the handle at the forehead, each horn the length of a man's hand. He dropped into a crouch and advanced on the unfortunate soldier who had been chosen to oppose him. His arms began to circle and pass in front of him, his wrists rotating the knives so that the blades flashed and flickered as they crossed and caught the sunlight. The movements speeded up until the unfortunate soldier was faced with two whirling circles of steel. If he held out his sword then Serpicus could see no other outcome than that his arm would be lopped off. The soldier had come to the same conclusion. He put his shield up in front of himself and looked at Severus with such a piteous expression that every man who saw it burst out laughing.

Severus didn't smile. He looked at the two men with a critical eye and then turned to one of the laughing soldiers.

'What would you do if a Cretan came at you like that?'

The laughter quieted but didn't die as the soldier considered the question.

'Run like hell, I should think,' he said eventually, with a rueful expression. Everyone laughed again.

'An honest soldier, there's a novelty,' said Severus and he laughed too, a strange sudden barking sound. It was the first time Serpicus had heard it. It didn't sound like it saw much daylight.

'Come on, anyone,' Severus said, the laugh disappearing as suddenly as it had appeared. 'There are a bunch of these Cretan bastards and one of them is coming straight at you just like Snake did to Diomedes a minute ago. The knives are coming right at your head. What are you going to do about it?'

'Use a very long spear?' said Diomedes, the soldier who had originally faced the Cretan. Serpicus listened critically. Now that he wasn't in immediate danger he was standing up and thinking hard. Not the bravest soldier in the bunch perhaps, but he wasn't going to be caught out next time. Maybe he was one to watch.

'Not such a bad idea,' said Severus. 'Though if he once got past it there is no way to recover.' He turned to the Cretan. 'What would you suggest we do if we run up against your countrymen?'

'Push Snake out in front of us and let him sort them out, he's the expert,' drawled another soldier. Everyone except the Cretan and Severus laughed.

Serpicus watched as the Cretan stood up and slipped the knives back into their sheaths each with a single deft movement. The soft leather wallet held them safe but made it easy to find what he needed. As the wallet opened Serpicus saw a line of shining blades, all of different lengths and shapes. The Cretan took out a small knife, the sort of thing you'd use to peel an apple, and folded the wallet before putting it away carefully in his shirt.

'You can indeed keep a Cretan away for a time with a long spear,' he said, looking carefully down as he used the fruit-knife deftly to clean his thumbnail. 'Even better if there are two or three of you with spears so he can't work his way around to the side of you.' He looked at the nails on his other fingers appraisingly. 'But don't let him get too close or the spear won't save you. And it will only work if there is one Cretan. If there are two men then one or the other will get you.'

'Remember that. Spear possibly fine for dealing with one Cretan,' said Severus. 'Anyone got any other ideas?'

'Bash him with a shield and then hit him with an axe,' said another man, leaning backwards against a wooden post with his arms folded.

Severus said nothing, but looked around enquiringly.

'Archers,' said one of the two soldiers that Severus had hit in the face on the first day. Serpicus remembered how the blood had dried and covered his lower face like a mask. 'Lots of arrows. Don't stop till the buggers look like dead hedgehogs. Don't need to get anywhere near the knives.'

Snake looked at them both with dark eyes and nodded his head slowly. 'The arrows might work,' he said gently, as if turning the idea over. 'If the Cretan stood still long enough to let the archers shoot at him.' Serpicus had a sense that someone was about to learn something. 'Of course, he might not.'

The Cretan's arm flickered forward like the striking

head of his namesake and there was a flash of sunlight on metal and a soft dead sound, followed by a shout of surprise. The reclining soldier swore and jumped upright. The fruit-knife was quivering in the wood next to his face, an arrow's width from his cheek.

'Bastard!' he hissed. He pulled out his sword and advanced on the Cretan, who stood still and impassive. Severus put out a restraining hand and the soldier subsided into resentful muttering. The Cretan looked thoughtful and spoke seriously.

'The long spear works so long as the Cretan has no knives to throw,' he said, 'but keep your shield up.' He smiled. 'Just in case.'

'Remember that,' said Severus, looking around the men. 'Spears fine in principle, but watch out for knives.'

'It is true that you can shoot arrows from a distance at a Cretan with a knife,' the Cretan said. 'You can even, as you suggest, try to bash him with a shield and then hit him with an axe.' He walked over to the post and retrieved his knife. He held it up next to the soldier's face. 'You can indeed do all those things,' he said quietly. 'But don't expect him to wait for you while you make up your mind what to do.' He tapped the blade against the soldier's breastplate. 'Whatever you decide, you'll only get one chance to kill him. Don't miss.'

Severus looked around. 'Right,' he said. 'Let's get on with practising that bashing and hitting.' He looked hard at the soldier whose cheek Snake had grazed with the knife. 'Just in case you get lucky and the Cretans allow you close enough to do that.'

15

Serpicus and Galba sat watching the men training. Brutus had got bored and was cantering a horse along the side of the exercise field, practising a Thracian trick that Galba had described to him. It involved jumping off his horse with both hands on the saddle pommel, hitting the ground with both feet and then jumping back on again. Serpicus suspected that Galba had been only half serious when he described it, but Brutus declared himself determined to master it. Watching him, Serpicus felt that he'd probably succeed eventually, if he didn't kill himself first.

Serpicus glanced at the drilling soldiers. Decius was in the centre of their ranks. Severus had refused to take the youngster if he didn't train with the others. Decius hadn't argued, and although at that precise moment, practising manoeuvres at double-time in the midday sun carrying a full pack and weapons, he looked as though he was about to fall flat on his face with exhaustion, Serpicus suspected he was rather enjoying himself.

Serpicus had to admit that Brutus and Galba had been right. Severus was exactly the right man to organize the expedition. Within a few days of him taking over, the soldiers were moving as a unit. Once the soldiers were working to his satisfaction, Severus left them in the charge of one of the ex-officers named Scipio, a man with a diagonal scar on his face who, it transpired, had been broken back to the ranks for hitting an officer.

'Insubordination?' said Brutus doubtfully, when Severus told him. 'What if he does the same thing to you?'

Severus shook his head. 'Do you know the penalty for hitting an officer?'

Brutus thought about it. 'In the field, usually immediate execution. In a camp in peace-time, you'd get maybe a hundred lashes, all of your pay for the next hundred years or so would be used to pay off the quartermaster's gambling debts, you'd lose anything remotely resembling a privilege for at least two lifetimes, you'd get several months in solitary while being beaten half to death every night by all the other officers, and when they eventually let you out of solitary it would be latrine duty every waking moment. If you were lucky. And any time there was any fighting to be done, you'd be placed right in the centre of the front rank every time.' Brutus shook his head. 'It's better to hit an officer during a battle, execution is kinder.'

Severus did something with his lips that might have been a smile. 'Scipio hit an officer during a battle. In Galicia. They were attacking up a slope and were under heavy fire, rocks, arrows, anything the defenders could find. The officer ordered his cohort to advance into a suicidal position. Pointless, stupid. Scipio refused to pass the order to his men, and, when the officer threatened to court-martial him, Scipio hit him. Broke his jaw. Then he left the officer under a tree while he led his men in a flanking movement and captured the position with only light casualties.'

Galba blinked in surprise and let out a low whistle. 'He disobeyed a direct order to attack and then hit the officer?'

Severus nodded. 'Exactly.'

'Then why isn't he dead?'

'That's my point. If Scipio was just insubordinate, or couldn't control his temper or was plain stupid, there wouldn't have been a court martial. We all know that his commander would have just carved him like a goat there and then and sent a limb to each of four different countries.' Severus leant towards Brutus, who was still looking puzzled. 'Think about it. Whoever his commander was, he must have thought Scipio was more useful alive and insubordinate than dead, or he wouldn't be here. So, useful, pig-headed and brave. A man to have near you, no?'

Brutus shrugged. 'True. Although he still might be angry and stupid as well as useful, and his usefulness might be something we can't use.'

'We'll find out soon enough,' said Severus. 'Meantime, he's my lieutenant.'

Severus handed over command and walked away. Scipio started bawling orders with the air of a man who knew what he was doing.

'Where to now?' Serpicus asked, looking at Severus' back.

Severus didn't answer, but he was heading towards the docks.

'Come on,' said Brutus happily, punching Galba on the shoulder. 'I want to see this.'

A carriage took them to Ostia, leaving them to walk the last few hundred paces on their own. Brutus, Galba and Serpicus trailed in Severus' wake, smiling like schoolboys following a teacher on his way to catch out other boys misbehaving. The dockside was in turmoil along almost its entire length, with a dozen big ships being loaded and unloaded at once. The only oasis of calm was directly opposite Blaesus' ship. The same pile of supplies was on the wharf, each case and sack with what looked like a large 'J' daubed on them carelessly in rust-red paint. The letter might have been Blaesus' mark, or it might have been for the ship's name, the *Juno*. Whichever it was, the supplies were mostly still on the dockside, not on the boat. Even the one man who had been loading earlier had disappeared.

Severus walked onto the small pier at which the *Juno* was moored and wandered along it for the length of the ship. The dockers who should have been loading the ship were dozing or playing dice in a ragged group, sheltering from the sun in the shadow of the stern. Cinna the captain was nowhere to be seen. He had made the ship ready, in the sense that the rigging was set, the oars were shipped, the hull was caulked. Loading the supplies he obviously felt wasn't his responsibility.

Brutus sat on a wall nearby. Galba and Serpicus gathered around him to watch.

Severus went straight up to the biggest docker, a huge man with a broken nose who was very comfortably stretched out on a big pile of nets. He was taking enthusiastic bites out of a blood-sausage big enough to feed a normal family for three days.

'I would bet a month's pay that that sausage is part of our stores,' muttered Serpicus.

Galba nodded. 'Presumably they're working on the idea that if they can delay loading the stores for long enough then they won't have to do the job at all because they'll have eaten everything.'

'Just shut up and watch,' said Brutus.

Severus stood in front of the men and cleared his throat. 'Who's in charge here?' he asked mildly.

The big man carried on chewing rhythmically and made a motion with the sausage that might possibly have been an acknowledgement, might perhaps have been a dismissal, but was most likely a graphic mime of what the centurion could do with his question. Severus scratched his head with one hand. His shoulders were slumped and the deeply sun-browned skin of his scalp showed through his sparse silver hair. He looked like someone's grandfather dressed up in his old legionary's uniform for a veteran's parade. He spoke to the big man, still using the mild tone.

'Do I take it that you're the foreman of this group?'

The sausage jerked sideways again. 'Piss off, old man, we're busy,' the big man growled, confirming the dismissal possibility. He belched loudly in a way that made you very glad you weren't down wind of him.

'You're the one who's in charge of getting the *Juno* here loaded, yes?' Severus said, moving to within arm's length of the big man, still scratching his scalp. The sun was now behind him and the foreman couldn't see his face. He squinted up at Severus for a long moment, then took another bite from the sausage and closed his eyes again without speaking. There was a still silence, broken only by the sounds of chewing. The other dockers grinned at Severus and nudged each other.

Then the foreman lifted a haunch and broke wind noisily and at length in Severus' direction. Serpicus could swear that the whole lower edge of the old man's cloak rippled in the breeze. Brutus sat up and looked at the situation keenly.

'He might just regret doing that,' he said.

At which point Severus' weight shifted slightly and he became a centurion again.

The hand that was scratching his head formed a fist and his arm swung down with all his weight behind it. Some instinct warned the foreman far too late. His hands were coming up when the tightly clenched fist smashed onto his throat. The sausage flew through the air in a graceful parabola and landed at Serpicus' feet, where two small dogs pounced on it and tore it apart between them. The big foreman made a terrible choking sound and rolled onto his side to face the centurion, both hands clawing at his shattered throat. Severus shifted his weight smoothly and his foot stamped down deep into the big man's gut. Then he reached down, seized a

166

handful of hair and dragged the retching man effortlessly up into a sitting position in front of his friends.

The other dockers were still chuckling at the foreman's treatment of the centurion when they were presented with the big man's face as he gasped for air. His protesting voice was a shallow bubbling rasp through the blood that filled his mouth. He could hardly breathe.

Severus held the foreman's head up long enough for everyone to see clearly what had happened, then let go with an expression of distaste. The big man toppled slowly sideways to the ground and lay moaning hoarsely. Severus stepped over him and approached the dockers, who visibly retreated at his approach.

The centurion spoke quietly but clearly. He leant forward, his posture relaxed but close enough to let them feel his presence.

'Now, listen to me very carefully.' He looked around so that they were all included. 'You useless poxed motherfuckers are going to have every single sack of those stores carefully packed in the hold of that fucking boat by nightfall, or I will be back here and I will come looking for you.' He leant forward a little further. 'I never forget a face and I always find the people I'm looking for.' He stood straight again. 'So. Here's the plan. I will return here tonight, with lots of soldiers, and that pile of stores will be on the boat. Not only will that be true, but you will all be standing here beside the boat, and then the soldiers and I will go on board with you and together we will all consult the stores manifest and compare it to what we've actually got on the ship. If there is anything not here that should be, then I will hold you all individually responsible for anything missing.' He paused and looked at each man in turn, and then down at the big man on the ground. 'And this fat warthog owes me a sausage at the least.' Severus paused and looked from side to side at the group of men. 'That's the plan. I won't be repeating myself after this, so let's do the questions now. Is anyone not absolutely clear about what I'm saying?'

The dockers looked at the moaning body on the ground. Some of them looked mutinous, others looked scared, but none of them would meet the centurion's eye.

'Good,' said Severus cheerfully. 'Now, before you start loading, I expect some of you will want to nip back to your beautiful homes to collect the items belonging to us that you've no doubt been looking after on our behalf. They no longer require your personal protection and can be brought back here without fear. The rest of you can start shifting the stores onto the ship straight away.' He stepped back and looked down again. 'Oh, and some-body should probably make sure this pig doesn't die.' Serpicus could hear the big man's breathing from where he sat.

Severus walked away without looking at them. Brutus jumped down off the wall.

'I don't know about you,' he said with a smile, 'but I'm going to see if I can buy that old man a drink.'

16

Aelius Sejanus, from his Servant:

> *Our agents report that the departure of the* Juno *has
> been successfully delayed. The expedition will depart on
> the morning tide. I have already left Rome and am
> preparing to put the next stage of your plan into effect.
> The necessary people have been contacted and the
> appropriate arrangements made for the arrival of
> the* Juno.

The night before they left Ostia, Severus gathered all the
men together in a dockside warehouse that belonged to
Blaesus. A couple of wineskins were passed around, and
there was good fresh bread, olives and a huge well-hung
sausage, blood-red with rare-cooked meat and laced with
as much garlic as anyone could stand. They were in a
good mood, filled with the expectancy that new
comrades and the anticipation of the unexpected bring.
Severus stood up in front of them.

'We're leaving tomorrow, so pack your things tonight and be ready at dawn.' This wasn't a surprise, but there was a low hum of satisfaction. Severus waited for it to die down.

'We've been training together long enough to get to know each other. I selected you myself and you haven't let me down.' He paused. 'Well, some of you could wash a bit more . . .'

The men laughed at this, and one legionary in particular named Monobazus was pushed about roughly by his friends.

'. . . but as soldiers, fighting men, I couldn't have asked for more.' He put both hands on his belt. 'So, let's be clear what's going to happen.' He paused and looked around. 'We're going to Germany.'

A rustle of conversation started. Severus raised his voice and cut across it.

'Yes, Germany. As some of you may already have heard, there is an uprising of some sort up there at the moment. The Seventh, Eighth and Tenth Legions are marching north to sort it out.' Severus smiled. 'Those of you who were in the Tenth with me will know that the rebels are in for a nasty surprise.' Serpicus could hear the pride in Severus' voice. Several of the men sat up straighter too. Severus smiled in the direction of Monobazus and went on. 'And for those of you who don't know the Seventh, if I tell you that Monobazus was in the Seventh, and they considered him to be a bit of a girl because of the amount of washing he was always doing, you'll appreciate that the rebels will be getting more than one nasty surprise when that lot appear upwind of their doorstep some fine morning.'

There was a lot more laughter, and the fragrant Monobazus was pushed around a lot more, treatment he took in good part.

Severus called the room to order with a look.

'So. Let's get it straight right now what our job is. The Germans will have their hands full with the legions, they won't have time to worry about us. We are going to have nothing to do with any revolts or whatever else may be taking place in Germany. Our job is to go to a village called Gelbheim, collect a wagon and come home. Straight in, grab it and straight out again.'

'Just like that,' said one of the soldiers.

'Yes, just like that,' said Severus, 'and if you interrupt me again I'll come down there and rip your balls off.'

Everyone laughed, including the man who had spoken.

Severus looked serious again. 'I want everyone to be very clear on this before we go. We are not going there looking for a fight. Everyone comes home, all right?' The listening legionaries smiled at the old soldier's maxim. Severus looked serious. 'But we have to be realistic. There is a war on just now, or something like one, and we'll be walking through the middle of it. We're obviously not Germans and we aren't soldiers either, so no one will trust us and we'll do the same for them.' He looked around. 'So this isn't a simple animal hunt, and there may be trouble. You will be well paid for this, but you may not think it's worth it. If so, you should leave now, you'll be paid for the time you've trained here and no more will be said.' He looked round, looking at every face individually. 'But hear me now. If you stay after tonight, you are in, no going back. I expect your full commitment. Now's your chance.'

He stopped and waited. Everyone looked around. No one got up to leave.

Severus looked satisfied. 'Right,' he said. 'From here on, everyone is a fully paid-up member of the expedition, and I own your ragged behinds until you're dead or the job is done and we're safe home, whichever comes first.'

Scipio cleared his throat. 'So, what's it all about?'

Severus shook his head. 'No need for you to know at the moment, and it's important word doesn't get out. For now, all you need to know is that we're marching north into Germany. Soon as we get anywhere close I'll tell you what's going on.'

There was a pause. Monobazus put his hand up. 'Um, aren't the Alps in the way?' he asked.

Severus grinned. 'And they say education is wasted on idiots.' Everyone laughed. 'Bring clothes to wrap up warm, all right?'

Scipio put up a hand. 'May I ask who the commission has come from?'

Severus hesitated, and looked around. Serpicus took a step forward.

'I can't tell you that and I can't tell you exactly what the job is either, because, as Severus said, if word gets out then the whole damn thing goes down the Cloaca Maxima, unhappy client, no one gets paid. However, I can assure you that the client is an important man.

Very important. If we pull this off, we could all be set up for a long time.'

The men looked around, grinning at each other. They'd forgotten the Alps already.

'Right, let's get some sleep,' snapped Severus. 'We leave with the tide tomorrow.'

17

To Aelius Sejanus, from his Servant:

The expedition has arrived in Genoa. The crossing was calm and event-free.

There are twenty soldiers with Serpicus. Most of them are Romans and in my estimation can be relied on to support the legitimate authority when their options are presented to them in the right way. The centurion Severus is harder to judge, but I shall have opportunity to assess his loyalty during the journey, and like all men he will no doubt seek to preserve himself. In addition to Serpicus are the boy Decius, the Thracian, Galba, and the other German confederate, Brutus. These four cannot be trusted.

The men have not yet been told what the purpose of their adventure is. They are impressionable and excitable. It will not be difficult to stir them up when the time comes.

The expedition leaves shortly for Germany. I have

*been in contact with our agents on the way, and the
arrangements are being made.*

Genoa was not as big as Rome and its port was nowhere
near as big as Ostia, but it was big enough to take all the
largest galleys in the Imperial fleet at once, and it was an
important transit point for goods and people from the
mainland to Rome, so it was always busy. Two huge
breakwaters curved around the circular harbour like the
horns on the head of a stag-beetle, and there were close-
packed ranks of ships of every size and description along
the inside of both of the horns.

The expedition arrived as the sun was losing its
strength. The *Juno* crept into the harbour against an
unfavourable tide and slipped into the one remaining
space left on the temporary holding pier. It seemed that
there wasn't room to spread a cloak without hitting a
ship, packed together in both directions like a huge
pontoon bridge. Brutus and Serpicus walked down to the
small hut that acted as the administrative centre of the
port. Decius, who had been seasick for most of the completely calm voyage, caught up with them as they got
there. Once the ship had tied up he had jumped into the
water to clean off the sweat of the previous three days,
dried himself, dressed, and run after them. He appeared
at Serpicus' side as they applied for a berth for the ship.

The harbour-master, a squat man with a legionary's
tattoo on his left forearm and a deep purple scar running
the length of his face, was sitting at a desk outside the
hut. The table was overflowing with papers and slates,
and a further sea of rolls of parchment surrounded him

and lapped at his ankles. He looked up at them with frank dislike.

'You want a berth.' It wasn't a question.

'Yes, please,' Serpicus said brightly.

He sighed heavily. 'Of course you do. Every bugger in the Mediterranean wants me to give them a berth today.'

He didn't say anything else, but went back to puzzling over a heavy roll of parchment. They waited. He carried on reading. They carried on waiting. Brutus cleared his throat in a way that Serpicus had heard before, and so moved in order to be close enough to get in front of him if Brutus decided he had had enough. He was going red in the face in a way that always meant trouble for someone. Serpicus had a vision of the harbour-master floating in the harbour below them, surrounded by his desk and all his papers, while Brutus worked to uproot the hut so that he could throw that in after him too. Serpicus shook his head hastily and held up a finger to indicate that he was giving the scarred man one more chance. Brutus subsided slightly and Serpicus cleared his throat. The harbour-master put a gnarled finger on his place on the document and looked up at him irritably. Serpicus fought down the feeling that Brutus had probably had the right idea, and smiled winningly.

'So?' he said.

'So what?'

Last chance, he thought, and then he would let Brutus do his worst. 'So, do we get a berth or not?'

The harbour-master sighed the sigh of the deeply and unjustly put-upon and looked past them out over the mass of ships at anchor.

'There aren't any berths left anywhere near the centre. You'll have to go over there.'

They looked at where he was pointing.

'Is that place even in the harbour?' said Brutus, squinting as he peered towards the horizon. 'Why not chuck us back into the ocean and be done with it?'

'Don't tempt me,' growled the harbour-master. He then growled quite a lot more, about how it was a public holiday and half his staff were off, how a dozen boats had come into the harbour after a storm and were still being repaired so he couldn't shift them even if he wanted to, which he did but there it was, and how, while he was sure Brutus' and Serpicus' mothers cared deeply about them, the problem of getting their one small boat settled in a satisfactory berth seen against the task of organizing the entire harbour was truly as the dust under his feet, as far as he was concerned. He hoped that his meaning was plain. The nearest available place for the *Juno* to tie up was next to the far point of the right-hand horn of the harbour, and they could take it or leave it. Either way, there was nothing else he could offer them so they could now stop bothering him and fuck off so he could get on with his job.

Serpicus turned and had a quick look around the harbour while Brutus carried on arguing the toss with the tattooed man. Looking around, Serpicus couldn't, in fairness, see a spare berth anywhere other than where the harbour-master had shown them, but of course fairness to the harbour-master had nothing to do with it. Serpicus turned back and added his voice to that of Brutus. Everyone was getting close to losing their temper when

Severus walked casually up the pier and stood behind the harbour-master. For a moment Serpicus thought the centurion was going to deal with the harbour-master as he had dealt with the foreman on the dock at Ostia, but instead Severus folded his arms and shook his head with a sad smile on his face.

'Jupiter,' he said, 'if they've started to give grown-up responsible administrative jobs to a reprobate camel-fucker like this one, then the Empire truly is heading to hell in a dung-cart quicker than I would have thought possible.'

The harbour-master whirled round and dropped into a fighting crouch. Severus beamed down at him. 'How are you, Graptus, you old fart?' he said, in an affectionate tone Serpicus hadn't heard him use before. The harbour-master stood up and his scarred face split into a smile.

'Severus? Is it you?'

Severus smiled back in a way that admitted it was him, and the scarred man let out a yelp of pleasure and jumped forward and seized his arm in both tarred hands.

'What are you doing here? I heard that you were dead.'

Severus shook his head. 'It was much worse for me. I heard that you were alive.'

The harbour-master laughed uproariously and punched him on the arm in a way that most men would have said tested the limits of affection.

'Come on, let's go and find a place we can get a drink. We've a lot of talking to do and we need refreshment to keep our throats in order.'

'Good idea,' said Severus, indicating his comrades

with a nod of his head. 'But first you have to stop fucking around with my friends here and get our lovely ship a decent berth so that we don't have to walk for half a day just to reach the city.'

The harbour-master turned to them with a look of incredulity. 'These ignorant barbarians are with you?'

Severus put one scarred forearm around his shoulders and gestured with the other. 'Gentlemen, may I present ex-centurion Graptus, an old friend from the German campaigns.' He pointed to his colleagues. 'Graptus, may I present Brutus, Serpicus and Decius, some of the Germans that Rome brought home from the same campaigns. Oh, and that short fat one waddling towards us is Galba.'

There was a strained moment while everyone looked at each other, and then Galba arrived beside them, out of breath and sweating and cursing the distance that the *Juno* was moored, and everyone laughed at the same moment. Graptus shook hands with the four of them.

'Come on,' he said. 'Let's get that drink.'

'What about the boat?' asked Brutus. Graptus turned and looked out over the harbour. He ran a finger thoughtfully down the scar on his face and then motioned to a tall dark-skinned man standing nearby to come over to him. The man walked over without lifting his feet off the ground and looked at them with no interest. He seemed surrounded by a sort of gentle gloom.

'Cato.'

'Yes, Graptus?'

The harbour-master slapped a hand onto his shoulder. 'You know those Phoenicians who arrived the other day, the ones you don't like?'

Cato raised an eyebrow. 'Those Phoenicians? The ones moored over there?' He pointed at a graceful ship berthed nearby at almost the exact centre of the forehead between the two horns of the breakwater.

'Yes, the same Phoenicians who insulted you, your gods and your country.'

'Because I didn't leave the Emperor's business and attend to them immediately? You mean *those* Phoenicians?'

Graptus nodded and smiled cheerfully. 'That's right, them. Please go and tell them that if their rat-infested slum of an apology for a boat is still fouling the waters of this, the Emperor's most beautiful harbour, next time I pass by, then I'll have their goods impounded, their boat sunk, and their heathen carcasses dragged off to jail. Would you do that for me?'

What Cato did wasn't exactly a smile, but Serpicus got the definite feeling that the expression on his face was what would have been a smile on anyone else's.

'And I should perhaps tell them that this command is in the name of the Emperor?'

Graptus smiled. 'Most certainly in His name, may the Gods protect Him.'

Cato went towards the Phoenician ship. If it is possible to slouch with a spring in one's step, that's what he did.

Graptus looked pleased. 'He'll enjoy doing that. They weren't very nice to him when they arrived. Come to that, they weren't very polite to me either.' He spat into the ocean. 'I've never had too much time for Phoenicians even on a good day. To be honest, if they hadn't bribed me so incredibly well I probably wouldn't have let them stay here at all.'

Serpicus looked at the little harbour-master, unsure if he was telling the truth or joking. He stared right back and let him wonder.

'Come on, barbarians,' Graptus said, slapping Brutus on the shoulder. 'Let a Roman show you what a real drink tastes like. The wine here is the best in the Empire.' He looked at Brutus and his expression became dubious. 'Mind you, I'm sure we could probably find some of that asses' piss you barbarians call beer. That is, if you haven't a taste for a civilized man's drink.'

Brutus stopped as if he had walked into a wall and turned, shoving a thick forefinger into the little man's face.

'Call me a barbarian if you want, Roman, and I'll maybe even see it as a compliment, but no one insults German beer to my face.'

Graptus looked at Severus, then at Brutus, then back at Severus. He shrugged at the old centurion and inclined his head at Brutus.

'I like him,' Graptus said. 'He's buying the drinks.'

It was a long evening. Graptus and Severus' acquaintance went back a long way and covered an enormous amount of ground, and they told almost all of it before they'd let anyone leave the tavern. By the time they arrived back at the port it was very late. The Phoenician ship was gone and the *Juno*'s captain was happily supervising the final details of taking its place. Cato was waiting at the quayside without any appearance of impatience.

Graptus looked at the *Juno* and clapped his hands. 'Well done, Cato, well done,' he said carefully with a minimum of slurring. 'They give you any trouble?'

'They were very angry,' said Cato, dolefully. 'But they were no trouble.'

Graptus looked serious. 'The Emperor's business.'

'Indeed,' said the dark-skinned man.

'In the name of the Emperor,' said Brutus rather loudly, and tripped over a thick rope. He didn't get up again.

Severus beckoned a couple of guards down from the ship. They hauled Brutus up the gangplank by his armpits and dumped him on a pile of canvas. Severus followed him up the plank, stepped over him and beckoned to Serpicus.

'Just time for a drink before bedtime, eh?' he said.

'Most certainly,' Graptus said with enthusiasm and stepped forward.

Serpicus was just sober enough to know he probably shouldn't have one, and drunk enough not to care. He followed the harbour-master rather unsteadily into the prow of the boat and sat down heavily on the bare deck. The men were mostly asleep on the stern of the ship, amongst the sailors. There was no rule that said that officers slept in the bow and the ranks in the stern, but that's the way it happened on every ship in the Empire.

Serpicus tilted his head back. It was perhaps an hour before dawn. The stars were impossibly bright.

Graptus flopped down nearby and Severus lay down flat on the deck at his feet. The centurion produced a wineskin from somewhere, took a swallow and passed it to Cato, who had come onto the boat and sat down on the other side of Graptus so quietly that Serpicus hadn't noticed him.

Graptus cleared his throat, propped himself up against the gunwale and spat noisily over the side. Then he settled back and closed his eyes. Severus did the same on the other side, so that he faced him. Their feet almost touched as they stretched them out. Cato sat upright without support. Serpicus was reclining on a sack of something soft that smelt of fish.

There was a silence, during which Graptus looked at his fingernails with mild interest.

'I've known for three days you were coming,' he said eventually, in an offhand way that had nothing offhand about it.

Serpicus blinked at him. 'Us? We didn't know that much ourselves. How?' Cato was looking at Graptus intently. Serpicus had the feeling that there was something unsaid between them.

Graptus tugged at a cuticle. 'Not you, necessarily, but someone like you.' Cato seemed to relax slightly.

'Keep talking,' said Severus, sitting up. He immediately looked a lot more sober than he had a few moments before. Serpicus was dimly aware that, as he looked around him, Graptus was inspecting his fingernails with the seriousness and focus of a rational man, rather than the disbelieving intensity of the reeling mind. Of the others, Cato had been sober all along. Decius was unconscious on a pile of rope half-way along the dock. Brutus was sitting across from him with the dangling jaw and blank expression of a stunned bullock.

Serpicus shrugged; just him awake and struggling then.

Graptus decided that his fingernails were satisfactory and looked back up at them.

'I heard that men in Ostia were being paid to work slowly loading a certain ship, and that men here were being paid to unload it the same way when it reached Genoa.'

'This ship?'

Graptus nodded. Severus and Serpicus exchanged glances. The centurion looked serious. Serpicus suspected he just looked confused. He hoped that someone understood what was going on.

'Why didn't you tell us before?' asked Severus.

Graptus shrugged. 'Wasn't sure what to make of it.'

Severus took the wineskin from Graptus and passed it to Cato without drinking. 'What else do you know?'

'A ship from Rome berthed here, half a day before you. Cato was paid to inform the captain when you arrived.'

'And he did so?' Serpicus asked, glaring at Cato. The dark man bore his displeasure without fear.

'Of course he did,' said Graptus, before Cato could reply and in a tone that suggested Serpicus was being stupid. 'A ship's arrival at a place like this isn't exactly something that can be kept secret for long. I'd rather Cato got the money than someone else. If it's any consolation, they got the worst berth in the entire harbour.'

'And, of course, Cato can now tell us all about them, whereas another man would not,' said Severus, with a warning glance at Serpicus.

Serpicus knew he hadn't thought of that, and probably

184

should have. He opened his mouth and then closed it without speaking.

'Exactly,' said Graptus. He looked at Cato as if his assistant was about to do something clever.

'They are Romans, on their way to take command of the forces being sent to put down the rebellion of the German tribes,' said Cato. 'The leader is a tall man, maybe forty, with dark hair, cut short. He is serious, and looks like a soldier. A scar on his cheek, the left, I think – no, the right. Another man is with him. Younger and bigger. He has fair hair and a strange, high-pitched laugh. Not, I think, a soldier.' There was a hint of scorn in his voice. 'It is said that they are brothers, though there is little resemblance. Both are expensively dressed but the older man's clothes are simple whereas the other is a fop with gold leaf down the edge of his tunic.'

Graptus shrugged. 'Never seen them.'

Serpicus felt a cold stone appear in his stomach. He forced himself to think. 'You say a scar on his cheek?'

Cato nodded. 'The right one.'

Severus looked at Serpicus appraisingly. 'You know them?'

Serpicus nodded. 'Just a moment,' he said. He walked across the deck to the side furthest from the pier and kept going. The water closed over his head, colder than he had expected. He emerged sneezing and spitting. He grabbed a rope that hung against the hull and pulled himself up the side and back onto the deck. He ran his hands back over his hair and slicked the water off, and sat down again on the pungent bundle of ropes.

'Better?' asked Graptus. He used a tone of voice that

sounded like an indulgent uncle watching boys getting into scrapes that he saw coming but let them find out for themselves. Serpicus felt it was the sort of voice that was going to get annoying if he used it a lot. Graptus grinned at Severus. 'You teach them to swim, they just can't resist showing off, can they?'

Severus chuckled. 'It's walking they have difficulty with.'

Serpicus tried to growl but it just made drips fly across the deck. He used his sleeve to wipe the excess water off his face.

'Those two men,' he said.

Severus looked at him enquiringly. 'You know them?'

Serpicus nodded. 'So do you, or at least you've heard of them. Marcus and Consilius. Sejanus' cousins.'

Graptus raised an eyebrow in surprise and then frowned. 'Both of the Partner's two Gilded Bollocks here in person, eh? Why would they be following you?'

Serpicus concentrated. Nothing made much sense. 'I doubt Blaesus trusts us. Maybe he's planning on making sure we don't try and make a run for it or something.' Serpicus knew it was weak, unlikely. Blaesus had his family, he knew Serpicus would return if he was still alive.

'There is more to tell you,' said Graptus. He glanced at Cato, who nodded.

'They weren't the only group who paid me to tell them when you arrived,' he said.

Brutus sighed, broke wind loudly and pulled himself to his feet. 'You lot just aren't going to let a man sleep, are you?' he said. He stepped onto the gunwale and disappeared over the side.

'Is this some sort of German ritual after drinking?' asked Graptus mildly, watching the water settle.

A few moments later Brutus appeared again. He stood dripping on the deck, bent over at the waist and shook himself vigorously. When he stood up his long red hair was wound around his head like seaweed.

'Now,' he said clearly. 'I think perhaps everyone had better share everything they know.'

Serpicus told them about Blaesus and Decius and his family and the bear, all of it.

When he was finished the sun was washing the dark from the horizon. He felt light-headed in a way that had nothing to do with the wine.

Severus was frowning at Cato. 'And you say there is another group of men interested in us?'

Cato nodded. 'Those are the ones I know of, the ones who bribed me to tell them when you arrived. There may be others who bribed someone else or who didn't need to bribe anyone at all.'

'You're doing well out of us.'

Cato smiled. 'Indeed. I have also been told that they have been scouring the taverns and hiring mercenaries at high wages for a short contract.'

Severus was thinking hard. 'So. We have the sons of our employer following us for no apparent reason apart from their little spat with you, and don't forget that they are supposed to be putting down the obviously small matter of an uprising in Germany, and at least one group of men following us as well. Why?'

'Presumably because they either want the bear for

themselves or at least want to make sure that Blaesus doesn't get it?' suggested Brutus.

Serpicus shrugged. 'Or for any one of a dozen other reasons we know nothing about.'

'It's like a game,' Graptus said to himself.

Galba looked gloomy. 'Or a military campaign.'

Serpicus looked up at the night sky. 'That too. They have a lot in common. But let's assume it's peaceful until we know any different.'

Galba shook his head. 'Actually I'd prefer to assume the opposite.'

Serpicus smiled. 'Fair enough. Do we agree that it isn't in their interests to do anything until we have the bear?'

Severus grunted agreement. 'That seems reasonable. They'll allow us to do the work and then try and take it from us on the way back.'

'They might kill us as soon as possible to prevent us getting it at all,' Brutus said.

Severus shook his head. 'True, but then no one gets it. That's possible, but it doesn't sound Roman. They all want it.'

Serpicus looked at the faces around him. 'So. Game or campaign, we carry on, showing as little of our hand as possible and waiting for them to reveal theirs.'

There was no reply.

'We haven't really got a choice, have we?' he said.

18

They set off three days later. Cato had been right about the bribery. The dockers in Genoa treated the cargo from the *Juno* like some strange and potentially lethal material that they had never seen before. The expedition ended up unloading most of it themselves, which at least meant that less of it got stolen than usual. Once it was off the boat, the dockers, presumably encouraged by the fact that none of them had died suddenly as a result of handling it, suddenly found the supplies immensely desirable, and Severus had to mount a full-time guard on the dockside to prevent the expedition setting off with nothing except that which they carried on their backs. They were glad to leave Genoa. Graptus gave them a couple of wineskins to remember him by. They promised to bring him something back in return when they passed through on the way home.

'Fine,' he said, 'anything. Just don't bring me any bloody German beer.'

As Serpicus was putting his wineskin in what he

hoped was a safe place amongst the baggage, Brutus caught his eye. The big man inclined his head slightly towards where the men were arguing in a melee about storage space a short distance away. Serpicus looked where Brutus was indicating and saw Cato threading his way unobtrusively between the soldiers towards him. Cato caught Serpicus' eye in a way that told him that he wanted to speak. Serpicus indicated with a gesture that Cato should circle round and meet him beside a nearby column by the corner of the courtyard.

The dark man leant against the column as he waited for Serpicus in a way that was so resolutely casual and unconspiratorial that it was utterly suspicious. Serpicus pulled him round to the far side so that no one could see them. Brutus had sauntered after them, and now propped himself against the pillar while he ate some fat black olives with single-minded attention. No one could get past him to overhear the conversation.

'Any news?' Serpicus asked, feeling that Cato would hardly have come if there was none.

'Graptus sent me to tell you that Marcus and Consilius left Genoa with their men last night, heading north. The rumour amongst the men is that they will go through the mountains together and then split up, circle around and meet up at Anthropae.'

'Please thank Graptus, and my thanks to you too.'

Cato gave him a slight bow. He seemed to hesitate.

'Is there anything else?'

He raised a hand slightly, lowered it again, then said in a rush, 'May I ask a favour?'

'Of course.'

'Graptus has suggested that I might ask if I might accompany you. Would you be willing to have me?'

Serpicus thought for a moment. 'Why?'

He looked slightly embarrassed. 'Graptus feels that I may be of more use to you than I am to him. He has told me that he wishes to employ a more ... vigorous assistant, and that I should seek alternative employment.' He gave him a quick nervous smile. 'For myself, I have been in Genoa long enough to be glad of the chance of a change. I have always been curious to see the lands to the north.' Serpicus looked at him with a raised eyebrow, and Cato saw it. He glanced down at his feet and then back at him. 'I was a soldier myself, for three years.' The nervous smile again. 'Not a very good one, I admit, but we saw action.'

'We can always use more soldiers. Who were you with?'

'I was with Antoninus in Gaul, in the Seventh Legion.'

Serpicus paused for a moment, then made a decision. 'If Graptus can do without you, you are welcome. How long do you need to prepare?'

He grinned shyly. 'Don't wait. Set off when you are ready. You'll be on the Comum road. If I'm not back here by when you leave then I'll catch you up.' He made the hand gesture again. 'Thank you. Thank you very much.' Serpicus watched him walk briskly away with a lift to his stride.

'What's he up to?' drawled a voice from the other side of the pillar.

'What do you mean?' Serpicus said, coming round to stand beside Brutus. A scattering of well-sucked olive

191

stones surrounded his feet. He jerked a thumb at Cato's back.

'Does that seem right to you?'

'What?'

Brutus squinted against the sun and looked over the harbour. 'Busy place like this, must be coming up to the busiest time of year, and the harbour-master quite cheerfully tells his right-hand man – the man who, as far as we can tell, does most of the work around here, as well as being the only man he seems to trust – that he can go off on an expedition which might take months, might be dangerous, might never see him again.' He gave the last olive stone a final careful examination between his front teeth and spat it out. 'Does that make sense to you?'

Serpicus pursed his lips in thought. 'I don't think it was exactly a favour. I think Graptus sacked him, so Cato wanted a job and didn't want to explain why.'

'You think so? Did Graptus ever complain about him? Show the slightest sign of dissatisfaction? I got the feeling Cato was doing a pretty good job. And it isn't something you can train someone to do in a week. I wouldn't sack someone unless they were doing more harm than good. Is that the impression you got from Graptus?'

It wasn't. Serpicus was confused. 'What are you saying? That Graptus has a reason? Maybe he wants to keep track of us and is sending Cato as a spy? What reason would he have to do that?'

Brutus shrugged. 'No idea. It just seems a bit odd to me, that's all.'

'Or maybe Cato just likes travelling?'

'Ah, you mean he's leaving and he hasn't told Graptus?' Brutus pondered it. 'I hadn't thought of that. Makes more sense, I grant you. Explains why he asked us so close to departure, so Graptus wouldn't find out till it was too late.' He paused and then another thought struck him. 'Is Cato a slave?'

'I don't know. Do you care?'

'Only that Graptus might send people after us to get him back.'

'Then we'll give him up. He isn't our concern.'

Brutus pushed himself upright off the pillar and kicked absently at a few olive stones. 'Fair enough.' He was getting at something and Serpicus didn't know what it was.

'I'm not sure what it is you're trying to say.'

'Just speaking my mind, that's all.'

'Trust no one, eh?'

Brutus looked at him seriously. 'On this expedition, no, I don't.'

'Present company included?'

Brutus said nothing, but smiled.

They walked in silence back to the ship. Cato had told them that he served with the Seventh in Gaul. A couple of Severus' men were from the Seventh. They could be counted on to find out very quickly if he was lying. Legion veterans always immediately asked new men claiming to have been legionaries who they had served with, and they hated it when they caught civilians pretending to be one of their number. They had plenty of ways of finding out the truth, ranging from asking innocent-sounding trick questions to hanging suspects upside down over the latrine in the dysentery hospital. Serpicus wondered for a while whether he should be worried about Cato, and then decided he wasn't that day's problem. He put Cato on the list of all the other things he had to think about and was putting off, like whether they were going to survive the month.

19

Aelius Sejanus, from his Servant:

*The expedition left Genoa yesterday and is making good
time. It is as yet unclear to me what the exact route will
be, but I assume it will head directly north until we come
near the area controlled by the rebellious tribes, and
then swing west to get as close to our destination as
possible before exposing ourselves to the possibility of
meeting hostile barbarians.*

*I have been entirely accepted by most of the soldiers
of the group. In particular I have become the confidant
of the young German, Decius. Some of the auxiliaries,
particularly those who do not speak Latin well, are
naturally suspicious of anyone not of their race, but they
are of no consequence. I will concentrate on the leaders
and all will follow from that.*

They set off soon after and Cato caught them up by
nightfall. He brought further news; men had been

recruited to pursue them from Genoa. They were lightly armed and travelling fast, no more than a day behind the expedition.

Five days' march brought them to Comum, which was the point where any fashionable Roman would have said that Italy – and therefore civilization – ended, and *terra incognita* – a barbarian land covered in eternal darkness and infested with cannibal hordes – began. Comum was the point, as a rich senator once put it, beyond which a Roman citizen could not walk with his money hanging in a bag at his waist while holding his blind virgin daughter by the hand and feel they were both absolutely safe. (The senator's listeners would have known that this statement ignored the fact that that same Roman and his daughter most certainly wouldn't have been able to do any of those things just a light javelin's toss from the Forum in Rome either, but no doubt they let that pass.)

The change hit Galba particularly hard. He spent most of the march wrapping himself in a thick cloak and bemoaning the prospect in front of them.

'No baths,' he said sadly. 'No massage. No steam rooms. Freezing water. Nothing but dirt, lice, smells and sweat, and all of it wet and cold.'

'Never mind,' said Brutus cheerfully. 'We'll soon find you a nice river and chuck you into it. It'll be exactly the same.'

Galba looked at him resentfully. 'Unless the river comes from a hot spring, I very much doubt it. I can always rely on the Germans to choose the uncivilized alternative.'

Brutus put a heavy hand on his shoulder and leant

forward to whisper loudly into his ear. 'Welcome to my country, you soft Roman tart.'

'I'm not Roman, I'm Thracian,' snapped Galba. 'Not that you'd know where that is.'

Brutus grinned. 'They have soft Roman tarts there too, do they?'

Galba suddenly frowned, reached into his cloak and pulled something from his chest. He looked at the wriggling louse between his fingertips with distaste and then flicked it at Brutus.

Brutus shook his head sorrowfully. 'Maybe if you were still painted blue they wouldn't want to chew on you quite so much?'

Galba shook his cloak and rearranged it around himself. 'I don't need to do anything except stand next to you, the smell drives them away faster than a lighted branch.'

Serpicus smiled. And so it went on.

The men were settled in a barn next to one of the local taverns with instructions to relax, stay sober and not get into any arguments. Serpicus reckoned that he could count on them for at least the first of the three. He sat in the tavern with Galba, Brutus and Severus in a side room and talked. Decius sat nearby, listening. A rough pigskin map of their route was on the table in front of them. The wine bottle went round, but everyone was watering it heavily and it was more for form's sake than real drinking. They were all taking things a bit more seriously as the temperature of the air dropped.

Serpicus looked around at his companions.

'I want us all to be clear what lies in front of us.

Everything out in the open and on the table now. If anyone has any problems or misgivings then now is the time to say so. Let's not have unnecessary arguments on the way.' They all made noises of agreement. He nodded to Severus to start the discussion. The old centurion looked serious.

'We have covered around twenty leagues a day so far. Assuming similar weather, similar terrain and an unlimited supply of shoes we can go on at the same speed more or less indefinitely.'

Brutus turned his cup slowly in his hands and looked at it with a distant expression. 'But we can't assume any of those things. The weather will change, it always does. The terrain from here into Germany is first mountains, then mostly forest, hills or marsh and sometimes all three.'

'And we've no idea where the good shoe shops are either,' said Galba.

Severus pointed at the map. 'Indeed, but there's nothing we can do about any of that.' His finger moved left, tracing a line north, and tapped a dark spot on the pigskin. 'We will stay on the present road until we reach this point here. It's the most direct route, and it takes us to the edge of Transpadana.' On the map, a fortress of triangles swallowed up the road and spread out to the edge of the skin in each direction.

'The Alps,' said Brutus quietly.

'The Alps,' agreed Severus. 'We haven't got a month to spare, so we have to go straight over them. We take the shortest way, through the Hinterrhein Pass. It's steep, but the snow isn't too bad this time of year.'

'Won't be much fun coming back though,' said Brutus in the same soft voice.

'True, but I don't know of an alternative,' said Severus, with the slightest hint of irritation. 'The Hinterrhein takes us slightly east of where we're actually going, but the alternative is to become mountain-climbers and none of our men have suggested much aptitude for that.' He took a contemplative sip from his cup. 'Then we swing west again and head straight due north for Augusta Trevororum.' He pointed at another smudge on the other side of the mountains. The line on the skin that indicated where the road joined the south side of the Alps didn't emerge on the north side. Galba squinted at the map mistrustfully.

'Is there actually a road to Augusta?'

Severus made a dismissive gesture. 'More of a decent track than a proper road, but it's passable. More important, it'll keep us on a reasonably straight route for the Treveri while keeping us away from the Leuci and the Lingones.'

Brutus looked up. 'They're south of the Rhine. I thought the tribes on the south side of the river weren't involved in the revolt? I heard it was the mad bastards from the north who were rebelling, like the Mattiaci and the Chatti. Are the southern tribes joining in now?'

Severus shrugged. 'The news isn't clear. I suspect those who know what's going on aren't telling anyone the full extent of the rebellion, in hopes that the other tribes won't join in. It's always hard to know who is involved and who isn't. The Mattiaci and Chatti are certainly in revolt. Other tribes who haven't actually declared war will probably be assisting them, either with supplies or with volunteers. The Marcomanni for one will certainly be sympathetic. And even the tribes who are peaceful will provide safe haven for the rebels. And there will be renegades from every tribe, men who will never accept Roman rule.' He looked down at the map. 'And you can bet that there will be men from the Mediomatrici and the Ubii involved somewhere, whether officially or unofficially. There always are.'

Brutus and Serpicus looked at each other but didn't speak. Severus was being tactful, he had just mentioned the tribes living either side of the Treveri without suggesting that the Treveri were in any way involved. Everyone knew that rebellions like this one always brought the discontented, the angry and the just plain bored to the surface. Just because the Treveri weren't officially allied to the rebels didn't mean there wouldn't be men from their tribe involved. Perhaps men they knew. Serpicus wondered if events had taken a different turn, if Brutus and he had not been taken to Rome, whether they might not be in the forests at this moment, sharpening their weapons and praying to the gods to send them another Varus.

And there was another problem. Brutus, Decius and Serpicus were Germans, and there were Spaniards, Gauls and a smattering of other nationalities amongst the auxiliaries, but almost all of their legionaries would, to any German, appear Roman. Everyone on the expedition habitually spoke Latin and usually wore bits of Roman uniform. As far as any Germans they might meet were concerned, they were Romans, marching through conquered territory during a rising against Roman rule. Even the tribes who were not presently in revolt against Rome remembered Germanicus' enforced peace and bore her no love. The expedition would have to hide their armour or they would probably be ambushed on sight. Even that might not save them. Bands of unidentified men were not likely to be allowed to travel unchallenged, by either side.

Severus continued. 'We march north, staying close to the west bank of the Rhine, and head for the lands of the Treveri.'

'Which takes us straight through the lands of the Mediomatrici,' said Brutus.

Severus met his gaze. 'Yes,' he said levelly. 'But short of a three-hundred-mile detour through Gaul and then swimming a very big river, there is no way of avoiding them that I am aware of. But it's your country. Do you know another way around?'

Galba frowned, putting a deep line in the bulb of skin between his eyes. 'Do we need to worry about the Mediomatrici?' he asked casually.

Brutus looked serious. 'You aren't a Treveri or a Roman, so you don't have to worry,' he said. 'They'll only put a sword in you. They have a real pleasure lined up for the rest of us.'

'Oh, that's all right then, and there's me getting all upset for nothing,' said Galba. 'I'm glad I'm only getting killed. What's the much worse thing than that they'll do to you then?'

'They'll set the dogs on us.'

'Dogs?'

'Hunting dogs. Jaws like bear traps. Once they shut their teeth on you, you can cut their heads off and they still won't let go. They aren't big enough to kill a man on their own, but they enjoy trying. And if six or so of them catch you, you'll end up just a pile of rags spread across a mile of countryside.'

It was turning into one of the extended jokes that only Brutus found funny. Serpicus intervened. 'They use a knife to make a cut in your belly, here. They pull the rope of your guts out. They nail your guts to a post. Then they set the dogs on you. You can choose between running away or standing and fighting.'

Brutus guffawed at Galba's expression. 'And you'll need at least one hand to hold your guts up high,' he said gleefully, 'or the dogs will be fighting over them like it was a fresh garlic sausage.'

Galba looked at him critically. 'I'm glad we're not going near any barbarians then,' he said, and straightened one leg to push hard with his foot on the edge of Brutus' stool. Brutus let out a surprised yelp and crashed to the floor.

Severus leant forward and put his forearms on the table. 'So, we are all agreed that it will be necessary to proceed quietly and unobtrusively through the lands of the Mediomatrici?'

Brutus, still chuckling on the floor, held up a finger and pointed at Serpicus and then himself.

'We know some of the country round there, it touches on our own.'

'Mine too,' said Decius.

Severus nodded. 'We're going to need all that knowledge.'

'Don't worry, we'll look after you,' Serpicus said. He hoped that the fact that the Treveri were allies with the Mediomatrici would protect them, but walking through Germany accompanied by a couple of dozen Romans didn't make him feel very secure about it.

Galba tapped a fingernail on the table thoughtfully. He could focus his attention when he chose. 'Let's assume we make it through to the village unscathed. It sounds unlikely, but I suppose it's possible. At least on the way there we can try to walk through the forests quietly and hope we don't run into anyone. There's hope. But on the journey back we'll have a bloody great animal with us in a cage on a cart. We'll have to use the roads, or at least what they use instead of roads. How can we hide then?'

Severus looked serious. 'Travel by night, slowly, while saying our prayers.'

Brutus glanced at Galba and shook his head. 'You were right, we're all going to die.'

Severus sat up straight and looked around him. Suddenly he was an officer of Rome again and it wasn't a democracy any more. 'We'll meet those problems when they come. My two main concerns now are these men from Genoa behind us on the one hand, and the fact that there are several legions in front of us led by men who don't like Serpicus on the other. If we run into them we'll probably be interned.'

'Oh good,' said Galba. 'I'd forgotten about Marcus and Consilius. There I was, thinking that at least there isn't going to be anyone in front of us stirring things up.'

'We can't do much about the Romans. Not only do we not know what their plans are, we don't know where they are either. I propose that we deal with the group behind us. There are fewer of them, and with them gone then at least we will know what direction to look in for the enemy.'

Brutus and Galba both sat up. 'Suits me,' said Brutus. 'I was beginning to wonder when the fighting would start.'

'One other question.'

Something in Severus' voice made everyone look at him.

'What?' asked Brutus. Serpicus had a feeling he knew what was coming.

Severus took a breath. 'There's no polite way to say this. The men know that you are from Germany. They are wondering where your loyalties lie.'

Brutus sat back, his eyebrows raised. 'What are you saying?'

Serpicus leant forward quickly. 'It's a natural question. The answer is simple. The Treveri aren't at war, and even if they were it's not our fight. We have a job to do, and we're being well paid for it. And if that isn't enough for them, remind the men that my family are hostages for the return of this expedition. That, for me, stands in front of any other loyalty.'

Severus looked steadily at Serpicus and then nodded slightly. Brutus growled agreement. Serpicus looked at Decius. The young man hadn't spoken. He'd spent more than half of his life in Rome. Germany must be a distant memory for him. There was no way of knowing what returning would stir up in him, and no point in worrying about it. Serpicus leant over Severus' map.

Severus' plan was simple. The pursuers didn't know where the expedition was going, so they must be staying fairly close and following the tracks. All Severus' men had to do was stop and wait for their pursuers to catch up, then slaughter them at will.

'I like it,' said Galba. 'It's simple, it's brutal, it's unimaginative.' He looked around, his gaze lingering just long enough on Brutus. 'I suspect that's probably going to become the theme for this trip.'

They left at dawn and marched along the road until they were at the bottom of a narrow gully that rose in an even gradient for a five-minute climb. Shale-covered slopes rose sharply on both sides. Large rocks were scattered amongst clumps of tough bushes along the gully floor. There was a slight indentation in the cliff to their right, a high thin flake of rock wide enough to hide perhaps six men. If, that is, the enemy kept walking and didn't look back. The other ambushers would have to use the rocks and small trees that dotted the ground.

Severus stroked his chin. 'Plenty of cover.' His men looked at the bushes rather dubiously but said nothing.

'Not much height advantage, though,' murmured Brutus. 'Not when there are more of them than us.'

'Enough though. The main problem will be to concentrate the two halves of our force quickly enough.' He turned to the men and indicated that they should stand close to him. 'Listen. There are a bunch of cut-throats on our trail.' Serpicus saw several men glance involuntarily back the way they had come. 'They probably outnumber us, but they are a gangrenous rabble with no discipline and no spirit. So we're going to stop here, ambush them, cut a few hearts out and try and find out what they're up to. So don't kill all of them, all right? Take prisoners.' He looked at them confidingly. 'Break their heads by all means, just don't kill them, all right?'

The men smiled grimly and returned to checking their weapons.

Severus turned and beckoned to Scipio and Soldi, the legionary with the broken arm, who followed Severus around like a dog. Brutus had protested mildly at the choice of a man who couldn't actually lift a sword to lead a band of soldiers, but Severus had refused to discuss it beyond asking if he had the right to choose his own lieutenants without reference to anyone else. When he was assured that this was the case, he walked away before anyone could put a 'but' on the end of the sentence.

Serpicus felt a hand on his forearm. It was Snake. The Cretan drew him to one side.

'We talked to Cato, the new recruit, last night.'

'And?' The Cretan paused. 'If you have something, give it to me.'

The Cretan shrugged. 'The others were happy enough, he knew what he was talking about. I just don't trust him.'

'Any particular reason?'

'No. Just a feeling.'

'Fair enough. Keep an eye on him and let me know if you come up with anything more definite.'

The Cretan nodded and went after Scipio, who was striding off to carry out Severus' instructions. The plan was simple. Half of the men, including Serpicus, Galba, Brutus and Decius, would go to the top of the hill and hide. The remainder, under Severus' command, would conceal themselves at the lower end of the gully. When the pursuers were safely inside they would be caught between the jaws of the attack. Severus retraced his steps a few hundred paces so that he could check how far back the men behind the rock would have to go so as not to be seen.

'Of course,' Galba mused to himself in a way that everyone could hear, as they prepared to follow the group heading up the gully, 'there are a number of assumptions here that don't necessarily follow.'

'And now you're going to cheer us up by telling us what they are,' muttered Brutus, bending to pick up a branch to use as a staff.

'Indeed. For example, we're assuming that they do not outnumber us significantly.'

'Anything else you have to tell us that might make us feel that we might just last the day?'

'Yes, actually. We're assuming that we're better soldiers than they are.'

Brutus stopped in his tracks and pointed with his sword back down the hill to where Severus was return- ing. 'See that old man down there?'

'Severus? Of course.'

'Well, I'll give you a choice.'

'What?'

'You can go down there and tell him that his plan is doomed to fail, partly due to his incompetence at planning and partly because he hasn't trained his men properly.'

Galba frowned. 'Bad idea. What's the alternative?'

Brutus leant forward until his face was almost touching Galba's. 'Shut the fuck up, all right?'

The brisk climb didn't take long but most of them needed a short time at the top to recover. They then watched as Severus and Snake ran up the hill to where they were waiting. Severus stood without any sign of breathlessness in the centre of the small group and gave out orders.

'If they know what they're doing, they'll have scouts out in front of them, and they will be looking for you so stay well hidden. Everyone stays put, no sound, no attack. Let the scouts go past us. Once the scouts have signalled back to the main force that it's clear, the men at the top of the hill will grab them as quietly and as efficiently as they can. Remember, we need them alive. Don't go for them too soon or you'll be seen, and then you'll have to kill them so they can't warn the others.'

Galba opened his mouth. Serpicus kicked him hard. Galba closed his mouth and sulked. Severus didn't notice the kick or the expression, or didn't show it if he did.

'Once the main body is near you at the top, we'll come out behind them and get their attention. They'll probably attack us.'

'You think?' said Galba with a smile.

Severus didn't reply, but he looked at Galba for long enough and in such a way that Galba stopped both the smiling and the talking. Severus continued.

'You lot at the top let them come back down the gully, and once we've engaged them and got their attention you will attack them from behind.' He looked around.

'Clear?' Everyone nodded. 'Any questions?' Galba cleared his throat in a respectful way.

'What if they don't attack you?'

'Then they'll come pelting up the hill to get away from us, in which case it'll be your job to stop them until we get up here to help you.' Severus looked around and the trace of a sardonic smile hovered on his lips. 'Remember, timing is important. If they see you too early, we'll lose the element of surprise and they'll massacre us.'

'And if we leave it too late they'll massacre you anyway.'

Severus' smile hardened into reality. 'That's the size of it. So mind you get it right.'

'Or we'll come back to haunt you,' said Snake, running his thumb along the edge of what looked like a butcher's knife.

'We won't need to,' said Severus. 'Get it right or we're all fucked. End of story.'

There was no more to say.

Severus trotted back down the hill. Brutus and Serpicus scrambled to the far end of the gully and sent the Cretan ahead over the brow of the hill. There were fewer large rocks for cover, but plenty of thick vegetation. This was mostly sage bushes, which sent up their scent of smoke and trodden grass when anyone pushed past them. The men dispersed themselves and hid. Serpicus walked up the end of the gully, trying to imagine himself a scout for the approaching force. Apart from a foot belonging to Cato, he couldn't see any trace of an ambush. He left it to one of the soldiers to explain to Cato what would happen to his foot if it gave them away, and they settled down to wait.

The sun was just starting to sink when one of Severus' men came stumbling up the slope and burst through the sage-brush towards them.

'They're just coming up the hill to the gully,' he panted, kneeling beside them.

'How many?' said Brutus.

The soldier hesitated. 'Twenty-five in the main group, more ahead of them scouting.'

Outnumbered, maybe two to one.

'Arms?'

'Side arms, a few spears. They don't look much like soldiers.' Serpicus got the feeling the man's pride was hurt.

'Let's hope they aren't,' Brutus said quietly. 'Right, everyone ready.'

Serpicus looked around. Every man was in a crouch, ready to move. Several of them were smiling at the thought of combat. He made a mental note to make sure that a couple of these smiling men were in front of him when they all ran back down the hill. Given their enthusiasm it seemed only fair to let them have first crack at the enemy.

Brutus peered around the side of a large rock at the head of the gully. 'Here they come,' he called softly, looking around him with a fierce expression. 'Get your bloody heads down.' Several men withdrew behind their bushes.

'What do you see?' Serpicus whispered.

Brutus lay on the ground so that he wasn't silhouetted

against the horizon and peered round the side of the boulder. 'The good news is that they aren't soldiers, that's for certain. Just a bunch of wharf rats, fit for shoving knives between drunken men's ribs in the dark and sneaking up on sleeping people.' He sat back behind the cover of the rock and looked at the edge of his sword meditatively.

'What's the bad news?' Serpicus asked.

Brutus hissed to the man who had come up the gully from Severus' group. 'Soldier?'

The man looked up. 'Sir?'

Brutus held up both hands, with a thumb and forefinger held down on one hand. 'How many fingers?'

The man looked uncomfortable. 'Five, sir?'

Brutus sighed. 'Thought so. Can't bloody count.'

Serpicus put his head carefully around the rock and looked down the hill. Two scouts were walking carefully on either side of the track towards him, looking from side to side. Perhaps forty more men were a good spear-throw away behind the scouts, coming towards them in a ragged but menacing group, led by a big man wearing some sort of chest armour and carrying a large sword. He looked familiar but Serpicus couldn't place him.

None of them had looked back yet and seen the ambush. The setting sun was in their eyes, which probably helped.

'Get ready,' Brutus said.

Like most plans, it started well. The scouts walked past the hiding men without seeing them. The scouts were both small wiry men with skin burnt dark by the sun and dried by the sea-wind. The sun reflected back at them off their drawn swords. Serpicus pressed himself back behind the bushes. He could just see Cato curled into a ball on the ground like a hedgehog, every extremity tucked in. Whatever the soldier said to him had worked.

Seeing nothing, the scouts turned at the summit, waved to those behind them and then disappeared over the hill.

'I hope the Cretan is still awake,' whispered Brutus.

As if in reply they heard two quick sounds, like someone hitting a horsehair mattress hard with a fist, followed by the noise of a soft weight hitting the ground. There was a sharp metallic scrape and then silence. Brutus looked at Serpicus and made a thumbs-up. 'If he'd caught the sword before it hit the ground, perfect,' he said.

They could hear the main group of men coming up the gully towards them. The pursuers were making no effort to keep silence. For a moment Serpicus thought something had gone wrong, that Severus thought they were not as far up as they really were, and that his fifteen soldiers would have to jump out and attack all forty of them on level ground. Then, just in time, a fearsome yelling started from the foot of the gully.

The pursuers turned in confusion, milling like startled animals. Not soldiers, or very poor ones. Some raised their swords and yelled obscenities back down the hill, while those closest to the rear pressed back, trying to get away in case of arrows. The big man with the breastplate pushed his way down the hill through them. He took in the small size of Severus' force in a moment and issued

212

a volley of orders. Whatever he was now, he at least had once been a soldier. He snapped instructions at his men and took about two thirds of his force with him at a run back down the hill. The remaining third was detailed to stay behind to prevent an attack from the rear, the very thing the ambushers were intending.

'Shit,' muttered Brutus.

Serpicus could see why. If they attacked the men left behind, the ambushers would be taking on a force the same size as their own, whereas Severus was heavily outnumbered. The rearguard could hold them up while the larger force dealt with Severus, and then the two could combine again to finish off Serpicus.

Serpicus hesitated, knowing he had to charge, but knowing also that to do it too soon would doom the strategy to failure.

Then the rearguard did the one thing that made their defeat certain.

If they had been soldiers, accustomed to taking and obeying orders, they would have stayed where they were told. The ambushers would have charged them, and – at best – would have been badly mauled right there even if they had broken through. But they were wharf rats and cut-throats. They saw nothing threatening them at the head of the gully, their scouts had given no warning, and their comrades were attacking an inferior force. They were missing an obvious victory, losing easy pickings. With shouts of encouragement to each other they charged back down the hill after their friends.

Brutus jumped up. 'Come on,' he called over his shoulder.

'No more than four against one,' muttered Galba, getting to his feet.

'About right odds against those idiots, I'd say,' growled a soldier as he pushed past Serpicus. It was one of the two who had had his nose broken by Severus on the first day. The other one was right behind him.

In a moment all of them were moving down the hill after Brutus. The ambushers were under strict orders not to make unnecessary noise as they approached, in the hope that they might be almost upon the pursuers before they realized they were there. As Serpicus ran down towards them with his blood pounding in his head he could see that they were going to need the surprise. Severus was heavily outnumbered and already in trouble. His men were stood in a tight defensive circle. They were doing a lot of damage, but they were taking punishment too. As Brutus and his men stumbled down the hill Serpicus saw one of Severus' men go down, and then another. Then one of the pursuers spun round to avoid a blow. He saw the reinforcements and for a moment was frozen in surprise. Then he let out a yell.

'Run!' yelled Brutus, and flung himself headlong down the slope.

Several other men turned as Brutus, by now running flat out, crashed into them. The man who had seen them first threw his sword away and started to scramble up the side of the gully. The loose shale shifted under his feet and he slipped back down on his back to where the broken-nosed soldier who had shoved Serpicus aside was waiting for him.

Any soldier knows that the true test of a fighting force

is when it is pressed hard on one front and is then attacked from behind. A centurion will justify the seemingly aimless days of marching and drill by pointing to the trust it creates. The only hope for survival in such a situation is that the front rank will continue fighting while relying on the rear to turn and defend their backs. An undisciplined force will not trust those around them. They will immediately resort to every man for himself. This was Severus' plan. His numerically inferior force fought as one unit, whereas the superior numbers fought as individuals. Unless one of those individuals is Hercules, the unit will always win. Although, like rats trapped in a corner, if the individuals have no path of retreat, they will not give up without a fight.

The ambushers were still outnumbered two to one, and Serpicus' portion were sprinting straight at him. The faster of the two, a tall thin man with a shock of black hair, held his sword high as he ran and brought it down at Serpicus' head with a roar of defiance. Serpicus deflected the impact on his shield and swayed to his left, allowing the man to overbalance, and slashed at him as he went past. The end of his blade caught the muscle of the thin man's right shoulder, and he dropped the sword with a howl.

The other man, fatter and slower, was more cautious. He came at Serpicus crouching down low with a short spear in his hand, and Serpicus had to jump sideways to avoid the thrust. His left foot came down on a sharp rock and he stumbled onto one knee. The fat man's face contorted in a grimace of triumph and he leapt after him. Serpicus swung without real hope of hitting anything.

The fat man pushed the blow aside and lifted the spear. Serpicus made himself as small as possible behind the shield and waited to see what he would do.

The fat man's head snapped back and a fountain of blood leapt up from the side of his throat. Brutus pulled his shield away from the dying man's neck and bashed the man's head again with a sideways swing, knocking him to the ground. Blood sprayed from his torn mouth. Brutus picked up the spear and tossed it to Serpicus, in-dicating behind him with a pointing finger. Serpicus swung round and thrust upward with the spear into the guts of the man whose shoulder he had cut. The thin man dropped the knife held in his left hand and made a choking sound. His hands clawed at the spear as if pulling it into himself, then he fell sideways and lay still.

Brutus and Serpicus stood back to back and looked around. Serpicus saw Decius on the ground, with a helmeted man above him with his sword raised. Decius was scrabbling frantically for a shield lying nearby, but he wasn't going to get to it in time. Then a figure jumped onto the helmeted man's back, holding his wrists and dragging him backwards. They crashed to the ground with the helmeted man on top. The man on his back was pinned down, but still held onto his wrists and prevented him using his sword. A moment later Decius was onto him, hitting him over and over again with a large stone. The helmeted man jerked convulsively and then lay still. Decius hauled the prone body to one side and helped his rescuer up. Serpicus thought the man looked like Cato.

The fight was almost over. The charge down the hill

had caught the pursuers in a vice and pushed them together so that they had no room to take advantage of their superior numbers. Added to that, they had no real will to fight unless it was clear that they would win, and it was only a matter of time before they threw down their swords and begged for mercy. That time arrived almost immediately.

Severus' soldiers took no little pleasure in knocking them to their knees in a narrow circle. They pulled the prisoners' hands behind them and tied them roughly together. Severus strode towards Serpicus, pausing to rip the shirt off one of the prisoners as he passed by in order to clean the blood off his sword. There was blood down his sword-arm and a sizeable dent in his armour high on the left shoulder, but he seemed unharmed. He pulled the torn cloth down the blade of the sword and tossed it aside. There was a lot of blood on the shirt.

He was smiling as he came to stand by Serpicus. 'That was a good trick you pulled,' Severus said, 'not showing yourselves, waiting for them to come back down after the others like that.' He put a hand on Serpicus' shoulder. His mouth was still smiling, but his eyes were hard. 'If you ever do that again and it doesn't work, I'll be waiting for you in Hades and we'll have words, I assure you.'

He turned away and went to supervise the further kicking and cuffing of the captives.

'We couldn't come any sooner,' Serpicus said.

'He knows,' said Brutus.

There were three men dead, all from Severus' group. A further dozen were wounded, just two of them severely. Set against that the twenty dead of the attackers and hardly one of the remainder without a wound some-where, and it was a clear victory by any calculation. Severus moved amongst the kneeling captives and then bent over slightly with a cry of recognition and hauled a groaning man to his feet. Blood was flowing freely from his scalp and he was limping badly. It was the big man, the one with the breastplate who had led them. Serpicus recognized him now too; it was the docker whose throat Severus had crushed back in Ostia.

Severus placed the point of his now fairly clean sword against the man's side and pushed him away from the group of prisoners towards a clump of rocks, beckoning a soldier to follow him. Brutus and Serpicus looked at each other and followed. They rounded the rocks to find the big man on the ground on his back, twisting sideways so that his bound hands were not trapped underneath him. The soldier was looping a cord around his ankles. Once the man's feet were secure, Severus dismissed the soldier. The point of the centurion's sword moved from the big man's ribs to his throat. Severus motioned Brutus and Serpicus to sit down.

Severus grabbed the man by the hair and pulled him upright without ceremony. The centurion's knees went into his back and the sword came round until it rested across the prisoner's throat. Serpicus could see that the edge of the sword was roughly serrated from the blows it had given and received.

'His name is Josef,' the centurion said. He leant forward until his mouth was by the man's ear. 'Now,' he said cheer-fully. 'These gentlemen are going to ask you some questions, which you are going to answer, understand?'

Josef twisted until his head was almost facing that of Severus and then he spat straight in the centurion's face.

Severus didn't flinch or wipe the spittle off. Nor did he hit Josef hard on the head with the handle of his sword, which is probably what most men would have done. He grabbed Josef by the jaw and dug his fingers deep into the big man's stubbled cheeks. Josef thrashed and struggled but the centurion's grip was unrelenting. Eventually Josef realized that he was achieving nothing and came to rest. Severus released his grip very slightly.

'As I was explaining,' he continued, in exactly the same tone of voice, 'these are the rules. These gentlemen will be asking you some questions. You will answer them.' The fingers bit into the cheeks again. 'Anything other than a completely helpful answer will lose you an ear.' He paused to let that sink in. 'An educated man like yourself will no doubt have worked out that that gives you two opportunities to be stupid before the ears are all gone. Then I will cut your throat and we will go back to the other side of these rocks and see if anyone else in that bunch of monkeys you brought here wants to be as stupid as you.' He pulled Josef's head sideways so that their faces almost touched. 'Understand?'

Without waiting for an answer he turned the man to face Serpicus, put his arm round the man's neck so that he was immobilized, placed his sword against the top of the man's ear and said, 'Ask.'

Josef's eyes were dark and angry. Serpicus leant forward, hands on his knees. 'Who sent you?' he asked, hoping to sound authoritative.

Josef looked as if he was about to spit again and a low

guttural sound was all the reply Serpicus got. Severus tightened his grip on the man's neck so that he couldn't breathe and then pulled his sword sharply back and down in one swift movement. The jagged blade flashed as it moved.

The prisoner let out a choked howl. Severus had released the pressure on his throat just enough to allow the noise to be heard, doubtless for the benefit of those sitting listening on the other side of the rocks. Blood poured from the man's ear onto Severus' arm. The centurion grabbed the man's hair and swapped the sword from one hand to the other. His arm went around the man's throat and he rested the sword on the man's remaining ear.

'One to go,' he said cheerfully.

'All right!' shouted Josef. 'I'll tell you what you want to know.'

Serpicus reasoned that if someone had just cut his ear off it would probably make him forgetful, so he repeated the question. 'Who sent you?'

Josef looked sullenly at him, his teeth grinding and his eyes wild with pain. 'A Roman. He came to Genoa a few days before you and hired me to raise a group of men to follow you.'

'Why?'

'To stop you.'

'Why?'

He paused. 'I don't know.' Severus' sword pressed against the skin of his ear and his voice rose. 'I swear it!'

Serpicus motioned Severus to relax. 'Describe the Roman.' Josef frowned. Description was, no doubt, not something he spent a lot of time doing. 'Age? Height? Colour? Anything unusual?'

'Thirty years old, perhaps less.' He gave Serpicus a smile with one side of his mouth. 'We find it hard to guess a Roman's age, the years treat them so much more lightly than ourselves.' The smile disappeared as Severus' sword drew a drop of blood from his scalp.

'Get on with it, barbarian,' the centurion growled.

'Maybe as tall as you, maybe a little shorter. Dark hair, cut like a Roman soldier.' A trace of animation crossed his face. 'A scar, from his eye to his mouth. Arrogant, as all Romans are. The marks of a soldier on his right arm.'

He paused. Severus leant forward to speak into his remaining ear. 'Finished?'

Josef showed his teeth. 'He was rich, or his master was. I was not the only man he talked to.'

'Anything else you can tell us?'

'That is all I remember. Romans are like pigs, covered in shit it is hard to tell them apart.'

Serpicus reached out swiftly and touched Severus on the wrist, or Josef would have lost the other ear for certain. The centurion looked at him with disbelief. Serpicus shook his head. 'Take him back and put him with the others.'

Severus stared at him for a long moment, and then pulled Josef to his feet. 'Come on,' he growled, and sliced the bonds of his ankles with the sword. 'Now, please, make a run for it,' he said. 'Make it easy for me.'

Brutus and Serpicus were left sitting on the rocks. Blood spattered the ground in front of them.

'Recognize the description?'

'A scarred Roman soldier of about thirty could be a lot of people, but I'd put my money on Marcus.'

'But why? It doesn't make sense.'

'That's what I don't know.'

Severus came back. He had splashed water on his arm where Josef had bled on it, and was using something to dry it that looked a lot like Josef's shirt.

'So,' he said, sitting on a boulder. 'What do we know?'

Brutus looked at his feet. 'Blaesus sent us and is now trying to stop us.'

Severus thought for a few moments. 'Doesn't make sense.'

'No, it doesn't.'

'We could split up,' Brutus said.

'Why?'

'Two small groups, less likely to be seen.'

Severus shook his head. 'Twice as likely to run into trouble, and half as equipped to deal with it. We stay together.'

20

Serpicus was standing at the highest point of the Hinterrhein Pass, in the narrow space between two facing cliffs. The path cut through the summit of the mountain as though a god had reached down and drawn a huge fingernail across the summit. His breath rolled out in front of him like a cloud coming in over the sea. He looked back over the steep path they had climbed. The snow had come early. The rain stopped and then froze, and then the slate sky went quiet and the first flakes slipped from it down towards them.

The unshaven men stood around him, surly with cold, their cloaks wrapped tightly. They were hungry too. Several of the pack animals had slipped or panicked on the narrow mountain ledges and plunged over the edge, taking much of their food with them. Every man had made it to the top.

Serpicus turned and looked out towards the way they were going. To Germany. His homeland.

The snow stopped like a fraying tablecloth about

half-way down the mountain slope and gave way to scrub and sporadic trees. Then, as the incline swept down towards the valley floor, the forest thickened and fanned out in every direction into a huge uniform carpet of deep green as far as the horizon.

Serpicus looked at the forest in silence. Somewhere deep within it the legions were cutting their way towards the rebellious German tribes. He wondered if the soldiers were thinking of the story of Varus, wondering if the same fate awaited them.

They camped overnight at the highest point, not because it was sensible but to enjoy the fact of finally getting there, then rose early because of the cold and set off down the other side of the mountain.

The track on the German side was narrower and steeper than the ascent, and where the streams normally flowed over the rocky path the water had frozen so that every step was dangerous. Severus made everyone dismount. The animals were less likely to slip without the weight of a man on their backs, and if an animal went over the edge he didn't want it taking any of his men with it.

Serpicus was tired. He felt as if he'd been walking for a year and been cold for most of it. He concentrated on removing himself mentally from his immediate physical situation, a trick that soldiers and other men who spend a lot of time in physically uncomfortable situations learn. The body is still cold, the feet are sore and the legs exhausted, but the mind sees it from a way off, as if it is happening to someone else. The part of him that was not concerned about where he was putting his feet was thinking about a warm day lying in his wife's arms. The situation was developing nicely, and by the time he realized that his horse was limping badly he was uncomfortably aware that the men behind him – Snake and Cato amongst them – had noticed it much earlier and were now looking at him critically.

'Probably a stone in his hoof,' said the man immediately behind Serpicus. Cato was behind him and peered over to look at the horse's cocked foot, then nodded agreement.

Serpicus grunted with annoyance. He pulled the lame horse off the path and waited until all the others had passed him. Once he was alone he bent down to inspect the animal's foot.

If he hadn't been cold and tired he would have registered immediately that the horse's shin was swollen, but as he reached down for it he was looking away, wrapping his cloak around himself against the bitter wind. His fingers dug deep into the puffy flesh and pulled.

The horse knew that his hands had always been gentle, so its reaction was one of shock and surprise as much as actual discomfort. It stamped the sore leg down, pulling Serpicus off balance, and then twisted sideways to get away from him. Its broad hindquarters thumped against his shoulder, and as Serpicus shifted to keep his balance his feet moved from under him on the ice. He reached out to use the horse to steady himself but his numb fingers slid off its rough coat. He made a final grab for the animal's tail, and missed.

Through the cold fog in his mind, the thought penetrated that he was going to fall.

Time stopped.

He felt himself toppling impossibly slowly backwards towards the slick ice at the edge of the path and the sheer cliff beyond it.

At the very last moment, while his feet still had a little purchase, he bent his knees slightly and pushed sideways. Instead of landing entirely on the ice his upper body landed at an angle, partly on a patch of snow next to the ice. His mind was suddenly working furiously, but his limbs felt as if they were immersed in a viscous liquid. He spread his arms out wide and jammed his hands hard into the snow, hoping to catch a root or a rock. His scrabbling fingers found nothing but more ice, smooth and unforgiving. He was sliding slowly but inexorably down the slope towards the edge.

He must have called out, because the others knew what was happening to him. He heard Snake call a warning and then saw Brutus jump towards him with a shout, but the lame horse continued to turn, its hooves rattling on the stones and blocking Brutus' path. Brutus yelled at it in frustration and the horse reared away from him, spinning and kicking backwards at another man who tried to grab its head-collar. As Serpicus slid slowly towards the edge he could see Brutus' legs behind the by now thoroughly frightened horse, trying to get around it. There wasn't going to be time to reach him.

Serpicus dug his hands into the ground with all his ebbing strength. He felt a fingernail bend backwards and snap. He wondered why it didn't hurt more.

Then, from the other side, he heard a shout. He turned his head and saw a slim figure sprinting towards him. He

226

opened his mouth to tell the man not to come too close or they would go over together, but it was too late. The man dived forward onto the snow and skidded on his stomach towards Serpicus. As he did so he brought his arm over his shoulder like a discus thrower. Clutched in his hand was the corner of a cloak. The other end of it billowed towards Serpicus and flapped onto the snow beside him. Serpicus grabbed at it with both hands and hung on. For a few moments he stopped sliding, then his weight started to pull the prone man forward over the ice. For a moment Serpicus thought of letting go of the cloak to avoid taking them both over the cliff, but the brief delay was enough. The man let out a gasp as Snake and Brutus landed on top of him simultaneously with an audible thump, followed moments later by several others. Serpicus felt himself stop moving. Then he heard an unpleasant sound.

'Don't pull it,' he called, 'the cloak, it's starting to tear.'

'Someone throw him a bloody rope before we all go over,' panted Brutus. Decius appeared behind Brutus with a coil of rope which he threw forward. Serpicus grabbed at it with one hand. His numb fingers couldn't feel the rough hemp at all. He knew he wouldn't be able to hold on much longer.

'Grab hold of the boy,' Serpicus gasped. 'I'm heavier than he is, I'll take him over.'

'Don't you let go,' said Brutus, making sure that there were enough bodies on top of the man holding the cloak before he went to help Decius. Once Serpicus was sure that Brutus had a firm hold of the rope, he let go of the cloak and wrapped both hands around it. Everyone scrambled to their feet and a dozen hands helped to haul him away from danger.

Serpicus lay on the ground, trembling with shock and breathing like a lung-speared boar. Brutus handed him a full wineskin.

'Thanks,' Serpicus gasped, and raised it to his lips.

'Better drink a toast to laughing boy over there,' said Brutus. 'He's the one who stopped you falling.'

The man who had thrown him the cloak sat up coughing, leaving a perfect human outline in the snow made by the impact of Brutus and the others landing on top of him. Serpicus raised the skin in salute.

'Many thanks,' he said, and only then realized with surprise who had saved him.

Cato waved a hand in breathless dismissal. 'It was nothing,' he said, coughing painfully and spitting earth-stained snow from his lips with an expression of distaste.

Serpicus drank deeply before passing the skin to Brutus. Brutus helped Cato to his feet and put the skin in his hand.

'Go on, lad,' he said softly. 'You've earned it.' Cato looked grateful and finished off the little wine that Serpicus had left.

Serpicus got stiffly to his feet and went forward to clasp Cato's hand. Over Cato's shoulder he saw Snake leaning back against a rock with his arms folded, deep lines of thought in his forehead. It had been a close call.

'I am in your debt,' Serpicus said.

Cato shook his head and smiled. 'I was closest to you, that's all.'

228

'You could have gone over with me. I won't forget it.'

Cato studied his outline in the snow. He took a deep breath, as if reinflating himself. 'It was nothing, truly,' he gasped. 'But you will, I hope, understand, if I say that, if there is a next time, and we have not by then worked out an alternative way of saving you that doesn't involve everyone jumping on top of me in the snow, I will be letting you die without a second thought?'

Serpicus grinned at him and slapped him on the shoulder. 'Fair enough.' He looked around. 'Now, where's that bloody horse?'

The rest of the descent was accomplished without serious incident. At a point half-way down, as the snow thinned, they stopped by a gushing spring to water the horses and rest. The sun came out and even the few limp rays it cast raised their spirits a little.

Serpicus was peeling off his damp clothes to inspect himself for injuries when he looked up and saw Snake standing nearby. The Cretan was tossing a short-bladed knife a few inches in the air and catching it as it fell. The sharp blade flickered in the light of the low sun as the knife spun on its axis. Snake caught it by the handle every time without apparent attention.

'That was close, up there,' he said, indicating back up the mountain path with an inclination of his head.

Serpicus agreed. 'Lucky,' he said. 'If Cato hadn't been there I'd be lying down in the valley now, making a lot of crows very happy.'

Snake said nothing and carried on rhythmically tossing the knife. Serpicus stopped undressing and looked at him searchingly.

'What's wrong? You want to say something?'

Snake frowned and, with a flick of his wrist too fast for Serpicus to follow, sent the knife six feet through the air into a dead branch lying on the ground nearby. They both watched the handle quiver.

Snake seemed to come to a decision.

'I was on the wrong side of the horses when you started sliding. That's why I couldn't get to you sooner.'

Serpicus smiled. 'I know,' he said. 'Everyone was. Don't worry about it. Luckily Cato was close.'

Snake bent forward and retrieved the knife. 'I saw his face.'

Serpicus waited. 'So?'

'He hesitated.'

'I was sliding over a cliff. I'd have hesitated myself.'

Snake shook his head. 'He watched you slide. He did nothing.'

'I'm not surprised. No one moved at first. It takes a while to react to something like that, especially when you're freezing cold.'

'He smiled.'

'What?'

Snake looked absolutely serious. 'I saw him. He saw you slipping, he watched and he smiled.'

Serpicus didn't know what to say. 'What are you saying? That he wasn't going to save me? Then why did he? It would have been easy enough to have let me go.'

Snake shook his head again. 'He changed his mind. He saw you go, he smiled, and then he suddenly pulled his cloak off and started running. I don't know why.'

There was a pause.

'That's ridiculous,' Serpicus said.

'I know. I already knew it would sound like nonsense when I said it. But I know what I saw.' Snake shrugged. 'I wanted you to know.'

Serpicus waited, but the Cretan had apparently finished.

'Fair enough,' he said. 'Thanks. I'll remember what you said.'

'Let's hope you won't need to,' said Snake and walked away, brushing past Brutus as he went.

'What was all that about?' the big man asked, watching the Cretan's retreating figure.

Serpicus shrugged. 'I don't really know. He says Cato thought twice before saving me.'

Brutus made a face. 'I'm not surprised,' he said. 'He could easily have gone over the edge with you.'

'That's more or less what I told him,' Serpicus said. 'Snake says he saw Cato watch me slipping, then changed his mind. Says he smiled.'

'They've never got on, those two,' said Brutus. 'Maybe there's trouble brewing. I'll keep an eye on both of them.' He knelt down and put his cupped hands in the stream, then brought them up to drink. 'I've got a bigger worry than those two falling out,' he said.

'What?'

'The snow. It's cold today all right, but the winter has hardly started. I'm wondering how the hell we're going to drag a bloody great bear in a cage over the Hinterrhein in a month's time when there's a blizzard blowing in our faces and five feet of snow and ice on the ground?'

Serpicus said nothing. His family would die if he couldn't get the cage over the Pass. Therefore the cage was going over, there was nothing else to say. How, he had no idea.

21

The rest of the journey down the mountain passed without serious incident. Apart from a sore finger Serpicus had no lasting damage, but the cold had got into him and he was glad to be moving towards the lowlands.

For several days the countryside was strangely deserted. They passed villas without inhabitants, fields without workers. Ragged figures watched from a safe distance and returned to scavenging when the heavily armed group were safely on their way.

Then the land became less fertile and the villas fewer and smaller. They rode past thick clumps of trees and undergrowth, often too thick to pass through. A day more and they were on a low ridge. The great forest stretched in front of them, dark and silent.

Galba and Serpicus rode on ahead to scout the forest edge taking Scipio and Cato with them. Brutus and Severus stayed with the main body. The idea was that if either group met with Germans then either Brutus or Serpicus should be around to explain who they were.

Decius wanted to come and scout too but they made him stay behind with Brutus and the main group.

The trees in this part of the forest were unusually sparse and relatively easy to pass through, although the rough bushes still scraped like coral against a rider's legs and long black thorns still snagged at his clothing and scratched at his exposed skin.

A steady damp drizzle laid a fine spray on Serpicus' jacket, the sort of rain someone hardly notices until their clothes are utterly sodden. Serpicus smiled and tilted his head back so that it could fall on his face. He didn't mind the rain. After seven years under an Italian sky he'd forgotten what honest rain felt like. His sun-leathered skin soaked up the moisture like an open mouth.

'Look.'

Galba pointed to the ground. Tracks were clearly visible. Scipio swung down off his horse and knelt by them, tracing the indentation in the soft earth with a forefinger. Then he stood and looked up and down the trail. He raised his hand in a signal for the others to stay where they were and he loped off on foot. They waited in silence, the bored horses chewing at their bridles and flicking their tails idly.

Scipio returned a little later. One of his fists was closed around something.

Galba leant forward and folded his arms on his horse's neck to give himself a place to rest his chin. 'Any ideas?'

Scipio nodded. 'Two people. A grown man on a horse, and a woman or a boy on a pony. The man's horse was lame.' He pointed to the prints on the ground. Serpicus leant forward to look. Now that Scipio had pointed it out, he could see that there were two sets of hoof-prints, and that they were different sizes and depths, and that one of the larger hoof-marks was less well defined than the other three. Easy when you knew how.

'How long ago?' asked Galba.

Scipio opened his palm and offered the contents up to them. 'Any idea what that is?'

Serpicus looked at it, and then stared unkindly at Scipio. 'I was a chariot driver. I work under the arena every day. If there is one thing I know more about than anything else, it's horseshit. I'm an expert on it. If the Senate needs to know about horseshit I'm the man they call for. Don't offer me a handful of it and then ask me if I know what it is.'

Scipio grinned. 'Fair enough. And you hunt and trap animals for a living, so you must know a bit about tracking. So, what does this fine specimen tell us?'

Serpicus took some of it in his hand, feeling slightly ridiculous, and thought hard. It was round and quite dry, soft to the touch. 'Not much. It's cold, so not very recent. It isn't rotted, so less than – what? – a week old?'

Scipio nodded with pursed lips, like a sympathetic teacher with a slow pupil who may just get there if he is given long enough. 'Anything else?'

Serpicus thought harder. 'Yes. It hasn't lost its shape.' He patted his sleeve and the fine mist came off in drops on his hand. 'This wouldn't be enough to do anything to it for a good while, but there was heavy rain at around dawn today. It must have been dropped after that or it wouldn't be this shape and it wouldn't be as dry.'

He thought Scipio was going to burst into applause.

'Excellent. So, the horse laid it between dawn and a short while ago. Anything else?'

Serpicus had the feeling he was back at school. He'd never liked school. 'No, it's just horseshit.'

Scipio leant forward and prodded it with a finger. 'Even texture. This horse only eats grass.'

'It's a horse,' said Galba. 'That's what horses eat.'

Scipio got back on his horse. 'German horses, yes,' he said. 'Roman horses, on the other hand . . .'

'Hay,' said Serpicus, with a gesture of acknowledgement. 'They eat hay.'

Scipio nodded with satisfaction. 'Just so. No dry grass fibres in the shit, ergo, this is not a Roman horse. So, do we follow them?' The lesson was apparently over.

Cato leant forward on his horse's withers. 'Might they perhaps be Romans riding German horses?'

'Or Romans who've run out of hay?' asked Galba.

'Or Romans trying to put us off the scent by cleverly denying it to their horses?' said Cato.

'I doubt it,' said Scipio. 'For one thing, because they think everyone is frightened of them, it wouldn't usually occur to Romans that they needed to disguise their tracks. For another, we're in Germany and there's a rebellion going on. Romans in this sort of situation typically tend to go around in large heavily armed groups, not on their own with women or boys for company.'

Galba looked at Scipio wide-eyed. 'Can you tell all that just from looking at one piece of shit?' he asked.

Serpicus and Scipio grinned. Serpicus didn't get Galba's joke. He chewed on Scipio's reply for a few moments, and then nodded. 'Fair enough. So, if they aren't Romans, do we need to keep following them?'

Galba and Serpicus looked at each other, and Galba raised an almost hairless eyebrow. 'They're your people. I only know about Romans, not Germans. You know the best way to approach them.'

Serpicus thought about it for a moment. Finding the Treveri was the point of the expedition. A man and a boy would be harder to track than a war party of men, but less likely to lie in ambush for them.

'We'll follow them, see if we can catch them up, but let's go carefully. Try and see them before they see us.'

Scipio gestured towards the tracks. 'Shouldn't be too hard. That lame horse is in trouble. The rider will need to keep a slow pace and take a lot of rests or he'll soon be walking home.'

They pushed their horses forward and for the next hour they followed the tracks in silence. The imprints were clear in the damp earth and had not yet filled with water. The two riders weren't far ahead.

Cato pulled his horse up beside Serpicus and Scipio. 'We could save some time here,' he said, pointing up the track.

Serpicus paused and looked around. The track was heading straight towards the base of a steep hill directly in front of them. If the riders were heading north they would have to skirt around the hill, there was no way a lame animal could have climbed it. Cato pointed, drawing a line in the air. Serpicus looked along the length of his arm and saw what he meant. There was an animal path cutting a jagged but clear line from the track up the side of the hill. If the riders were going around the hill, the pursuers could climb and cut across their path, perhaps even overtake them. Of course, if the riders were going around the hill but heading east, then the pursuers would miss them and have to swing back in a wide arc until they crossed their trail again. Serpicus made a decision.

'Galba and I will take the hill. You wait for Severus to catch up and then carry on following the trail. If we can see them from the top we'll come down and introduce ourselves. They shouldn't be too frightened by just two of us. If we can't see them or find their tracks, we'll wait and meet you at the bottom of the hill on the northern side. Carry on following them if you have to but don't let them see you. Wait until we catch up with you again. All right?' Scipio nodded and pulled his horse around, and the rest of the men followed him. Cato looked as though he wanted to make another suggestion, but then stayed silent. Galba was already tackling the path. Serpicus heeled his tired horse after him.

The hill was stony, and the path was narrow but it was there. Galba and Serpicus wound their way up the hill and breasted a ridge near the top. In front of them and on all sides the forest spread out into the distance. A pale sun broke through the clouds and Serpicus sat up in the saddle as the warmth hit his face. They had been under dark clouds and the trees for days. It was good to see bright light again.

He looked around. Below them on the north side of the hill Serpicus could see two horses picking their way around the trees. Scipio had read their tracks well. One was an older man, with silver hair and dressed in a long robe, and he was accompanied by a boy on a pony. As Serpicus watched, the two riders stopped to share a skin of water.

From high above them on the hill, Serpicus and Galba had a panoramic view of the trail the two riders were following and what lay in front of them. Which meant that Serpicus and Galba had an excellent view of the six Roman horses lined up in wait behind a dense thicket about a bow-shot down the hill.

Two bored legionaries were looking after the animals. Galba and Serpicus dismounted, pulled their own horses back under cover and moved forward so that they could peer down over a large rock without being seen. 'Where are the rest of them?' whispered Galba.

Serpicus shaded his eyes and looked carefully. For a moment he couldn't make anything out. Then he realized what he was looking at. There were dark outlines in the trees and bushes on either side of the track that could be men. He waited a little longer and saw one of them move, then another.

'I can see five or six men in the trees waiting for them.'

'Look,' said Galba. He pointed back along the track, behind where the two riders now stood. There were soldiers there too, about the same number. They were on horseback, but still behind the trees, waiting for something, a command or a signal. They had let the two riders pass without revealing themselves.

'Ambush,' Galba said softly.

Serpicus nodded. 'What are they up to?' he said. 'There are at least a dozen Romans, there may be even more down there who are better at hiding than the ones I can see. Why sneak up on them? Why not just go and get them? Why would they go to all this trouble to ambush a boy and a man on a lame horse?'

Galba shrugged. 'Maybe he's a great warrior?'

'He'll need to be,' Serpicus said grimly. There was something about the silver-haired man that reminded him of someone. 'I'm going down to have a look,' he said.

Galba looked at him doubtfully. 'Are you sure? If there's going to be a fight I'm not sure we should get mixed up in it.'

Serpicus swung back onto his horse and urged it forward. 'I think I know who that is down there, and if I'm right then I know why they have a dozen Romans out to catch him. Stay here, I'll be back.'

The route directly to the bottom of the steep hill was clear enough, but it wasn't an option for Serpicus. The horse would have got a few steps and then tipped over and gone head first the rest of the way and Serpicus would have gone tumbling straight after him. There was a goat track at a sharp angle down the hillside, precipitous but possible. The horse picked his way down it and Serpicus concentrated on counting Romans. The path brought him onto a small shelf of rock which was almost directly above the two slowly moving riders. From there the hill dropped all but vertically to the track. Serpicus vaulted off the horse. He crouched low and edged closer, trying to keep out of sight of the soldiers. He picked up a stone and threw it overarm with all his strength down towards the road. The stone fell short, hit an outcrop and bounced high, landed a few steps in front of the pair of riders and clattered on into the forest. The old man looked at it and then reined the horse back to see where it had come from.

Serpicus looked down at his long face and thin beard and felt the warmth of memory flood him. He knew for certain who the rider was.

The old man didn't shout or give any sign of recognition. He stopped and waited, as if watching to see what Serpicus would do. Serpicus gestured emphatically back along the trail, then as emphatically up the way the two riders were travelling. He couldn't at that moment think of a good mime for 'Roman', but he felt it probably wasn't necessary. His agitation obviously meant trouble, and trouble usually meant Romans. The old man pulled the horse hard round away from the hill and towards the forest. In a moment he and the boy were in the trees and out of sight.

'You've made some enemies down there,' Galba said as Serpicus breasted the hill dragging his horse behind him and sat, gasping for breath. Serpicus looked back down the hill. Mounted Romans were approaching at speed from both ends of the track. One of them, an officer by his helmet plumes, waved most of the soldiers into the trees after the man and boy. He waited on the track, his horse pawing the earth, and looked up at the two men on the steep hill. It was too far away for them to see his face, but Serpicus felt he could have taken a fair guess at his expression.

'Not a happy man,' said Galba. 'What do we do now?'

'Wait, I suppose,' Serpicus said. 'They'll get bored and move away and then we can ride on.'

241

'What happens if they catch up with the old man and the boy?'

Serpicus smiled. 'They won't.'

'You're very certain. His horse was lame and the Romans are just behind him. It's odds on they'll catch him in no time.'

'If I weren't an honest man I'd take that bet,' Serpicus said. He looked back down the hill. 'They'll not catch him.' He picked up a rock and tossed it in the air, feeling its weight. 'You want a real bet, how much says I can knock that blond bastard's helmet off from here?'

'Good idea,' said Galba, shaking his head. 'You've only ruined his ambush, he's hardly likely to be seriously annoyed yet, let's pelt him with rocks and make absolutely sure.'

They retraced their path to the top of the hill and watched from behind a clump of bushes. Soon the Roman soldiers came back out of the trees, slower and much dirtier than when they went in. The officer was still on the road, and he kept looking up the hill back at where Serpicus and Galba had disappeared from sight. He took his helmet off and wiped his forehead on his sleeve. His hair shone a bright yellow-blond in the sun. Serpicus remembered where he had seen hair like that before. Weeks before, standing in the entrance to the Palace of the Partner, when a young Roman with hair like straw threatened to kill him for no reason at all.

Serpicus smiled. At least Consilius now had a reason.

242

22

When Serpicus was a boy his father told him that Gelbheim was the first proper settlement in Germany. Serpicus suspected that almost every village in Germany probably made the same claim. However, standing on the low hills that separate the great winding silver rope of the Rhine from the land of the Treveri and looking across, it was easy to see why a displaced people walking across the German plain searching for a place to settle might choose to live in the place now called Gelbheim. The Treveri lived in several dozen villages, each with its own chief and distinct identity, but they all called themselves Treveri, and they all acknowledged that Gelbheim was the first, the village from which their fathers came.

The river Talis, a tributary of the Rhine and at this point only a few leagues from its apotheosis, wound wide and slow like a well-fed snake through the broad green fields that followed it on both sides. Serpicus remembered the rich black earth, and how if a man crumbled it in his hand it smelt of life. Everyone in Gelbheim knew a man who knew a man who had met a traveller, and how the traveller told the Gelbheimer how, only the day before, he had driven his spear into the black earth beside him while he stopped to piss, and how by the time the traveller had finished there were broad leaves and heavy fruit growing from the spear-shaft. Crops leapt up thick from the ground, dark wide-bladed grasses brushed along the deep bellies of the horned cattle that grew fat in the fields. Every other tribe bordering their territory knew that the lands of the Treveri were the finest in Germany, and throughout their history almost all of their neighbours had tried to take it away from them. But it was said by their druids that the feet of the Treveri had sunk deep in the soft soil like roots, and that there was no tearing them up. If the Treveri were to leave this place they would surely wither and die, and so they had no choice but to fight for their land like heroes, to the death or to victory. What is certainly true is that they had defended their land successfully against every attack ever made on it, and did it with a ferocity that had deterred any new attempt for over twenty years.

The village itself was on a tear-drop-shaped piece of land contained by the last bend of the river Talis before it straightened out for its final rush to join the Rhine. The river curved around the village like a mother's arm around a child, surrounding the wooden houses on three sides. This made the village hard to attack and even harder to retreat from. The Gelbheimers had become expert boatmen, using a coracle of willow and oiled deer-skin that was so light that it could be carried easily by a small child and yet would support a fully armed warrior on the water. Every Gelbheimer boy learned from his father how to make them, and looked forward to the day when he would make one for himself. It was a solemn part of the ritual of becoming a warrior, and no other man would ever use it except him.

The coracles were called *seges*, in honour of Segestes, chief of the Treveri at the time of their greatest danger. Generations earlier, the village was besieged and completely surrounded by a hostile alliance of tribes. There was little food left and hardly a man in Gelbheim was left uninjured after several days of desperate fighting. Some of Segestes' councillors advised him and his personal guard to take to the river, to leave the village and save the line of his people from extinction. Segestes heard them in silence, then left the council chamber without replying and walked down to the river-bank. The whole tribe, gathered outside the council to hear the debate, followed him. Segestes stood over the coracle he had built many years before. He raised his foot and then brought it down on the craft with all his strength, smashing it beyond repair. There was a silence, and then Caspar and Vladmir, his two greatest champions, walked silently to his side and did the same to their own boats. With a loud cheer every man ran forward and within moments there was not a serviceable coracle left on the river-bank. With no possibility of escape left, the Gelbheim warriors returned to the battle filled with new strength and without fear. In a great struggle lasting two days and a night the alliance of tribes was driven from the lands of the

Treveri. Segestes was killed fighting at the head of his men, and in his honour the boats were named for him.

A good lesson was learned that day by the Treveri, about how men fight, and why. Since that day, if in a fight a chance to encircle their enemy on all sides arose, the Treveri had always declined it. Their enemy was always left an avenue of retreat. The Treveri knew that they would rather fight a man who keeps looking over his shoulder at the possibility of self-preservation, than a man who has no escape remaining to him and therefore has nothing left but the possibility of making a glorious end for himself.

Serpicus took a deep breath, preparing himself to return to the place where he was born. There was a constriction in his throat. It was a cold morning. He blew his nose on a cloth. Cold air can blur the vision and also make it hard to swallow sometimes.

They were camped next to an upright stone as tall as a man. On it were intricately cut lines, swirling around and back so that they formed the shapes of waves rolling up a beach. Below these designs were more geometric shapes, angular and solid, fitting together like jagged stones. It was a useful landmark if they needed to return to the same place.

Galba stood beside Serpicus' horse and pleaded with him. 'Try and come back to get us before this bloody rain starts up again, please?' Serpicus smiled and urged his horse forward, following Brutus and Decius down a narrow trail that followed the slope of the hill that was the horizon for the villagers.

The three of them circled around to approach the

village from the front. The last thing any German village wants to see, at any time but particularly at a time of insurrection, is twenty or so heavily armed and foreign-looking men moving purposefully towards them out of the morning gloom. In their position Serpicus knew that he too would sooner throw a spear first and ask questions afterwards. No one wanted to give the villagers any excuse to mistake their intentions.

It was early, and the village was still quiet. The grass was wet and cold and a thin memory of mist still covered it and clung to the horses' legs. A string of smoke curled slowly upwards from behind the wooden walls, either the last of the night fires or the first of the morning's. Immediately in front of the palisade was a cleared area grazed freely by goats and cows during the day, to remove even the suggestion of cover for any attacker.

On each side of the main gate, well within bow-shot of the sentries, the pens that protected the animals at night were arranged in neat rows. There were other similar areas inside the village where the animals were kept when there was the risk of an attack; the fact that the animals were still outside presumably meant that Gelbheim was not expecting trouble. Serpicus wondered if it was therefore safe to assume that the Treveri – or at least this branch of them – had not joined the rebellion. Yet.

The river-encircled teardrop of land on which the village stood was an outcrop of rock, a grey, hard, speckled protrusion of stone. Its hardness was, the Treveri presumed, the reason why the river had not worn it away. The village was thus the highest point in the valley. When the rain fell hard and the Talis flooded, the entire valley floor was covered in water, except for the rock that the village sat upon. It was this regular flooding that made the land fertile, and the villagers happily salted their meat and dried their vegetables all summer in preparation for the weeks when the fields all around them were underwater and the only way out of the village was to paddle a flimsy coracle over the cold and dangerous floodwaters to the hills on either side of the valley.

Serpicus looked at the village and the memories swept over him. There was no stone wall around the village, for the Treveri, although no longer nomads given to wandering across the countryside, still moved the boundaries of the village from year to year as the population varied and the floods dictated. A stone wall would have been impractical, too constricting. So they had built the defensive wooden palisade near the top of their teardrop of land, running from where the river bent away from its own line to where it curved back again to resume it. It was constructed in rectangular overlapping sections, which could be dismantled quickly and realigned as and when necessary. Sharpened stakes pointed up and outwards from the base of the parapet, to discourage attackers from climbing up it. The line of stakes swung in a broad rank in front of Brutus, Serpicus and Decius as they approached, then curved inward, funnelling the approaching travellers as it would any attacker towards the main gate, forcing them to pass under the arch that loomed over the approach to the village.

There were usually three guards on the wall, one on

the gate and one at each end of the palisade, where it met the river. The guards would have plenty of time to rouse help by the time an attack covered the open area in front of the gate, so not many were needed. The two by the river were insurance; in practice, if the man on the gate was awake, the others could sleep.

Serpicus knew that several other men would be patrolling the river-bank behind the village. He could see that the river was unusually high, the rain had swelled it until the turbid water lapped the top of the bank. Broken trees poked thin branches up from the surface like fingers, and a dead sheep swollen until it resembled an over-filled wineskin came down the river, turning in slow circles.

A sorrowful-looking dog wandered without intent across the clearing between the three new arrivals and the gate. It saw or smelt them and looked up, one foot poised. It watched for a while as they moved steadily towards it, and then barked once before trotting away, its job apparently done.

A face appeared over the palisade immediately above the main gate. It looked steadily in their direction for a short time, then disappeared. A few moments later it reappeared at ground level, framed by the gate and supported by a body that in a young man would be described as 'solid', whereas in an older man would more likely be called 'stout'. He was still just about young enough to carry it off, but was at the point where he was going to have to grow younger again or the epithets were going to get less kind. He drew himself up, drove the butt end of his spear into the ground near his foot and held the top end out from his body at arm's length, at the angle that guards all over the world seem to adopt instinctively. His face was small and round and surrounded with a halo of red curls that stuck straight out from his head, making him look like an aggressive tomcat.

Decius spoke to Serpicus without turning to look at him. 'Do you know him?'

'I don't,' said Brutus.

'His name is Hansi,' Serpicus said.

Brutus leant forward squinting. 'Is that really Hansi?'

Serpicus nodded. 'He's got fat. Maybe we have too, he doesn't seem to recognize us.'

'Speak for yourself,' muttered Brutus. 'I've hardly changed at all.'

The guard let the three horsemen get quite close before speaking. Full daylight hadn't arrived yet and there was mist behind them. Serpicus thought that it must look to the guard as though they were dark wraiths, risen from the earth.

'Good morning,' Brutus said, pulling the horse to a halt just over a comfortable spear-throw away from the guard and keeping his hands in clear sight.

The guard looked at them with mild curiosity for a few moments. 'Good morning,' he replied. He looked at them some more. 'You aren't from our tribe,' he said, 'because I don't know you. You aren't travellers because you have no supplies. You aren't attackers because there aren't enough of you and no one is throwing spears at me. So, who goes there?'

'Friends,' Serpicus said. 'At least, we were once.

We've been away a while, but I know you. Don't you recognize us, Hansi?'

The guard's amiability disappeared and his grip on his spear tightened. 'Just because you know my name doesn't mean I know you,' he snapped, 'and I don't much like it. You look and sound and smell like Romans to me. You've three heartbeats to explain who you are before I come over there and put a doorway in your chest.'

'It's been a long time, but I've changed less than you.' Serpicus held his hands out from his body in a way that he hoped was unthreatening. 'Don't you remember the day we went to spy on the girls down by the swimming hole, and you overbalanced and fell in and got caught, and the Chief made you swim around all day until you were almost drowned and even the girls begged him to let you come out?' He got down from the horse and walked a few steps closer. 'You were thinner in those days.'

'I'm a better swimmer now, and unlike you I don't have to spy on the girls any more.' Hansi leant forward and peered at them. 'You sound like a Roman but you do look a bit like Alraic who was there that day. I don't know who the kid is. The other one is big enough and ugly enough to be that thug called Carvanus who used to be from Glaudern, but the Carvanus I knew then wasn't anything like as fat as this one.' He looked quizzically at Serpicus. 'You only went out to fetch a bucket of water and it's been, what, seven years? Where the hell have you been?' Serpicus smiled as he felt a prickle of recognition at the unfamiliar names.

Brutus lost patience and pushed his horse forward to walk quickly towards the village. 'Being held hostage for your good behaviour, you fat peasant, or we'd all have been home long ago. Now stop fucking around and let us in. We're cold, we're soaked through, we're starving, and most of all we need a drink.'

A huge smile split the guard's round features and he rushed forward to reach up to Brutus. 'It is you,' he said, pointing delightedly at Brutus and then turning to Serpicus with his arms spread wide. 'I never thought I'd see you again. Actually, I never thought of you at all, which is the same thing. What are you doing sneaking around here this time of the morning?'

'Just visiting,' Serpicus said, disentangling himself from Hansi's exuberant embrace.

'Business or pleasure?'

'Business, but we were hoping for some pleasure too,' said Brutus, swinging his leg over his saddle and dropping down to the ground. Decius was already there and looking around with wide eyes as they walked towards the village.

'Excellent idea,' said Hansi. He walked over to a young warrior who was dozing nearby and planted his toe hard between the boy's ribs. 'Look after the gate for a while, I'm going to take these two in.' The boy staggered to his feet, wiping sleep from his eyes. Hansi looked at the boy critically and pointed at the three riders. 'If any more of these pretend Romans turn up, you make them stay here until I get back, all right?' He leant forward and grabbed the boy's shoulder. 'All right?'

The boy made a sound of assent, stumbled sleepily forward and leant against the gatepost with a heartfelt yawn. Hansi strode off shaking his head, and led them towards the centre of the village.

While Brutus explained to Hansi how Alraic and Carvanus had become Serpicus and Brutus, Serpicus looked around. He knew where they were going. Little had changed. The Chief's house was in the middle of the village and was the largest on view, but it wasn't a palace and it didn't belong to him. He lived in an unprepossessing corner of it. The large hall that made up the rest of it was used for village meetings and any sort of celebration. The villagers always called it just 'the Hall', whether they meant the Chief's house or the meeting place. He didn't mind. The Treveri set little store in possessions – apart from weapons – and their glory was measured in the number of heads a man had taken, not by how big his front door was.

A couple of guards were dozing outside the entrance to the Hall. As Hansi and the others approached they straightened up into a slouch.

'What do you want, fat boy?'

Hansi visibly bristled. He glanced back at Serpicus to see if he had heard. Serpicus kept his face neutral and looked casually around at the village. Hansi shoved his chest out at the guard. 'Visitors.' He leant forward to the guard and said, slightly more confidentially, 'And if you ever call me that again, I'll break your back.'

Serpicus thought that the guard didn't look too frightened.

The patchwork of heavily furred skins that curtained

the entrance to the Hall was pulled back from the inside, revealing a tall and deeply tanned man whom Serpicus didn't recognize. He was wrapped in a long cloak of silver fox edged with something grey.

'What's going on?' the tall man asked. Serpicus noticed that his voice was not thickened with sleep. He had been awake for some time.

The guard pointed at Hansi and then the three visitors. 'The fat man brought these men into the village.'

Hansi's hands tightened into fists at that but he said nothing. Serpicus took note. The tall man in front of them was a powerful person in the village, or Hansi would not have bothered controlling himself.

The tall man looked at them in a way that made them stand up straighter. 'You are welcome.' He looked at Hansi. 'Is it too early in the morning for introductions?'

Hansi looked dazed for a moment. Serpicus smiled to himself. It was probably all a bit too much for the guard. Then Hansi got hold of himself and stood to an impression of attention.

'This is Alraic, from our village, and this is Carvanus, from Glaudern. They were taken hostage by the Romans seven years ago and are now returned.'

Hansi looked at Decius blankly and apparently decided that there was nothing to say about him. Serpicus put a hand on Decius' shoulder. 'Decius. From Praunberg, although he has family here. His people called him Sigmund.'

The tall man nodded and smiled at Decius. 'Then you are twice welcome.' He stepped aside so that they could come into the house.

They gathered just inside the door. The room was dark and simply furnished. A wide bed with no one in it, covered by several thick furs. Two chairs either side of a low table, and stools at the end. A fireplace with a cooking pot on a rack at the side of a damped-down fire.

The tall man gestured to them to sit down. 'My name is Balant. I am a visitor here. Have you travelled far?'

Serpicus saw no point in lying. 'From Rome.'

Balant looked at him for a long moment and sat down beside him. 'Really?' he said mildly. 'You must be tired after your journey.' A thought seemed to strike him. 'Have you come all this way, just the three of you?'

Brutus looked back over his shoulder towards the entrance. 'There are more of us up in the hills.'

Balant looked at him appraisingly. 'You left them out there while you came down to the village on your own? They are not Germans then?' Brutus hesitated and then shook his head. Balant stroked his chin while looking at them appraisingly. 'Romans, perhaps?'

'Some,' said Serpicus. 'A mixture. Germans and Greeks as well.'

Balant stood up. 'I see. I suggest you go and fetch them. They will be cold and hungry.' He looked enquiringly at Hansi, who seemed unable to move.

'Bring Romans? Into the village?' asked Hansi falteringly.

'Of course,' said Balant. 'Rome is our friend.' He looked at Brutus. 'Is she not?'

Brutus smiled. 'I can't vouch for Rome, but I can promise you that if someone brings those men on the hill down here and gives them a hot meal they will

255

happily swear eternal brotherhood with the whole village.'

Balant returned the smile coldly. 'Then the sooner you bring them here the better. Hansi will accompany you.' Brutus hesitated, then realized what Balant intended. He gestured to Decius to come with him and went out, with Hansi bringing up the rear.

Balant indicated to Serpicus that he should sit, and took the chair facing him, a wide seat with high arms shaped like an inverted stirrup. As he sat the silver fur cloak fell open, revealing a smoothly muscled body. The body of an athlete. A thin white scar with a jagged turn at one end ran right across his chest, and several other smaller ones marked his torso. He had seen battle. Serpicus found himself wondering how he would manage in the arena.

Balant dipped a horn cup into a metal bowl beside the fire and handed it to Serpicus. It held a spiced liquid, heavy and warm, tasting of honey. Serpicus recognized it immediately. German mead, the sweetest battle-axe to the brain a man could experience. He hadn't tasted it for seven years. He drank, and the warmth of the remembered past flowed down his throat.

Balant sat back in the chair. He took a small cup of mead himself but held it cradled in his hand while he watched his guest drink.

'So,' he said. 'You're here to buy our animal.'

Serpicus blinked with surprise. Somehow he had supposed that the secrecy that surrounded their expedition when they were planning it in Rome was general.

'We're here to collect it, yes,' he said.

Balant rolled the stem of the cup between his fingers, and seemed to hesitate. 'There may be a . . . difficulty. Concerning the arrangement.'

Serpicus took a deep breath. 'I wish I could say that I am surprised,' he said.

Balant cleared his throat and concentrated on looking at the cup, as if performing a slightly unpleasant duty. 'I should point out that the arrangement to sell the animal was made between Cruptorix and Blaesus. The agreement was concluded over a year ago. Many things can change in a year.'

'For example?'

'Perhaps most importantly, Cruptorix is no longer Chief of Gelbheim.'

Serpicus thought for a moment. When he left the village Vonones had been Chief. It wasn't the time to find out what happened to him. Serpicus could remember Cruptorix. A big man, fleshy rather than fat, with a loud laugh, a truly heroic moustache and a capacity for beer like a bottomless bucket. He had never seemed to mind his daughter's friendship with Serpicus, but Serpicus had always felt intimidated by his size and vigour and stayed away from him when he could. But men always spoke well of him.

'Is he dead?'

Balant nodded. 'The summer solstice celebrations. He led the revels from the front as always. He was the last man standing at the end of three days and nights. He picked up a barrel of beer and drained it then fell down dead. The druid says his heart just burst.'

Serpicus looked solemn. 'I am sorry to hear it.'

'It was a good life, and a happy death,' Balant said. 'But it does put your purpose in jeopardy.'

'Why so? Can we not just renegotiate the agreement with the new Chief?'

Balant shrugged. 'Perhaps. I am sure that, when the hunting party returns, you will be able to raise it then. But there are other issues to consider. Some members of my village – in fact not just from our village, but several of the neighbouring ones as well – have decided that the white bear is sacred to the god Wodan.' Serpicus' heart sank inside him, but he tried to look merely interested. Balant hesitated, as if waiting for him to react, and then continued. 'The druids have yet to pronounce on this, but you will appreciate that if the druids decide that the bear is sacred then it will be difficult for us to let you take it.'

Serpicus worked to keep his face impassive. 'No chief to sell us the bear, and the tribe turning it into a god. Is that all we have to worry about?'

Balant permitted himself a smile. 'You will know that there is a revolt against Rome in parts of Germany. The Treveri have not joined the revolt, but neither have they decided what their position is.'

'If they are not at war, then there is no reason why the bear should not be sold.'

'Some of our people feel that the idea of selling anything at all to Romans – and for entertainment most especially – when many of our brother tribes are at war with Rome is, shall we say, inappropriate? You will know that even if the Treveri decide not to join the revolt, they are unlikely to support Rome.' His gaze met that of Serpicus. 'I would be less than honest if I did not tell you that, even before we find out where the druids stand on the issue, there is already a good deal of resistance here to the idea of taking the bear away.' He made an open-handed gesture and looked at Serpicus with the politician's expression which takes for granted that an intelligent man of the world like Serpicus would – naturally – understand his position.

Serpicus felt a wave of exasperation roll over him and waited until his self-control returned before replying.

'May I be honest too?'

Balant smiled. 'I have tried to be, I would expect the same from you.'

'I shan't try and persuade you by pointing out that we had a business arrangement.' Balant smiled again. Serpicus was getting a little tired of his smiling. Balant reminded him of one of the men who walked around the arena during the intervals between events, smiling and shaking hands, accumulating favours and influence. Not bad, exactly, but ambitious and sometimes dangerous. 'Nor, I suspect, does the fact that we have travelled a long way and lost good men to get here mean much, nor that we will probably lose more good men on the way home whether we have the bear or not.'

Balant made an apologetic gesture. 'All this is no doubt true, but as you say, it is regrettably unlikely to carry much weight.'

'I thought not.' Serpicus leant forward. 'Then let me tell you what my situation is, and you will perhaps understand why I cannot let anything come between me and taking that bear back to Rome. My wife and family are under Blaesus' protection.'

Balant opened his mouth while raising his head slightly. 'Ah,' he said softly. 'That explains it.'

Serpicus looked serious. 'It was made very clear to me what my family's fate would be if we failed to carry out our commission. I tried to make plans to get them out if this trip went wrong, but Blaesus has his spies everywhere. They are trapped, and thus so am I.' Serpicus looked at Balant and gave him his smile back. 'So, now you understand my position.'

Balant looked thoughtful. 'Then,' he said, 'for everyone's sake we must hope that the druids say they have got enough sacred objects to be getting along with, and that the people are in a mood to be persuaded that entertaining Romans is something to be supported.' He stood up. 'And now we should go and greet your companions from the hills.'

Serpicus stood up, wondering how it was that a man from Glaudern was deferred to in Gelbheim, and where the power lay in the village. As usual, things weren't as simple as he had hoped.

23

They left the house, taking the guard with them. At the gate, they stood in the shelter of the ledge that ran along the top of the palisade to wait for the rest of the expedition to arrive from the hill. The guards leant casually but alert against the palisade base, chewing on some dried meat as they watched Brutus and the others approach. Hansi was walking proudly beside them and so came in for some ribald comments which he pretended not to hear. Balant met the group of men inside the gate and greeted them. They gathered in a tight group as Serpicus made introductions.

'This is Severus.' He was about to say more, then stopped. Severus was a military man, that was obvious. The rest of the explanation could wait. Balant held out a hand. The centurion's hesitation was so slight that it could have passed for nothing, but Serpicus saw it and knew Balant saw it. The two men clasped hands and looked at each other appraisingly, like two boxers before a bout, respectful but without backing down.

'What do your men need?' he said simply.

Severus nodded acknowledgement. 'A good wash, food and sleep, in that order,' he said.

Balant smiled. 'Hansi will show you to where you can sleep. I will have food brought to you soon.' He started to say something then looked over Serpicus' shoulder and fell respectfully silent.

'I owe you a debt of thanks.'

The voice was familiar. Serpicus turned around. A long face with a silver beard was looking at him. A boy stood close behind the old man, balancing a hooded hawk on his arm.

'I am Bocalas. You were on the trail yesterday.'

Serpicus took the outstretched hand in his own. The old druid's grey eyes looked through him into his thoughts, as they always had. 'Yes.'

'You warned us about the Romans. They would have caught us if you had not given them away to us.' Bocalas' voice was clear, as Serpicus remembered, but softer and with a dry edge, like the wind pushing autumn leaves over flat stones.

'It was just luck that we happened to be there.'

'Nevertheless. I am in your debt.' Bocalas moved his head in salute. There was a pause. Serpicus waited, but nothing more came.

'You don't remember me,' he said.

The old man raised an eyebrow. 'Should I? You speak our language, you are from our tribe, but I . . .' A smile began at one corner of his mouth and spread across his face like a cloud revealing the sun. 'Alraic? Is it you?'

Serpicus smiled, feeling almost bashful. 'It's been a long time.'

Bocalas took Serpicus' hand in both of his. 'But why did you not come back? We thought you were dead.' Serpicus shrugged and smiled, hoping the old man wouldn't pursue his reasons. He didn't care to go into them. He gestured towards Brutus, who grinned and strode towards them. Bocalas looked far more surprised than he had when he realized who Serpicus was. 'Carvanus, from Glaudern? You here too?' Brutus nodded and they clasped hands in the same way.

Serpicus saw Galba behind Bocalas giving him a wry look over the druid's shoulder. He mouthed 'Alraic? Carvanus?' silently at him. Serpicus indicated Galba to Bocalas.

'This is Galba, a friend from Rome. Unfortunately he does not speak our language. And he knows us by our Roman names, Serpicus and Brutus.'

Bocalas nodded to Galba. Serpicus heard a sound behind him, and turned. Decius was looking at Bocalas eagerly.

'And this is Sigmund, from Praunberg, now more usually called Decius.'

Bocalas looked startled. 'Sigmund? Who I used to chase out of my house? Who never stopped asking questions and who had three more questions for every answer?' Decius blushed and looked at the floor. Bocalas took his hand. 'I see it is you. Welcome home.'

Word had spread through Gelbheim of the arrival of a group of Romans. The villagers gathered to watch. Serpicus could see people nudging their neighbours and pointing at himself and Brutus, and eyeing the arrivals speculatively. Serpicus had to admit that his men were an unprepossessing sight: travel-stained, unshaven and weary. The two groups of people stood and looked at each other. A number of the villagers were carrying swords. Although Brutus had had the foresight to tell the men to disarm before they came down the hill, presumably their arms were close at hand in their packs or under their cloaks. The villagers were looking at them curiously. The men didn't look anything like Roman soldiers, but they didn't look much like Germans either. They didn't speak the language, and it was only a matter of time before a villager heard some of them talking and recognized it as Latin.

Balant stepped forward and raised his arms. 'We welcome our guests from the south,' he said in a loud voice and with a welcoming smile.

'From the south, eh?' chuckled Brutus to himself. 'Who's he fooling?'

'Just look happy,' said Serpicus out of the corner of his mouth, at the same moment that he caught sight of Cato, still in his blanket. If anything the man's face was more mournful than before.

Balant spoke quickly to two men who went off in different directions. He gestured after them to Serpicus.

'They have gone to bring everyone to meet in the Hall,' he said. 'I shall explain what is happening. We don't want any sort of misunderstanding.'

The only sorts of misunderstanding that Serpicus could think of all involved bloodshed on a sudden and plentiful scale, and he wanted none of it. As they walked

264

to the meeting hall he explained in a low voice to Galba and the rest of the men who didn't speak German what was happening. Galba saw the sense of it. He pulled Serpicus a little to one side.

'This Balant,' he said. 'Whose side is he on? If the Treveri join the revolt, would he be in it with the rest of them?'

Serpicus shrugged. 'I don't know him,' he said. 'But if the whole of Germany was fighting against Rome then it would be difficult not to join in.'

Galba looked fretful. 'All this smiling isn't going to last,' he said. 'I vote we get a bath, eat all their food, grab the bear and push off back to Rome at the earliest opportunity.'

'Suits me,' said Severus, who was listening nearby. 'It feels like we're sitting on a nest of sleeping snakes.'

Serpicus said nothing. He was home for the first time in seven years, and he was still trying to work out how that felt.

24

The introductions didn't take long. Balant explained that the new arrivals had come to the village as traders. He didn't specify the nature of the trade. The Germans looked suspiciously at the dark skins and military appearance of many of their visitors, but enough of the Gelbheimers remembered Serpicus and Brutus to allow trust to overcome fear. Although no one was taking bets that it would last.

They were allotted a large comfortable barn near the village centre. They went off to get some sleep, while the villagers prepared a feast of welcome. The soldiers were up again by the afternoon. They hadn't seen civilization for a while, and intended to make the most of it.

First, washing. Every man except Galba stripped himself naked and ran into the river. Even Cato cheered up enough to join in. Galba said the river was too cold for washing, and he looked so dirty and so miserable that the villagers took pity on him. They put several large pots of water on the fire and when it was warm they stood Galba in a large barrel and poured it in around him. The river was too cold to stay in long. When the men came running back up to the village to warm themselves by the fires they found Galba in a barrel of hot water, steam rising around his pink face and a seraphic smile upon it. He was still smiling when they had finished tipping the barrel over and rolling him around in it for a while.

Then, eating. A sheep carcass turned slowly over a large fire, and a huge pot of beans and pulses bubbled gently on one side. There was bread, in huge rough loaves to be broken in the hands, and game birds, fat pheasant and pigeon roasted in earth ovens near the river and brought by slaves to the party. The sun sank over the hills as the feasting began.

Then, finally, beer. Serpicus realized just how much he'd missed it. He lifted the leather cup and smelt his childhood in the wheat and hops, an aroma of the damp black earth and of his country. He liked wine as much as the next man, and the Empire produced some very fine examples, but, as Brutus never tired of pointing out, wine isn't a proper drink for a German party. Wine whispers, beer shouts; wine sits on a couch and talks behind its palm, beer lies on the dry ground and shouts happy propositions at passers-by; wine eats with two fingers, beer uses both hands; wine brings a sour taste from the gut to the mouth and an apologetic smile, beer breaks wind in your face and laughs at you. Wine, thought Serpicus, is Blaesus and Rome, beer is Brutus and Germany.

Decius toyed with a cup and looked distant. Serpicus

thought he recognized in the young man's face the same feeling that possessed him – a strange form of happiness mixed with an unexpected uncertainty. Galba sat next to the youngster. Galba, who like most Thracians would drink anything at all so long as it had the desired effect, sat back, swallowed the contents of another cup and looked around with the air of someone entirely at home. It seemed he had forgiven Serpicus and Brutus for leaving him and the others on top of the hill for an hour while they talked in the village, and his tour of the village in a barrel hadn't punctured his good humour either. He looked benignly down the length of the table to where the rest of the men were sitting, and then spoke to no one in particular.

'So, where's this famous chief then?' he said cheerfully.

'Out hunting, apparently,' said Brutus through several mouthfuls of pheasant. 'And don't think you can be disrespectful, because if he doesn't take your head off for it then I will.' He jabbed the leg-bone at Galba for emphasis.

Across the table from Brutus, Serpicus picked several small partly chewed pieces of pheasant off his cheek. 'I remember Cruptorix loved hunting. When I left the tribe he was the greatest hunter for leagues around, the greatest our tribe had ever seen, that anyone could remember.'

Galba, sitting beside Brutus, sniffed in a manner not exactly dismissive but one which might be interpreted that way. 'Shame he isn't alive, it sounds like we could have used him as a partner in the business.'

Brutus poked a leg-bone at him again like a long finger. 'Not that Cruptorix would have lowered himself to do a job like ours, but he'd have been bloody good at it if he had.'

Galba dabbed deliberately at several glistening spots of grease on his tunic. 'No doubt he would. However he isn't here, and nor is the new chief, which suggests that the hunting hasn't been too good.'

Brutus swallowed and took another large bite. 'Or maybe he's killed so many animals that the pack-horses' bellies are scraping the ground and they can't raise a trot between them.'

Galba looked sorrowfully at the state of his tunic. It was like sitting beside a blizzard, with bits of food taking the place of snow. He did his sniff again, this time louder. 'We'll no doubt find out soon enough,' he said.

There was a sudden change in the atmosphere in the Hall, as if an exciting piece of news had been passed around to all the occupants simultaneously. Serpicus looked around. He sensed that something was about to happen, without knowing how or what. Most of the men were looking towards the door, and he saw Cato's face look interested for the first time since they had crossed the border into Germany. Sounds of arrival came from outside.

'Looks like we'll find out sooner than you thought,' grinned Brutus. He nudged the man sitting next to him. They'd recently made friends over a large jug of beer, which for Brutus constituted a sacred and eternal bond. Brutus had been telling him stories about Hannibal's elephants until his eyes looked as though they might drop from his head. 'Hey, Max,' he said. 'Who's coming?'

'Chief,' the nudged man said, raising his cup in a toast as he picked himself up off the ground. 'Been hunting.'

The iron-studded doors at the front of the Hall swung wide open, letting in a breeze which caught the edges of the brightly painted shields hanging on the walls and gave out a low ringing sound as they rolled back and forth against the stone. The wind cleared the wood-smoke that clung to the high rafters, and the cold air woke up all but the insensible.

The men sitting at the table nearest the door stood up and a path cleared through the crowd. Two men came in, guards lightly armed for escort duty, stained from the hunt. They stood facing each other, one either side of the hall opening. There was a slight pause, during which Serpicus had time to look around and see the expectancy on everyone's faces, and then five women came in. Four of them stood at each corner of an invisible box of which the fifth was at the centre. The four were all tall, muscular and had the weapons and confidence of warriors. For a few moments Serpicus couldn't get a good look at the woman in the centre, then someone moved sideways and he saw her clearly.

She was wearing a light bronze breastplate polished to a deep burnished glow, and the sword at her side almost touched the ground.

Serpicus blinked, and the curtains of the past parted as if pulled aside by a lover's hands.

He stretched out on his back and put an arm across his eyes to block the light. The trees around him were higher than the sky. The druids say that the branches at the very top brush against the feet of the gods. Sometimes, they say, when the wind is right, you can hear them murmur their pleasure as the soft fronds sweep back and forth against their toes.

'What are you doing?'

He hadn't heard her, as usual. He usually pretended that the wind and his concentration prevented him from hearing her approach, but the truth was that he never heard her. She was twelve years old, and she could move casually through the forest, across ground covered with sharp pebbles and dry sticks, and make less noise than the best hunter creeping up on a nervous deer. When she really didn't want to be heard, she could reach out and touch him on the shoulder before he knew she was there.

'Watching the sky,' he said.

She turned her head until it faced upward and narrowed her eyes. The forest was dark; the eyes became accustomed to it. If you turned your face as if you were looking up a smoke-hole the bright light would make you flinch.

He blinked and turned so that he could see her. Long dark hair fell over her shoulders, so dark sometimes that only the brightest sun could reveal the deep fires that hid within it. Its sleek depths were unusual; her mother was red-haired and her father fair, like most of his tribe.

She looked down at him and grinned. 'What do you see?'

He stared at her. He had promised himself that he would always speak the truth to her. Recently he had started to hide his real feelings from her. He had felt things, wanted to do things that he didn't understand, and this made him embarrassed and uneasy when he saw her. He knew she was puzzled and even perhaps hurt by the change in him, and he knew that more than he valued his life he didn't want her to be hurt. He knew she was open with him, so he had resolved to be the same with her. The idea of telling her even a tenth of what boiled in his heart was more frightening than a hundred rabid Romans charging towards him, but he held onto his courage. He felt his cheeks grow warm and somehow forced himself to reply without stammering. 'Your hair.'

She took a lock and looked at it critically. 'Why? It's just hair.'

'No it isn't.' She frowned. He felt the world slow down. His breath seemed to run out. 'It's beautiful.'

She shrugged. 'Hair is hair.'

'No. No, it isn't.' He felt a fist around his throat, and at the same time he knew that he had started something and if he didn't finish it he would never have the courage to speak again. 'It's yours, it's your hair. That's what makes it perfect.'

She looked at him for a long time. Her narrow fingers turned the lock of hair slowly as if she was testing it for texture. Then she let it go and reached out with the same hand until the back of her fingers touched his cheek.

'I'm going to like being married to you,' she said.

Serpicus stared at her as if she was a ghost. When he had been taken to Rome she was just coming to womanhood and was thin as a spear, with a tangled rope of hair hanging down her back. Now she was almost as tall as he was.

Her shoulders were broad and supported arms of long and clearly defined muscle. He saw how her waist tapered and then swelled slightly into narrow hips. Her skin was paler than he remembered, but her hair was as lustrous as ever and had grown almost to her waist. It flowed across her shoulders and, shining softly in the firelight, poured down her back like a frozen fall of dark water.

Serpicus took a step forward and then remembered his manners and stood still, waiting for the Chief. The new arrivals should be introduced as a group first. Then he could speak to Drenthe. And there was pleasure in watching her again. Serpicus had hunted leopards in Syria, and there was a smooth rhythm to her movements that reminded him of them when he watched her. The torch-light struck a silver helmet she carried in her hand and flashed from it around the hall. He watched as she strode across the room to go to stand by the Chief's chair. Serpicus was impressed. Just to be one of the Chief's bodyguard was a great honour, to lead it meant she had done well. There could be little doubt that the Chief would have claimed her. He was proud for her. He also felt a soft hand touch his heart. He knew that his memories were of two different people in a very different time, and yet he felt that a part of her was his alone.

Serpicus smiled to himself at how the memory stirred within him. He watched her walk towards the Chief's chair, to take the most trusted guard's position immediately behind it. A high honour indeed.

But she didn't go behind the chair. She sat in it herself.

A great shout of acclamation went up and she smiled and raised a hand in easy acceptance of it.

Brutus leant across to Serpicus. 'Close your mouth before a bird flies into it. They might take it amiss for you to make it so obvious you've noticed her.' He flicked a piece of bread at Galba. 'You too, pink boy.'

'She's the Chief?' Serpicus whispered.

'Indeed she is, and more,' Max said, waving his chicken bone enthusiastically in her direction. 'Go on, tell me you wouldn't follow her to hell and beyond.'

Brutus took a big bite from a pheasant leg. 'She's handsome enough,' he said, 'but I like a little more flesh on a woman.'

Galba rested his head on his hand and looked at her with a wistful smile. 'You're missing the point. She's a racehorse, not a brood mare.'

Max took a deep swallow from his cup, belched heroically and then nodded vigorously. 'That's right. If you're going to be charging towards the enemy, you don't want to be following someone who makes you think of your warm bed.' He slapped the palm of a hand on the table with drunken seriousness. 'I love my wife and I want no one else, but when you follow her . . .' He smiled, and swung round to get another glance at Drenthe, then turned back and said, as if confiding in them, 'When you follow her you don't mind the thought of dying, so long as she thinks well of you.'

Serpicus sat and watched Drenthe in silence as the shouting filled the room. She raised a hand again and the cheering died away. Most of the men sat down.

'I have news,' she said, her voice strong and clear. 'I

could wait and so not risk disturbing your digestion, but a warrior can eat and talk at the same time, no?'

The men chose to take that as a compliment, as well as being an acknowledgement of the futility of trying to get between a German warrior and his food. Dozens of men with full mouths grunted and banged their approval loudly on the wooden tables with the bone handles of their knives, and then carried on eating as they listened.

She looked at them with a half-smile and then made a signal towards the back of the Hall. A small muscular man pushed his way past the tables, taking a lot of good-humoured abuse on the way. There was a deep sword-cut on his left shoulder that had been recently cauterized, perhaps even earlier the same day. He had two hessian sacks in his right hand, one small, the other larger and heavier. He raised them both high to avoid a drunken warrior's flailing hand. A dark fluid dripped steadily from the smaller bag.

He reached the foot of Drenthe's chair and held the small bag open in front of her. She reached into it and, with the air of a fairground magician, pulled a man's head from it by the hair. A helmet came out too, hooked by the chin-strap, then the strap snapped and the helmet fell and rolled across the ground towards Serpicus, glinting in the firelight. Those nearest it, including all those who had arrived that day with Serpicus, could clearly see the silver chasing on the sides and the coarse horse-hair crest on the crown, dyed a distinctive red ochre. An officer's helmet.

A Roman helmet.

A hiss of surprise and excitement went around the

room. Serpicus looked down the long table towards Severus and his men. They had stopped eating and were looking uncomfortably down at the helmet. Even those who were not Romans looked wary. Severus caught Serpicus' eye and shook his head meaningfully.

Someone picked the helmet up and handed it back to Drenthe. She held it high above her head like a trophy, so that every man in the room could see it. Blood was splashed up one side and had blackened the sweat-stained leather that lined the inside of the rim. For a long moment there was dead silence. Then everyone began to shout at once.

'This isn't good,' murmured Brutus, holding a fresh pheasant leg in front of his face but not eating it.

'Most especially not good for that Roman,' said Galba quietly, without looking up from a close inspection of his knuckles. Serpicus looked down the table again. Severus had risen from his seat to look at the helmet, and then sat down again with a face of stone. Cato was looking around with lowered head as if to see what other men thought. Scipio sat still, and his face left no doubt at all what he thought. Most of the men looked as if they agreed with him.

All around them was pandemonium. The majority of the Treveri seemed to be acclaiming Drenthe, cheering and applauding as they pointed at the helmet, but there were a significant number who argued with them, who shook their heads and pushed their shouting neighbours away from them angrily. Like most people, Germans don't like being pushed and nor do they like people who spoil a celebration, and several fights were in different

276

stages of breaking out when Drenthe stood up and raised her arms. The warriors stopped arguing and separated, snarling at each other across the tables. Drenthe waited, still with the same half-smile, like a schoolteacher sure of her class, until there was almost total silence. She held the helmet in front of her and looked at it as a lawyer would hold a final crucial piece of evidence.

'We hunted all morning, and killed well,' she said. 'There is enough meat to salt for many winter days when the floods come.' There were a few half-hearted cheers and then silence. The hunt wasn't the story any more.

She continued, looking round, gauging the audience. 'We were on our way home, riding through the low woodlands near the boundary of our land with that of the Mediomatrici, when we were attacked.' A low growl came from several points in the room and she nodded gravely. 'A coward's arrow came from the trees and struck Lothar in the shoulder.' A note of passion entered her voice. Serpicus wondered what Lothar was to her. 'He was riding between myself and the woods, or the arrow would have hit me instead.' There were shouts of alarm at this. She quieted the sounds with a gesture. 'Brave Lothar lies in the druid's house and the arrow is in his shoulder yet. The druid says that he will not fight again this year, but he will live, and he will ride with us in the spring.'

The knife-drumming came again, a brief but fervent noise. She waited for it to finish. Serpicus saw Decius looking at her as if he'd never seen anything like her. Which, of course, he probably hadn't.

'More arrows followed the one that struck Lothar, but

we were already riding towards them and the arrows missed. Romans came at us from the woods and we fought with them.' She paused and looked at the short man who still held the larger of the two sacks. He paused dramatically, then turned it upside down with a flourish. There was a loud crash as half a dozen empty Roman helmets landed on the wooden platform in front of her. Blood seeped across the boards and dripped to the floor. There was another cheer and she waited for it to finish. 'As you can see, one German is worth ten Romans. Even wounded Lothar helped kill a man, fighting left-handed and with no shield.' The cheers came again, longer this time. 'We killed these, and the rest of them ran away, many of them wounded.' She paused. 'We lost Gallus to a Roman spear. He died bravely, and we will honour him.' She bowed her head in a movement of respect. As she did so, a tall man in a sleeveless leather jerkin jumped up on top of one of the tables and raised his arms in the same gesture that Drenthe had used earlier. She heard his feet hit the planks and looked up again. She paused a moment and then made an open-palmed gesture to him. 'Calryx will speak.'

The man called Calryx looked around the room. His eyes were dark, penetrating. Serpicus had seen the same eyes in a man preaching outside the arena one day. He had spoken of the doom that awaited the Romans if they did not amend their ways and worship the true God. The games had been about to start, and amongst the hurrying crowds no one was waiting to find out who the true God was, but Serpicus remembered the intensity of the man's eyes and the way he spoke. He had been driven by an absolute certainty, the sort of single-mindedness that goes beyond sense and self-preservation; the eyes of a man who will happily die if only he can get men to listen to him first.

'I say that this is the day that many of us predicted and which many of you denied would ever come. I say we should arm ourselves now and join the revolt against Roman arrogance and tyranny, the revolt we should have joined when it first began. It is our shame that we have allowed ourselves to be persuaded to hold back for this long. I say we should fight alongside our brothers, the Lingones, the Chatti, and the Mediomatrici. I say . . .'

Calryx had more to say, but tumultuous cheering drowned him out. He jumped off the table to a pounding on the back from his friends. Serpicus looked around and saw that the men who responded most enthusiastically to Calryx's speech were all sitting around him. Those who sat silent with glowering expressions and their arms tightly folded were all on the other side of the room. The tribe, it seemed, was divided, to the extent that those on the two different sides sat only with those who agreed with them. This was unusual. Among the Gelbheimers as with all the villages of the Treveri, decisions were always made communally, and if a man failed to persuade his friends of the strength of his argument and position then tradition dictated that he accepted their decision, went with them wholeheartedly and took the consequences whatever they were.

Serpicus wondered if things had changed. He wondered also if the strains of war were enough to divide the tribe, or if Roman gold had come into some men's hands.

Drenthe raised a hand and the noise subsided enough for her to speak. 'I hear what Calryx says, but we should not jump to action before we have fully understood the situation. If this was an assassination attempt, then the Romans have failed, and many of them paid heavily for their failure. If it was the start to a campaign against us, then we are now fully warned and more than ready for them. If it was a group of deserters, or a lost group of soldiers thinking they saw an opportunity, or even an honest mistake,' she smiled, and some laughed as she said it, 'which it might have been, for we know that all Germans look the same to them, as all Romans do to us, and they may have thought we were of the Chatti . . .' and at that many of the men laughed for it was well known that the Chatti looked more like pigs than Germans, though they were still of course better-looking than most Romans. She raised her voice over the end of the laughter. 'Whatever their motives, we will find out soon enough, and if we must fight then we will. The Romans may even come to us and try to explain away what happened. But . . .'

'No!'

Calryx roared his disapproval, and a small tightly bunched group of men behind him joined in enthusiastically. A shadow crossed Drenthe's face as she waited for them to tire of their shouting. When it was possible to be heard again, she spoke.

'Calryx, again you reject a road that leads to any destination but war, as you have done ever since the

280

revolt of the Chatti against the Romans began.' Her voice hardened. 'I am Chief here, and my word is this. If we must fight then we will, and when we do then let any man who comes against us beware for we will fight hard, harder than they will believe possible.' She paused. The tall man looked sullen but he kept silent. She continued in a lower voice. 'But we must take counsel. The Romans are many and they fight hard too, and although we have had great victories against them, they have also beaten us. When we win, they lose soldiers, and soldiers are easily replaced. When they win, they kill our menfolk, burn our crops, take hostages, destroy our lives.' She looked around slowly. 'Whoever the final victory is to, if we fight then there will be bare hearths in many houses and a cold bed beside the fire before the fighting is over.'

'You think that we would lose, and so you say we should not fight,' said a man standing beside Calryx, in a deep voice that carried all around the room. Calryx put a hand on the man's shoulder to quiet him and waited for silence before speaking.

'You say that we must wait until we feel the flames touch our skin before we act. I say that you are sleeping while the bed you lie in is on fire. We have been attacked by Romans, the same Romans who are attacking our brothers only a few leagues away, but you say we should wait.' He spat sideways onto the ground. 'You care nothing for the honour of the Treveri.'

There were some shouts of approval and a lot more of angry disagreement. Drenthe's four bodyguards stood with their hands tense around the pommels of their swords, like dogs waiting to be released into the chase. Drenthe paused, looking at Calryx as if he was a strange animal that had wandered into the hall by accident. When she eventually spoke her voice was measured, holding in check the emotion that made her eyes flash and the colour disappear from her cheeks save for high on the bones under her eyes.

'Calryx feels passionately, and he speaks in ways that, once he has had time to reconsider his words, he will not wish to repeat. The honour and lives of the Treveri are my first concern, as always.' She let a pause fall. Calryx looked every bit as angry as before, but he said nothing. She continued, addressing the whole hall.

'I do not say that we would lose a war, and I do say that there are worse things than losing. I do not say that we should not fight, but I do say that we should consider well before we fight.' There was a loud muttering from the group behind Calryx and she glared at them until they subsided. 'I will take advice and counsel, and the druids will perform the sacred rituals, as always.' She drew herself up to her full height. 'But hear me now and hear me well.'

Her hair glowed in the torch-light like iron cooling from the blacksmith's fire, and her eyes and her voice filled the room with her authority.

'I promise you, if the decision is for war, then I will lead you in battle against the Romans and I will strike the first blow and many after it, and there will be no going back until we have driven the invader from our lands.' She looked hard at Calryx. 'But first I say, in front of you all, that I am Chief of our village. I will take counsel, but if I decide that there is to be no war, or war tomorrow, or war in the future, then you will accept my decision.' Her word was absolute, like two flat pieces of wood slapping together. 'The people of the Treveri are threatened. This may be the greatest danger they have ever known, and at such a time I will have no dissension. We stand together, as Armin showed us, or we fail. Accept my word on this, finally and for ever, or else put your hand on your sword now and challenge me here, in front of the tribe; I will have it no other way.'

She stared her challenge in a circle around the room, finishing with Calryx and his supporters.

There was a long silence. Serpicus realized he was holding his breath, and suspected a lot of other men were doing the same.

Slowly, without breaking their locked gaze, Calryx walked forward towards Drenthe and drew out his sword with a shrill metallic ring. Everyone but Drenthe tensed as they watched and leant forward, waiting. He held the blade against his forehead in salute, then reversed it and held it out to her, handle first. Without speaking, every man in the hall did the same. A hundred swords left their sheaths with the harsh sound of a whetstone on a scythe. Drenthe reached forward, took Calryx's sword and reversed it again, giving it back to him with a graceful gesture. Serpicus tensed. If Calryx was going to strike at her, this was the moment, as she held the blade of his sword pointed at her breast and offered him the handle. After a moment Calryx took the sword and stepped back. Drenthe gathered her cloak, turned and left through an opening at the back of the hall. Her four women strode after her. Calryx sheathed his sword and left the room, followed by his men.

Serpicus smiled at Decius, who appeared entranced, his eyes fixed on the place where Drenthe had disappeared. Severus was deep in conversation with Scipio and several of the others. Cato was nowhere to be seen.

Serpicus got up and went to stand by Severus. The centurion looked up and gave him a guarded look.

'An interesting evening,' he said.

'How much of that did you understand?'

Severus indicated one of the Gallic auxiliaries. 'Felix here has enough of the language to make sense of most of it.'

Serpicus nodded. 'We should discuss what's happening here.'

Severus stroked his chin. 'Is anything about to happen?' Serpicus shook his head. 'Then we should wait until the evening is over. We will talk then.'

Serpicus hesitated, then agreed. Better to find out as much information as possible first. He returned to his seat.

Brutus and Max had found another jug of beer and had sat down again together, deep in conversation. Serpicus pulled up a stool beside them. Max smiled at him amiably with unfocused eyes. He had emptied his cup more than once that evening.

'When I left here seven years ago, Vonones was Chief of the Treveri,' Serpicus said. 'Now Drenthe rules in his stead. Is she not too young to have been his wife?'

Max looked puzzled. 'Wife? Her, married to Vonones? Hardly.'

'Then how is it she sits in the Chief's chair and speaks for him?'

Max opened his mouth to speak, then closed it again. It was plainly the sort of story that needed adequate and proper preparation. He poured more beer into all their cups, made himself comfortable and started his explanation.

'You left seven years ago, you say?' Max did some arithmetic on his fingers while looking up with narrowed eyes at the smoke-blackened roof of the Hall as if the answer might be written there in the soot. 'Yes, Vonones was still Chief then. He died about five years ago.'

'A fine man. He fought well.' Brutus made an upward motion with his cup and drank. They all followed his example. 'Did he die in battle?'

Max shook his head. 'The fever. It took many of us that year. He fought the sickness for a long time, longer than anyone, until we thought he must have beaten it, but it left him too weak, and he died.'

There was a silence.

'So, who took his place?' asked Serpicus.

Max screwed his forehead up in thought. 'Galan.'

Serpicus didn't know the name. Brutus looked surprised. 'Galan from my village? The Chief's son?'

'If you are from Glaudern, yes.'

Serpicus was puzzled. 'How did the people of Gelbheim agree to have an outsider become chief?'

Max drank and shook his head, not quite separating the two actions. 'He was no outsider. He was betrothed to Drenthe.'

Brutus nodded, wiping his face absently. 'So Galan becomes Chief of the tribe.'

Serpicus drank deeply to give himself time to think. 'So Drenthe speaks for Galan?'

Max shook his head again. 'Galan was killed on a cattle raid three years ago.' He looked genuinely upset. 'He was a good chief, and it was a pointless waste. No glory in it, not even any decent cattle.'

'Then who was chief after Galan?'

'Cruptorix, Drenthe's father. He died a year ago.'

'So Drenthe is a widow?' Serpicus told himself that he was asking the question without any motive, but he had to admit that a part of him was interested. He remembered once walking past a house he had lived in and seeing that the new occupants had let the shrubs that he had planted die. The feeling was similar. He knew it was none of his business, but a part of him still cared.

Max drank. 'Yes. She has yet to remarry.'

Brutus nodded his understanding. 'An unusually high casualty rate amongst chiefs of the Treveri, it seems,' he said. 'So, the man we met when we came here.' He clicked his fingers at Serpicus. 'What was his name?'

'Balant,' Serpicus said. Max looked confused for a moment. 'Tall, sun-browned, twenty-five summers, perhaps a few more?' Max's brow cleared.

'Ah, yes, that Balant. It's a common name. A good man. He's Galan's youngest brother,' he said. 'He divides his time between here and Glaudern. There were three brothers. All good men. The eldest brother, Salix, is Chief of Glaudern.'

'So Balant is a guest here?'

Max became thoughtful. 'Actually, I'm not sure what

to call him. He's a friend to this village, for certain. He has helped guide us well.'

Serpicus hesitated. 'So he and Drenthe are . . . ?'

Max grinned and brushed the thought aside with a gesture. 'No, no. Balant has a wife in Glaudern. He comes here to visit his brother's grave and to advise his brother's widow. When she needs it.'

Brutus let out a raucous laugh. 'So how did the men take the idea of a woman leading them?'

Max smiled, almost sheepishly. 'Even now it seems a strange thing to think of.'

'The men accept her?'

'Most of them. Some of the men are . . . still unsure.'

'Yes, I think we saw some of that earlier,' Brutus said, looking across to where Calryx had sat with his supporters. Max glanced across to the same place and nodded.

'Yes, Calryx was no friend of Galan's but he accepted the will of the village to have him as chief once he had married Cruptorix's daughter. However, without Galan, Calryx has no intention of accepting Drenthe. When Cruptorix died he . . .'

Max's voice was drowned by a loud cheering. Everyone looked up to see what was happening. Out of the corner of his eye Serpicus saw Cato returning from the direction of the latrines.

Drenthe had come back into the Hall. She had removed her armour and replaced it with a simple white linen robe. A silver circlet held her hair back from her face and a thin silver torc lay at her throat. Both shone in the torch-light.

287

'So what is the situation now?' Serpicus asked.

Max leant forward. 'Once Cruptorix had been buried, there was a Council, as you would expect. Every man, woman and child was there, it was a good party. Then Bocalas stood up – you can always rely on the druids to take charge if no one else seems to want to – and asked who was to be the new chief. Galan had no sons, his widow Drenthe was Cruptorix's only child. No one had the right of succession. One of Calryx's friends proposed him. There was a vote. The village split. Calryx had maybe a third of the village behind him. We argued all night. Even though he didn't have a majority, Calryx demanded that he be accepted as chief as there was no other candidate.'

'You can see his point,' said Brutus. 'Better any chief than no chief.'

Max nodded. 'True, but the larger part of the village wouldn't have Calryx at any price. When you get to know him a bit better you'll know why.' He took a drink and looked reflectively at his empty cup. Brutus filled it up for him again. 'Anyhow, Bocalas sits all night listening, and then, just as dawn breaks, he stands up as though he's had enough of the wrangling, bangs his staff on the ground, and says he is going to go to the forest to consult the gods on the matter.'

'I bet Calryx loved that thought,' chuckled Brutus.

'He hated it,' said Max, 'but he didn't have a better idea and we had to admit that the discussion was going nowhere, so we all went off to bed and waited for Bocalas to come back.'

'And he did?'

'Three days later. We all gathered round and he stood in front of us and said that he had fasted for three days, and on the third night the gods had sent him a vision.'

'Let me guess,' said Brutus.

'Exactly,' said Max. 'I'll spare you the details – I've forgotten most of them anyhow – but the thrust of it was that Drenthe was to be chief for two summers, with the help of a small group of advisers.' He pointed a knobbled finger at Brutus. 'Want to try and guess who they were?'

Brutus smiled. 'I think I'd be able to.'

'Two of the village elders, plus Bocalas himself, Balant and Calryx.'

'Sounds sensible,' said Serpicus thoughtfully. 'A couple of neutrals, the druid, an outsider and the man who she needs to keep closest to her. Bocalas would make a good politician.'

Max nodded. 'She has done well for the village. She doesn't rush into things, she isn't too proud to take advice, and when she makes her mind up to do something she goes at it like an arrow at a target. And she fights as well as any man and better than most.'

'A fine woman,' Brutus said, in respectful tones.

Max looked serious and banged his cup down on the table. 'A man, for all she's a woman!' he said emphatically.

Serpicus tried to think of an intelligent way of replying to this and failed, so nodded vigorously instead. 'I can see what you mean,' he said.

Max shook his head. 'No, you can't. Not until you've seen her fight.' He banged his cup again on the table and leant towards Brutus, half closing an eye as if aiming the words at him. 'She can stand up to strong men and meet them blow for blow, and then suddenly she twists away and steps to one side and there is a flash of steel and they look down and their guts are on the ground and they have no idea how it happened.' He shook his head in baffled admiration. 'She is like a cat. She has never been beaten.'

'What happens once the two summers are up?' asked Serpicus.

'She stands for election again,' said Max, 'and the gods will decide. Anyone may stand against her. Calryx will definitely stand, and there are probably one or two others though they haven't much chance. Calryx is the main contender. If Drenthe is confirmed, she'll be chief for good and there's an end to it. If she loses, then she stands down and there's an end to it too.' Max looked around. 'Now I've talked enough. Can I please go and try to find someone prettier than you lot who'll have me for the night?'

Brutus put a hand on his arm. 'One more question, and then you can go and talk to that dark woman over there who has been looking at you so hungrily for the last hour.'

Max spun around to look. 'Really? Who? Where?'

Brutus squeezed his arm. 'In a moment. First, tell us, when does Drenthe's time as chief end?'

'A month, I think, perhaps a little longer,' said Max. 'Now, point me in the right direction, will you?'

When Max had climbed unsteadily over a table to get at the woman Brutus said was eyeing him – which Serpicus was sure came as news to her – Serpicus, Galba and Brutus looked at one another speculatively. Decius leant in so that he could hear what was said, though his eyes were still on Drenthe, as they had been since she came back into the room.

'You are going to tell me sometime what all that was about, aren't you?' said Galba. Not speaking German was causing him pain, he was missing out on all the details.

'D'you suppose that little fracas we saw earlier was the start of the election campaign?' asked Serpicus.

Brutus nodded. 'Probably. Just what the tribe needs, an election during a war.'

'They aren't at war yet.'

'Tell it to those Romans,' said Brutus, jerking a thumb at the blood-smeared helmets piled in the corner. 'And I suspect we'll have a deputation or two coming to us shortly, wanting to know whose side we're on.'

Brutus squinted down the table at the expedition, and Serpicus did the same. Most of them were surprisingly sober, and several of them were looking unhappily at the pile of Roman helmets. Severus leant forward and signalled.

'A word, before the night is over?' he said. Serpicus opened his mouth to reply and Severus shook his head. 'Not here,' he said.

'They're Germans. They don't speak Latin.'

'You're Germans, and you do,' Severus said.

25

They went back to the barn.

One side of the building was piled high with hay for the winter. Sides of salted and cured meat hung from the rafters on metal hooks. The village cats sat waiting below while hundreds of rats ran along the beams. Every so often a venturesome rat would slide down a hook and feast on the meat. The cats ignored it until the bloated rat turned to climb back up again. More often than not it couldn't get any purchase on the smooth metal, and either fell off or would still be there, gripping the carcass, when a villager next came in to check. Either way, the cats always won.

Serpicus and Brutus sat at the single table which, with two low benches, made up all the furniture in the building. Decius and Galba stood nearby. Severus and Scipio sat on the bench on the other side of the table, as spokesmen for the rest of the men who arranged themselves in a ragged but attentive clump behind them. Serpicus saw Cato with the men and wondered which way he would jump when the time came. He had nothing to gain by staying to fight; he'd surely leave.

Severus hadn't wanted to have the conversation in front of their hosts, and Serpicus could see why. The centurion came straight to the point.

'We signed on to come here, to Gelbheim, and escort an animal back to Rome. We knew there was a war going on, fair enough. We're soldiers, if there's fighting to be done then so be it.' He looked at the men behind him, and they made noises of assent. 'But we assumed that if there was any fighting to be done it would be against the locals or attacks by bandits. None of us expected to be sitting here listening to people talking about killing Romans as if it was the accepted local pastime.'

Serpicus tapped a finger on the table. 'So you're worried that you might have to fight Romans?' Several men grunted agreement, and Severus looked quickly around the room before replying.

'That's most of it,' he said. 'I'm not too keen either about staying here and making friends with people who may very soon end up fighting Romans. Life is complicated enough. I don't want to end up caught between them and having to choose sides.'

Brutus looked up. 'Does Severus speak for all of you?'

There was some shuffling, and three men pushed through the front row of listening soldiers. One of them was Snake, the Cretan. As always, he was wearing the soft leather waistcoat that held his knives. He spoke for them.

'I am a Cretan. Rome tells me I am no longer a Cretan or a Greek, that there is no Greece or Crete any more, that we are all Romans. If this can be done with the stroke of a pen, if it is so easy to make a man a Roman, then I say it is not worth much and it is as easily undone. I will fight for my people or for my friends, or for who pays me the most, or for whom I please, but I owe no debt to Rome.' He indicated the two men with him. 'Frank and Bertrand are Gauls. Their fathers both died fighting Germanicus. They owe Rome no debts either.'

Severus looked at them sternly. 'And if I say that I am a Roman, will you fight me?'

Snake shook his head. 'We do not fight men who say they are Romans. We fight Rome. Romans may be many kinds of people, including Cretans and Gauls, even Germans. But for us, Rome and the Empire, it brings only one thing, the death of those we care about and the end of independence.' He indicated the village around them. 'We all heard how Rome has already attacked these people here without provocation.' He looked steadily at several faces in the group. 'You are all our friends. We will gladly fight at your sides against anyone who threatens you, but if you say that you are for Rome regardless of whom Rome decides you must fight, then we must part now and hope our eyes never meet over the top of a shield.'

Scipio leant forward. 'We only have the Germans' word that the Romans attacked them first. It could equally well have been the other way around. Doesn't the story strike you as suspicious? When was the last time you saw a Roman ambush which left seven dead legionaries and only one dead German?' He waited for an answer. The men looked at each other and many of them murmured agreement. Scipio continued, looking at Snake. 'If Romans come to Gelbheim to demand that the village lays down its arms, and if the villagers resist them, will you join with them against us?'

Snake paused a long time before replying. 'If I join with these people, and if you join with the Roman army and fight these people, then yes, I will fight you.' The two Gauls nodded their support.

Severus looked at Snake and nodded slowly. 'I see.' He turned back to Serpicus. 'Regardless of who started it, Romans have been killed today, and there seem to be plenty of men in Gelbheim who think it was a good idea. Rome will call it a rebellion even if the villagers decide for peace. The legions will come to Gelbheim and there will be war. We must make up our minds now, because if we do not then they will be made up for us very soon. Do we stay with these people and fight against Rome, or shall we stick to our mission and leave as quickly as possible, while we are all still together?'

Before anyone could answer him, the door opened suddenly and crashed back against the wall. Calryx stood in the doorway, framed by the torches held up by his men behind him. There were as many of them as there were men already in the room.

'So,' Calryx said with a sardonic smile. 'The Romans stay to hear us talk openly, then leave to hold their own debates in secret.'

The four men around the table stood up. Galba and Decius moved close to Brutus and Serpicus and the rest of the men came around the table so that they all faced Calryx. Serpicus almost smiled at the way allegiances could change in an instant. He looked at Calryx. 'What do you want?'

Calryx stepped forward until he was close enough to reach out and touch Serpicus on the chest. 'War is coming. When it does arrive, we do not want Romans in our village, even if they have eaten our food and call themselves our allies. When we fight we do not want to know that they are standing behind us with bare swords in their hands.'

Serpicus sensed movement behind him and glanced at Severus. The centurion had put his hand on his sword. Most of his men had done the same. It looked as though everyone in the room had heard enough talking and was ready to move on to the next stage. Serpicus stood up and moved in front of Severus so that Calryx could not see the centurion's sword-arm. 'You want us all to leave now?'

'Yes.'

'And is this your Chief's order?'

Calryx bit back the reply that sprang to his lips. 'I lead the Council,' he said evenly. 'There will soon be a new chief. In the meantime I give the orders here.'

'Not while I live,' said a new voice clearly from behind Calryx's men.

Calryx's group of men parted and Drenthe came through the space, flanked by the four guards who accompanied her everywhere. She walked past Calryx and then turned to face him. The women stood around her in silence, their muscles tensed and ready to move.

'What does this mean?' she asked. 'These men are our guests.'

Calryx's face flushed. 'I am removing these Romans from our midst. They are probably all spies, and even if they are not then they are a liability.'

Drenthe was staring straight into his face. 'They are strange spies indeed, to arrive as they did. You know that some of them are as German as you or I. You also should know that, even if every one of them was a direct blood relative of Tiberius, they have eaten our food. They are guests here.' She looked straight into Calryx's face. '*My* guests.'

Calryx trembled with anger and then visibly got control of his temper. 'And when the Romans come and attack us? Do you suppose these men will fight with us then?'

Drenthe lifted an eyebrow. 'I don't know. Just now, it doesn't matter. They are guests, under my protection, under the protection of our village. If you insult them then you insult the hospitality of the whole village. You insult me.' She paused. 'Only someone who cares nothing for the honour of the Treveri could even think of acting as you do.' She paused again, to give him time to remember where he had heard that phrase before. 'Is that clear?'

Calryx let out a noise closer to an animal growl than a human word. He turned and swept back out through the door. His men turned and followed him, muttering darkly.

When they were all gone, Drenthe took a deep breath and let it out slowly, blowing the conflict after them. Then she turned to face Serpicus.

'I'm told you have a new name now,' she said quietly

with a smile. 'It has been a long time. We must find an opportunity to talk about the old days. Meanwhile, will you translate what I say to your men?'

Serpicus opened his mouth and found himself unable to speak. He made a sound that he hoped would suffice as a reply. Her voice became a leader's. 'We must all be honest with each other. You have eaten and drunk here and so you are our guests, but that does not make us allies. Our friends tell us that the legions are marching towards this village as I speak. War is coming, although I do not wish it and when it arrives it will not be our doing. If you are still in Gelbheim when the legions arrive, I can understand that this will place some of you in an uncomfortable position. If any of you wish to depart, you are free to leave now and I suggest you do so quickly. You will be escorted to the limits of our territory and then you may ride in any direction you choose.' She looked at Severus appraisingly as she gave his translation time to catch up, then continued. 'If you decide to stay, I am sure you will already have realized that these are dangerous times. If you decide to take a chance and then Gelbheim is attacked, you will, of course, have the right to choose not to join in our fight.' She smiled. 'I will have you put in irons so that it is plain you took no part in defending the village. If we fail to repel the attack, then how sympathetic the legions will be to your position will, I am afraid, have to be a matter between you and them.'

There was a pause. Serpicus was aware that many eyes were upon him. He spoke.

'As some of you know, my family's safety depends

upon the success of this expedition. I shall attempt to get the animal out of here before the legions arrive. However, we must wait for the druids to agree to us taking it, and I have no way of knowing how long that will be. I shall understand if any of you feel that you can't wait and take the chance of being trapped here.'

Snake and the two Gauls stepped forward and stood behind Brutus and Serpicus. Galba moved sideways until he too was beside them. Decius moved less obviously, but there was no doubt which side he was on. Severus and the rest of the men stayed where they were. Drenthe waited until she was sure no one else was going to move and then nodded once to Severus and his men.

'So be it. You will be given horses if you have none and you may keep your weapons. I will arrange your escort to the border.' She turned to Serpicus. 'Those who stay will be billeted with families in the village. I would not have it said that our allies were left to sleep in a barn.' She turned swiftly and left the building.

Severus' men moved away smartly to gather their effects. Decius came from behind Brutus' broad back into the light. He looked utterly miserable. Serpicus caught his eye. 'Are you sure about staying?'

'I don't know what to do,' he said. 'I feel as though whatever I do I lose something.'

Brutus snorted. 'Welcome to the big world, my lad,' he said. He dropped his pack onto the floor and sat on the table.

Another figure appeared beside Decius.

'I have no love for Rome either,' he said. 'If you are going to stay here, I would like to stay with you, to see

299

if I can help.' They all stared at Cato, who stared back.

Serpicus stood up and held out his hand. 'I hope it won't be necessary, but if it comes to that, we're glad to have you.'

Cato clasped his hand and grinned at him. It was the first time Serpicus had seen his gloomy face change.

Serpicus turned away and saw Snake standing in the shadows, his face impassive, watching.

A short time later Serpicus was standing outside Drenthe's quarters, a wet skin of drizzle gathering on his clothes. The guard outside seemed to expect him and waved him towards the door. Serpicus raised a hand to rap on the frame and then hesitated. He didn't know what he wanted to say to her. He knocked twice, hoping she would begin the conversation.

A serving girl opened the door and stepped aside to let him enter. She looked at Drenthe for instructions and was dismissed with a smile.

The room was warm and dry. Drenthe sat in a chair near a small fire. Her hair fell around her shoulders and caught the firelight. She gestured to a chair facing her without speaking. When he sat down she passed him a cup of warmed wine and lifted her own cup to him. They drank. Serpicus watched her over the edge of the cup as the spiced wine rose to his head.

She sat back in the chair, apparently completely relaxed.

'So,' she said, smiling warmly. 'What shall we talk about?'

He hesitated. He still wasn't sure if she knew who he was.

'The bear?' he said. 'I wasn't sure if . . .'

She held the cup in front of her mouth in both hands without drinking. 'The situation is complicated. I understand that Balant has already explained to you what the problems are?'

Serpicus nodded. 'Yes. He was pessimistic. Do you see the druids as an obstacle too?'

'Perhaps. But the price is a good one. If the money is properly shared around amongst the right people, then I suspect that many men will find that their objections are not nearly so hot as they thought.'

Relief flooded through him. 'So you have made a decision?'

'No. The Council is split, but the majority is just in favour of the sale. For now. That could easily change. The decision is mine, for as long as there is one to take. I wanted to talk to you before making it.'

'What can I tell you?'

She sat back in her chair and looked amused, a curve of the lips that tossed Serpicus backwards through the years.

'For a start, you can tell me whatever happened to that big clumsy boy with the sleepy eyes and sticking-out ears who used to follow me around all those years ago?'

Serpicus stopped breathing for a long moment. Then his own face creased into a grin. 'Oh, he was wondering what happened to the skinny girl with the pony-teeth and the hair like straw who liked to pretend that she didn't notice him following her around.'

Drenthe's smile reached her eyes. 'It's good to see you again.'

He allowed himself to look at her properly, openly, for the first time. 'And it's good to see you.'

There was a silence, but they were both comfortable with it.

'You were married?' he said, knowing the answer.

'I was.'

'I'm sorry.'

She looked at him curiously, and he looked straight back, neither of them quite sure what he meant. She decided to take him at face value.

'He was a good man.'

Serpicus nodded. 'I have heard it said so.'

She tapped a finger on her cup. 'And you are married now?'

'Yes.'

She paused. 'And so, should I be sorry too?'

There wasn't a reply he could think of, so he said nothing.

'And you must leave soon?' she asked.

'If I do not return with the bear, my family will die in the arena.'

She looked directly at him. 'You have children?'

'Two.'

A shadow stroked her face. 'I see. Then you should go back quickly.'

'Yes,' he said. 'You had none?'

She looked into her cup and spoke slowly. 'It seems the gods want me for a soldier myself, not a bearer of them.'

'Again, I am sorry. Perhaps . . .'

She shook her head and lifted it. Her eyes were shining in the firelight. 'No. It cannot be. Will not be. There are . . . reasons. It does not matter.' She smiled again, differently, a deliberate movement of the lips that rose through time and through pain, defying them. 'I thought, once, that you and I might have . . .'

Serpicus needed to move. He leant forward. 'I thought it too, once,' he said. He looked at her frankly. 'I never forgot you.'

She laughed, and a tear spilt down her cheek. 'I never forgot you either. And yet, somehow, life seems to have gone on for both of us.'

He could think of nothing to say to that. She looked up at him and a tight fist gripped his chest. Everything stopped moving, pinned to the tension between them.

And then the noise started.

Somebody and something – the butt end of a spear, or the handle of a sword – was pounding on the outside of the door.

They both turned slowly to look. Serpicus turned back again, but she did not. She wiped her face dry and said in a controlled voice, 'Yes?'

The door opened immediately. A man was standing outside. He stepped in. To be as wet as he was would mean either taking a swim fully clothed or standing on guard in the rain for half a day. Serpicus presumed it was the latter.

'I'm sorry to disturb you,' the guard said breathlessly. 'There is something you must know.'

303

Drenthe stood up with a concerned expression. 'What is it?'

He gestured over his shoulder. 'The gate. You can see . . . there are . . .' He stopped, his agitation leaving him without words. 'You should come to the gate.'

In the distance Serpicus could hear excited voices and shouting. The village was being roused.

Drenthe looked at Serpicus as she spoke to the guard. 'I will be there immediately.'

The man withdrew, closing the door behind him. She put a hand on Serpicus' forearm and indicated the thin fabric of her clothing with the other. 'I must get dressed,' she said. The warmth of her hand entered his blood.

'Of course. I will . . . of course.' He headed for the door.

'Serpicus?'

He stopped and turned. She stood with the red glow of the burning logs behind her. The shadow of her body was outlined with glowing fire.

'We will speak again, yes?'

'We will,' he said.

The cold air after the warm house was like a slap in the face. He turned his face up to the rain and, breathing deeply, waited for it to wash him clean.

26

'How far do you think?' said Serpicus, jumping off the ladder to stand on the walkway beside Brutus.

Decius shook his head and said nothing. Brutus squinted into the night, a dark cloak made impenetrable by the heavy rain. If there was a moon it was completely hidden behind the clouds. 'Three hundred paces?' he said.

Standing beside him wrapped tightly in a thick cloak, Galba shook his head. 'Impossible to judge,' he said. 'You don't know how far away they are or how big the fires are. They could be very big fires a long way away, or they could be very small ones but quite close.'

Brutus looked at Galba as if seeing him clearly for the very first time. 'Yes, Archimedes, I know that,' he said with heavy sarcasm, 'but then, he asked, and so, to please him, I'm guessing. It's approximate. And, of course, if I was a Roman and I was building a line of fires to cut off this place, I know where I would put them, and so I do know roughly how far away they are. And

I've got a bag of coins that say that my guess is closer to the truth than yours, whatever that may be.' He made a disgusted sound and stared back out over the wooden wall. 'Bloody accountants,' he muttered, 'thinking they can do a soldier's job.'

'How big is your bag of coins?' said Galba, from between teeth rattling with the cold like bone dice in his mouth.

Brutus narrowed his eyes. 'Are you trying to start an argument?'

'No, I . . .'

Galba's reply was cut off by Drenthe's arrival. She came up the nearest ladder three steps at a time and jumped off it onto the walkway behind the parapet. Decius stepped back to give her room and almost fell off the walkway. She was now wearing her armour, and her bearing was a commander's. She peered out into the gloom as Brutus had done. 'What the hell is that?' she said softly.

Serpicus stood behind Brutus and said nothing. The guard who had escorted Drenthe to the wall pointed over the parapet, moving his extended arm from one side to the other like an actor addressing an audience.

'The Romans arrived after dark. When the fires started, Orodes took a few men and went out to see what was happening. They had posted cavalry at the fires, expecting us to come. Orodes was nearly caught.' Drenthe put her hand on the shoulder of a dark, heavily bearded man standing nearby. Serpicus assumed he was Orodes. The man stood taller at her touch and grinned cheerfully at everyone nearby. Decius watched Drenthe's hand intently.

306

'Lucky for us that Roman horses are so slow,' Orodes said.

Galba stood between Brutus and Serpicus. 'I wish people would speak Latin,' he said mournfully. 'Would someone please tell me what's going on?'

Brutus folded his arms on the top of the parapet, like a father about to embark on an explanation to a dull-witted child. He pointed out into the gloom. 'Well, you see those pretty glowing things all in a line out there?'

'Yes,' said Galba, sounding as though he was grinding his teeth together as he spoke.

'Well, those pretty things haven't been put there so that you can admire them. Oh no. They belong to the Romans, who are very nasty men with sharp swords who don't like us very much, and they've built those fires all across the neck of this particular bottle that we're in so we can't get out of it.' He paused. 'Anything there you're not clear on?'

Galba shook his head. 'No, all admirably clear, thank you.' He turned to Serpicus. 'Why does he have to be such a horse's arse all the time?' he asked in a loud voice. Brutus responded with a low chuckle.

Serpicus looked around. Severus and the rest of his men were on the ledge on the other side of the gate, looking out at the fires. He nudged Brutus and indicated towards them.

'They aren't happy.'

'I'm not surprised. I'm not delighted myself.' Brutus looked at Severus and became thoughtful. 'All right,' he said. 'We should try and get them out before the attack comes. If we can.'

307

Serpicus thought about that. 'If they just walk out of the gate it'll look as if they are going over to the Romans,' he said. 'The Germans won't let that happen.'

Brutus coughed and spat. 'That may be true,' he said. 'But if any of them are still here when the Romans come in through that gate, they'll get slaughtered along with the rest of us.'

Serpicus put a hand on Brutus' shoulder and squeezed gently. 'Thank you,' he said. 'And to think, there I was, in danger of worrying about someone else.'

Drenthe stood with her arms folded, watching over the parapet. Balant was standing beside her, occupying himself by trying to find a better way of arranging his heavy cloak against the rain. Drenthe stood without moving. Most of her men seemed content to do the same. Waiting was apparently something that the Gelbheimers were good at.

Brutus shivered, looked around and then whispered to Serpicus. 'Is this entirely necessary? Couldn't we take turns to go inside and get warm?'

'Welcome to your country, you German tart,' Galba said, looking pleased with himself.

The villagers wandered aimlessly along the walkway, watching the distant line of fires as if hypnotized. Serpicus found himself standing next to Orodes.

'Any idea what happens next?' he said.

Orodes shrugged. 'They've got us cut off. We can't get past their lines, and they can see that the river is too swollen to allow us to escape. They've got pickets out across their front line, though I suspect they'll be too busy getting close to the fires to be paying much attention to us. You wonder why they ever leave Italy, they miss the sun so much.' He turned his head and spat on the ground. 'I think that, for the moment, the sword is in their hand. We must wait and see.'

'They'll attack.'

Orodes looked at Serpicus as if he was slightly simple. 'I imagine they didn't march right across Germany just because they needed the exercise. They'll want a few Treveri heads to take back to their families, if only to prove they weren't just sitting around enjoying themselves all the time.'

Serpicus looked out at the fires again and learned nothing he didn't already know. He was cold, wet and miserable. Nothing was going to happen. The Romans were following regulations, as always. They wouldn't attack until their camp was built, their situation secure and they'd done a proper reconnoitre of the situation. He gestured to Brutus to follow him and went over to talk to Drenthe. Decius was still standing nearby, doing his best to look military. Serpicus suppressed a smile.

'I want to go and see what's going on out there,' he said, pointing towards the fires.

Drenthe shook her head. 'Orodes tried that, and nearly didn't return,' she said.

'No, not on horseback. As if we were Romans.'

'What?'

'Brutus and I know the army, we both speak army Latin. Most of the men who came with us are wearing bits of legionary uniform, it's a dark night, we only need enough to be convincing. We'll creep out towards the nearest fire until we're as close as we can get, then we'll walk along the line. They'll all have their heads down looking at the fire, they'll assume we're a patrol. Then we'll go into the camp and see what we can find out.'

Drenthe pursed her lips. 'It's not a bad idea.' She looked enquiringly at Balant. He nodded.

'Anything we can find out will be useful,' he said. 'But – and forgive my stating the obvious – it'll be dangerous.'

'I don't care,' said Brutus. 'They'll have dry tents and hot food.'

Everyone smiled.

'Another thing,' said Serpicus. 'The men who came with us, is your promise of safe conduct still good?'

She looked surprised. 'Yes, but I don't see how . . .'

'I'll talk to them,' said Serpicus. He motioned to Brutus, Galba and Decius to follow and went across to where Severus stood on the walkway and gestured to him to join them on the ground. Severus jumped down like a man twenty years younger. He even somehow managed to look drier than anyone else.

'We're properly screwed now,' the centurion said.

'You certainly are if you stay here.'

Severus looked surprised. 'What choice have we?'

'A chance. Collect up all the bits of uniform we have. Give it to the worst swimmers. They come with us. We slip into the camp between the fires and then they walk out the other side.'

Severus lifted an incredulous eyebrow. 'That'll never work, they'll be spotted.'

Serpicus shrugged. 'Possibly, although given the weather and the fact that they will be Roman soldiers in

Roman uniform, I doubt it. Once they're in the camp it's every man for himself. Rendezvous back at the place where you waited while we came into the village, head south. You'll have to ditch the uniforms.'

Severus glanced around the village. 'Why would they let us go? They'll surely assume we'll join the legion.'

Serpicus looked serious. 'If I can persuade the villagers to let us take you out, you'll have to give your word not to fight against the Treveri.'

Severus frowned. 'That could be tricky.'

Serpicus nodded. 'If the Romans catch you they'll execute you as deserters or else co-opt you into the legion. You'll be dead or you'll be back here fighting us. And if you run into any of these Germans and you're wearing uniform I wouldn't fancy your chances. Your only hope is to get through the camp and head for Italy.'

'We haven't much chance in civilian clothes either.'

'You can always stay and try your luck here,' Brutus said.

The centurion gave him a grim smile. 'Fair enough. What about the rest of them, the ones we haven't armour for?'

'They get into the river and go downstream.'

'They'll be drowned.'

'There's that chance, but I don't think so. We'll give them skins to keep them afloat. They'll be swept a good way downstream and it'll be a long walk back by the time they manage to get out, but the Romans are only guarding this side of the river. They won't see anyone go past their pickets so long as they keep to the far side of the river. There's no moon. It's too dark and there's too much floating in the river already to notice. The guards will be staying close to the fires and feeling sorry for themselves, not checking the river. Anyhow, as you pointed out, the alternative isn't promising. But if anyone has a better idea, they're welcome to try it and good luck.'

Severus looked thoughtful. 'We're bound to lose some. But I'll grant we don't have much of a choice.'

'Tell them to be quick, whatever they decide,' said Serpicus. 'We need to leave before dawn, while the Romans are still getting organized.'

Severus nodded and strode quickly away towards the barn which held their equipment, gesturing to the men to join him.

'Come with me,' said a sepulchral voice at Serpicus' shoulder.

Serpicus flinched and then did his best to pretend he hadn't.

'Bocalas,' he said, aware that he sounded guilty of something. 'What is it?'

The druid had a fresh torch in his hand, the flames hissing as the rain landed on it. The boy stood silently behind him, the hooded hawk on his arm. Bocalas gestured that Serpicus should follow him and turned away without speaking. Serpicus looked around. All the others were heading for the barn to put together whatever equipment they had. No one was watching him. He went after the druid.

The rough path was in rain-swept darkness apart from Bocalas' torch, which was getting steadily less brilliant in the downpour. Bocalas strode confidently ahead.

Serpicus navigated his way unsuccessfully between a series of puddles. The boy followed, seeming to know where the deeper water was.

Bocalas led them to a door in the wall of a small barn.

'What's this?' asked Serpicus, shaking the water from his boots.

Bocalas still didn't speak, but raised his head and inhaled sharply. Serpicus did the same and immediately caught a rank smell, definitely animal but unfamiliar. He had a feeling he'd smelt something like it before but had no idea when.

'What is it?' he said. Bocalas opened the door and stepped aside to let Serpicus enter.

A deep growl came from inside the barn and Serpicus knew at once what he had been brought to see.

Serpicus had seen bears before. Two years earlier there had been a craze for black bears in the arena, the bigger the better. A rich man who possessed a huge black bear said that the bear was the most powerful of animals, and that he would bet on it to fight any other creature. His friends immediately sent animal catchers in every direction to find animals to fight it. The bear killed a buffalo easily and a lion with difficulty, before being badly mauled by a tiger and retired by its owner. By then the craze had bitten deep – bears were brought to fight other beasts in combinations that no normal bear would have found itself. The competition everyone wanted to see was a bear against a shark, but no one could agree on the depth of water that would give an advantage to neither side, and so the contest never took place.

Serpicus had also seen smaller, brown bears, which

were in less demand as they were less ferocious in aspect and in character. However, he had never seen, and he knew of no one else who had seen, a completely white bear.

He expected a cage but when they entered the small hall there were no bars. There was a smell, the same as the one he had smelt outside but much stronger, heavy with both musk and oil and mixed with the queasy odour of rotten meat from the dozens of bones that lay strewn on the floor. The hut was divided into two unequal parts by a partition made of thick tree-trunks split lengthways and driven deep into the earth. The section into which the door led was about a quarter of the floor-space of the hall. The wooden wall rose up higher than Serpicus' head. A ladder leant against it, giving access to a small platform near the top. Bocalas indicated that Serpicus should climb. He pulled himself up gingerly. From behind the wall he could hear a deep gurgling sound, and the rustle of something large moving about.

Serpicus stepped onto the platform and looked over carefully. The floor had been dug down on the other side, making the wall higher on that side. The floor was strewn with straw. In several places there were areas reddened with dried blood.

And there, in the centre of the space, was the biggest bear Serpicus had ever seen.

Its head was long and pointed, unlike the round-faced brown bear, and much larger than the black bears he had seen. It looked up at Serpicus and made a curious up and down motion of its head as it stared at him. Its fur was indeed white, or, more accurately, a smoky yellow.

Serpicus supposed that the yellow colour was mostly dirt. The bear would no doubt be cleaned up before the crowd saw it in the arena. He'd known brown bears dyed black for the arena, so he didn't suppose that the Master of Games would have any scruples about putting this one through a pool of whitewash to make it shine in the sunlight and show off the blood of the men who came to fight it.

Serpicus looked back down at Bocalas.

'What do you think?' asked the druid.

'I've never seen anything like it,' Serpicus whispered. 'It's magnificent. And huge – how on earth did you get it into this place?'

Bocalas smiled. 'Brave young men with long stout sticks, lots of ropes and a freshly slaughtered cow for bait,' he said. He motioned Serpicus to stand to one side, and climbed the ladder. When he was standing next to him, he put a hand on Serpicus' chest and pushed him gently to arm's length.

'Watch. Don't move or speak,' he said.

He leant over the wall and made a guttural sound deep in his throat. The bear looked up. Its head moved up and down and then it rocked back so its weight was over its hindquarters. Then it stood up like a man. Its head and paws reached easily over the wall. Serpicus felt himself flinch and forced himself to stay still. Bocalas was within easy reach. One swipe of its paw and he would be lying broken on the ground.

Serpicus watched as the man and the animal stood within touching distance. Neither of them moved or made any noise for what seemed a very long time. Then

Bocalas made the sort of sound that a man might make to a guard-dog which has got up to check the source of a sound, telling it not to worry and go back to sleep. The bear slid back down into the pen. Serpicus breathed again.

Bocalas turned and smiled, pleased with the display.

'Do you control it?' asked Serpicus.

The druid shook his head. 'No man controls him,' he said. 'But he enjoys our conversations. I believe he respects me, as I respect him.'

Serpicus stood and looked down at the bear, which looked back with indifference. The size of the task in front of him became all too obvious. Blaesus hadn't mentioned that the bear was twice the size of any animal Serpicus had seen before. Getting it into a cage that could hold it and dragging it several hundred leagues along roads that were mostly mud and pot-holes while keeping it fed and alive was a bad enough prospect, without having to dodge irate warriors from the Treveri objecting to the removal of their sacred animal. And then getting it over the Hinterrhein Pass, and through the winter snows that stood between them and Rome. All that was in front of them, assuming that somehow they could get it safely out of the village past several thousand besieging Romans. Serpicus shook his head.

It was impossible.

He looked down at Bocalas. The druid had a seraphic smile on his face that suggested he was privy to Serpicus' thoughts.

'I don't envy you,' he said.

'I don't envy me either,' said Serpicus. He slid down the ladder. 'Do you have any suggestions?'

Bocalas' face looked serious, although Serpicus suspected that the shine in his eyes was amusement as well as torch-light. 'Have you considered divine intervention?'

'Actually, it's strange that you should mention that,' said Serpicus.

He had made a lot of sacrifices to Mercury when he had been a charioteer. Maybe he still had some credit with the gods, if their remit operated this far from Rome. He was about to find out.

27

Bocalas looked at Serpicus in a way that seemed to go through him and out of the back of his head.

'You said you owed me a debt,' said Serpicus.

'Are you sure that this is what you want?' Bocalas asked again. 'The Romans are coming, it is a strange time. Perhaps you are too eager?'

'It's what I want,' Serpicus said.

Bocalas looked at him seriously for a while. Eventually he spoke in a quiet voice. 'To ask the gods a question is not like asking a shopkeeper what he has for sale today. Sometimes the gods do not reply. Sometimes they do reply, but not to the question we have asked. Sometimes they reply, but their answer may seem playful or even hurtful.' He paused. 'Sometimes they lie, sometimes for a reason, sometimes for no reason we can see.'

'But sometimes they tell the truth,' Serpicus said.

The old man nodded. 'Yes, sometimes they tell the truth.'

Serpicus sat up straight. 'Then I will take that chance.'

Bocalas looked at him once more and Serpicus saw that he had made his decision. The old man blew out the torch and Serpicus heard him moving around in the gloom. There was a rustling sound behind him and then someone – presumably Bocalas' silent boy – placed a cloth bag over his head and pulled it tight over his eyes. The cloth was thin, but the evening was already nearly over; he could see nothing. A deep emotionless voice – not that of Bocalas – told Serpicus to put his hands out, rest them in front of him and follow where he was led. His hands settled on thin shoulders. As soon as Serpicus complied, he heard the noise of the door to the barn opening, and whoever was in front of him started walking slowly in the direction of the forest.

Serpicus had no idea who he was following, nor how long they walked for, nor how deep into the forest they went. It could have been that they walked for a good distance in a straight line or for a long time in a series of small circles. The ground underfoot was flat, like a well-worn path, with nothing to step over or walk around, that much he knew, and little else. He soon stopped thinking about it and turned over in his mind what lay ahead. He knew nothing, so his imagination had full rein. He remembered that, when he was a child, he was told stories of what the druid's ceremonies were like, and he had nightmares about them, all the children did. It was possible that the stories were designed to keep the children away from the druids' sacred places. If so, they succeeded.

In Rome, after the German campaigns, veterans

regaled dinner-parties with tales of the druids' debauchery, of ceremonies of licentiousness and human sacrifice. Serpicus had always been fairly sure that these stories were not true, but, as he walked into the forest like a blind man with his hands outstretched on a stranger's shoulders, he realized he had no idea what was about to happen. He knew that they were on a small island connected to the rest of the world by a neck of land which had a Roman army camped across it, and yet he heard no shouts and smelt no fires. He heard the noises of a forest at night, and yet there was no forest on the island, and he walked for a long time, much longer than it would take to cross the village.

He had questions, but no answers. He dealt with the confusion by allowing the questions to slip away, until his mind was only aware of walking and listening.

The shoulders in front of him came to a sudden stop. Large hands took Serpicus by the wrists, lifted them off the shoulders of his guide and let them drop by his sides.

'There is a seat beside you,' said the deep voice. 'Rest a moment.'

Serpicus stretched out a hand and found a flat rock beside him at waist height. He was tired after the walk, but wondered if whether he sat or not was some kind of test. He compromised by leaning against it as casually as he could.

A short distance away he heard the *aak-kraak* sound of the hawk, made deep in its throat.

Serpicus knew it must be dark but he could see no torches through the cloth around his eyes. The air was cool and damp. The ground was sodden from the rain. He listened hard, trying to anticipate what would happen, but there was almost complete silence. He heard the scrape of metal on rock, and then the faint but exact click of two pebbles striking each other. Of the normal forest night sounds, Serpicus could hear nothing. No hollow owl-call, no rustling as a fox or rabbit passed through the undergrowth, no yelp or growl or whine. The atmosphere thickened. His senses seemed unnaturally sharp in the silence, and yet he had no idea what was going to happen. He wondered if the feeling of anticipation was real or a product of his blinded imagination. The forest around him was wound tight like a catapult, waiting for something to happen.

Serpicus stood still for what seemed a very long time.

He was suddenly aware that someone was standing next to him. Then there was a voice, unnaturally loud as it broke the silence, and Serpicus recognized Bocalas' tones, but more stern and formal than before.

'In a moment I will take off your blindfold. Do not look to left or right, there is nothing to find out and it does not matter where you are. The God is in front of you. Stand before him and wait for your answer.'

'How shall I know when to ask my question?'

'Do not speak. The God already knows what you wish to ask him.'

The cloth bag was lifted over Serpicus' head in one movement, as if a conjuror were revealing his head to an audience, and he blinked in the sudden light of several torches placed in carved holders in a number of large stones set out at intervals nearby. Two large braziers glowed red and yellow, one at either side of a low altar.

Immediately in front of him was Bocalas' outstretched hand, holding a golden cup.

'Drink this,' Bocalas murmured. 'It will help you hear the God's voice clearly.'

Serpicus took the cup. The metal was warm. The liquid inside it was dark like wine and tasted of bitter herbs. It was strong but not unpleasant. Immediately he drank he felt fumes rising from deep in his belly, roiling in dizzying circles to his head. His mind had never been so clear and he felt wonderfully well. Everything came into sharp focus. Even though it was dark beyond the torches he could see every twig on the nearby branches, every blade of grass on the ground, every hair in Bocalas' beard. It was a feeling of absolute clarity, as though he could understand everything.

'Go to the altar,' said Bocalas.

Serpicus wondered if it was another test, if he should kneel or not. He waited, unmoving. It seemed the best thing. When the God appeared he would know what to do.

Suddenly Serpicus knew the God was there. Not because he could see or hear him, but because he just knew, could sense it. The God had appeared inside him.

A bright light appeared in front of him, as if he had been in a dark room and opened the door to the rising sun.

You seek knowledge of your loved ones.

The voice was light and musical, and strangely emotionless.

'Yes.' He wasn't sure if he had spoken out loud or not.

They cannot speak to you here.

His heart thumped and rolled around in his chest. 'Shall I never speak to them again?'

You will speak again, one day soon.

He didn't know what he should say. He waited.

You seek knowledge of the battle to come.

'The villagers do not seek to fight. They wish only to be permitted to continue their lives as they always have done.'

The voice became thoughtful. *Change surrounds us always.*

'But the Romans worship other gods of their own. Do not you, our own gods, protect us?'

Sometimes men think they serve one set of ends, but the gods have other plans. Nothing is certain.

'Will the village fall to the Romans?'

A pause.

You ask too much.

There was a heavy silence. Then Serpicus felt himself turned around by large hands, as if he was a doll in a child's game made to face another way, and he saw . . .

He saw Antonia in a pure white tunic that reached to the ground. She was standing against a background of thick mist, her hair spread out around her as if on a pillow. Her hair had the deep reddish glow of the setting sun. She was smiling languidly. He felt a warmth in his heart, which cooled as – somehow – he became aware that the person she was smiling at was not him. Without warning her face changed, tensed, as if she was suddenly lifting a weight from the ground. The glow of her hair darkened and began to flow outwards onto the mist like tendrils of thick smoke. Serpicus knew the smoke was blood.

Her eyes widened, then closed.

Then darkness.

Serpicus waited, his heart not beating.

'What does it mean?' he whispered, almost silently.

The darkness lifted. Bocalas was beside him, and the boy stood nearby. The hawk was nowhere to be seen.

'Bocalas, what does it mean?'

The druid's face was impassive. 'You asked the question, only you can understand the answer.'

The strength drained from Serpicus' legs and he sat down heavily. Bocalas looked at him. For a moment Serpicus thought the druid was going to call him a fool, but then the old man's expression softened. He lifted his robe and sat down beside him.

'I'll let you into a trade secret,' he said.

'What?' asked Serpicus.

The druid gave him a wistful smile. 'I've known a lot of men who have undergone what you've just done. Every one has asked the same question, wanted to know what the vision meant. I've given every man the same answer, and every man has gone away to come to his own decision. And do you know what?'

'What?'

Bocalas' expression turned rueful. 'Every single one of them was wrong.'

Serpicus stared at the darkness for a long time without speaking. Then the druid and the boy helped him silently to his feet and they made their way slowly back the way they had come.

28

The village was in turmoil. Heavily armed men with stern expressions were everywhere. Some paced purposefully, looking around as if enemies might jump out at them at any moment. Others stood still, tense and expectant, waiting. Serpicus stopped a fierce-looking warrior.

'What's happening?'

The German's eyes narrowed. 'You were with those Romans. Stay away from me if you want to live.' He pulled his arm free and walked quickly away.

Serpicus hurried to the barn. It was surrounded by armed men. Some of them stood on agitated guard, others were engaged in furious argument. Serpicus looked around and saw a familiar face, red with passion.

'Hansi, what's happened?'

Hansi turned to him in surprise. The man he was arguing with reached for his sword. Hansi's hand went out to stop him. 'It's all right.'

'It bloody isn't,' said the man. 'He's one of them.'

'One of who?' asked Serpicus.

'A Roman,' he said. 'A bloody assassin.'

Serpicus' expression of bewilderment gave Hansi time to grab the man's wrist and push the sword back into its scabbard.

'He's not a Roman and he certainly isn't an assassin. He was born here, he's one of us.'

The warrior looked at him doubtfully. 'Men change,' he said. 'Men can be bought. Even Germans.'

Serpicus pulled Hansi around to face him. 'Will someone please tell me what's going on?' Hansi looked at him with curiosity.

'You don't know? Where have you been?'

'With Bocalas. What happened?'

'One of your men killed a guard and tried to kill Drenthe.'

Serpicus felt his heart dip and lurch. 'What? Is she all right? Who did it?'

The man beside Hansi narrowed his eyes. 'Does it matter who? You brought them into our village. They ate with us and all the time they were planning to betray us. We should kill you all, now, and be done with traitors.'

Serpicus concentrated on the important things.

'Where is Drenthe?'

'You think we would tell you?'

Serpicus fought down his exasperation. 'Don't be stupid. Take my sword, tie my hands if it'll make you feel better, but I must see her.'

Hansi looked at Serpicus, then reached out and pulled the sword from his belt. 'You must understand the situation. Walk in front of me, don't try and get beyond my reach, don't do anything sudden. If you move too fast or do anything I don't like, I will kill you, understand?' He pushed Serpicus forward and walked behind him, just out of reach, the sword pricking the skin between his shoulders. The other man strode behind him, fingering his sword and muttering darkly.

They went to a small house behind the Hall. Hansi pushed Serpicus against a wall and hammered on the door. There was the sound of footsteps inside. The door opened slowly and light from a torch fell onto the ground.

'Who is it?' said a female voice. Hansi stepped into the light, pulling Serpicus by the arm. The voice became alarmed. 'What do you want? Why have you brought him here? He should be in the barn with all the others. He's one of them.'

'No, he is not,' said Drenthe's voice from inside before Hansi could reply. 'Let him in.'

'But he . . .'

Drenthe said something indistinct and the door was grudgingly opened. The guard stood beside it looking suspicious, her sword drawn and ready. The other three were between Serpicus and the inside of the room, their eyes alert and their weapons ready. Serpicus stepped through the doorway and the woman nearest him put her hands on his shoulders and spun him around, then pushed him roughly against the door and searched him thoroughly for weapons. Serpicus said nothing until she was finished, then turned and raised his hands in warning.

'I am unarmed. I am of your tribe. That is enough.'

The woman moved towards him angrily.

'Leave him,' said Drenthe. She sounded weary.

The woman hesitated but didn't lower her sword or take her eyes off Serpicus as he went over to Drenthe. Everything about the four guards oozed suspicion. Even if Serpicus had been an assassin, he didn't think he would have had a chance to strike.

She was sitting on a low stool near the fire. There was fresh blood on her forearm and more smeared down her thigh. An old woman was using a broad-bladed knife to smear a foul-smelling ointment around a deep cut on Drenthe's left shoulder. She winced as the cold metal crossed the wound.

'What happened?' asked Serpicus, kneeling beside her.

'You should know,' said the woman who had searched him. Serpicus ignored her.

Balant strode into the room, a drawn sword in his hand. The women all jumped forward with their weapons ready, then relaxed slightly as they recognized him. Serpicus stood up, not wanting Balant to be above him.

Drenthe looked up and nodded to Balant, then growled with pain as the old woman made a final pass with her spatula and raised the wounded arm up so that she could bandage it.

'Who did this?' demanded Balant.

'It was the tall thin one who came with you,' Drenthe said, looking at Serpicus.

Serpicus thought for a moment, then Snake's warnings rose up inside him. 'Do you mean Cato?'

'I don't know his name. After you left he came to me

and said that you needed to see me, that I was to come alone.'

Serpicus leant forward. 'I never sent any message.'

'That's what you say,' snarled one of the guards.

Drenthe smiled faintly at him. 'I know. I should have realized,' she said.

'What happened?' said Balant.

'He showed me into this house, saying that you were waiting for me here. As I came in I must have sensed that something was wrong, because I turned around just as he struck at me. His knife missed my throat, or I would not be here.' She looked at the bandage with distaste. 'Once I had my sword ready he hesitated, then he heard footsteps and ran out into the dark. By the time I got to the doorway he was gone.' She smiled at the women standing beside her. 'Then these four came running up. They had disobeyed my strict orders, came creeping after me. I owe them my life, again.'

Balant pointed at Serpicus with his sword. 'She got this wound because of you.'

Drenthe put a hand on Serpicus' arm as he turned to defend himself. 'It is not his fault that the assassin used him to attack me, but mine that I did not suspect that someone might do so.'

Balant looked seriously at Drenthe. 'You defend him for the sake of the past, but you do not know if he is still to be trusted.'

Drenthe looked at Serpicus and then at Balant. 'I know him. I trust him. The tall thin man is the guilty one, and him alone. Find him for me.'

'I have men searching the whole village,' said Balant.

He stood and extended his arm to Serpicus. 'If Drenthe trusts you then I must too. I am sorry for what I said.'

Serpicus took his hand. 'Thank you. I ask that you go to the barn where my friends are. Your men there are angry and blood will be spilt.'

Balant nodded. 'I will. I suggest you stay here for now. It is safest for everyone.' He turned and left.

Serpicus furrowed his brow, thinking hard. Cato had earned his trust, not least by saving his life. And yet there could be no doubt. He was a spy, an assassin. Everything had been a front, a trick. Serpicus looked at Drenthe's wound and felt sick. Snake had warned him about Cato and he had ignored it. As a result of his misjudgement she could have been killed.

Drenthe exhaled slowly as the woman finished bandaging her arm. 'Do you know why anyone would want to do this?' Serpicus shook his head and stood up. She looked at him enquiringly.

'I must see that my friends are all right, and help them get ready to leave,' he said, and hesitated. There was more to her question. 'I don't know who Cato was or why he did this,' he said, 'but I shall find out.'

To Aelius Sejanus, from his Servant:

> *I am now with the legion camped around Gelbheim. I deemed it proper to leave the village once I had gained all the intelligence I could. The woman Drenthe is wounded, possibly fatally. It was not possible to stay to verify this. The village is entirely surrounded and completely secure, and no German will pass in or out.*

Preparations are well in hand for the attack on the German village. I have personally taken command of the intelligence-gathering operation. I have also assured the General of my support, while ensuring that he is aware of the consequences of failure.

I shall write as soon as the village has surrendered, informing you of the situation.

Looking out of the door of the barn, Serpicus guessed that the dawn was perhaps an hour away, although the clouds were so low and grey that the day was never likely to bring much relief from the dark. It was raining hard again and bitterly cold.

'Just the weather for a swim,' Galba said cheerfully. Several of the men looked at him in a way that made further remarks unlikely.

The soldiers had emptied their packs and stripped off the motley collection of legionary armour and clothing they wore. Added together, there were just about enough pieces of uniform between them for five men and a centurion to look reasonably convincing. At least, they would 'On a dark night when no one is doing inspections,' as Severus put it with a sorrowful shake of the head. All of them were missing some piece of equipment, but there was enough to get by. Severus in particular would pass for a centurion unless someone looked too closely, except that he was older than most and he didn't have a helmet. Age wasn't really a problem, but no centurion would be seen without his helmet while on a campaign. The plumes were a jealously guarded privilege and it would be strange for him to be seen without one.

331

Brutus came back into the barn and tossed a bundle to Severus. He caught it and unwrapped a centurion's helmet, with full plumes.

'That poor bastard we saw at supper?' said Severus.

Brutus nodded. 'I had to thump someone who was about to run off with it for a souvenir.'

Severus looked at it thoughtfully and then tried it on. It was far too small.

'I'll carry it,' he said. 'At least I've got the thing, I can always say that the chin-strap is broken or something.'

'Actually, the chin-strap *is* broken,' said Brutus.

'Then that's decided.' Severus looked critically at the five men dressed as legionaries and shook his head slowly. 'The sorriest lot of soldiers I've ever seen,' he said. 'It's just as well it's raining. Keep your cloaks wrapped around you and hope no one notices that you're only half dressed.'

The men who didn't have uniforms would have to swim to safety. Severus insisted on overseeing the preparations, making sure that they smeared themselves thoroughly with the pungent goose-fat that an unwilling cook had given Decius. Each man tied two inflated wineskins to his belt and slung two more under his arms.

'Wrap your weapons in your cloak and tie it to your back,' Severus said, moving down the line. 'It'll help keep you the right way up. It's every man for himself on the water. As soon as you hit land, try and regroup, but don't waste time.'

Serpicus took over. 'Start walking north. There is a crossing about ten leagues upriver beside a hill shaped

332

like a lion's head. Head south-east until you hit the road home.'

Severus looked at them with something that might have been affection. 'We'll wait for you at the Hinterrhein. Don't be late. Anyone who drowns will have me to answer to.'

Scipio looked up from spreading a final fist of goose-fat onto his chest. 'Hell, we'll get there first, we'll wait for you.'

Severus looked affronted. 'Ten sesterces say we beat you by a day.'

'Ten sesterces for every day we beat you by.'

'Can I bet too?' said Brutus.

'No non-participants,' said Scipio quickly with a laugh which died in his throat. There was an uncomfortable silence. Those who were leaving looked at those who were staying. They had spent a month constantly in each other's company and now they were on opposite sides. Several of the men clasped hands with Snake and the Gauls. Scipio reached out his hand to Serpicus.

'I'm glad we came,' he said, and inclined his head before walking away. Severus walked slowly around the table and stood in front of Serpicus.

'I'm sorry for the way things are,' he said quietly.

A picture of Antonia and the children appeared in Serpicus' mind. He pushed it aside. 'It's not your fault,' he said. 'Everyone understands.'

Severus cleared his throat and spoke up. 'When you return to Rome, I'll back up your story. Blaesus won't have any grounds for thinking you cheated him.'

Serpicus did his best to look positive. 'I suspect

Blaesus won't be in a mood for listening, but I appreciate the thought.'

Severus looked at Brutus, Galba and Decius, and raised a finger to his forehead in salute. Then he turned to Snake and the two Gauls. 'You should come with us. When the legions come in over the walls, it won't be pretty.'

Snake stepped forward and held out his hand. As Severus shook it the Cretan said, 'Thanks for the thought. Will you please all fuck off now and stop making a sentimental mess out of it?'

There was a brief flurry of leave-taking, a call from Scipio of 'Everyone meets in the Four Cats by the Forum a year from today, last one there buys the drinks,' and then the men filed out of the barn and split into their two groups. A soaked and rain-chilled group of German warriors were still standing sullenly outside. Balant had warned them sternly off their original intention of hanging all of their guests from convenient branches, but they weren't happy about it. Most of them had gone back to look at the Roman fires from the wall, but a fair few had remained and appointed themselves as guards to ensure that their guests left without further trouble or delay. It was very dark and the rain made any sort of farewell difficult. Scipio shouted 'The Four Cats, don't forget!' again and then his men set off towards the river. Serpicus reckoned it was as good a way of parting as any.

He went with Severus and his five motley legionaries to the gate. They made sure that there were no lights shining behind them to reveal any movement, and then started to walk quietly towards the Roman fires.

A short time later, they were talking to a thoroughly miserable group of legionaries huddled beside a picket fire. The plan was working. The dawn was so dark, the hour so late and the weather so miserable that they got within ten steps of the fire before the shivering guards even noticed them. The legionaries jumped to attention at the sight of an inspecting centurion with an escort coming from the gloom, and were visibly relieved to escape the barnacling they knew they deserved. Severus made a few army jokes about the foul weather and the Germans' unattractively webbed feet which were received with enthusiasm, and the guards were beginning to wonder if all officers were really bastards by the time he saluted and set off towards the Roman tents.

Severus marched straight into the centre of the camp and indicated that they should form a circle around him. Guards were visible nearby but were watching from under what shelter they could find. Severus would not be overheard, and there was no reason for suspicion.

'All right,' he said quietly. 'Now we split up and get out of here nice and easy. The guards on the far side of the camp won't be expecting trouble. Take a spade with you and walk out like you know where you're going. Anybody queries you, you've got bad guts from this foul bloody German food and you're going to dig a big bloody hole for yourself and they are welcome to bloody well come and watch. Anybody queries that, the normal latrines are flooded and if he doesn't believe you he should go and look for himself but you aren't stopping. All right?' He turned slowly and looked up the hill where they had camped on the morning of their arrival. 'Soon as you get out of sight, double-time up the hill. We meet at the top, beside the stone with the carved lines. We wait for an hour and then we go. Anyone not there by then is on his own and will have to catch us up at the Hinterrhein. Any questions?'

There were none. Severus turned to Serpicus. 'Don't suppose you'll be coming with us?'

Serpicus smiled and shook his head. 'I'll take a look around, see if I can find anything out.'

'Good luck then. I'm sorry it has to be like this.'

'It's the only way. Don't worry.'

Severus smiled. 'The Four Cats, then?'

Serpicus touched a finger to his forehead in salute. 'The Four Cats.'

Severus and the others walked silently away.

Serpicus looked around, suddenly uncomfortably aware that he was on his own in the centre of the Roman camp. His cloak hid the fact that he was not wearing uniform, but if he was challenged it would not take long to find out who he was. He moved into shadow and circled around the centre of the camp. It was raining hard and there were few guards doing more than trying to keep dry. That made it easier to move around, but it also made him look suspicious as no one would be out in such weather without having to be. He moved quietly from shadow to shadow, stopping each time to listen and watch for guards, until he found a tent that was deserted. There were eight legionary packs with bedrolls in two neat rows, and spare equipment piled symmetrically next to each. He helped himself to an extra cloak to help his disguise. Poking around the tent he found a long Persian knife, which he put in his belt and then went out again. He headed back towards the centre of the camp, stopping to listen for a short while outside each tent, hoping to find out something useful.

Some time later he was cold and wet through and had listened beside what seemed like every tent in the camp without learning anything about the plan of attack on Gelbheim. He knew what the legionaries had had for supper, and learned the names of three brothels in Rome he'd never heard of and made a note of them for Brutus, but no plan.

Serpicus moved quietly towards a large tent with a canopy over the entrance. Two legionaries were standing on guard under the shelter. Canopies and guards meant officers. He slipped quietly behind the tent and crouched down to listen. There were subdued voices inside. He listened for a little time without being able to make out a thing.

As he stood up there was a soft sound behind him. He whirled round. A shapeless shadow moved nearby. He raised a hand instinctively to defend himself, then one of Vulcan's anvils fell out of heaven and landed on his head.

Serpicus knew that he was dreaming. In his dream he was sitting unconscious in a chair, and a flaming torch was being held just under his nose, as if the smoke would revive him. He could smell the flames, feel the heat, hear it crackling as it burned him. He opened his eyes.

He was sitting in a chair.

His hands and legs were tied.

337

His face was on fire.

For a moment he couldn't feel the landslide of pain he knew must be hurtling his way. And then it came, like a mountain collapsing on him. He threw his head back with a gasp and hit something soft behind him. There was a guttural gasp of pain.

'Ah, good,' said a familiar voice. 'He's awake at last.'

'Give me that fucking torch for a moment and I'll shove it into your face, see how long you stay asleep,' Serpicus hissed, shaking his head to relieve the pain. And then he knew who had spoken to him.

'He's broken my nose!' said a different voice from behind him, one he didn't recognize. By the harsh slurred accent, a soldier from the Tiber's east side, the worst part of the worst slums of Rome.

'Well,' said the familiar voice languidly. 'I suggest you hit him somewhere that won't stop him talking, check he is still firmly tied up, and then go and get someone to fix your face.'

There was a sound suspiciously like a chuckle of amusement. A fist like a toppling key-stone slammed deep into Serpicus' stomach twice in quick succession, then, as he arched forward with pain, smashed down onto the back of his neck, spilling pain across his shoulders and a blinding light into his temples. Serpicus bent over, choking and gasping for air.

The soldier with the broken nose put ropes around Serpicus' hands to hold them even more firmly to the arms of the chair, cursing softly as the blood streamed down off his chin.

'So, Cato,' Serpicus said, still breathing hard. His face

338

was agony. He fought to ignore it. 'I see you still do your own racking and branding. I gather most people in your position get their servants to do it for them.' He couldn't quite get his mouth under control, the sibilants were sending out spit every time he tried one. 'Good to know that the old Roman virtue of self-reliance is still alive in you, at least where torture is concerned.'

The philosophers say that when a man knows the hour of his death, it makes him free. That wasn't why Serpicus insulted Cato. Serpicus insulted him because the man was a lying two-faced bastard who had roasted half Serpicus' face off, and insulting him took his mind a little off the pain.

Cato held the torch to one side so that he could look closely at his prisoner. 'Oh, I normally do get someone else to do it,' he said casually. 'So tedious. The noise, the mess, you know. But in your case I'm delighted to make an exception.'

His voice was urbane, emotionless, inhuman as the rain falling on the canvas above them. Serpicus tried to prevent a shiver running across his body. Hearing it was like touching a dead man's face.

'Why did you go to all this trouble?' Serpicus asked. 'There are three legions outside Gelbheim. Drenthe is probably going to die anyway.'

Cato smiled. 'She's the key,' he said. 'Not only is she the leader of Gelbheim but she's holding the Treveri together. Kill her first and the revolt falls apart. As long as she lives there is a chance the other tribes may rise to help her.' He looked at a fingernail. 'Of course, as you say, she's going to die soon anyway.'

The soldier finished tying Serpicus' ankles to the chair-legs, then leant forward and spat a mouthful of blood into his face. He was close enough for Serpicus to smell the stale sweat on his clothes.

'Enough.'

Another voice.

The soldier stood to startled attention facing the entrance, then, dismissed, walked quickly from the tent. A tall figure came from behind Cato, took the torch from his hand and placed it in a holder. Near enough to bring back into use again very quickly, but a bit further away. The light showed Serpicus who the man was. Serpicus tried not to think about what his own face must look like, and nodded to him.

'Marcus,' he said. 'You here for the show too?'

Marcus folded his arms. 'No. I came to make sure that it was really you. Cato will perform the interrogation.'

'I'm flattered.' Every time Serpicus spoke he could feel the skin of his lips stiffening and cracking, and blood flowing slowly from them.

'Don't be. He started all this. He should be allowed to finish it.' Marcus smiled at Serpicus' expression and turned away. He walked to the far side of the tent and sat in the shadows near the entrance.

'You know that in time you will tell me anything that I want to know,' Cato said, settling himself against the edge of a table like a schoolmaster. 'The only issue you have to decide is how much pain you wish to endure before you tell it to me. As you're going to tell me anyhow soon, wouldn't you rather spare yourself the pain?'

'Depends,' Serpicus said.

340

'On what?'

'What you tell me.'

'That's unhelpful,' Cato said reproachfully, 'but I don't mind sharing. Especially seeing as we've already shared so much.' He paused and smiled amiably. 'You don't know yet just how often we've shared things, do you?'

Serpicus said nothing. Cato came around and spoke into his face. His breath smelt of goat's cheese and black olives.

'Remember when the steward came to the arena stables to invite you to dinner at the Palace of the Partner?' He waited. Serpicus said nothing, but he could see that Cato knew he remembered. 'Remember how you and your barbarian friends tied that pompous old fool Calcas up in knots?' Cato grinned and his voice rose slightly. He was enjoying himself. He paused, waiting to announce the surprise. 'I was there.'

Serpicus didn't know what Cato was going to say but he knew that he wasn't going to give him the satisfaction of a reaction. Now Serpicus' mind raced. He had known everyone who had been there that day, except Calcas the messenger and his slave, and one or two of the chariot drivers although they had all been at least faintly familiar . . .

The slave.

Something must have flickered in Serpicus' eyes. 'Ah. I see you do remember me, I am flattered.' Cato smiled and clapped his hands like an actor when a witness praises a performance long past. He leant forward, watching Serpicus' eyes. 'And that long conversation

341

with the Partner's uncle the next day, I was there too. When you spoke with Blaesus, I saw everything, heard every word you said.' He must have thought Serpicus' expression changed. 'Yes. It's true. Though you wouldn't have seen me, so you couldn't be expected to remember that occasion.'

Serpicus remembered. There had been shadows moving in the corners of the room. He'd assumed that powerful men are never alone.

Cato went on. 'I have to confess, when I met all of you again that day on the pier at Genoa, I did wonder if my faith in my disguise was justified, if I might have been over-confident. I wondered as you approached if changing my stance and growing my beard would be enough.' He smiled. 'Then in moments I saw that it was. Very gratifying, I have to say.' He stood in front of his prisoner. He was preening himself like an ageing courtesan.

'Yes, how you fooled us, a bunch of drunks in the dark, with your brilliant disguises,' Serpicus said. Speaking helped him ignore the pain. 'Disguises aren't all that clever. Wrap an arsehole in silk, it'll still look like all the other arseholes around it.'

Cato hesitated a moment. Serpicus wasn't surprised, he didn't really know what that remark meant either, but hoped Cato would take it as an insult anyway. Cato stroked his chin for a moment, and then with all his strength he smashed the back of his hand against Serpicus' cheek. The burnt side of his face. A heavy signet ring on Cato's middle finger ripped a gobbet of scorched flesh from Serpicus' cheek-bone, sending an iron lance of pain across his temples. It took everything Serpicus had not to howl like a whipped dog. Perhaps, he reflected as the pain ebbed slightly and he fought for breath, insulting Cato while roasted and tied up wasn't the best idea he'd had that day.

Cato inspected his hand thoughtfully, then picked up a cloth napkin and slowly cleaned the blood off the ring without taking his eyes from Serpicus' face.

'Of course,' Cato said, looking at the ceiling, 'that's not all that you and I have in common.'

Something snapped inside Serpicus. 'We have absolutely nothing in common,' he said. Cato's eyes opened wide.

'Oh, but we do,' he said. He leant forward and put his hands on Serpicus' bound forearms. 'After all, apart from anything else, we have shared loved ones. I got to know your lovely family really quite well in the regrettably short time that it took you to organize and undertake this trip.'

Cato smiled into Serpicus' face while he waited for his prisoner to realize what he meant. It took a moment.

A heavy red curtain fell across Serpicus' eyes. A huge bubble of pressure expanded in his head. He fought to control it. Cato was lying. Antonia had said nothing, nothing had happened . . .

Then the curtain fell back and he fought to control his breathing. Cato watched him carefully.

'Your children, Priscus, wasn't it, and the other? The little girl?' Serpicus said nothing, although the blood flowed through him as water flows through a storm drain. Cato shrugged and went on. 'Lovely children,

343

most amusing, bright, intelligent, almost good-looking for barbarians.' He paused and showed his teeth and Serpicus knew what was coming. 'And of course your wife, well, what a delightful creature she is, no? You are a lucky man, anyone could see that. Those eyes, that lustrous hair, what man would not want her? That beautiful skin . . .' His voice tailed away and he paused. Serpicus prepared himself as for a blow. Cato had a habit of hesitating just as he was about to drive the nail in deepest. The blood pounded through Serpicus' forehead. It was as if a sword was spinning in the air above his head and all he could do was wait for it to fall where it would. She said nothing, she said nothing . . .

'And of course, the tricks she knew!' He raised an eyebrow and spoke slowly, as if his thoughts were far away. 'One had to admire her professionalism. Like an Egyptian whore on heat, working her way in pairs through three cohorts of athletic young legionaries and all the way back down the line until every man was worn out, and she was screaming for more throughout. You are indeed a lucky man to have had all that for yourself.' He stood up, and his voice became wistful. 'Or should I say, you were.'

The sword fell and Serpicus felt its point scythe into his heart. Cato went to the table and poured a cup of wine. He let Serpicus absorb what he had said, let him pick it up, examine it, roll it around in his hands. Let him take a good look at how his life had just run up against the lip of a cliff.

It wasn't true. Couldn't be.

'You lie,' Serpicus whispered. There wasn't time. Cato

was already in Genoa when Serpicus arrived, so he couldn't have . . . but someone else could have given her to the soldiers. Cato could be embellishing something he hadn't seen himself, but that didn't mean it hadn't happened.

'You think so?' Cato asked. 'Which bit? All of it?' He took a sip of wine. 'I can produce the men I mentioned if you want, most of them serve in this very legion.' He took another sip. 'Fortuitously enough in fact, I believe both the guards outside were amongst those most entertained by your wife, shall I call them in to tell you about it?'

A great burning fist was crushing everything inside Serpicus' chest. He knew Cato must be lying. He knew Cato wanted him to ask, was waiting for him to ask, and Serpicus knew that he must ask, must know, and Cato knew it. So Serpicus asked.

'What have you done?'

'Done?'

'I was promised . . .'

Cato's eyes suddenly hardened. 'I promised nothing.'

'They were not to be harmed. Promised, by Blaesus. He speaks for Rome, for the Emperor.'

Cato shook his head. 'I am charged to protect the State. Promises – even those made by the uncle of the Emperor's Partner, and of course we have only your word for that – mean nothing when the security of Rome is threatened.'

'Threatened?' Serpicus felt as if he was living in a dream. He knew what had happened, that it was too late, and yet he was incredulous, arguing as if the situation could still be saved. 'In what way did I threaten the State, and how much less did a woman and two small children?' He laughed, feeling the skin on his face tear. 'I trap animals for a living. All I ever wanted was to be left alone, all I ever did was what I was told to do.' He realized he was trying to reason with Cato and hated himself for it, but there was nothing else he could do. 'I was told to fetch an animal for Blaesus and my family would be looked after.'

'Well,' Cato said. 'In a manner of speaking they were.' A thought struck him. 'Oh, I nearly forgot. It occurred to me that you might not believe my story, so I brought this for you.'

He pulled something out of his pocket, unlooped a leather thong and placed it over Serpicus' head.

Serpicus knew what it was without looking.

Cato waited. 'Nothing to say? After I brought that half-way across the Empire to give to you?' He leant forward with an air of concern. 'It is the right one, isn't it? Not another one like it in the world, the only one that matches yours, am I right?'

Serpicus was waiting for his heart to break in two as it must and let him fall insensible to the floor, but somehow it kept on beating. The amulet hung like a stone around his neck, pressing against his chest and stopping his breath. He was cold, colder than he had ever felt before, and he realized that he no longer felt any pain from the burn on his face.

'Listen to me, Roman,' he said softly. He could hear the skin cracking more as he spoke.

Cato tipped his head to one side in a parody of attention. 'I hear you.'

'I have one thing to say to you now, and then I will never speak to you again except at the moment of your death.'

Cato smiled and picked up the cup. 'Then you definitely have my full attention. What can it be that is so momentous?'

Serpicus took a breath and waited for it to flow out of him. It felt cold in his mouth, sharp against the metal of the blood and the tar of the burnt skin. A calmness filled him.

'You should kill me now.'

Cato looked amused. He took a sip of wine. 'Why should I do that? Just when we were having so much fun together.'

'You should kill me now, because I will tell you nothing more except this: that if I ever leave this tent alive then I will dedicate every moment I live, every breath I take, to hunting you, until you are under my sword, and then I will speak my wife's name to you and it will be the last thing you will hear.'

Cato seemed to smile, then the hand with the goblet smashed hard against Serpicus' mouth. Blood poured down his chin. Cato pulled a small leather bottle from his belt, unstoppered it and forced the neck between Serpicus' lips. Then he grasped Serpicus' mouth and jammed stiff fingers into his cheeks, forcing his mouth open. The pain from his face was beyond anything Serpicus had ever felt.

'Oh, you will tell me things,' Cato said softly, tipping a bitter liquid into Serpicus' mouth. Serpicus managed to spit some of it out, but he had no choice: swallow or choke. Most of it went down his throat. 'You will tell me everything I want to know, and then you will beg me to kill you, and when I have heard enough begging I will oblige you.' Cato tossed the empty bottle aside and started to scratch lines on the wooden table with the point of the Persian knife that Serpicus had stolen. 'Just as I did with your wife.'

Again, Serpicus waited for his heart to break, again somehow it still continued to beat beneath the heavy ice within him.

The sound of voices came from outside and the flap of the tent was pushed inward. A centurion entered. He saw Cato and hesitated.

'Yes?'

The centurion looked about to speak, and then saw Marcus sitting in the shadow. An expression of relief crossed his face as he turned from Cato and saluted Marcus.

'What is it?' asked Marcus, standing and walking forward into the light.

'A fire has broken out on the east side of the camp, sir.'

'Fires don't just break out, centurion. Someone starts them.'

Cato glanced at Serpicus and laughed harshly. 'Friends of yours?'

Marcus ignored him. 'How serious is it?'

'Five tents are beyond help,' said the centurion. 'Next to the horse feed store, which is burning as well.'

'Coincidence,' murmured Cato. 'Or, I wonder, perhaps a diversion?'

Serpicus was wondering the same thing himself, but since Cato had forced him to drink his mind was a dull edge.

Marcus snapped a narrow-eyed look at Cato and then fired orders at the centurion. 'Get the fire put out. Save what you can but douse the fire without wasting time. Double the guard all round and triple it on the side facing the village. Warn the pickets to be extra vigilant. They may still be here in the camp. Take them alive if you can, but don't let them escape.'

'Sir!' The centurion was already leaving through the tent flaps before his salute was finished. Marcus started to follow him and then stopped.

'I'm going to the west side. It's probably just a nuisance raid, but if they do attack it'll be from there.' He looked at Serpicus, hesitated for a fleeting moment and then ducked through the flaps. The sounds of men shouting and running came through the gap.

'So, alone together at last,' said Cato. He walked behind his captive and drew the point of the Persian knife down the back of Serpicus' neck, hard enough to draw blood. Serpicus felt it as if it happened to someone else. 'What do you think? Is it just a pointless raid? Or will your friends wait for us to be occupied on one side of the camp and then attack on the other?' He leant around so that he could see Serpicus' face. 'Oh, sorry, I forgot, you aren't speaking to me. That's a firm resolve, I'm sure you won't break your promise.' He leant close. 'Not even nailing your balls to a tent pole and hanging you up like a flag will open your lips, of course not.' He tapped Serpicus' ear with the blade. Serpicus

349

heard it like waves in a sea-cave. 'Of course not.' He leant closer still and almost whispered. 'But I have an entertainment for you that might change your mind.'

The dark clouds in Serpicus' mind thickened and closed around him, and he heard nothing more.

When the clouds parted again and Serpicus opened his eyes, every object was indistinct, as if the world vibrated as he looked at it. He was still sitting in the same chair, but he had been turned around and moved into the deep shadows at the side of the tent.

He couldn't move his head, but by looking down he could see that the ropes around his arms had been removed. He tried to clench a fist and nothing happened. He told his legs to move, but they remained still. The ropes were now unnecessary: he could not move his limbs.

He could feel that the drug was still inside him; his mind seemed clear but he couldn't concentrate. Everything he looked at was now surrounded by a strange vibrant light, like a skin.

He blinked and bit his lip hard. The clouds in his mind were still there. He felt nothing from his lip, although he could taste the salt metal of his own blood. He felt no pain from the burn on his face or the blows Cato had given him. The drug had removed all feeling.

The heavy chair he sat on was now facing into what looked like Cato's private quarters. A single low torch illuminated the room. The light barely reached the thin curtain dividing the room from the area in which Cato had interrogated him. He was sitting immobile in complete darkness.

A large draped bed was at the centre of the room, surrounded by cushions and rugs, and at the end was a low table supporting two wine cups, a small jug and a bowl piled with fruit. Serpicus wondered if this was the entertainment that Cato had mentioned; if the chair had been deliberately placed in this position so that he could see the food but not get to it.

And then he found out.

Cato pushed a curtain aside and sat on the bed. He had taken off his armour, and wore only a short light tunic like a boy. He picked up both the wine cups and sipped from one of them, rolling the wine around his mouth and then swallowing with intense satisfaction. He looked in Serpicus' direction with a strange expression, almost grave, and then lifted the wine cup slightly in a toast and drank from it.

Then the curtain parted on the other side of the bed and a woman came in, wearing a similar short tunic. Her face was turned away from the man sitting still in the dark, but then Cato stood and carried the wine cup around the bed to give it to her. She turned to take it, smiled, and Serpicus saw her face.

The clouds in his mind parted to let a light burst through them like a spear passing through water, and a great hand reached down with the spear and seized his vitals and dragged them out through his throat, choking the scream that rose inside him.

She turned, smiled at Cato.

Serpicus closed his eyes, squeezed them hard and opened them again. She glowed with the strange light that the drug surrounded everything with.

351

She was looking directly at him, just as Cato had done, but could not see him. Serpicus strained helplessly against his invisible bonds. He was almost close enough to touch her and he could not even tell her that he was there.

And then Cato leant forward and took hold of the front of her tunic. Very slowly, very deliberately, he pulled it down and away from her, until she stood naked in front of him. She stood still, her eyes and her mouth both just open as he moved around her, running his hands lightly over her skin.

Serpicus waited for her to produce a knife, kill him, stab him again and again until he was a bloodied husk.

Nothing happened, just an eternity of watching as Cato caressed her.

Which is how for a few moments Serpicus knew that it was a dream, a confection of the clouds in his mind. She did not kill him; therefore it could only be a dream. It could be nothing else.

Until Cato slid his hand over her hip and down her thigh and brought it up again across her belly, and as his lips touched her breast she sighed and let her head fall back so that her hair hung free down her back, and Serpicus knew that sigh, felt it cut through him like a ragged blade, and knew – knew, beyond doubt, as he knew he lived and loved her – that it was no dream, that she was real, knew that he must move and was helpless, must scream and could not.

And so Serpicus watched in silence while they lay and moved on the bed together, heard the familiar sounds she made and the soft words she used, saw everything.

Watched with tears flowing down his cheeks, watched and waited for the clouds to close and release him, to tell him that it was his imagination, while knowing beyond doubt, beyond truth, that it was real.

After a lifetime had passed, Serpicus opened his eyes again. A huge numbness was gathered in his chest, a paralysing clenched hand that went beyond pain into something that there were no words for. His mind was empty, as if nothing had ever happened to him.

Cato stood in front of him.

His enemy. He knew that.

The Roman put a grape into his mouth, then reached out and put one between Serpicus' teeth. Serpicus felt a flicker of feeling in his lips. The drug seemed to be wearing off. He waited. Cato turned his back to reach for wine, and Serpicus tried to move. His limbs were still too heavy to lift, but he could move some of his toes and the thumb of his right hand. Cato turned to face him again. Serpicus relaxed. It was simple. He would wait until his powers returned, and then he would kill Cato. There was nothing else in his life.

Cato reached out and pushed Serpicus' slack jaw upwards until his teeth split the grape and juice spilled down his chin. Cato ate another and glanced over his shoulder at the disarranged sheets behind him.

'I never knew barbarian women had it in them,' he said. 'When you're dead I think I may marry her.' He looked thoughtful. 'Or perhaps I'll just have her until I grow bored and then give her to my house slaves.' He gestured to Serpicus. 'What do you think?'

Serpicus struggled until his mouth opened enough to let words escape. 'Why ... why do you hate me so much?'

Cato looked mildly surprised. 'Hate you?' He thought for a moment. 'Do I hate you? I suppose it might look like that, though I wasn't really aware of it until now.' He tapped his chin with a finger. 'Not so much hate, actually, as just annoyance. You wife, your children, your friends, your ...' he leant into Serpicus' face ... 'self-satisfaction, it irritates me. And I don't like being irritated.' He stood up again. 'And so, I now have your wife, I have your children, and I've killed most of your friends.' He smiled. 'And I have to admit, I do feel an awful lot better.'

Cato's voice was becoming indistinct, and Serpicus couldn't see properly. He was confused and didn't know what Cato was talking about. Strange images passed through his mind. He remembered his burnt face. He remembered the pain and wondered where he was. He was suddenly unutterably tired. His mind was full of smoke. He stopped listening and allowed the exhaustion to flow through him. He closed his eyes, just for a moment.

He had no idea how much time had passed. He thought he heard a cry of surprise, and then felt the wind of someone running past him. His face hurt. He could feel again, though it didn't seem important. There was something he needed to think about but his thoughts wouldn't cohere long enough to remember what it was. He tried to open his eyes but couldn't. There was a distant thud and sounds of a scuffle, and then he heard a whisper, felt breath on his cheek. A familiar voice said, 'Gods, what have they done?' Strong hands lifted him.

'Can you walk?'

'Of course I can,' Serpicus said, his voice a soft croak. 'I've been able to since I was three.'

A dirty thumb pressed against Serpicus' eyeball and lifted up the eyelid, a feat beyond its owner. 'He's completely gone to Hades,' someone hissed. 'Get him out of here, fast as you can. We'll watch your backs.'

'What about the Roman?'

'Kill him,' Serpicus shouted, but no one heard.

It was still dark when Serpicus woke up again. He had memories of being surrounded by shouting, of screams of pain, of being forced to run when all he wanted to do was sleep, of falling several times, of freezing water, and then being dragged to his feet again just as he had organized the water into a comfortable place to rest and made to run some more.

Serpicus opened his eyes slowly. He was indoors, lying on a bed. He had no idea how he had arrived there. His wounds were bandaged and the pain was less than he expected. There was some ointment on his face. His thoughts were splashing around in his head like drunken otters; he couldn't get two of them to go in the same direction for more than a moment. Nothing mattered very much, anything troubling him was a long way away. He was warm, it was quiet, he needed no encouragement to go back to sleep. Which should have been enough to tell him that Brutus and Galba were likely to walk in at that moment. Which they did.

'Stop pretending to sleep,' said Galba. Serpicus looked at them through eyes barely opened and tried to look as sick as possible.

'Ungrateful bastard,' said Brutus, sitting on the bed beside him. 'We stay up all night, walk bloody leagues, fight off half the Roman army just for the fun of dragging him all the way back here, and he just lies there in a heap.'

The fog in Serpicus' head parted enough to make him sit up. A sharp shaft of pain made him groan. He felt as though he had drunk a lot of very bad wine, but he was awake.

'Ah, he's back,' said Galba. He was eating an apple, and had another in his hand which he held out to Serpicus. Serpicus was suddenly starving, and accepted it gratefully. He lifted it to his lips and saw that Decius was sitting silently by the door. Serpicus wondered how long he had been there.

'So, what the hell happened to you?' said Brutus.

Serpicus frowned and bit into the apple without thinking. Pain curled around his cheek. He froze, and took the apple from his mouth, broke it in half and chewed a small piece gingerly on the unburnt side. 'I remember creeping around the camp and getting hit on the head.' He paused. His lips hurt nearly too much to let him talk. 'Cato was there.' He took a breath and tried to speak without moving them. 'I remember Cato setting fire to my face. He knocked me about a bit and then gave me something to drink. After that it's all a blur.' Brutus and Galba exchanged a glance.

'Cato was there? You're sure?'

'He's an officer. A Roman. Some sort of high-up anyway.'

Brutus sat back and let out a long sigh.

'He knows everything about us,' said Galba softly to himself. 'If he's there, then the Romans know how many of us there are, how much food there is, where the weak points are, everything.'

'Doesn't matter,' Brutus said irritably. 'Anyone could tell them that.'

Serpicus finished his apple and looked around hopefully for another, but there weren't any. 'How did you know I was in trouble?'

Brutus shrugged. 'We didn't, though it did cross our minds when you didn't come back. We decided to raid the camp anyway, and if we found you were in difficulties and we had the opportunity for a heroic rescue, so much the better.'

'What happened?'

Brutus gestured to Galba. 'Get him to tell you. It was his idea.'

Galba tried not to look pleased with himself. 'Not really.'

'Tell him anyway.'

Galba sat on a low chair. 'It was quite simple really. We floated down the river until we were past the pickets but before we got to the main army. The river is high and fast with all the rain and there are plenty of tree stumps and dead cattle in it, so there wasn't any reason for them to worry about a few extra bumps on the surface. We landed behind the pickets and walked quietly past the sentries. They hardly challenged us, because they knew that any attack coming at them would be spotted by the pickets first and so most of them were asleep. Brutus had to kill one of them who had got up to take a piss, but apart from that it was easy.' Galba grinned at Brutus who shrugged.

'So how did you find me?'

'We kept on setting fire to tents until just about every Roman was busy fighting the fires except the guards around the big tent they had you in.'

'They didn't see you?'

Brutus smiled. 'A few of them caught up with us so we had to stop and deal with them. Didn't take long. We bashed the tent guards on the head, grabbed you and made a run for it. We got to the river, threw you in and we all floated back down to the village again.'

'There must be more to it than that,' Serpicus said, half closing his eyes with the effort of memory. 'Marcus doubled the guard when the fire started, I remember, I heard him. The fire woke everyone up. You can't have given them the slip, not just like that.'

Galba shrugged. 'It was dark, and raining. No moon-light.'

Brutus nodded. 'And there was a lot of confusion.'

'And we didn't waste any time.' There was a pause. Brutus snapped his fingers together.

'Oh, and the Roman uniforms probably helped.'

Serpicus burst out laughing and then winced with the pain. 'You stole Roman uniforms?'

'Hardly stole. The owners had no further use for them.'

Serpicus started to laugh again, then a dark sun came into his head and the clouds parted. Memory flooded back.

It was as if leather helmet straps tightened suddenly around his neck and he could not breathe.

Galba leant forward looking concerned.

'What's the matter?'

'Cato told me that . . . that Antonia and the children were dead.'

Galba looked as if Serpicus had slapped him. 'What? They can't be.'

They questioned him, and Serpicus had to admit that Cato hadn't exactly said they were all dead. He'd let Serpicus think it, and he'd produced the ivory token to underline it. Serpicus still felt there was more to remember, but it just nibbled at the edge of the fabric of his mind, refusing to come out. He let it be. He had remembered one thing. Perhaps that was the nature of the drug. He might remember more as time passed.

'He probably did it just to make you angry.'

'That worked,' Serpicus said.

Brutus bit his bottom lip. 'Can I be honest?'

'Why not?'

'He's got no reason to kill them. Let's say we succeed, bring back the animal to Rome. All he wants is a quiet life. He doesn't want the Man Who Brought Back the White Bear looking for him with a sword. He doesn't need to do it.'

'Maybe.'

Brutus put a hand on Serpicus' shoulder. 'If he keeps them alive, he wins either way. He can always kill them later if needs be.'

Galba and Serpicus looked up at him. 'And you were doing so well,' murmured Galba.

'I'm sure she's alive,' said Decius urgently.

Serpicus saw that the young man's serious face was covered in grime.

Serpicus looked at Galba. 'Is that smoke? Did he come to help get me back?'

Galba grinned. 'We wouldn't let him go and get you, so he helped with the fire starting. He was pretty good at it.'

A thought struck Serpicus. 'Was anyone else hurt?'

Brutus picked up his sword and pushed it at him. 'Yes, a lot of Romans.'

'Any of ours?'

Galba looked at him and nodded. 'A couple. They did a lot of damage, one way and another, before they died. The odds weren't good, they knew that before they set out.'

Serpicus held the sword without putting it on. Something hot welled up in him like boiling milk, something a lot like self-pity. 'So they died because of me.'

Galba dismissed the idea with a hand gesture. 'No, of course not.'

'Yes. It's true, isn't it?'

Brutus bent down and shoved his face into Serpicus. 'All right, yes, if you insist. They died because you needed rescuing, but they were volunteers and brave men, so I doubt they would have seen it as a waste and they certainly wouldn't blame you. Unless, of course, you are determined to make what they did into something useless by whining about it. They died fighting Romans, which is all they ever wanted to do, and they gave a bloody good account of themselves.' He stepped aside and gestured towards the door. 'So, can I suggest that you stop feeling sorry for yourself and put the sword on, and then we can all go and do the same ourselves?'

Serpicus stood up and shook his head to clear it. His ribs ached. His face burned and the blood pounded in his chest and head, but he could stand.

'Sorry.' He touched the tokens around his neck. 'You're right, I . . .'

Brutus raised a hand. 'It's all right,' he said gruffly. 'Come on. We'll all keep an eye open for that Cato, and if we can we'll drag him back here and you can roast him over a fire or something.'

And then Serpicus' mind cleared with an absolute suddenness and he remembered everything. In a moment, the nightmare was in front of him, as if it was happening again. He took a choking breath as if about to go underwater. He staggered and put a hand on Brutus' arm. His friend looked at him with concern.

'What's wrong?'

Serpicus opened his mouth to answer and then closed it again. He had a choice, and he made it. He pushed the memory away. The pain set hard, like a stone in his chest. He yanked tight the buckle of his sword belt. 'No one kills that bastard except me,' he whispered. 'No one.'

Galba and Brutus both smiled.

'Agreed.'

29

To Aelius Sejanus, from his Servant:

> *Last night I interrogated Serpicus the German, who the*
> *uncle of the Partner employed to lead the party charged*
> *with returning his animal. He and his confederates have*
> *thrown in their lot with the barbarian rebels. He had*
> *little of value to tell, and later died in an attempt to*
> *escape.*
>
> *The attack begins at dawn.*

The Roman camp ran from west to east across the neck
of the tear-shaped isthmus on which the village stood.
Facing the village the Romans had built a low wall of
wooden stakes, backed with piled earth and rocks to
about chest height, low enough for a defender to see
over and strike with a sword, but too high for an attacker
to jump in his stride. The stake wall had narrow gaps at
intervals of about twenty paces into which the Treveri
would be funnelled into killing zones if they tried to

attack. Forward of the wall, perhaps a hundred paces out, a line of fires spread out at an interval of a poor soldier's javelin-throw. Each warmed two soldiers. The pickets were not designed to be defensive – they would barely slow the Treveri down if they charged – but as look-outs and sentries, to warn those behind them. This allowed light sentry duty behind the wall, as there would be plenty of warning of any attack.

Serpicus stood on the walkway that ran around the inside of the palisade and wondered how the legionaries on the picket line enjoyed being placed as sacrificial offerings so that the rest of the army could get some sleep.

The Roman picket fires ran in a line across the village's only way out, like glowing rings on the fingers of a fist around its throat. The fires burned low in the steady rain. There were more fires burning all the way around the far side of the river's loop, cutting off any attempt to escape across the water, and a heavy boom of logs chained together with thorn bushes and metal spikes would be constructed and laid across the river downstream, to prevent anyone using the current to carry them away. It was too dark to see if the boom was already in position. Severus' men should have got away down the river in time, but it was impossible to be sure.

Serpicus pulled his cloak tighter around him. The damp air chilled his bones, but it helped soothe the burns on his face. His whole body felt as though a herd of wild animals had run over it.

Drenthe stood silently beside Serpicus. Serpicus didn't want to talk. Moving his jaw made the healing burnt skin crack open and bleed, and the druid had told him to stay silent if possible.

He had followed her while she went around the Treveri fires, silently willing the men to listen to her. Her main concern was discipline. The German way of fighting wasn't to stand behind a wall and wait for someone to attack, nor was it to wait for orders before acting. Germans fought as individuals. If they saw an opportunity, they charged forward. If a man saw a chance for glory then he seized it. Honour was paramount, success important but secondary.

Armin had taught the Germans another way and used it to beat Varus, and the lesson had been learned well. Drenthe spoke tirelessly, explaining what had to be done, reminding them of the need to fight as one, to obey orders. The fighters grumbled about it but she wore them down. They preferred to fight in the old way, but they liked to win as well. She asked for their word and they gave it.

What no one could be sure of was how well that promise would bear up in the battle to come.

Brutus came up onto the palisade beside them.

'Don't suppose they've gone away yet?' he asked.

'We're completely boxed in,' murmured Drenthe, peering out through the rain into the night and counting the fires. Her four guards stood silently nearby, checking the edges of their weapons.

'That's the way Romans like it,' Brutus said.

'What will they do next?'

Brutus and Serpicus looked at each other. Serpicus nodded to Brutus to speak.

'At dawn, draw up the infantry to frighten you. Attack with skirmishers to sow confusion.'

'What are skirmishers?' Drenthe asked.

'Archers and light cavalry. The cavalry will gallop around for a bit while the archers stand and fire a few arrows in our direction. They'll probably pretend to have a go at opening the gate, just to get your attention.'

Drenthe looked at the gate critically. 'That's not the real attack, though, is it?'

Brutus shook his head. 'They'll be hoping that you'll come out and fight. They want to draw you out, get some idea of your strength.'

'No need for that,' said Drenthe sardonically. 'If they didn't know already, Cato has by now given them all the information they'll need.'

Brutus nodded. 'True. Nevertheless, they will still do what they always do. That's the Roman way.'

'Then what?'

'Head-on infantry attack, archers on the flanks, cavalry in reserve for a break-out.'

'Cavalry,' one of her guards said thoughtfully. 'We haven't fought them before.'

Brutus grinned. 'Don't worry, they aren't much use as long as you stay within the village walls.' He pointed out in front of the main gate, indicating right and left. 'The infantry will be in three columns. The column on each side carries ladders to scale the walls, the centre column carries a battering ram, protecting it with the testudo.' Brutus saw Drenthe's expression at the unfamiliar word. 'Testudo. Tortoise. They put their shields above their heads so arrows can't hit them.'

'Ah, I have heard of this beast,' she said, raising her voice so those around would hear. 'Only a Roman could run into battle under his shield, bent double like an old man trying to get out of a thunderstorm, and think it honourable.' Her guards smiled grimly. 'So, three columns of men, one with the dreaded tortoise, two with ladders. Archers and cavalry around the sides. Is that it?'

'More or less,' Serpicus mumbled. 'It usually suffices against a village of this size.' He fell silent again, wondering if it was possible to be any less tactful.

Drenthe watched his confusion without expression. 'And does every village fall?'

Brutus and Serpicus glanced quickly at each other. Brutus cleared his throat. 'Well . . . yes, actually. Eventually.'

Drenthe looked at them for a long moment, and Serpicus thought he saw a faint smile on her lips. 'Thank you for the information,' she said, and turned to walk away. The guards went after her, silently forming a defensive box around her, two close, two flanking them. They were taking no more chances. She stopped to talk to a small group of waiting men, who then trotted off in different directions. After a final look along the palisade she went down the steps and disappeared into the village.

'D'you think we've upset her?' asked Brutus.

Serpicus shrugged. He had no idea.

The gates were opened quietly and a group of warriors went out and started digging a trench across the entrance. They dug silently, obscured by the rain and the gloom.

Behind the shelter of the palisade men and women were busy carrying water and oil to fill the cauldrons heating on the fires, and others tested and practised with the winches which would lift the scalding mixture onto the walls when the time came. Children carried rocks the size of a man's head up the steps and placed them in piles above the gate, ready for use.

Brutus and Serpicus occupied themselves explaining to the defenders what was likely to happen in the morning. As if by unspoken agreement they both passed over the bits about certain defeat followed inexorably by crucifixion and a painful death, and concentrated on the tactics that the Romans were likely to employ. Decius and Galba stood behind them and the young man translated. When the fun had gone out of that, the four of them went to the walkway and watched the Romans getting ready to attack.

By the time the dawn came, the Treveri working in front of the entrance had dug a trench as wide as a man's outstretched arm and more than waist-deep along the length of the gate. The rain had come down steadily all night and they were covered in mud and working up to their knees in freezing water. Drenthe had sent out replacements every half-hour, but even so the returning men came in stiff with cold. However, their efforts had produced results. A rampart of dark earth was piled up on the side of the trench facing the Romans. The rain had slackened slightly and there was enough light to see from the Roman lines that something was going on. A squad of Roman archers ran out to fire some speculative arrows over the earthen rampart at the diggers without success. A cavalry detachment trotted forward and had a look at the gate with its newly dug ramparts, but declined to advance within range of the Treveri waiting for them with taut bow-strings on the village wall.

The Roman custom was to attack at dawn, but the raid and the fire had wrecked their schedule. By the time the fires were put out and everything was ordered to the centurions' satisfaction it was late in the morning. A watery sun peered through a narrow gap in the clouds and warmed the defenders a little, but it still loomed dark and thunderous over the hills. Serpicus hoped it would rain all day; the Germans were stood on firm wood ramparts whereas the Romans were crossing wet grass and mud. Battles have turned on less.

The cloud lifted slightly, revealing the Roman troops deployed as Brutus and Serpicus had predicted. The infantry were in three square blocks across the field. The two outside columns were each sixteen ranks of men across and twelve deep. The centre was the same depth but half the width. The battering ram they held, a heavy log with a bronze ram's head mounted on the end, was slung by ropes from a wooden yoke resting on the shoulders of the centre four lines of legionaries, two on each side. The men outside the ram-carriers held their shields up to protect the carriers.

Drenthe appeared beside Brutus on the walkway, flanked as always by the guards, who hadn't left her side since Cato's attack. She stood listening to the distant shouts of the centurions drifting through the rain.

'They've been busy,' she mused.

Brutus grunted agreement. He leant forward and rested his forearms on top of the wooden palisade.

'Thank Zeus they didn't bring any decent equipment,' he said to Galba.

Galba ran his thumb along the edge of his freshly sharpened sword. 'True. If they'd brought their siege engines we'd truly be screwed.'

A Treveri warrior nearby looked at him with narrowed eyes. 'Siege engines? What are they?'

Brutus didn't look at him as he replied, 'If we're both alive at the end of today, ask me again and I'll gladly explain.'

The Treveri grinned. 'I look forward to it,' he said. 'Will they come soon, do you think?' He gestured at the sky. 'I'd rather fight before the sun gets too high.'

Brutus looked up at the heavy rain-clouds above them and smiled back at the Treveri. He leant forward onto the palisade and gestured at the manoeuvring Romans. 'Don't worry, so would they,' he said. 'They won't be enjoying this any more than we are.' He spat over the rampart. 'They'll be along shortly. Once their archers have stood out of range and wasted their arrows for long enough.'

'Be careful,' Drenthe said, and moved away down the palisade towards the gate.

'Always,' Brutus said.

There was a sharp low sound like an old bone hitting a hollow wooden tube, then the same twice more. Brutus grunted with surprise and swore. Serpicus stared at Brutus' left arm. Three Roman arrows were quivering in the palisade in front of him. One of them had pinned him to the wooden wall by the flesh underneath his left forearm. Blood flowed slowly down the arrow shaft.

'Hmmm,' Galba said, looking at the arm with a serious expression. 'Lucky they are out of range, or that might be really painful.'

Brutus looked at him with an unfilial expression. Serpicus was rather glad for Galba's sake that Brutus' arm was firmly held by the Roman arrow.

'Do you think you could perhaps do something about this for me?' Brutus said to Galba, breathing heavily and nodding at the arrow. 'I wouldn't normally trouble you, but I expect to have several thousand Romans attacking me soon, and having both arms free at that time would be an advantage.'

Galba leant forward and took a close look. 'It's only a flesh wound,' he said.

Brutus glowered at him. 'It's my flesh it's wounding, and I don't give a fuck for your opinion. I just want it out of me, all right?'

A Treveri soldier leant forward with a knife in his hand and cut through the arrow shaft near to where the head was buried deep in the wood. Several more arrows thumped into the wooden wall nearby while he was leaning forward. Serpicus flinched instinctively at the noise of the arrows, but the German stayed where he was and kept on cutting as if nothing was happening. Brutus didn't make a sound, even though each movement of the knife moved the shaft of the arrow in his forearm. Sweat pearled on his forehead and ran down his cheeks. When he was free he nodded a curt thanks and lifted his arm to look at the remaining part of the arrow. It was buried in his forearm almost up to the feathered flight.

'Hold still,' Galba said, taking hold of his wrist.

'I'll do it,' Brutus growled.

'It'll hurt less if you hold your arm steady and I pull it out.'

Brutus hesitated. 'Do it right then, or I'll shove it up your . . . ow!'

Galba held up the blood-smeared arrow and looked at it critically. 'Good and straight, just the way the Romans always make them,' he said. 'Shouldn't be much damage apart from the hole.'

Brutus looked at the blood flowing freely from the wound and then glared at Galba with ingratitude. 'I'll give you a hole to match it if you don't get out of my way,' he snarled. Everyone who heard him stepped aside, even people some distance off who could not possibly have impeded him. Brutus stamped angrily down the steps.

'Will he be all right?' asked Decius.

'It's a clean wound,' Galba said quietly. 'So long as the arrow wasn't dipped in dogshit, he'll be all right.'

They watched as, clutching his arm and holding it up over his head to slow the bleeding, Brutus walked over to the nearest of several small braziers spaced out evenly in a line close to the inside of the palisade, each with an anvil beside it. The fire was tended by a Treveri, a heavily muscled man in his middle years with sword-scars all over his torso. The man didn't speak, but he knew what to do. He looked briefly at Brutus' wound and wrapped a wet cloth around his hand so that he could take hold of the handle of a long thin piece of iron lying in the fire. He handed Brutus a full wineskin. Brutus took the skin and downed a large mouthful. As he did so, the man seized Brutus' injured arm by the wrist and pinned it against the anvil. He lifted the iron out of the fire. The tip was flattened to the width of a man's finger. It glowed a bright yellow-red. Raindrops snapped and hissed at the hot iron as they passed. Brutus glanced at it and the wineskin rose to his mouth again. When he lowered the skin he sucked in a deep breath, took hold with his good hand of a rope hanging from a stanchion, and nodded to the waiting Treveri.

Everyone nearby turned their faces away. They knew that many of them would be in Brutus' position later that day, no one wanted to think about what was about to happen.

Twice in quick succession there was a hissing sound like cold water poured onto a hot pan. Serpicus swallowed on a dry throat and looked back again. Brutus hadn't made a sound but he was leaning against the palisade supported by his grip on the rope. He was breathing hard and sweat bathed his face. Smoke was still rising from his forearm. The Treveri thrust the iron back into the fire. It would be needed again.

'Lucky to get your wound early in the day,' he said.

Brutus looked at him sceptically. 'Lucky,' he repeated, pondering the word like a philosopher. 'Well, possibly. I suppose so. In a sense.'

The man ignored him. 'If you get a wound early then the ice is still cold.' He pulled Brutus a couple of steps away from the fire and, forcing him to kneel, took his hand and thrust his arm into a wide basin. Serpicus had seen them filling the basin earlier. It was full of spring-water, with large chunks of ice from the cold-store floating in it. Brutus had taken two levels of pain already. An arrow through the arm was painful, the hot iron more so. Serpicus only knew one thing to be more painful than the hot iron and that was the cold water hitting the cap of blackened flesh that the hot iron had left over the wound. The water would make the wound-scar heal quicker, and, more importantly, it meant that – apart from some stiffness and a raging ache – Brutus would be able to use it in the fight to come. Without the cold water the flesh would continue to burn and blister, and by the time it stopped the arm would be useless for weeks.

Serpicus smelt the burnt flesh and lifted a hand to his cheek and touched it gently. It was sticky with the ointment that the druid had smeared onto it. The pain was constant but tolerable.

Brutus took a deep breath and let it out again slowly. The man who had cauterized the wound released Brutus' arm and allowed him to take it from the ice-water, inspected it closely and pronounced himself satisfied. A woman pressed on a herb poultice while Brutus tipped the wineskin up once more and held it to his lips for a long time. He lowered it, tossed it aside and belched like a bull.

'I hope those Romans come soon,' he growled, 'because the sons of bitches are going to feel a lot of pain this day.' He looked at the blackened flesh under his arm and then at the smiling men around him. 'And anyone who lays a hand on a Roman archer before I've killed at least three will have me to reckon with.'

Drenthe smiled and put a hand on his shoulder. 'Any captured Roman archers will be brought alive to our friend Brutus for judgement!' she shouted. 'Your Chief commands it!' Her guard smiled malevolently. The Treveri cheered loudly and started to make suggestions to Brutus as to what appropriate measures to take against a captured archer might be. By the time they tired of the game Brutus had a broad smile on his face and a fistful of ideas, and Serpicus was starting to feel quite sorry for any Roman with a bow foolish enough to get himself captured.

The deep bell tone of the Roman horns sounded outside the walls, and Galba and Brutus glanced across at Serpicus without speaking. Then the sound of feet marching in rhythm and the sounds of metal and leather rubbing and striking each other began, and over it the shouts of the centurions, keeping the lines straight. Drenthe looked over the palisade, careless of Roman arrows.

'The music may mean they are inviting us to a dance,' she called, 'but I doubt it.'

'We'll show them how Germans dance!' yelled a man from further down the line. Everyone laughed, and they faced outward towards the slowly advancing Romans. The villagers began shouting defiance at the Romans and encouragement to each other. Drenthe signalled to a man below and the cauldrons of oil were attached to ropes in order to winch them onto the walkway.

Galba and Serpicus were standing almost shoulder to shoulder. Brutus stood just behind them. Serpicus could smell burning from him. A torch passed in front of his eyes for a moment.

'Here they come,' he muttered.

'We're fucked, aren't we?' said Galba softly, without turning his head. Serpicus said nothing. They were outnumbered ten to one, and Cato had almost certainly told the Romans everything they needed to know about the village's defences. 'Oh yes,' said Brutus, almost under his breath. 'But we'll do it to plenty of them before they do it to us.'

30

The central group of legionaries marched at a steady rhythm across the plain towards the village. Their shields fitted together closely all around them and over their heads, so that they looked like a metal box with feet marching towards Gelbheim. The villagers could see the flat iron head of the battering ram, hanging from the yoke carried by the two central ranks and protruding just forward of the front line of soldiers. The columns of soldiers either side of those carrying the ram marched slightly in front, with their archers flanking them. A steady marching beat came from them, the sound of every legionary pounding the back of his shield with the handle of his short stabbing sword.

Serpicus could see the staff officers at the rear, gathered on horseback on slightly higher ground. The General was at the centre. He wondered if it was Marcus. And if Consilius was with him. A tall, thin man was at the back, obscured by the General and the helmet he wore. Serpicus knew that it was Cato. The warmth of a torch touched his face, and the nightmare flashed through his mind again. He pushed it away.

More villagers gathered on the battlements to yell abuse at the Romans. Brutus leant towards Drenthe and pointed. 'Their intention is to engage our defences at two points on the wall a good distance from the gate. They will try and prevent us concentrating our efforts on the main danger.'

Drenthe smiled. 'So the Romans on the flanks aren't dangerous?'

'Only the big ones,' said Brutus, smiling back at her. He looked quite cheerful. The wine, the ice-water and the herbs were apparently working. Drenthe looked along the battlement to right and left. Set faces met her gaze and nodded their readiness. Drenthe went to the left, to lead the men and women on that side. Serpicus went to the right. Brutus stayed in the middle to see to the defence of the gate. His size gained him respect amongst the Treveri; he was not their leader, but they would follow him. Decius stood beside him. Brutus insisted, said he needed him in case he needed a message carried.

Galba looked up at Serpicus and smiled. He had gone down to help with the cauldrons. He was a reasonable shot with a bow and almost completely useless with a sword. The Treveri had plenty of archers at the present; later on his skills might be needed.

The rain was falling heavily again. The clouds over the mountains were almost black. Men from both sides looked up at the sky. The gods were surely angry with someone, but no one yet knew with whom.

The cauldrons sat steaming on the battlement above

the gate. A third of the Treveri force was clustered there or nearby, ready for the real attack. The rest of the men and women were stretched thinly along the palisade. They knew what they would have to do; it remained only to see how well they would do it. The defence was as ready as it could be.

Drenthe raised an arm and then chopped downward. The archers drew their short bows while kneeling on the walkway, then leant over the parapet and let fly before swiftly returning behind the cover of the palisade. Half of them were detailed to remove as many of the Roman archers as possible, the remainder concentrated their fire at the front rank of the central square of legionaries. Serpicus looked between a crack in the wall and saw the first legionaries cry out and spin sideways, clutching at the shafts. The replying arrows passed harmlessly overhead.

'Concentrate on the men carrying the ram!' Drenthe shouted to the first group. 'Unless you see an officer, of course.'

Several men laughed, and the archers redoubled their efforts. It wasn't their traditional way to fight, and it wasn't heroic or glamorous, but it was working. The Treveri were doing real damage, while escaping serious casualties themselves. Cries of pain came from below the walls.

Serpicus knew what was coming next. 'Ladders!' he shouted, ignoring the cracking skin on his face. A dozen defenders grabbed the long forked poles that lay ready beside them and crouched waiting. A moment later the first wooden assault-ladder crashed down onto the tip of the parapet. The Treveri men with the forked poles yelled defiance. Serpicus held out an arm. 'Not yet,' he pleaded. 'Wait until the ladder is full of Romans.' They hesitated, remembered their promise, and stopped. They crouched just below the rim of the parapet and held the poles ready. Other ladders poked over the edge. Serpicus counted to five, forcing himself to go slowly, imagining the Romans on the other side of the wall, racing up the ladder.

'Now!' he yelled.

The Treveri warriors sprang forward, three to a pole, and jammed the fork against the top rung of the ladder. At that moment helmeted heads appeared above the top of the rampart. With a yell of effort the defenders pushed with all their strength. There were startled shouts as the ladders flew backwards and the heads disappeared.

Serpicus risked a look over the wall. The ladders were lying on the ground. Those who had been on them were either crumpled and unmoving or were broken and helpless on the ground. Two of the ladders had injured further men waiting underneath as they landed. All along the wall the ladders were being pushed away from the palisade to fall backwards on the tightly packed legionaries behind them. Serpicus knew that the tactic had taken the Romans by surprise. They hadn't been expecting the Treveri to have poles. If they had, then the Roman commander would have used grapnels to hold the ladders firm before his men ascended them.

An arrow thumped into the wood next to his head and Serpicus jerked back. 'They'll come back again soon,' he shouted. 'Keep your heads down.'

He was expecting hooks to hurtle over the parapet, but the attackers used a simpler tactic. The next wave of ladders were placed further back, and so the top hit the outside wall lower down, just out of sight. This made it harder for the Romans to climb over the top of the wall and jump down into the village, but it meant that the defenders either had to let them come in over the defences and tackle them once they were inside, or else had to lean out over the edge to get at them while they were still on the ladders, exposing themselves to Roman swords and to the archers on the ground. Men from both sides were dying all along the walkway. The shouts of both sides and the clang of metal rang all around. Dozens of dead and wounded Romans lay on the blood-spattered ground below the walls, but the villagers were heavily outnumbered and taking casualties, especially where their forces were spread thin.

Serpicus swung with the end of a broken pole at a helmet that appeared in front of him. The legionary fell soundlessly backwards. Serpicus dropped the pole and gasped for breath. Along the walkway he saw Calryx set upon by two legionaries, one from each side. One he chopped to the ground with a two-handed blow, but the other jumped from the palisade and landed yelling on his back. Both disappeared from view.

A giant legionary came over the parapet as if catapulted by a giant's hand and struggled for balance as he landed. Serpicus jumped forward and swung at him, but his foot skidded sideways on the blood and rain-soaked walkway, pitching him against the parapet. The big Roman threw himself sideways, crashing into two

Treveri men who were fighting with their backs to him. He backhanded one of them off the walkway with a vicious swing of his shield and swung wide with his sword at the other. The German stepped back against the parapet to avoid the blow. As he raised his sword to strike back he was cut down from behind by another Roman coming over the parapet, a dark man wielding an axe in both hands. A Treveri archer nearby leant over the parapet to get a better shot at the Romans on the ladder below him, and then staggered back with an arrow deep in his shoulder and fell onto one knee. The Roman axe-man howled with rage and slashed at him as he jumped down, hitting the archer's forehead a glancing blow. Serpicus saw blood spurt and the archer cartwheeled slowly sideways off the walkway and lay still. The big legionary turned towards Serpicus and swung a blow overarm at his head. The Roman leant forward as he swung, putting all his weight behind the blow, aiming to smash Serpicus' defence aside. As it came down the two men fighting behind Serpicus fell backwards past him and landed between Serpicus and his attacker. The big man's sword hit the German a glancing blow and went sideways, pulling him off balance. The fallen Roman came up on one knee and cut at his opponent as he brought his shield up, knocking the German back as he tried to get to his feet. Serpicus slashed to the side and felt his sword sink into the Roman's arm. The prone German picked up a small axe and swung with all his strength. The axe bit deep into the wounded Roman's side and he toppled on to the German. The two of them rolled off the walkway locked in a death embrace.

The big legionary stepped forward into the space and drew his arm back to stab at Serpicus in the classic legionary's thrust to the gut, in-up-out. Serpicus stepped back and swayed sideways, hacking down at the man's arm. The blow hit the sheath surrounding the man's forearm, drawing no blood but knocking it downwards. He stumbled forward slightly and Serpicus smashed his elbow into the man's face. He staggered back, shaking his head to clear it. Serpicus gave him no time to recover but ran forward and kicked at the man's knee with all his strength. The man let out a yell of pain and slumped sideways, spinning off the edge of the walkway and onto the ground. The impact drove the breath from his body, and three waiting women used their sharp knives to make sure it never returned.

Everyone in the village heard the first crash of the ram against the gate above the noise of the battle.

The central column had reached the walls.

Serpicus saw Brutus lean over the edge, and risked another look himself. The Romans had come prepared. The ditch and rampart the Germans had built in front of the gate made the Romans' task more awkward, but they clambered slipping and cursing up the rampart and then dropped a wide flat wooden bridge across the ditch. It made it hard for the men at the edges of the column to maintain formation and a number fell into the trench and were picked off by the archers, but it enabled the legionaries at the centre to bring the ram up against the walls. The men on the ladders redoubled their efforts to get over the palisade and draw the defenders' attention away from the main assault. The narrow walkway was a chain of swaying hacking combats.

Brutus gestured frantically to the men above the gate. Working in pairs they seized either end of the poles tied by ropes to the steaming cooking pots. They lifted them and put them on the top of the palisade, then tipped them almost simultaneously onto the attackers below.

The screams of the men outside the gate rose above the sound of battle, a gale of agony over the cries of the dying and the deafening crash and shriek of iron smashed against iron.

A second rank of cauldron-bearers ran to the wall. The scalding mix of oil and water splashed again onto the upraised shields, falling on the men to either side as well as those immediately below. Blinded men ran aimlessly and writhed on the ground, clawing at their faces while their skin bubbled under the oil.

Serpicus saw Drenthe signal for the next stage with a dramatic swing of one arm. The gods were smiling on her strategy, for at that moment the rain suddenly lifted. Women on the ground pulled tightly twisted straw bundles soaked in oil from beneath a shelter, thrust one end into a brazier placed nearby and then ran forward and hurled them over the rampart at the Romans. The blazing straw landed on the shields below in a shower of sparks which caught the oil. Black smoke and flame leapt upwards. Burning men reeled screaming away from the walls, breaking the close-packed ranks. The Treveri archers poured their arrows into the gaps.

The momentum of the attack was gone. The Romans had taken heavy casualties, and had no defence against the burning oil. The officers yelled orders and beat at the cowering legionaries with the flat of their swords, but it was clearly useless. The attack had failed. The legion could stay where it was and take more casualties, or it could withdraw in reasonable order while the soldiers still had a semblance of discipline. The horns sounded the retreat.

A loud cheer went up from the walls as the central column began to pull back, holding their shields above their heads to protect themselves as best they could. The testudo is extremely mobile going forward, but clumsy and inefficient in retreat, especially over broken ground soaked by days of rain and strewn with bodies. The archers on the walls made the best of the opportunity.

The defenders on the walkway fought with renewed enthusiasm, reinforced by the men who had defended the gate and who were now free to come to the aid of the men further along the walls. The Romans on the walkway were now trapped. Some jumped back over the wall, taking their chance on the soft earth below. Those who stayed were slaughtered to a man. The defenders yelled insults at the retreating Romans below. One man picked up a severed legionary's head and hurled it down on them. It hit a soldier's shield, bounced sideways and knocked the man next to him off balance. The Treveri cheered and looked around. In a few moments there wasn't an intact Roman corpse left in the village and the Treveri were vying with each other to see who could land a head furthest from the walls.

'Are you all right?' said a man next to Serpicus, pointing at his chest. Serpicus looked down. There was blood on either side of a cut in the front of his shirt like a wide red seam. He lifted the shirt carefully and looked through narrowed eyes. A shallow cut ran from his breast-bone to his navel. If he had been standing an inch closer to the thrust then his guts would have been on the ground in front of him. The man leant forward and pushed at the skin gently with his thumb. Serpicus tried not to flinch. 'Nothing much to worry about,' the man said, 'although you'll need to get some herbs on it soon to stop the bleeding.'

Serpicus nodded his thanks and dropped the shirt. 'You'll need a few of them yourself,' he said.

Blood was flowing steadily from a cut above the man's right ear. He put a hand to it with surprise, then winced and grinned. 'It didn't hurt until you pointed it out.'

Serpicus wiped sweat from his forehead with a sleeve without thinking and almost cried out. In the fighting he had forgotten his burnt face. Now the pain came back as strong as before.

A large hand gripped Serpicus' shoulder. 'Are you all right?' asked Brutus. Serpicus nodded.

'Yes. You?' Brutus was blackened with smoke and smeared with blood, but none of it looked to be his.

All around them was a frenzy of bandaging, replacement of weapons, dousing of fires. The German casualties were light; but they had expected that; the Roman advance had been a probing attack, to assess their spirit and readiness. The next examination would be more serious.

Once the heads were all used up, the defenders tossed the corpses of the Romans out over the battlements.

Some of the village councillors wanted to keep them, to let the Romans wonder what had happened to them and how many had been captured and how many killed, but the Treveri were past any such subtleties. Calryx, who had a deep cut in his scalp which streamed blood down his face, lifted his sword aloft. 'Let them climb our walls on their dead comrades' backs,' he shouted. 'They will spare none of us if they gain entrance; let us spare none of them who enter uninvited.' A cheer went up and the defenders began to toss the corpses back over the wall. In a short time there wasn't a Roman body left in the village.

A low growl of anger borne on the wind came across the grass as the legionaries saw how the Germans treated the Roman dead.

'That's done it,' Brutus murmured. 'We've upset them.'

31

Galba stood beside Serpicus on the walkway and looked across at the regrouping Roman formations. The shouts of the officers could be heard clearly. They pointed repeatedly towards the headless corpses lying in front of the walls.

'We should have treated their dead properly,' Galba said. 'They were brave men.'

Brutus leant back on the parapet and twisted his arm to inspect the wound on his forearm. The flesh was charred and black, but the bleeding had stopped. Decius came up with a handful of herbs which he pressed to the wound. Brutus winced and said, 'You think they would have given us any mercy if the situation had been reversed?'

Galba shrugged. 'I'm not talking about mercy. They'd have killed us, but I doubt they'd have thrown us back over the edge like rubbish.' He paused. 'Anyhow, even if they are barbarians, it doesn't matter. It doesn't matter what anyone else does, it's what we do. It's bad luck.'

Brutus leant over the edge and spat towards the corpses below. 'For them.'

Galba looked at him, suddenly furious. 'Stop that!'

Brutus leant backwards, surprised. 'Why?'

'They died bravely. You don't spit on brave men.'

Brutus looked at him in wonderment for what seemed a long time. Galba had his fists clenched and looked as if he might swing one of them at Brutus any moment. Decius looked ready to jump out of the way. Brutus held up a placatory hand. 'I'm sorry. I promise I won't spit on any more dead Romans.'

Galba looked a little mollified. 'Good.'

'Would it be all right to spit on the live ones?'

Galba hesitated, then smiled. 'Yes.'

'And pour hot oil on them?'

'Most certainly.'

Brutus clapped a hand on Galba's shoulder and laughed out loud, his expression mystified. 'I don't understand you, but you certainly make the place more interesting.'

'Pucker up, boys, here they come again,' Serpicus said quietly.

It was now the middle of the afternoon. It was getting colder and as Serpicus spoke the drizzle turned into heavy rain.

The Germans watched and waited as the Romans marched purposefully towards them. It appeared at first that they were arranged in the same formation as before. Serpicus and Brutus both saw the difference in the Roman ranks at the same time. Brutus leant towards Galba and nudged his arm. 'Look.' He pointed over the

388

central group. 'They've got all the archers lined up behind them. And I see smoke.'

They both turned to warn Drenthe, but she had seen it too. 'Get ready,' she shouted. 'Water carriers to their posts.' Decius jumped down off the walkway and ran to where a line of buckets stood ready.

'Here it comes,' said Brutus softly. In front of the walls, archers ran down between the ranks of marching Roman soldiers, their bows notched and ready. Smoke streamed from the tips of their arrows. They didn't stop to aim, just pulled, released and ran back to the fire pots again. Serpicus and the others on the walls watched the fluttering flames as the arrows passed over their heads. Some landed harmlessly on the ground and were stamped out. Others landed on the thatched roofs of the huts. The continuous rain had dampened the thatch and the flames on most flickered and died. Some arrows landed on dry timber and began to burn. Serpicus saw that the fire-fighters were obeying the orders Drenthe had given them before the battle started. 'Bury your valuables. They can be dug up again once the battle is won. Leave your houses if they are burning. Only fight the fires which threaten the defences.' The Treveri saw the fire-arrows hit their houses, the homes they had built with their own hands, and they did nothing except watch them burn.

A woman carrying a bucket of water ran past Serpicus, tears streaming down her face as she ignored her own burning home to fight the flames in the feed barn. Serpicus watched her run and his heart swelled in his chest. Romans said Germans were barbarians, didn't know how to take orders, had no discipline. Perhaps there was a chance after all.

Only one fire, started by an arrow that landed in some stored animal feed in a small barn near the far end of the front wall, was endangering the defenders. The rain fell steadily, which made ground treacherous but also took the fury out of the fire. Half of the fire-fighters ran to the feed store and soon had it under control.

The Treveri discipline meant that they had almost a full complement of defenders on the walls when the Roman line struck it. Again, the cohorts on either flank struck first. They pressed home the attack hard. The defenders in the middle, above and either side of the gate, watched uneasily, waiting for the centre cohort to arrive and begin its assault. The main attack would come at the gate; everyone knew it, but even so a few men, seeing their friends on the walkway hard pressed or cut down, cried out and ran to help them. But the main group stayed steady, and when the main attack came, they were ready.

Again, the ram smashed against the gate. Again, the oil and scalding water poured over the ramparts. The pounding of the ram continued. Brutus leant over, oblivious to the arrows that thumped into the wood next to his head. When he took cover again, his face was dark.

'They've got some sort of big oil-cloth over the shields on top, as if they're all under a tent. Most of the oil is flowing off the sides.'

Drenthe shouted, 'Save the oil! Use the rocks!' She jumped across to the pile of boulders and heaved one up onto her shoulder. 'Throw them all at the same place!'

she yelled, and hurled the boulder. Her guard did the same. The rocks pounded down onto the testudo.

Brutus looked at Serpicus. 'She's good, isn't she?'

Looking between the stakes Serpicus could see that the thick canvas cloth, so effective against the oil, was rendered useless by Drenthe's tactic. The rocks landed on the shields and slid between them, to be caught by the cloth. In places the cloth tore. Where the stitching held, the men under it were forced to support the weight of the rocks. In a short time the attackers were forced to cut the cloth to allow the rocks to fall through. Either way, it left gaping holes.

'Now, the oil again,' shouted Drenthe and was rewarded by screams from below as the unfortunate soldiers who had cut the cloth to relieve the weight were now scalded by boiling oil.

For a few moments it looked as if the momentum of the attack was lost, but then the centurions drove the legionaries forward again in a prearranged move. A small group of legionaries stayed with the ram and continued to pound at the gate. The other soldiers ran to each side, in groups of about ten men, each group carrying a ladder. The intent was plain; to keep the defenders occupied with protecting the gate while attacking at so many other points at once as to make it impossible to man the wall properly.

Ladders landed all along the length of the wall. Romans were already swarming up them before the ladders were secure. Men threw themselves over the battlements, and other men threw themselves forward to stop them, and in moments there were dozens of private fights all along the walkway. Legionaries fell backwards off the ladders, pierced with arrows, and the long pitchforks tipped many of the ladders backwards, but the clatter and thump of more ladders against the palisade kept sounding and more invaders swarmed over the walls.

Serpicus and Brutus stood side by side, hacking at the legionaries coming at them from two ladders close together. The Romans had been equipped with javelins, which they used to keep the defenders at bay while they climbed over the wall. Brutus had a long pole that he was using to push men off the ladder. Serpicus had only a sword, and had to knock the javelin aside and thrust down before the legionary recovered. The intention was to keep them at bay until the archers running along the walkway arrived, leant over, shot and ran on.

In the distance a horn sounded. Brutus and Serpicus exchanged a glance. The reserves were being thrown in. This was the final attack.

Enough Romans were now on the battlements to form up and fight back to back to clear a safe space to allow more of their comrades to join them unhindered. They presented a wall of shields to the defenders and moved forward, crowding them off the walkway. Brutus saw the danger and grabbed a nearby Treveri archer by the shoulder.

'Get a couple of others and go down below, shoot up at those bastards there.' The archer hesitated at any suggestion of leaving the battle. Brutus shook him impatiently. 'If enough of them get onto the walkway they can do real damage. Do it!'

The Treveri saw the sense of the idea. He yelled to two other archers nearby and jumped down off the battlement, rolling away to absorb the impact. He had an arrow notched before he was up again, and in moments two Romans had tumbled off the walkway and crashed to the ground nearby. One didn't move again; the other rolled and tried to get up and then gave a single scream as a woman put her knife to his throat.

'Good lad!' Brutus shouted down to the archer. 'Get some of the others.' Decius ran past with an armful of spears. Brutus grabbed him. 'Get the archers to shoot them from below!' he shouted. Decius nodded and ran on. Brutus charged forward and furiously belaboured the nearest enemy, who slipped and was forced to take a step back. Brutus glanced down then dropped onto one knee and ducked his head as an arrow flew past him and sank into the man's chest. In a movement Brutus swatted the toppling body out of his way and drove forward.

The archers were doing terrible damage amongst the attacking legionaries, but they were short of arrows. One shot a Roman and then ran past Serpicus to the fallen body to retrieve the arrow. The invaders were coming over the wall quicker than the defenders could kill them.

Serpicus heard a shout and spun round. Brutus was being attacked from three sides. He swayed to one side as a legionary battered at his shield with an axe and hacked at two others coming at him from the side. Serpicus jumped forward and slashed sideways as the axe-man came forward, cutting deep into his forearm. The axe fell from his nerveless fingers but he barely paused and flung himself at Serpicus with a shout.

Serpicus swung at him but missed and the man's good hand grasped at his throat. Fingers dug into Serpicus' burnt flesh like hot bronze. Serpicus battered at the Roman's face with the hilt of his sword. The man's features dissolved into a red pulp mixing with the rain to run down his neck and his grip faded. There were black stars of effort in front of Serpicus' eyes as he stabbed down to make sure the man was dead, and he paused for a moment, gasping for air. From the corner of his eye he saw a red-cloaked figure coming at him with his sword-arm outstretched. There was no space to back away. Serpicus slashed at the attacker's face as hard as he could. Instinctively the Roman jerked his head back. Serpicus used the moment to stand on the man lying in front of him and threw himself forward. The Roman got his sword up in time but was off balance. Serpicus knocked his arm aside and plunged his sword under the man's armour into his belly. They both fell to the ground.

A hand grabbed Serpicus' belt and pulled him back up. The Roman's blood was all over his chest.

'You all right?'

Half of Brutus' face was a mask of wet blood from a cut on his scalp, but his eyes were full of light above a wide smile. Serpicus nodded, still without breath.

'Thanks,' he gasped.

Brutus grinned even wider. 'Thanks yourself.'

There was a momentary respite around them. They looked warily about. The ground below the walkway was heaped with bodies. Decius ran past again, bending down to collect arrows and javelins. His clothes were torn and he was covered in mud but appeared unhurt.

Many attackers had been shot off the walkway by the archers who had dropped down onto the ground. Blood pooled around the bodies, Roman and Treveri both flowing into puddles mixed with rainwater. There were many more dead Romans than Treveri, but that was only partly good news. There had been a lot more Romans to start with.

'We might even survive this,' said Brutus and laughed. Galba appeared beside them, covered in blood, and he laughed too, without knowing at what.

Then, suddenly and with finality, they knew that Brutus was wrong and that they had lost the fight.

Beneath the screams and crashes of combat had been a steady pounding, a deep and relentless pulse that they had been too preoccupied to pay attention to. Now they heard it gain in volume, accompanied by a splintering crash. The men under the testudo had paid a heavy price, but the battering ram had finally done its work. Serpicus looked along the walkway. The defenders immediately above the gate were moving sideways, and the men and women on the ground behind the gate were moving forward to defend it. The gate was about to fall.

There was another crash and the end of the battering ram came through a panel of the gate like the nose of a shark before swinging back out again. A few more blows and the gate would be useless. Everyone knew that once the gate was gone the battle was lost.

There was no point in contesting the battlements if the gate was open. Brutus and Serpicus jumped down and ran, slipping and tumbling in the mud, to meet the imminent invasion. Every time the ram swung into the now-wrecked gate the Romans at the front of the testudo had to move their shields out of the way to let it through, and when they did the Treveri archers were ready and shot into the gap. One arrow took down a man at the very front and he fell into the ram itself. Another soldier quickly hauled the body off and took the dead man's place, and the ram swung again. A whole section of the gate splintered and hung uselessly sideways.

'Here they come,' said Brutus, and Serpicus felt the big man's shoulder touch his own.

'Get close to the gate,' yelled Drenthe from above them. Her guards were fighting in pairs either side of her, allowing her time to look around and assess the situation. Bodies were piled up in front of them, but the Romans kept coming forward. Drenthe pointed downwards with her sword. 'Don't let them get in and spread out.'

Even if the gate itself was destroyed, the gateway was still the place to meet the Romans. If the Treveri stood back then the attackers would come through and fight them in a wide front. Either way the defenders would probably die but the latter would be more certain and sooner. They pressed up against the wrecked gate and hacked with axes and swords at anything that came through it.

The rain was now coming down in a freezing torrent, carried by a cold east wind. The women fought beside the defenders, letting the village burn.

Brutus used a broken stave to beat at an arm that came through the gate. There was a howl of agony and the arm jerked back again. 'Just as well there are all these

Romans here to give us some exercise,' he shouted to Serpicus, the breath rasping in his throat. 'It'd be bloody cold if we were just standing around in the rain.'

There was a loud rending sound as the last gate support tore free of the wall and crashed inwards. The defenders jumped back to avoid the falling timber and the Romans seized their chance. In a moment they were through the gap and inside the village.

Serpicus saw Calryx surrounded by legionaries. He parried several blows and knocked a legionary backwards, then two men struck at him at once. He threw himself forward onto their attack, striking with his sword at the head of one and swinging his shield at another. Both men went down, but Calryx staggered and fell onto them. Others flung themselves forward and he disappeared beneath them.

The Treveri were now split into small groups, fighting desperately, and the Romans poured through the gate in a rush and swarmed between them. In moments the ground became a mix of blood, earth and water that splashed up their thighs while the rain poured down their faces and blinded them.

Brutus leant against Serpicus' shoulder. 'Watch out for the big one!' he yelled.

Serpicus had already seen him. A muscular legionary with the face of a boy came running straight at him, screaming as loud as he could, exactly as his drill-sergeant would have told him to. His sergeant would not have approved of the headlong charge or the sword held high above the head, and the legionary was about to find out why. Serpicus swayed sideways without moving his feet to avoid the downward blow and brought his sword in an uppercut aimed at the man's groin. The impact jarred Serpicus' arm into numbness as the sword hit the edge of the man's armour, plunged deep into flesh and hit bone. The Roman howled and spun away from him, twisting Serpicus' sword from his nerveless fingers. Serpicus hesitated and then let the sword go and picked up a spear from the ground. Another soldier swiped at him like an angry slave chasing a wasp. Serpicus ducked and came up jabbing with the spear-point at the man's face. He pulled back and Brutus slashed sideways at his throat. The man spun away with a scream, blood fountaining as he fell to the ground. A group of four legionaries jumped forward to take his place. One of them slipped as his leading foot landed and in trying to save himself he knocked the man next to him off balance and pulled him down. Serpicus thrust the spear as hard as he could into the back of the Roman on top and without waiting to see the result ran to the corpse of the first man he had killed. He pulled his sword free and raised it, just in time to block the blow of the legionary who had slipped. He had pushed the dead body of his comrade away, jumped up and attacked Serpicus almost in one movement and the fury of the assault pushed him back. Over his shoulder Serpicus could see Brutus hard pressed, and Galba on the ground near Brutus with a Roman on top of him and a knife at his throat. As he looked, Decius appeared and threw himself onto the man attacking Galba.

Everywhere they were outnumbered. They were finished. It only remained to decide the manner of it.

Serpicus blocked the first and second blows and stabbed forward at the legionary. The Roman blocked him easily and swept his still-numb arm aside, knocking him off balance and onto one knee. He was wide open. The Roman pulled his arm back to deliver the killing thrust. Serpicus was a pig tethered for the slaughter.

The Roman sank to his knees, and then fell slowly face forward into the carmined mud with his arm in the same position. An arrow protruded from between his shoulder-blades.

The man's death left a space for a moment, and through it Serpicus saw Galba, still on the ground but now on top of his opponent. Galba had torn the legionary's helmet off and was using it as a club, battering at the man's head. Decius was nowhere to be seen. Brutus had badly wounded one of his Romans and was pressing the other back. Serpicus jumped up to join him and another arrow hissed through the rain to land at his feet. Serpicus looked up and saw Drenthe on the walkway with a bow in her hand. She was indicating frantically to him but for a moment he couldn't see what she wanted him to do. She pointed over the wall. Serpicus looked through the gate out over the plain in front of the village but it was too dark to see what was happening. Then an enormous clap of thunder broke overhead, followed by three shafts of lightning in fast succession which lit up the entire area.

The thin neck of land where the river turned back onto itself to coil around the village was completely covered in dark rushing water.

The Roman picket fires, which had been placed exactly at that spot, were gone. Most of the main Roman camp behind the pickets was still just above the water line, but it was on low ground. It had been raining all day, so the water could only be still rising. Soldiers at the rear of the Roman attack were hearing the shouts of the camp attendants and were breaking ranks, running back to save what was left of their stores. The men in front of them heard their shouts and knew that their comrades were no longer watching their backs as they fought. The Roman attack faltered. If the attack failed, there was no escape except across the freezing rushing water, in the dark, exhausted and in full armour. The choice was stark.

The Treveri tactics were obvious and simple. Serpicus sprinted to where Brutus and Galba were standing back to back and holding off several legionaries. Without breaking stride he cut the nearest man down from behind.

'Follow me!' he shouted. He ran past Brutus and charged straight at the man standing between him and the gate. The Roman's eyes opened wide in surprise as suddenly the three Germans ignored everyone else and homed in on him. He instinctively moved sideways. They sprinted past him, splashing and yelling through the mud towards the gate. Other defenders saw their lead and ran to join them. A blood-spattered Roman officer charged at Brutus with a roar of anger. Brutus dropped a shoulder and drove his full weight into the man's midriff, then kept running, lifting the officer clear off the ground and sending him sprawling to one side, right into the path of Drenthe's guard who were running to help the fight at the gate. One slashed at his throat, another at his chest. Blood sprayed upward as the Roman jerked convulsively and lay still.

The Germans stood back to back in a line across the entrance to the village, fighting to keep the Romans outside from entering while making sure that those trapped inside didn't escape.

Serpicus ducked as a sword split the air above his head, spun sideways and thrust upward at the legionary in front of him. The blow missed and left him off balance. The Roman swung a mailed fist at Serpicus' jaw, knocking him to one side as an explosion of pain spread up from his burned face. A lithe figure dropped off the battlements to land beside the legionary and caved the Roman's head in before he realized what had happened. He toppled sideways into the mud. Drenthe's guard appeared and formed around her without a word being spoken.

'Thanks,' croaked Serpicus, trying to ignore the pain.

'The camp is being washed away,' Drenthe shouted. 'They will have to retreat.' She looked at Brutus and Galba, then Serpicus. 'You should save yourselves while there is time.'

Another sheet of lightning lit up the Roman camp. The water seemed to have risen even in the short time since Serpicus last saw it. The river was picking up the tents at the near edge of the camp and carrying them away on its swollen back. Men who tried to wade through it to recover their belongings were knocked over by the branches swept along by the current just under the surface of the water. Once a man was down, the fast-moving river rolled him over and battered him with loose equipment and debris. It would not be long before the Romans had no avenues of retreat left. Shouts of dismay were coming from the attackers' ranks.

A broken dagger of light flashed to the earth from the black sky and Serpicus saw Marcus, son to Blaesus and cousin of Sejanus, outlined by the light like a bas-relief on a wall. The General was on horseback, riding just behind the front rank of soldiers. His sword was in his hand and he was pointing forward with it like a statue. Then a legionary ran forward and stood in front of him, gesturing frantically back at the camp. Marcus pulled his horse sideways and looked back for a long moment. He glanced forward again to the faltering attack on the village walls, then back once more at the disappearing camp. Thunder rolled like huge stones on a wooden floor above him, adding to the roar of the battle. His frightened horse reared up and turned in a tight circle. Marcus came to a decision. He shouted to the trumpeters standing nearby and then turned his horse and pushed it into a canter back to the camp. In moments he was lost in the gloom.

'They're retreating!' said Brutus, breathing hard after knocking a man to the ground with the broken end of a spear.

It was true. The mournful note of the trumpets could be heard over the noise of the battle. Officers were shouting orders at the legionaries. The front ranks of Romans were slowly disengaging while the rear was already trotting back through the mud towards the camp.

A German with a throat wound that coated the front of his body with blood ran past Serpicus screaming, 'After them! Don't let them escape!' Drenthe reached out and grabbed his arm. He turned, his eyes wild, and lifted his arm to strike at her. Then he saw who it was and stopped, though his head still moved from side to side frantically as if angry bees were attacking him.

'They aren't running away, they're pulling back,' she said. She swung him around in front of her and pointed over his shoulder. 'Look. They are still in ranks, in good order. The reason we are still alive is because of the village walls. If we chase the Romans we will be a disorganized rabble. We will be caught out in the open and they will form up again and cut us to pieces.'

The warrior hesitated, and then his shoulders slumped. Drenthe turned him around and looked into his face. She slapped him gently across the cheek, smiled and pushed him back towards the village.

The only Romans still left inside the walls were either dead or wounded. The Treveri gathered in front of the gate and hurled insults as the remaining legionaries ran back towards their camp. A few of the Treveri had forgotten or ignored Drenthe's orders and could be seen chasing after the Romans. It was plain that some of the remaining warriors who had maintained discipline were watching them enviously. They weren't content with what they felt was an unnatural tactic, but they kept their promise.

Many of the buildings had been damaged by the fire-arrows, so the wounded were laid out in the Hall. While

403

the villagers worked frantically to rebuild the gate, Drenthe quickly went around the wounded, pressing a hand here, whispering a word there, and then gathered her remaining officers around her near the doorway. Every one of them was covered in mud and streaked with blood, their own and that of others. The dead and the wounded were reported and counted. Balant was nursing a deep cut in his left shoulder. The muscle was severed and the arm hung uselessly at his side. He couldn't lift his hand, let alone a shield. Bocalas cursed steadily as the boy handed him herb-smeared cloths to press against it. He had stopped the worst of the bleeding but he could do nothing about the useless arm except tie it up so that it did not get in the way. Drenthe was almost unharmed, but all of her guard were wounded. One of them had been struck on the head and was almost unconscious. The others carried a dozen cuts each, none of them serious in themselves, but they had lost much blood and needed rest, medicine and food. The champion Calryx was dead, lying at the centre of a circle of dead Romans, and many of the village's best men were dead or were so badly hurt that they lay on the ground, no longer able to fight. Brutus found his drinking friend Max run through with a spear and unable to talk, so he stayed with him until he died. The Hall was full of heavy breathing and soft grunts of pain as wounds were roughly bound.

Serpicus leant against the wall and waited for his breathing to return to normal. He was battered and exhausted, but compared to most of the men he was fighting fit. Galba had a nasty cut on his thigh and another on his forearm, and was holding one of Bocalas' poultices to each one. Brutus had a deep laceration across his forehead to add to the arrow wound on his arm. One of Drenthe's guards was sewing it up with soldier's stitches, a thread run loosely through the two edges of the cut from one end to the other and then back again. It was quick to do, and when both ends were pulled tight it closed the cut. It was fast and effective, but it left an ugly scar. Decius watched anxiously until Bocalas called him over.

Serpicus smiled at the expression on Brutus' face as the woman fixed his scalp. Not only was he not complaining at the pain, he was looking at her as a dog looks at the man who removes a painful thorn from his paw. Serpicus had heard the sort of things that Brutus usually said to the men who had attended his wounds in the past. His silence was in marked contrast.

Drenthe stood in the centre of the Hall and raised her voice. There was a silence.

'Everyone knows the situation,' she said. 'We have just a short respite while the Romans try and stop their camp from floating down to the Rhine.' Several men laughed harshly. 'We have hurt them badly, but they are not defeated. We are still trapped. They outnumber us and they have the advantage. Many of us are wounded.' She put a hand on Balant's shoulder as Bocalas finished binding his other arm tightly to his chest. 'If anyone has any magic potions or secret plans, this would be a very good time to produce them.'

'An invisibility spell would help,' said one of the wounded men. Everyone laughed. Drenthe stooped to help bandage the arm of one of her guard.

'Actually, I do have an idea,' said a quiet voice, dry like the wind moving across the cold forest floor.

For a moment no one realized who had spoken. Then Drenthe turned and looked at Bocalas.

'No hurry at all,' she said, 'but let's hear it.'

32

The warriors laughed at Bocalas' suggestion. Drenthe enquired softly if they had any better ideas, or any ideas at all. There was a slightly sheepish silence. She snapped orders. Bocalas took six men and left. The boy went with them, the hawk on his arm as always. Drenthe sent others to bring everyone left alive except the sentries into the Hall. It took a while. Most of the men and many of the women were carrying wounds which they hadn't considered serious enough to need treatment, but which slowed them down.

Their spirit was unbroken, but that was all they had left. If the Romans pressed hard, the Treveri would not be able to resist them.

Drenthe stood on a table and her village gathered around her in grim silence. She began quietly.

'We have done well. We held them until they broke down the gate, and Wodan saw that the gods of the river made sure that our efforts did not go unrewarded. Many Roman mothers will weep for their sons and many

Roman wives will go home to cold beds as a result of what we did here today.' There was a low growl of agreement which died away almost immediately. They wanted to know what they were going to do next. She looked around and smiled at them.

'We know what is coming. The Romans will regroup and they will advance again. We can wait for them, and meet them with our spears. We will kill many of them before the day is over, but we should not lie to ourselves. They outnumber us and our defences are already breached. We can make our stand, and it will be glorious, but they will win.'

The Treveri looked at each other and smiled. They were not afraid to die, and reckoned to take a few Romans to Hades with them before it happened. Serpicus felt a lump in his throat and looked down at the floor. Drenthe looked around again and gave them a different sort of smile. The Treveri seemed to have been waiting for this and were immediately attentive again.

'And of course,' she said, and her eyes glowed with pleasure, 'that's what the Romans will be expecting us to do.'

It took the Romans the rest of the day and much of the night to regroup and to rebuild the camp on higher ground. Several cohorts of shivering men were stationed close to the village to discourage any sort of escape, and the rest did the best they could with what remained of their equipment. By morning the camp was standing again, smaller because many of the tents were lost or beyond repair, and on higher ground.

The Treveri had not wasted the opportunity. The walls were rebuilt, the gate patched and rehung, the defences prepared again. Roman scouts rode close to the walls, peering through the rain, and were met with arrows and insults. The Romans could be in no doubt that the Treveri were preparing to make a stand. The scouts galloped away to report back. There was a lull. The Treveri waited, but no attack came.

'First light?' asked Drenthe. Serpicus and Brutus nodded. Roman officers loved the dawn.

The rain slackened off but in its place there was a cold wind that sliced through the cloaks of the guards on both sides and sent them scurrying back to the fires as soon as their relief arrived.

In the village, behind the walls where the Romans could not see, preparations for the morning continued.

They knew that the sun had risen that morning because the night became a little lighter, but it was hidden behind a heavy dark sheet of cloud. The Romans formed up as they had done before, but in different proportions. The centre was now by far the strongest block, a thick arrowhead of men, with the battering ram at its apex and a large force behind it ready to pour into the village as soon as it had done its work. This left only thin ranks of men to either side of the main force, a dozen ladders on each side and men to climb them. The flanks were a distraction, just enough to ensure that the Treveri could not afford to concentrate their whole force at the gate to meet the main assault. The Romans were planning on one knock-out blow. Both sides knew that the Treveri did not have the defences nor the manpower to block the blow for long.

The defenders looked over the wall and watched the legionaries manoeuvre. The Romans advanced in a steady rhythm. The point of the arrowhead moved off first, with the ram swinging between the centre lines, heading straight for the gate. Then the archers moved into position, clustered behind the men carrying the ram, ready to pick off any defender who raised his head above the wall. The flanking groups with the ladders advanced level with the archers, fanning out and looking for ill-defended places along the walls, aiming to arrive at the wall simultaneously with the first blow of the ram. The supporting ranks left a gap of twenty paces, then advanced in step with the ram.

The pattern of the fight was almost identical to the previous day. The Romans advanced and pounded the ram; the defenders poured arrows and rocks and scalding oil and water down on them; the archers on both sides picked off anyone unwise enough to show themselves; and all along the walls attackers prepared to climb and defenders stood ready to stop them.

The difference was the gate. The solid interlocking timbers had withstood dozens of blows, giving the defenders time to inflict heavy losses amongst the soldiers carrying the ram. This time that could not happen. The very first collision made the whole patched door visibly move inwards. A beam fell backwards, opening a gap. Those inside and outside could tell at once that it would not take long to shatter it. The advancing Romans could see a large wooden cart, like a giant box on wheels, being pushed forward to add weight to the defences.

'Ready,' shouted Drenthe, watching the approaching cart with her sword raised high.

The ram smashed against the gate again. Several planks in the centre fell to the ground, leaving a space wide enough for a man to get through. The defenders ran forward.

The ram struck again with a deep crash. The whole gate shuddered and two of the hinges burst free. A heavy beam which had been tied across the width of the entrance burst its bonds and swung erratically backwards, knocking a man over and smashing against the side of the cart. The Roman lines behind the ram drew their swords and started to shout encouragement at each other.

All along the walls heavy ladders crashed against the wooden palisade stakes. Iron-helmeted men yelling encouragement to each other swarmed up the steps.

Drenthe screamed one word.

'Now!'

As the first legionaries vaulted the top, concealed men crouched on the walkway leapt up and hacked furiously at them with swords and axes. The Romans were taken by surprise. As the ram approached, the defenders had shown themselves in force in front of it, and then left a skeleton defence to resist while most of them ran unseen to the walkway. When the attackers came over the wall expecting a token resistance they met almost the full force of Germans waiting behind it. They were completely outnumbered. The Treveri killed most of them in a few moments. The defenders picked up the legionaries' bodies and flung them back over the wall, deliberately aiming to knock as many men off the ladders as possible. Apart from a few scattered fights, in moments the walkway was clear of Romans.

Drenthe screamed again.

'Back to the gate!'

Every one of the Treveri who was on the walkway turned his back on the wall and jumped down. Serpicus hit the ground hard, knocking the remaining breath out of himself. He felt as if every part of him was cut or bruised or broken. He rolled to absorb the impact.

In the sky far above him he saw the hawk, suspended in space. The battle sounds around him dropped to a distant roar. He lay still, watching the bird circle above him. Then it slipped sideways on the breeze and disappeared, heading south. Home.

The screams of the wounded and the sound of the ram pounded against his ears. He jumped painfully to his feet and ran with the others to the gate, where the defenders were pushing the square cart forward until it was close to the wall.

The ram struck the exact centre of the gate, punching a hole clean through it. The planks and spars splintered and cracked. As a defence, it ceased to exist. The Treveri saw the Romans drop the ram and take a deep breath for the cheer that would propel their charge forward as well as encourage those behind them to come to their assistance. The archers on both sides drew their bows and loosed arrows as fast as they could through the gap.

Drenthe signalled furiously with her sword-arm and Bocalas, who had been lying prone on top of the box, stood up, swinging a heavy hammer. A Roman arrow drove deep into his thigh. He dropped the hammer and sank onto one knee, faltering for a moment, then the boy appeared at his side and put the handle of the hammer carefully back into his hand. Bocalas gathered his strength and struck left and right, then two arrows thumped into his chest and he toppled backwards.

The boy smiled up at the sky as if he was standing in a field on a quiet summer's day. Then he crumpled slowly to the ground, turning as he fell so that Serpicus saw the arrow in his neck and the thin cord of blood that flowed from his still-smiling lips.

The Romans howled as they pushed forward. The fastenings of the box flew out under the blows from Bocalas' hammer and the front dropped down like a ramp, landing with a crash at the feet of the onrushing attackers.

The front line of legionaries looked into the darkness inside it and came to a dead halt, milling in confusion as if a steep cliff had suddenly appeared at their feet.

A harsh growl was heard over the shouts of the soldiers. A huge white head slowly looked out. For a moment nothing happened, and then a stray arrow skimmed the bear's muzzle before thumping into the wooden cage behind it.

The bear let out a deep roar and sprang forward. In two bounds it reached the Roman line. The first man was smashed to the ground by a massive paw. A centurion leapt forward and stabbed at it with a short spear, wounding it in the shoulder. The bear swatted the spear away and caught the centurion's arm, tossing him aside like a handful of rags. It let out a roar and plunged on, deep into the Roman ranks.

Drenthe opened her mouth in a wordless scream and hurled herself forward. The Treveri let out a great cheer and every man and woman poured into the gap left by the bear. The Roman front line disintegrated. The bear ran straight forward heading directly for the Roman camp, roaring with anger and pain. Blood streamed down its chest and its feet were wet with gore. Arrows hung from its side and there was a cut on its head but it only ran faster, maddened by the smell of blood and the panic surrounding it. The Treveri followed howling in its wake, hacking and stabbing at the stunned enemy as they ran.

Serpicus and Brutus sprinted shoulder to shoulder, the breath rasping into their lungs. Decius appeared from one side, his face spattered with someone else's blood, and dropped in behind them, watching their backs. Serpicus swung at a Roman who appeared in front of him. Half of the man's face was torn off but he was still fighting. The man's sword spun away as Serpicus rammed an elbow into the remains of his face and ran on. In front of him Brutus bent to pick up a spear and without breaking stride threw it underarm into the guts of a legionary coming towards him. The man screamed and fell across his path. Brutus tried to jump but caught a foot on the man's body. He stumbled and Decius threw out an arm to steady him. Another Roman leaped in front of them and then fell, an arrow in his eye, as the Treveri came up around them. Serpicus saw Balant sidestep a Roman spear-thrust and then drive his sword deep into the legionary's side. Another man jumped forward from behind Balant, and Serpicus yelled a warning, drowned out in the clamour. Balant stepped back to pull the sword out and was turning for the next attack when a whirling axe from behind split his head open. He dropped from sight.

'Head for the camp!'

The bear swung left and the three men did the same. Serpicus saw Galba at the edge of his vision, running high-kneed as fast as he could, hurdling bodies without breaking stride. The bear ran headlong through the camp, scattering men and equipment, knocking aside anyone too brave or too slow to get out of its way. The Treveri saw their opportunity and ran with all their strength into the space behind it. It was as if a giant foot had come down into a shallow pool of water. For a while there is just a space where the foot has been; then the water seeps slowly back. Behind the bear for a short while there was nothing. Then legionaries began to reappear in ones and twos, as if drawn back to the animal's tracks, some dazed, some intent on re-forming ranks. As they came together again, another foot smashed down onto them as the pursuing Treveri poured forward in the bear's wake, howling as they cut the Romans down where they stood.

A thin legionary saw Serpicus and ran hard and straight at him. Serpicus ducked a sideways slash of his sword and struck at the man's head. The legionary dodged easily and moved in close, jabbing his fist twice into Serpicus' midriff. Serpicus knew he must not drop his head, but his wind shot from him and he had no choice. He tried to spin away but the Roman stepped across his path. Then Serpicus felt a blow on his hip, knocking him out of the way, and a large shape came between him and the man trying to kill him. Serpicus smelt familiar sweat and smiled as he gasped for breath. By the time he was able to stand up, Brutus and Decius had knocked the Roman lifeless to the ground.

The three men looked around. The bear was gone, leaving the Romans in confusion. The main body of the Treveri were still running through the camp, and the Romans who had been besieging their village shortly before now had no one to fight, and were now trying to regroup and pursue them.

Galba joined them, with flushed face and matted blood all down the front of his tunic. He saw Decius looking at it. 'Don't worry,' he gasped, 'most of it doesn't belong to me.'

Serpicus turned to follow the Treveri to wherever it was they were going, and the world stopped.

'Come on,' said Brutus, pulling at Serpicus' arm. He didn't move. Brutus looked to see what had paralysed Serpicus and his head jerked back in surprise. He opened his mouth to speak and then let out a harsh warning instead as two Romans came running round the side of a tent and saw Serpicus standing motionless. Brutus jumped forward and knocked one legionary's arm up, then drove a fist into the man's face. Without pausing he threw himself at the other soldier, who had knocked Decius to one side with a vicious blow to the head and was now charging at Serpicus. The soldier was armed only with a club, but Serpicus wasn't defending himself. He swung at Serpicus' head as Brutus crashed into him.

The club would have smashed Serpicus' skull, but the impact of Brutus' charge took the force out of the blow and knocked it off-course. It hit Serpicus high on the temple. He dropped to the ground as if his body was suspended by strings and the club was a scimitar passing through them.

Serpicus saw her.

He could smell her skin, feel the soft touch of her breast against his cheek.

Another dream, he knew, like all the others.

'Wake up. Please wake up.'

Her voice was hushed and urgent.

He opened his eyes.

She was leaning over him. Holding his head in her hands. Stroking his hair. Pressing his face to hers. Her tears wet on his eyelids.

He looked, saw her.

His eyes burned at the sight of her.

His memory full of her on a bed. With his enemy. Writhing. Moaning. He pushed the pictures away.

They looked at each other in silence.

Brutus knelt beside them. In his hands were the reins of four horses, their eyes rolling and their flanks trembling, their mouths foaming from the battle and made skittish by the noise and flames. 'We have to go,' he said urgently. 'They're getting organized again. Any minute now they'll be coming through here after us.'

Antonia took Serpicus' arm. 'Can you stand?'

He didn't speak, unable to trust himself, his mind empty of words. He allowed himself to be helped up and pushed onto the back of one of the horses. Antonia sat behind him and wrapped her arms around him to hold him on. Brutus rode in front, Decius and Galba watched their backs. They kicked the horses into a canter and rode hard away from the camp.

33

To Aelius Sejanus, from his Servant:

> *The village has been destroyed and the insurgents killed
> or captured. The assault was less than a total success
> owing to the loss of much valuable equipment in a flood,
> due to the camp being placed near the river, a location I
> specifically advised against. I shall be able to give
> complete details of this failure on my return.*
>
> *The body of the Treveri woman has not been found yet,
> but reports suggest that she perished early in the attack,
> most likely as a result of the wound that I inflicted or as
> part of the military operation against the village. It seems
> probable that she is no longer an obstacle.*
>
> *I shall return to Rome directly.*

Once out of sight and hearing they pushed the horses fast
towards the hills, keeping to the low land, avoiding the
horizon. They galloped when the land was flat, walked
fast when it was broken or uphill.

Galba came up beside Brutus and spoke softly. 'The horses won't be able to keep this pace up for long,' he said.

'Let's hope the Romans have the same problem,' Brutus said grimly. 'We need to get into the forest before they catch up. We'll lose them there and the horses can rest.'

Galba said nothing. There was no alternative. Either the horses would make it or they wouldn't. More pressing was the state of his friends. Decius was complaining of a sore head and blurred vision. Serpicus was visibly dazed and Antonia was still holding him onto the horse's back.

Serpicus said nothing, did nothing. He wanted to hold her for a day without moving, but the images in his mind wouldn't fade. He felt as if his mind had hidden what he saw in the tent from him. Then she appeared and the sight of her had been too powerful for the chains that bound his memory. Now they were free, and they scorched his thoughts.

At last Brutus called a halt. They were on a slight slope with a stream at the bottom. Decius tied up the horses, not daring to hobble them in case they were needed in a hurry, and went slowly down the hill to bathe his head. Serpicus slid down off his horse's back and he and Antonia sat under a stunted tree without moving.

'You two rest,' Brutus said. 'We'll take a walk around.' He shouldered his spear and walked away with Galba.

Serpicus leant back against the tree and tried to put his thoughts in order, but they defeated him. He was wounded and exhausted, and his memories were whirling round like snowflakes in a blizzard. His children, the way she lay on Cato's bed, their house in Rome, the sounds she made as Cato touched her, her smile as she rested her head on his chest . . .

He didn't know what to say and he couldn't say or do nothing, so he reached into his pocket.

'Here,' he said.

She looked quizzically at his hand and then her eyes opened wide with delight. She took the leather thong and put it around her neck. The half token lay at her throat. She stroked his hand with a swift gesture. 'I thought it was lost, that I'd never see it again.' She touched the token gently with two fingertips. 'The Romans took it.' She frowned. 'How ever did you find it?'

'Did they hurt you?' he asked suddenly.

'Who?'

Serpicus couldn't speak for a moment. Then it came, a rasping sound. 'The legionaries.'

She looked puzzled. 'No. What do you mean?'

His throat seemed to be closing. 'Cato said that they . . .' He couldn't finish.

She smiled and shook her head. 'Whatever he said, he lied,' she said softly. 'None of them touched me.'

One did, he thought, and his voice returned.

He knew that he was doing something more wrong than he had ever done, and he still did it. The words poured out, with all the pain that filled him.

He felt her body grow cold and tense, as if she had died and stiffened in a moment. She pulled slowly away from him and sat up.

421

'You didn't ask that,' she said. 'Tell me again what you just said, and this time lie to me, please.'

Her eyes were soft, her voice filled with tears. For a moment he felt his questions freeze on his lips, then the hot pain inside him melted them and they tumbled out. He tried to sound reasonable and he heard his voice accusing her and he didn't care what she'd done but he still couldn't stop. The images and sounds spilt out and flooded over both of them, the scene in the tent, her words, her face, her movements, everything that he had sat and watched in silence in the dark, and which had clawed at his gut like an iron grapnel since that moment. Like blood from a deep wound it poured from him, flowed until he was empty and felt nothing at all except his own anguish.

She didn't speak for a long time, but looked at the ground. He wished desperately that she would speak.

Then, so slowly he wasn't sure if she was doing it, she lifted her bowed head. Her eyes were dry, full of anger. She reached up to her neck and took the ivory token in her fist. With one short tug she ripped it from her neck. He felt his heart tear from its roots as she did it, and suddenly he was free. He knew he loved her, how stupid his questions had been, how little it mattered. He closed her open fingers over the token and pressed them gently, sure of himself.

She looked at him as if he was a stranger.

'Always,' she said softly.

'No doubt,' he said, with emphasis, willing the edges of the torn fabric of their life to meet and join again.

She smiled a little, and opened her fingers. The

token fell to the ground and they both looked at it.

'I'm so sorry,' he said.

She reached up, her face blank, and touched his cheek with an infinite gentleness. He almost closed his eyes with relief.

Then she stood and started to walk away.

'Where are you going?'

She didn't reply. His mind tilted and he moved forward in confusion, and then with a lurch of the heart he ran after her until he was close enough to reach out and hold her arm.

She turned and her expression thrust a knife into his chest. Anger, perhaps pity, but no love.

'Listen to me well,' she said, sounding like she was choking, 'for we will never speak again.'

He opened his mouth to protest, and then shut it again.

She took a breath, calmed herself. When she spoke she was in control, though her voice trembled and stumbled with suppressed passion.

'That bastard Roman came to our home – *my home* – and sat at my table . . . and told me that if I wanted to live, if I wanted . . . wanted our children to live, if I wanted you to live, I would have to do . . . do what he told me.'

She seemed to choke, then coughed and spat. She tossed her hair back and looked up into his face, held the words up for him to see.

'He explained my situation to me.' She smiled. 'In detail.' A tear ran down her cheek. She ignored it.

'The choice was simple. If I tried to escape, the children would die. If I resisted him, the children would die. If I ever looked anything other than entirely delighted to receive his attentions, if I didn't scream with pleasure at his slightest touch, the children would die.'

She paused. Her breath was coming in tight short bursts. She stood close to him and whispered into his face.

'Do you . . . can you . . . have any idea what that is like? Can you imagine what it means to wish a thousand screaming tortures upon a man, a man who threatens the lives of your children, and to . . . and to have that man pawing at you, whispering love into your ear, pushing himself into you? And while he does it you must *encourage* him, cry out for pleasure, beg for more?' Tears were now streaming down her cheeks. Her voice rose. 'Try, Serpicus! Try and imagine that! And while you do it, while you try to imagine what that feels like, imagine what more you would yet do to protect your family.' She stepped close to him and her eyes burned into his. Her voice stuttered with pent-up rage. 'Tell me that you would not bend over an ox-cart and spread yourself while a whole legion took turns at you, and do it willingly if you thought it would protect your children. Tell me you would not laugh and beg them for more if that was what it took to keep the children safe.' She was just a finger-length away, spitting her anger into his eyes. 'Tell me it isn't true!'

He couldn't face her. Her words struck him like hammers. He stepped back.

'Yes,' he said, almost inaudibly.

She moved forward, leaning towards him, looking up into his face. 'What? Yes what?'

'It is true. You are right. I would do it all. Yes, of course. Of course.'

She stepped back from him. 'I would too,' she said. 'I did.' She paused, looking at him as if he was her enemy. 'That's what you *saw*. What I must live with.'

He sank to the ground. His head was full of noise and he could neither hear nor see. The world no longer meant anything to him.

He lay there for a time that had no length, and then he felt someone shaking him.

He opened his eyes. His head was still unclear, but he could make sense of the world again. He knew who he was, what he felt, what he must do.

Brutus shook him hard. 'Come on,' he said. 'It's time to move on.' He looked around. 'Where's Antonia?'

Serpicus shook his head, trying to snap himself fully awake. 'Isn't she here?'

'No. I'll take a look around.' Brutus looked at him as if about to say something, then didn't. 'You stay here,' he muttered, and stood up. Decius was revealed behind him, looking serious. The two of them went off together.

Serpicus sat on the ground and waited. The memory of what he had done ached like a bad tooth. He lifted and turned it over in his mind repeatedly, as if expecting to find something different under it. Something on the ground caught his eye. He reached out for it. It was the ivory token, lying where she had dropped it.

There was a loud crack nearby as a branch broke. Serpicus rolled sideways and reached for a weapon.

'It's me!' hissed Brutus, running bent double across the clearing towards him. Serpicus started to stand

and Brutus put a heavy arm on his shoulder. 'Stay down!'

'Where's Antonia?'

Brutus hesitated and didn't look at him. 'Hiding, or gone. Nowhere that I can see. She took one of the horses.'

Serpicus knew from his face that she had spoken to Brutus before she left. He struggled to stand up. Brutus pushed him back down again. 'Stay where you are. There are people out there.'

'I don't care, I have to . . .'

Brutus knelt in front of Serpicus, took him by both shoulders and hissed into his face. 'If they're Romans then what you have to do is absolutely nothing because otherwise it'll be the last thing you ever do, understand?' Serpicus didn't reply and Brutus shook him roughly. 'Understand?'

'Yes.'

They crawled forward to the edge of the clearing, and Brutus lifted his head very slowly. Serpicus watched, and saw his face spread into a wide grin. He stood up without troubling to conceal himself. Serpicus heard a surprised voice nearby, and then running feet. Something that felt uncomfortably like a sharp spear-point was pressed against the back of his neck. He turned very slowly to see who was behind him, expecting to get a blow on the head. Instead he was allowed to turn all the way. One of Drenthe's four bodyguards was behind him, holding the spear. Two others were quickly scouting the clearing. The fourth was standing next to Brutus, looking at him in a way that suggested that the smile on Brutus' face was more than just a social pleasantry. She was a handsome woman, hard-muscled and scarred. She wore a yellow boar's tooth on a worn leather thong at her throat.

'Hello,' she said. 'We thought you'd got lost.'

Brutus smiled down at his new friend. 'Not a bit of it,' he said. 'We thought we'd take a rest and let you find us.' His new friend laughed with a cheerfulness and enthusiasm that the comment didn't really deserve.

'Like we found this one,' she said, and pointed at Galba, who was sitting on the ground nearby looking sheepish.

'Are you all right?'

Serpicus turned. Drenthe was in front of him. Her leather armour was stained with blood and smoke and her hair was in matted ropes around her head, but she looked unharmed.

'Yes,' he said, without inflection.

She opened her mouth to speak but then said nothing, as if something about him had told her that there was nothing to be said. She looked around and spoke to Brutus.

'We must keep moving. The Romans will not be far away.'

'Where to?'

She shrugged. 'Any direction will do. Our people are all around us.'

Brutus frowned. 'And will they take us in? Even after what happened at Gelbheim? Would they risk the same?'

The woman beside him looked as if she had only just prevented herself from reaching up and ruffling his hair affectionately. 'This is not Rome,' she said gruffly. 'You have been away from Germany for long enough to forget, or you would know that what happened at Gelbheim makes it more likely that they will take us in, not less.'

Brutus looked almost ashamed. 'Of course.'

Decius appeared from some nearby bushes. He had worked his way back up the hill until he was close enough to see who the new arrivals were. Drenthe looked at him and smiled in welcome. He blushed and looked down, then up again.

'That boy's growing up,' said Brutus.

Drenthe and Brutus inspected the horses.

'What do you think?' Drenthe said.

Brutus looked at the animals and shook his head. 'So long as we just walk then they'll be able to carry someone. Try and gallop them and they won't get over the next hill.'

'I agree.' Drenthe directed her bodyguards to take up positions around them. 'You ride slowly, in a straight line. Our horses are fresher. We will circle around you and warn you of anything ahead.'

Brutus started to protest, then stopped. There was no other sensible course of action. They set off with Drenthe at the front and Decius and Galba just behind her. Serpicus sat inert on his horse like a sack of damp corn, feeling their eyes upon him. They all knew Antonia, yet none of them had commented on her disappearance. There was only one explanation; she had spoken to Brutus before she left, and he had told the others. There was nothing for them to say, so they stayed away from him.

The horses picked their way carefully forward, their heads low with exhaustion. Drenthe's bodyguard formed pairs and rode one in front and one behind, with the other two acting as outriders, riding a bow-shot either side of them, back and forth just below the horizon. The pairs changed over every half-hour so that the horses could rest.

The bodyguard who had Brutus' special attention galloped up from behind them, her hair streaming out behind her like a banner. The outriding pair came in from either side to meet her and escort her in. Drenthe turned at the sound of the horses' hooves behind them and called out, 'What's wrong?'

The bodyguard sat tall in her saddle and looked back from where she had come. She pointed behind them and a little to the west.

'Romans. Coming this way. They saw me.'

Drenthe looked around. They were on an open stretch of grassland between two areas of thick woodland, without cover or natural defences. The horses were exhausted. The Romans would just ride them down.

'How many?'

'Twenty, perhaps more.'

Brutus looked around. 'Not good odds,' he said.

Drenthe looked at Serpicus and then at Brutus and shook her head slightly. 'The forest begins again on the other side of the hill.' She pointed west. 'Make it to the trees and you will be able to hide there.'

Decius drew his sword. The chipped and scarred edge rattled as it left the scabbard. 'And what about you?'

'I thought I would see Rome.' Her voice was wistful.

'It seems my visions were wrong.' She smiled and gave a little shrug as she drew her sword. 'Not for the first time.'

'No.'

Drenthe looked up in surprise. Her bodyguard looked at the other two women, saw their expressions, and then repeated it. 'No.'

'You have an alternative?'

The woman pointed with her spear at the hill. 'We stay here. You push on for the forest. Romans have bad memories of Germans amongst the trees. They will fear ambush, they won't follow you.'

Galba shook his head. Brutus moved forward, frowning. 'But there are only three of you. It's hopeless, you'll die for no reason.'

She smiled, and took her bow from her pack. 'One German is worth five Romans any day. We will slow them down, reduce their numbers at least, perhaps even stop them altogether. That's a reason.'

'But you cannot hope to win.'

The other two bodyguards nodded fiercely. 'If you leave now, it will be for a reason,' said one of them. 'If we stand here and debate it, it will certainly all be for nothing.'

'I will come with you,' said Brutus, looking at her as if he had suddenly found something after searching all his life for it. She shook her head with a smile.

'No. You must look after Drenthe. Don't worry, we will kill many Romans and then we will follow you.' She reached to her throat, closed her hand around the tooth that hung there and pulled hard. The leather cord snapped and she tossed the tooth to Brutus. 'Keep that for me till I return.' She swung her horse's head away to the rear of the small column and the three women galloped hard back down the slope.

Serpicus looked at Brutus, who was staring at the ivory-coloured tooth in his hand.

'Come on!' snapped Drenthe. 'If they are determined to get killed to save us, let's make sure it isn't wasted.'

All five horses were exhausted. The hill grew steeper and they had to dismount, dragging the unwilling animals up the slope until they reached the top.

Serpicus saw all three of his friends looking at him surreptitiously. He didn't know what they were thinking. His memory burned him, the pain and guilt filled him. He had nothing to say. He ignored them.

When they arrived at the top they paused to look back.

At that exact moment a riderless horse galloped through the trees. A red cloth flapped under the saddle.

'Roman,' said Galba softly.

In the next few moments two more horses came into view. One was wounded and dragged his foreleg.

'Recognize them?' Decius asked.

Brutus shook his head. 'Might be Roman, might not.'

The wind was blowing into their faces from the direction of the fight. They listened, straining for a sound.

'I think I can hear something,' said Galba. 'Metal.'

They all heard a high-pitched scream, rising and falling to a whisper.

Then it went quiet.

Men appeared at the tree-line. Serpicus counted them.

Eight, nine, ten, about half of them on horseback. A pause. Then two more, both mounted. One was slumped forward in his saddle with an arm hanging uselessly. Two men slid awkwardly off their horses and lay stretched out on the ground, not moving. Another had both hands raised to his head and was held onto the saddle by two companions.

Drenthe stood beside them and looked down at the stricken Romans. 'Apparently my guard did well,' she said in a level voice. 'Once the Romans pull themselves together they'll follow the tracks. There will be others. Rest a moment. I'll go ahead, make sure there isn't an ambush waiting.' Brutus watched her go.

'She's a cold bitch,' Serpicus said, almost to himself, and spat on the ground.

Decius whirled around and strode towards Serpicus, tugging at his sword, fury on his face. Brutus held out an arm in front of him. Decius tried to push the arm aside but Brutus didn't move. Decius snapped the sword back into its scabbard and turned away.

Brutus moved close to Serpicus. 'Don't think you're the only one who feels anything,' he said seriously. 'There is more at stake here than your domestic problems. If you think she doesn't care then you aren't looking hard enough.' He began to turn away and then looked back. 'And if you ever say anything like that again, I'll put you on the ground myself.'

Serpicus looked at him dully. Galba stepped between them and pushed Serpicus away, his face expressionless. Serpicus could see how hard his friends were trying not

432

to judge him. He wondered why he had said what he did about Drenthe.

They heard the sound of another horse coming from the other direction. It was the fourth bodyguard, returned from scouting in front of them. She trotted up to them and looked around. She realized immediately that something had happened.

'What's wrong?' she said.

Brutus looked back down the hill. 'Your friends just made a meal of those Romans,' he said.

She looked in wonderment down at the remains of the Roman pursuers. 'They went alone?' she said. 'Just the three of them?' Brutus nodded. 'And you let them? You let them go without me?'

'We didn't know where you were,' said Drenthe, breathless from running back up the hill. 'They knew what had to be done.'

The woman's face hardened. 'You let them fight without me? Let them die and me live?'

Drenthe drew herself up. 'This isn't a time for thinking about yourself.'

'We swore an oath.'

'The gods will understand.'

'I should have been with them. We have always fought as one.'

'You were not here, or you would have accompanied them. Now I need you alive and here.'

The bodyguard drew her sword. 'I cannot stay here while their work is not finished.'

'It would be a waste,' said Drenthe. 'Stay. There will be other opportunities to avenge them.'

She smiled. 'You ask what I cannot give. My oath binds me.'

'Your oath is to me.'

She made a courtly gesture. 'My oath to you is great. You are my Chief. My life is yours to command, and I will die for you.'

'Then I command you to live now.'

The bodyguard pointed down the slope at the Roman soldiers standing and lying on the grass at the edge of the trees. 'Not while my sisters fight down there and I stand here.' She kicked the horse's flanks once and cantered down the hill, the horse's front legs jabbing rigid into the turf.

Brutus let out a sigh and drew his sword. Drenthe put a hand on his arm.

'Stay,' she said. 'This is not your fight.' Brutus didn't speak. He smiled at Drenthe, then held up a palm to Decius to indicate that he was to stay with her. He and Serpicus exchanged glances. Galba held out a hand which Brutus clasped briefly and then he pushed the horse forward. The slope allowed the tired animal to get up speed. By the bottom of the hill both horses were at full gallop and thundering straight for the soldiers at the tree-line.

There were a dozen dismounted soldiers in front of them. Eight could still ride and carry a sword. As soon as they saw the woman coming down the hill towards them with Brutus not far behind the officer jumped onto his horse, shouting orders. The other soldiers tried to join him, but the horses were still nervous from the fight and several of the legionaries had difficulty keeping them still enough to get on their backs. The wounded men tried to mount too, but needed help and so delayed their friends. By the time the two riders reached the Romans only half a dozen men were mounted and riding to meet them. Brutus held his sword at his side. The woman with him rode with an arrow fitted to her bow-string and two more clamped between her teeth. Her first shot took the officer through the upper sword-arm. He dropped his weapon with a hiss of pain and swung away. Before the sword hit the ground another soldier was falling from his horse with an arrow through his side. There wasn't time for a third shot and she hurled the bow at the men closing on her and drew her sword.

Two Romans rode straight at Brutus, one approaching from each side. Serpicus watched, the situation cutting through the fog in his mind. His friend was in a bad position. A horse-soldier is trained never to allow this situation to develop; whichever one he strikes at, the other has a clear chance at him. Had Brutus been carrying a shield he could have dropped the reins, blocked one attack with the shield while striking with his right arm and hoping that his horse would keep galloping straight, but he had only a sword.

Serpicus stood up on the crest of the hill and called out involuntarily. He had seen this fight before, and the lone fighter always lost. Brutus was a dead man. Serpicus was too far away to see exactly what happened next, but he saw Brutus' arm come up high, and the sun catch his blade as it twisted in his hand. The Roman on his right threw his arms back and fell from his horse. The other Roman reached Brutus a moment later and slashed down at his head, but Brutus was no longer there. He had swung his legs over and jumped down holding the pommel of his saddle. His feet hit the ground as the Roman's blade flew across the horse's back where he had sat a moment before. The horses were past each other and he leapt back into the saddle. He was safe, but unarmed. He swung the horse to the left, to where Drenthe's bodyguard had run into a clump of four Romans. She had unhorsed one and left him dead on the ground and was now fighting a second man who was defending himself left-handed, his right arm smashed and useless. The other two were working their way around behind her and she had to keep changing the angle of her attack to stop them striking her from behind. Only the ferocity of her assault and the nimbleness of her mount were keeping them out of reach, but she was hard pressed.

Brutus rode up behind the Roman with the broken arm and, as the Roman raised his sword to chop down at her, seized the man's wrist and yanked it backwards hard. Serpicus thought he heard the sound of the bone cracking from where he was standing. Brutus snatched the man's sword and smashed the pommel backhanded into the man's face. With both arms broken the Roman had no defence, and the blow sent him backwards over the horse's rump.

'He's good, you have to give him that,' said Galba judiciously.

Now the odds were even. Serpicus saw one soldier raise his sword to parry a blow, but Brutus brushed past his defence and a moment later the soldier rolled sideways, his head caved in. At the same moment the bodyguard feinted left then swung right and her sword went under the soldier's guard and into his side.

They turned to face the remaining Romans. There were five of them, but only one was armed and still on horseback, and he was leaning forward, bent over as if hurt. A couple more seemed fit to fight but were on foot. The other two were kneeling on the ground, obviously badly wounded.

There was a pause. For a moment Serpicus thought the Romans would charge, then he saw the two dismounted men take a step backwards behind the wounded horseman. They were defending their casualties, not pressing the attack.

'Leave them,' he murmured urgently.

Brutus walked his horse slowly in an arc around the Romans and went into the forest. The woman stayed, watching the Romans, who didn't move.

'What's he doing?' asked Decius.

'Looking for more Romans. Can't get enough of them,' said Galba.

'Looking for my guards,' said Drenthe, watching intently.

For a hundred heartbeats nothing happened, then Brutus reappeared alone and went back to where the woman was waiting. Drenthe shielded her eyes to watch as the two horses walked slowly back past the injured Romans. Suddenly she gasped and cried out, 'Watch him, look . . .'

Serpicus saw one of the Romans raise a bow behind the woman's back. Decius called out quietly, as if realizing it was too late and too far. The woman beside him

437

toppled backwards from her saddle and fell to the ground.

Brutus didn't hesitate. In a moment he was amongst the Romans, slashing with his sword. The man who had shot Drenthe's bodyguard died at once, his head split as he fumbled with the bow. The other uninjured man turned to run and lost his head to a single swing of Brutus' sword.

The three remaining men knelt with their hands raised in surrender. Brutus advanced on them with his sword raised, then stopped and turned the horse and went back to where the woman lay still. He looked down at her for a long moment, then pulled the exhausted horse round and rode slowly back up the hill.

Serpicus took several quick paces forward until he was standing beside Brutus. He put a hand on his friend's arm and looked up into his face. Brutus smiled, but his expression was strained. Drenthe came to stand beside Serpicus carrying a waterskin and motioned that Brutus should get down off his horse. He shook his head.

'Better stay put,' he said quietly.

Serpicus and Drenthe could both see a red stain on Brutus' tunic and blood running steadily down his thigh and off his saddle. If he once got off his mount he might not be able to get back on it.

Galba came up beside Brutus. The two men looked at each other and both nodded silently. Decius saw the blood and gasped involuntarily. He put a trembling hand on Brutus' arm.

'It's all right, lad,' Brutus wheezed. 'Doesn't hurt.'

Drenthe turned away decisively and remounted.

'All gone?' she asked Brutus, looking back at the forest.

He let out a sound like a sigh. 'Surrounded by dead Romans. It must have been some fight.'

She nodded slowly, as if considering the information. 'They kept their promise,' she said simply, and turned away. 'Come, there will be more Romans. The forest will protect us.'

34

They rode their tired horses through the trees until late afternoon. Decius rode beside Brutus all the way. At the beginning Brutus growled at him to keep his hands to himself, but by the end Decius was preventing him from falling to the ground, and Galba was doing the same on the other side. The stain was spreading across Brutus' tunic and blood was dripping off the end of his foot.

The forest thickened and they slowed, allowing the animals to rest.

They came to a clearing. The ground was dark and mossy underfoot. The trees around it were almost leafless and the weak sun in the northern sky barely filtered through the thin branches.

'Better give the horses a break,' Drenthe said. Serpicus could feel his mount trembling with exhaustion underneath him. The animal's wind might already be broken; even if not, he would take a long time to recover.

Serpicus went to help Brutus off his horse but was told by a silent look to leave him alone. The wounded man warned Decius off the same way, and then very slowly dismounted. He slumped against a fallen tree covered in dark moss.

Serpicus swung stiff legs off his horse and slid off the saddle. The toe of his shoe hit something solid in the thick grass, something like a large stone, but it wasn't heavy and it made a dull metallic noise. He bent down and picked it up.

It was a Roman helmet.

The leather straps were almost rotted away to thin knotted strings and the metal was covered with verdigris, but the shape was unmistakable. He turned it in his hands and a peaty smell rose from it.

'What's that?' asked Decius. Serpicus passed it to him without answering. Decius took it and his eyes widened.

'Romans? When have they come this far into the forest?'

Galba appeared behind him. 'Didn't they teach you any history?' he said. He took Decius by the arm and turned him around. 'Look.'

The trees were closely arrayed and cloaked in shadow, and Decius had to lean forward to see where he was indicating. He let out a startled yelp and took two quick paces backwards before peering intently into the gloom. He looked as if something large and unpleasant might be about to come flying out of the forest straight at him.

Serpicus glanced around, and suddenly saw what Decius was looking at.

Every tree looked misshapen in the shadow. The straight dark lines of the trunks were broken up with bulbous knots that looked like cooking pots, and strips of

441

material hung from them as if cloth and sticks had been roughly bundled together and tied there.

Except that they weren't cooking pots, or bundles of cloth, or sticks tied together.

Serpicus moved closer to the nearest tree. A rounded protuberance half-way up the trunk suddenly resolved itself. He saw teeth, eye-sockets, and the white bone of the skull. The left side of it was caved in and there was an arrow driven deep through one of the eye-sockets.

Next to that tree was another. A thick branch extended almost horizontally at chest-height, and from it three skeletons hung upside down, nailed through the ankles to the living wood. One leg on the nearest skeleton had worked free, as if struggling to release itself from its bonds, and it now hung sideways like a broken piece of rigging. A breeze moved the branches, and from all around the forest there was the groan and clack of bone rubbing on bone. Everywhere he looked, Serpicus saw bones nailed to the trees, bits of what might once have been men hanging from branches, and skulls lying on the ground like mushrooms. There were broken weapons too, and everywhere under their feet rotten pieces of uniform and equipment.

Serpicus had been here before. He knew what this place was.

'Varus' legions,' he whispered softly.

Decius looked at him. 'Varus? The one who lost the Eagles?' he said.

'Yes.' Serpicus looked around and a shiver ran across his shoulders. 'Even when the Romans eventually defeated the tribes and retrieved the Eagles, Germanicus never found exactly where Varus' last stand took place. He tortured dozens of captives, but they never spoke of it. No one would tell him where it was.' Serpicus realized that he was almost whispering. 'This is a sacred place.'

'Anywhere in Germany where a Roman dies is a sacred place,' growled Drenthe. She trotted off to scout the clearing.

Decius looked around. Everywhere the empty skulls of men leered back at him. 'There must have been hundreds of them.'

'Three legions in total, and their camp followers.' Serpicus gestured to the west. 'There were bodies strewn all along the trail, but the final fight took place some distance away.' He could remember it all, see the story-tellers around the camp fire, hear their voices rising as they told the tale. 'The Romans had been in the dark for days, and we had killed hundreds of them without them even being able to see us. Romans are used to the sun; it was as if they sought it out before they died. So they pushed deeper into the forest, looking for a clearing. When they found one, they made their stand.' Serpicus looked around. 'It was a larger space then. There was a great fire that day. The flames cleared the land so that the trees were able to grow back more thickly than before.'

Galba looked at him with curiosity. 'You were here?'

Serpicus nodded. 'I was too young to fight, but I was here.'

Decius looked around. 'Have you noticed how quiet it is?' he said.

Serpicus listened. He was right. No birds, no rustling

undergrowth, no animal cries. They seemed to be the only living things there.

A branch snapped and everyone turned towards it. Drenthe came out from the gloom. 'Nothing useful that I can see,' she said. 'All the weapons were taken away. Everything left behind is broken or rusted through.'

'Nothing left but spirits,' Serpicus said, surprising himself. Drenthe raised a wry eyebrow.

'I never had you down for a superstitious man,' she said.

'I'm not,' he said, feeling embarrassed.

'If it is true that something lives on after a man dies,' said Decius, 'then this is the sort of place where you would be able to sense it.' He had a strange expression on his face.

There was a pause. Drenthe stood with her fists on her hips and looked at them both with amusement. 'Did your grandparents have a lot of fun sending you to sleep with ghost stories?' she asked.

There was a sharp report nearby, a branch cracking under its own weight. Decius and Serpicus both jumped and then pretended they hadn't.

'There are Romans chasing us,' said Drenthe. 'D'you think perhaps we should give that matter some attention?' Serpicus shook himself as if to get rid of a damp cloak that someone had draped over his shoulders, and tried to look attentive. She pointed towards the afternoon sun. 'They will come from that direction. We can either go back into the forest and hide, or we can stay here.'

'Come on then,' said Decius. He turned to help Brutus,

who was sitting leaning against the fallen tree with his eyes closed. His skin was pale. He held up a hand.

'I've come far enough,' said Brutus in a distant rasp, quite unlike his normal voice. 'I'm going to stay here.'

His face was lined with pain. Serpicus bent over him and started to lift his shirt to check the wound underneath. Brutus put a hand on Serpicus' arm to stop him. The touch of his palm felt dry, like onion skin left out in the sun all day.

'Leave me alone,' he said quietly. 'I'm done. I can't walk, I can't ride. I can't stand being dragged through the forest any more. Give me a bow and a sword and leave me here. I'll keep them talking long enough to give you a chance.'

Decius shook his head. 'No. We won't leave you.' A tear ran down his cheek and he sat down on the fallen tree beside Brutus. He looked around at the others. 'We can't just leave him.'

Brutus managed to smile at Decius. 'You know you must. My day is almost finished. No point in us all dying here.'

Serpicus glanced up at Drenthe. She met his gaze for a moment and then looked away. Serpicus took Brutus' hand and held it. Galba came and stood beside him. Brutus smiled and Serpicus felt his fingers press against his palm. 'Go on, you two,' he said huskily. 'Say hello to the girls in Ox's for me.'

Galba leant a bow and a dozen arrows against the tree. 'You think they'll remember you?'

Brutus smiled. 'Oh, I think one or two of them will.' A brief shadow of pain passed over his face. 'Drink my health with them when you see them.' He winked slowly at Serpicus. 'Go, now. The Romans can't be far away.'

Serpicus stood up and pulled Decius to his feet. 'Come on,' he said. Decius hesitated and wiped his sleeve across his eyes. Brutus looked at Decius for a long moment, winked at him and then turned away.

Decius stood looking at Brutus, his face contorted with grief and indecision. He looked at Serpicus for help. Serpicus stepped forward and handed Brutus his sword. For a moment Serpicus thought that Decius was going to hit him. Then the tears started to run down Decius' face. He turned away and plunged into the forest.

Brutus watched him go. 'Look after him for me,' he said.

'Of course,' Serpicus said.

Drenthe silently raised the handle of her sword to her forehead in salute. Brutus nodded to her and she turned to follow Decius. Galba followed, leaving Brutus and Serpicus alone.

'What exactly would you like me to tell Ox's girls for you?' Serpicus asked, uncomfortably aware that his voice was roughened with emotion.

Brutus thought for a moment. 'Just tell them that I always meant what I said, at least I did at the time I said it.' He held out his hand. 'Now fuck off like a good fellow and let a friend die in peace.'

Serpicus grasped his forearm in the Roman way. Brutus smiled. Serpicus could only meet his eyes for a moment.

'We'll meet again in Hades,' Brutus said hoarsely. 'But no need to hurry, eh? Now go, quickly.'

Serpicus turned away and it felt like tearing a barbed hook from his heart. He didn't dare look back, but trotted to the edge of the clearing to where Drenthe and Galba were waiting.

'Where is Decius?' he asked.

Drenthe pointed into the forest. 'That way. Easy enough to follow. He . . .' Suddenly her eyes opened wide and she reached out, grabbed Serpicus by his breastplate and dragged him into the trees.

Serpicus didn't have to ask what was going on. He threw himself flat on the cold ground and then, keeping low, he peered cautiously over a large fallen branch in front of him. Galba appeared next to him, on the other side from Drenthe.

Brutus was sat on the moss-covered trunk, hunched and still. He looked like a farmer resting after a hard day; in a land where farmers wear armour and carry swords and bows.

The Romans were on the other side of the clearing, led by a tall centurion. Three or four men clustered behind him. To their right and left Serpicus could see other men appearing through the trees. The Romans had learned at least one lesson from Varus; the value of advancing in small groups, far enough apart to allow freedom of movement and to prevent the enemy concentrating his force, but close enough to support each other if one group was attacked.

A Roman officer came into view. Serpicus' hand tightened on his sword handle, and he saw Brutus lift his head.

Consilius.

A branch cracked behind them. Serpicus whirled around.

'What the hell are you doing here?' he hissed.

Decius came towards them in a running crouch. 'We have to help him,' he hissed, peering through the branches. Drenthe held him down with one hand and put the other on Serpicus' shoulder.

'This is the way he wanted it,' she said. 'Respect the way he chose to die.' Decius lay down again, his anguish clear on his face. Serpicus felt paralysed, like a bird watching a snake.

The centurion walked to stand beside the fair-haired man and they conferred briefly. Then Consilius stepped forward and stood a few paces from Brutus with his arms folded.

'So, old man,' he said, the sound carrying clearly to every side of the clearing. 'They have abandoned you. Typical Germans. Even pack wolves do not leave their injured behind.' His clear, arrogant tones carried easily to where they crouched in the cover of the forest.

Brutus looked up at him. 'They do, if it is for the greater good, as you would know if you knew even half so much as you pretend,' he said. He reached out and seized the stump of a broken-off branch and slowly stood up until he was facing Consilius. Sweat was pouring down his face with the effort and he had to pause a few moments to get his breath. 'And I am not so much an old man that I cannot best you if needs be.' He was taller and broader than the Roman and leaning towards him. Consilius took half a step back and dropped a hand to his sword. 'You can dream, old man,' he said.

The Roman's sword came out of the scabbard in his left hand so that he held it like a theatre assassin's dagger. He feinted towards Brutus, who swayed backwards to avoid it, and then tossed the blade to his right and swung backhanded. Brutus was forced to step back and struck his heel against the rotten tree. For a moment it looked as if he might retain his balance but then he toppled over backwards. He hit the ground and Serpicus heard him groan with pain.

Consilius jumped up on the tree-trunk and let out a short bark of satisfaction. Brutus lay below him, one foot still up on the trunk, trapped between the branches of the tree. The Roman stepped down beside him and held out his sword.

'I send you to Hell,' he said. 'Don't make any immediate plans, your friends will be following shortly.'

'I'll see you there,' hissed Brutus, and, raising both hands, he made a circle between the forefinger and thumb of his right hand and thrust his left thumb up through it, jabbing it at the Roman.

Consilius lunged forward with the sword outstretched and Serpicus heard Brutus make a sound as if he had been punched hard in the stomach. The Roman shifted his balance and then pushed the sword forward again with all his weight. Then he withdrew it, pulling himself upright as he did so.

The blade was stained red half-way to the hilt.

Brutus lifted himself up briefly then fell back again. He tried to prop himself up on his elbow, and then slowly slid back against the branches and lay still. For a moment there was nothing but silence.

'No!'

From the side of the clearing a howling figure ran out with a sword upraised, heading straight for Consilius. The Roman instinctively took a step backwards. He trod on a branch and for a moment was unsteady. The banshee reached him and brought the sword down with all his force. Consilius regained his balance at that instant and held up his own weapon, blocking the blow. The ring of the impact rang round the clearing and the force of the attack sent Consilius stumbling sideways. The Roman soldiers hesitated, then moved forward to help their captain.

'Decius, stop!' shouted Drenthe, and she stood up so that everyone could see her. Decius paused his attack.

'You go, now, quickly!' he said, his voice high with grief. 'I will kill him and follow you.'

The Roman soldiers surrounded Decius and held out their spear-points towards him.

Drenthe held up a hand. 'Stop,' she said, in a quiet, steady voice full of command. Consilius saw her and nodded to the centurion. He snapped a brisk order and everyone stood still, waiting. Serpicus held her by the arm.

'Don't do it,' he said urgently. Drenthe smiled at him.

'It's all right,' she said simply, and waited for him to release her. When he did so she stepped out from the protection of the trees.

'Consilius,' she said. 'Let the boy go.'

Serpicus felt as if the heel of a large man's hand had thumped into his chest. 'No,' he said softly.

Consilius looked at her and then at Decius, and

smiled. 'Why should I do that?' he said. 'I already have the boy, we are twelve, you are one.' He looked at Decius, and then beyond Drenthe, to see Serpicus and Galba emerging as well. 'Well, three and a half perhaps. Still good odds. I have all of you now, without releasing or fighting anyone.'

'Not so.'

A spear-throw from where Consilius had appeared from the forest, six men appeared. Three were in something approximating Roman uniform, and the rest were dressed in an assortment of German leather and Roman metal, though it was hard to tell exactly what as they were wrapped in furs against the cold. They were led by a centurion past retirement age. The men behind Consilius hesitated. The new arrivals walked across the clearing and stood beside Decius.

'By all the gods,' Serpicus said slowly. Severus turned and looked at him, and dropped one eyelid in a lascivious wink. Serpicus shook his head in disbelief. 'Not dead, then?'

'Not yet,' the centurion said. 'And the gods had nothing to do with it.'

The two men clasped hands. Severus looked at Serpicus and smiled. 'It's a strange thing,' he said, 'but the closer we got to Rome, the less we wanted to get there.'

Serpicus returned the smile, and nodded his thanks to the men behind Severus. The two groups faced each other over Brutus' body. Consilius stood in front of his men and fixed his eyes on Drenthe. His gaze burned and he swung the sword loosely from his wrist as if he was preparing to run through all of them to get to her.

Serpicus looked around. It was an interesting situation. There were six in Severus' group, plus Decius, Galba, Serpicus and Drenthe. Consilius had fifteen men with him, but several of those looked like beardless recruits only just out of basic training and the others didn't look keen to die for their leader, whereas all of Severus' men were hardened fighters. In a straight contest, head to head, the odds were that there wouldn't be a winner. There might just be one person left standing at the end, and there was no guarantee who that might be.

There was a long pause while every man in the clearing looked at the man opposite him. They fingered their swords and looked from face to face, and no one made the first move.

Severus cleared his throat. 'Centurion,' he called out casually across the clearing while looking critically at the edge of his sword. The centurion standing beside Consilius looked at him suspiciously.

'What?' he shouted back.

'How's the leg?'

The centurion looked down instinctively, then back up again with narrowed eyes. 'Sore in cold weather. Why?'

'I just wondered,' Severus said, looking at his feet and scuffing the damp earth with the heel of his boot like a schoolboy. 'I wondered if any of my spit was left in it still.'

The centurion leant forward, his eyes narrowed. 'Severus?' he said softly.

'Publius,' replied Severus with a smile. 'I thought it was you.'

452

Consilius held out a sword at shoulder height so that it was across his centurion's face, preventing him from moving any closer to Severus. 'You are a Roman soldier,' Consilius called to Severus. 'Would you fight us, legionaries like yourself? Your brothers?'

'If necessary,' said Severus with a shrug. 'It's happened before. But we'd rather not.' He looked back at his men. 'In this situation we see ourselves more as . . . honest brokers. Referees, if you prefer.' He pointed at Consilius and his voice hardened. 'And you are no brother of mine or any of my men. What you do here has nothing to do with serving Rome and everything to do with your own vanity and ambition. We want nothing to do with it, and your men should have nothing to do with it either.'

'Don't try and subvert my men,' Consilius snapped. 'You are already insubordinate at best, traitors at worst. A Roman soldier knows his duty. None of my men will join you.'

Severus looked at Consilius for a long moment. 'I have a suggestion,' he said.

'I don't want to hear it.'

Severus shrugged again. 'It's a good offer.'

'I will make you an offer,' Consilius snarled, stepping forward and pointing with the sword. 'Give me the German bitch immediately and I will consider not crucifying you. Anything short of that will mean I nail you all up for the crows.'

The centurion behind Consilius stepped forward and pushed his commander's sword-arm down. 'I want to hear what he has to say,' he said.

Serpicus saw Consilius' jaw harden. The fist clenched around the sword and the bicep contracted and for a moment Serpicus thought that Consilius would bring the sword up hard into the centurion's throat. The two men stood facing each other, close enough for their breath to mingle. The centurion met his gaze steadily. Consilius slowly relaxed.

'Very well, we'll hear him,' he said. 'It might be amusing. But no tricks.'

'No tricks,' agreed Severus. 'I suggest a duel.'

Consilius barked an incredulous laugh. 'With champions? How quaint.'

Severus let a pause fall before continuing. 'You' – he pointed with his sword at Consilius – 'you fight her.' He swung the sword round like a teacher pointing at a pupil until it was aimed at Drenthe, then left it there while turning back to Consilius. 'If you win, you have got what you want, and everyone goes home. If you lose, everyone else has what they want and everyone still goes home.' He paused. 'You agree?'

'No!' said Decius, his cheeks turned white with just a point of red under each eye. The boy was looking at Drenthe in a way that was unmistakable, as a man looks at a woman. Serpicus reached out and closed his fingers around the muscle in Decius' arm to quiet him, wondering for a moment how he had failed to see that the boy had become a man. His thoughts piled up inside his head. The duel was a risk, but Serpicus thought that Severus knew what he was doing. Consilius' thoughts were racing across his face for everyone to see as he counted the odds. Single combat was dangerous, but so was a pitched fight involving everyone in the clearing.

Decius turned to Serpicus, his face anguished. 'Stop them,' he said. 'He'll kill her. Don't let it happen.'

A cold finger stroked Serpicus' heart for an instant and then vanished. He said nothing.

Drenthe looked at Decius reproachfully. 'Thanks for the vote of confidence,' she said.

Severus slouched and tapped his sword aimlessly against his leg as if he were waiting for someone habitually late. He looked up and across the clearing at Consilius and his voice became deliberately slow, mocking his indecision. 'I don't know why you hesitate,' he said mildly. 'After all, that's why we're all here, isn't it? To kill her?'

There was a silence. Drenthe looked at him with real surprise. 'To kill me? Why?'

Severus didn't take his eyes off Consilius. 'That's what this was always about. They wanted you dead.'

Drenthe lifted an eyebrow. 'Very flattering. Who, exactly, is it wants me dead?'

'Sejanus, his generals, his tame senators. They looked around for some Germans who could get into Gelbheim without being challenged, and then got Blaesus to send them to fetch his bear for him. That's why Serpicus and Decius are here. They were cover for Cato. He'd never have got into the village, let alone near Drenthe, if he hadn't been with them.'

It was Serpicus' turn to look incredulous. 'But what about the animal?'

Severus made a dismissive gesture. 'You are animal trackers, so he used the bear. If you'd been professional drunks Blaesus would have said there was a drinking festival he needed you to attend for him. If you were acrobats, he'd have said he'd contracted to provide the Gelbheimers a circus.' He glanced at Drenthe. 'They wanted her dead, and they needed someone to get Cato into the village so that he could do it. Everything else was garnish.'

Serpicus shook his head in slow disbelief. 'But why would they kill her? She was keeping the Treveri out of the rebellion when just about every other German tribe was joining it.'

Severus pursed his lips and looked hard across the clearing at Consilius. 'A good question, and one you'd have to ask that smooth-faced bastard over there. Why would a Roman senator want to kill a leader who was trying to keep her tribe out of a war against Rome?' He looked at Serpicus. 'Think about it. Imagine you're an investigator. You're looking into a murder and you don't know who did it. What's the first question you'd ask?'

Serpicus thought for a moment. 'I suppose . . . you'd look at anyone mentioned in the will? Ask who benefits from the death?'

Severus nodded. 'Very good question. So, ask it.'

Serpicus hesitated, dazed by what Severus was saying. Then Drenthe's voice spoke up clearly. 'Who benefits from a war with the German tribes, and why?'

'Exactly,' said Severus. 'Perhaps when we return to Rome we should ask that question.'

'This is entertaining nonsense,' Consilius called across the clearing. 'You know nothing about . . .'

'Perhaps,' interrupted Severus. 'But you will notice

that everyone here is now giving the matter some thought.' He paused to let Consilius look at his men, who were listening with surprise and curiosity to the conversation. 'So, do you fight, or will you leave here now?'

Serpicus could see that Consilius in fact had little choice. His honour and pride were in question. Added to that, Severus was asking uncomfortable questions. If there was a conspiracy then the longer the talk went on the more time it gave to everyone to think about it. Serpicus wasn't surprised when Consilius made the best of it. He looked at Drenthe and drew his thin lips into a smile.

'Winner takes all. You agree, bitch?'

Drenthe smiled back. 'You like that word too much,' she said, holding out her sword towards him and drawing circular shapes in the air with a steady movement of her wrist. 'I'll carve it between your shoulder-blades like a tattoo so that your boyfriends will have something to read when you bend over for them.' Consilius scowled and turned to adjust the straps of his armour without reply.

Serpicus remembered Consilius' smile from the first time they had met. He also remembered what Consilius had said then. He called them 'the Partner's Germans'. Not 'Uncle's Germans', which would have meant that Blaesus was in charge. 'The Partner's Germans'. Sejanus. Sejanus had arranged it, through Blaesus. It went even higher than they thought.

Severus looked enquiringly across the clearing at Publius, the centurion standing by Consilius, and called to him. 'Centurion?'

Publius looked up.

'One rule. We hold the ring only. No interference, no help nor hindrance, not by anyone, not your men or mine. Agreed?'

Publius hesitated, glancing instinctively at Consilius, and then nodded without waiting for an order.

Drenthe leant towards Severus with a movement of her head as if agreeing to the terms. 'Can we trust them?' she asked softly.

Severus did something between a nod and a shrug. 'Consilius, let's be frank, probably not. He'd break his word to himself if he thought there was advantage in it. Publius, maybe. I used to know him. He also owes me his leg and therefore his career from a wound he got in Parthia. That counts for something. Against that, he's a lifer soldier and he can't be far off his pension. Consilius owns his nuts and the army owns his soul. I think he'll want to be honest if given the chance, but don't bet your summer villa on it. Let's not push him unless we have to.'

'We should run, just run,' said Decius, the skin on his face a stretched mask of worry.

Serpicus looked at Drenthe. She seemed calm about the prospect of fighting a man much larger than herself. 'Is this the only answer?' he asked.

'Yes,' said Drenthe. She looked at Decius, who didn't speak but stood beside them as tense as a drawn bow. 'Don't worry. I'll kill him quickly and then we'll be on our way.' She reached out quickly and brushed her fingers against his cheek. He tried to take her hand but it was gone before he could hold it.

'I'm the only one who can end this,' she said to all of them, her face serious. 'This way, the Roman dies, I am satisfied, and the rest of us live.' Decius' face betrayed his thoughts and she smiled. 'Or I die, and he is satisfied, and the rest of you live.' Serpicus wondered what would happen if Consilius won and was not satisfied, but said nothing.

Severus leant close to her and spoke softly. 'I've never seen him fight, but I know what men say about him. He is quick, and he knows all the tricks. He is right-handed, but he usually fights with his left because of a spear he got in his right shoulder a few years ago.'

Drenthe nodded slowly, gazing across the clearing at Consilius. 'That should help.'

Severus shook his head. 'Not really. He fights almost as well with his left.'

She looked amused. 'Any more good news for me?'

Severus shook his head. 'Not really, but one thought. My experience of pretty boys is, no matter how good with a weapon they are, if you wave something pointed and sharp in front of their faces, you get their full attention.'

Drenthe flexed her wrist until the joint made a sound like frozen river-water when a man on the other side steps carefully down onto it from the bank. 'I find that's true of most people, but I take your point.'

Consilius cinched the final buckle on his armour and turned to face them, his sword outstretched.

Drenthe moved towards Serpicus and beckoned Decius close. She spoke to both of them softly, hardly moving her lips. 'You know what Severus said earlier, about how if Consilius won then everyone would be satisfied and go home quietly?'

'Yes.'

'Fuck that. If he kills me I want you to spread his guts all over the forest floor.'

Decius and Serpicus glanced at each other and Serpicus spoke for both of them.

'You can count on it.'

'That means I will win or lose equally happily.' She spat on her hands and rubbed them together. 'I hope those four girls are still waiting for me on the river-bank, we can split a bottle together at Wodan's table tonight.'

Galba had been standing silently nearby. He leant in towards Serpicus. 'As you'll have noticed, I'm waiting here silently on events, or more correctly, on translation. You will, of course, let me know if you need me to fight anyone?'

Serpicus gave him a wry look. 'If the time comes to fight, I suspect you'll work it out without my help.'

Consilius walked steadily forward ten paces and stopped, his sword held up at an angle across his belly. Drenthe advanced until she was just out of reach, her sword-arm hanging loose by her side. Serpicus wondered why Consilius had not complained about the fact that her sword was half as long again as his. Perhaps he wanted her to have to handle the extra weight.

She stood looking utterly relaxed. Serpicus watched carefully. She was confident, perhaps over-confident. Perhaps she didn't care. Or perhaps she was up to something. They all stepped back to give the fighters room.

'Any bets?' Galba murmured to Severus.

'Lousy odds,' the centurion said. 'Let's face it, he should win. She might surprise us. Three to two on the Roman.'

'I'll take those odds,' a soldier beside him said. Serpicus recognized him as one of the two Gauls who had fought beside Drenthe at the gate when the final Roman assault came. 'She's better than any woman I've ever seen, and she's got more balls than most men.'

Severus nodded slowly. 'True. But he's bigger and stronger and he knows his way around with a sword.'

Decius turned on him, fear clawing at his face. 'Then why did you suggest the fight?'

Severus spoke without turning to face him. 'Because she's mean and she's fast and she's been fighting every day since she bit the midwife's finger. And she wants to fight him. She wants him dead for her village and her tribe, while Consilius only wants to kill her because it's his job and it's the sort of thing he likes doing.' Severus looked around into the dark forest surrounding them. 'If I believed in such things, I'd say the people who died in Gelbheim might even be watching this little fracas from wherever they are and cheering her on. Now shut up and watch. And keep half an eye on those other Romans, they might try something.'

Serpicus looked at Consilius' soldiers. He doubted that. They were content to let their commander do the fighting for them; win or lose, either way they would all be going home after the fight.

Serpicus thought Consilius would rush to the attack at once, but he dropped into a crouch and began to move sideways, still facing her, crossing his legs in the gladiator's walk. It was a good way of moving across the uneven and slippery ground. Drenthe made no attempt to shadow his movements, merely turned in a slow circle so that she continued to face him.

It soon became obvious what the Roman was doing. The ground he was moving over was up a slight incline. If Drenthe allowed him to move unimpeded he would eventually have the advantage of the higher ground. It wasn't much, but any fighter would normally value it, and any fighter who was conceding height already would surely be concerned at adding to the disadvantage. Drenthe watched him move but didn't seem concerned.

'Why doesn't she stop him?' murmured Decius.

In a few more steps Consilius was at the highest point. It was clear what he was going to do next, and he did it. He paused for a moment, and then came at her, shuffling forward in short steps so that his left foot was always in front of his right, and with his sword-arm held high.

Serpicus watched, assessing the fight. The normal defence to such an attack would be for Drenthe to raise her sword above her head to parry the threatened blow. However, Consilius was taller and heavier than Drenthe, and was attacking from slightly above her. He would be confident of breaking through any attempt to block his stroke. Alternatively, once he was committed, she could duck and move quickly to her left, hoping to cut at him as he went past. Serpicus didn't like her position. Her movement would have to be swift and exact to escape him, and Consilius would make sure that, while all his strength would be behind the blow, his weight would still be centred. If he failed to connect he still wasn't going to overbalance and could then immediately follow up while she was getting back her balance.

The clearing was absolutely silent as the attack came. Decius opened his mouth to shout a warning but it was pointless. Consilius loomed over her. She raised her sword to shoulder height, but otherwise didn't react. His sword came overarm and down on her head like a blacksmith's hammer on an anvil.

Except that her head wasn't there any more.

Consilius knew there wasn't time for her to get her sword high enough to deflect his blow, so he was anticipating that she would drop low and move to her right. His sword would then pass over her left shoulder and she could then strike under his arm at his side. So instead of striking at an angle from left to right he cut down and to his left, so that a step away would not save her.

She stepped a little to her right, but not to get away from his sword. As his arm descended she jabbed her own blade forward in a short uppercut. Consilius instinctively arched his torso but she was not aiming at his body.

There was a frozen moment when the two of them were close together, staring into each other's faces, neither moving, and the watchers could not see what had happened. Then Consilius' fingers spread wide. The sword carried on and fell harmlessly to the ground. She stepped forward and picked it up.

Her own weapon was embedded in Consilius' forearm. She had let his own momentum drive his arm onto her blade. It went in above his wrist and came out the other side.

Consilius staggered and his mouth opened in a gasp of pain. Then he stood upright, looked at Drenthe and took hold of the hilt with his right hand. He watched her face as he pulled the sword from his own arm. Blood streamed down his arm and off his elbow, darkening the snow. When it was out he breathed out a long breath and laughed.

'You can't beat me, bitch,' he said, panting. 'I fight with both arms.'

'Then let's hope for your sake that you fight better with the other one,' she said, and slashed down at his neck.

Consilius blocked the blow and the three that followed it, then pressed his own attack, pushing her backwards. Blood was dripping off his hand and falling to the ground freely. Any soldier could see that a man could only fight for a short time with a wound like that before the pain and loss of blood slowed him down. Consilius had to win the fight soon or it would be taken away from him. Drenthe only had to defend herself and wait, and they both knew it.

He swung wildly at her head. Drenthe swayed from the waist like a Persian dancer and took a short step back. Serpicus saw her foot stop above the ground and then slip sideways. Something round, a helmet perhaps, rolled away from under her heel. Consilius saw her stumble and moved quickly forward, swinging at her like a drunken harvester. As Drenthe fell backwards to the ground the two swords connected with a tearing crash. The impact twisted the hilt in her hand and the sword spun away from her. Consilius jumped forward and kicked the sword out of her reach. She rolled to one side to retrieve it and he moved quickly forward to get between her and the weapon. She made a despairing lunge at it and missed. Consilius swatted her away with a blow to her temple with the back of his good fist. She rolled away again and came up on one knee.

Decius stepped forward instinctively. The Romans across the clearing tensed. Severus' hand shot out and landed on Decius' shoulder. The young man tried to pull away and then gasped with pain as the centurion's thumb dug deep into the top of his arm. 'All right, I'll stay,' he hissed. Severus relaxed, but pulled Decius back and sat him down on a rock nearby. The Romans saw what happened and took their hands off their swords.

Consilius' fist clearly dazed her. She threw herself sideways to avoid his next attack, rolling through the wet grass. Consilius stepped forward with his sword upraised and then stopped as his foot stood on a branch which gave way with a loud crack. It was only a few inches off the ground but he hesitated for a moment and she was away from his reach. A few yards away from him she stopped rolling and came up in a crouch, her hands on the ground. Her fingers clutched and closed and she pulled something from the grip of the grass. A heavy legionary's spear, blackened by age and damp.

Severus looked up to see what Consilius' Romans were doing. The centurion had his hand on his sword-hilt and was leaning forward, looking across the clearing. Severus folded his arms in an exaggerated way, gestured to Decius, and called out across the clearing.

'Neither help nor hinder, agreed?' The centurion

hesitated, looked at the ancient spear, slippery with mildew, and relaxed. 'I don't think he's looking for a fight,' Severus said contentedly to himself.

'We should help her,' said Decius. 'She doesn't stand a chance.'

Galba spoke without turning. 'You need to have more faith, boy,' he said. 'You want to bet?'

Decius shook his head. 'I wouldn't bet on a life,' he said.

Galba pursed his lips in mock disappointment. 'And I thought we had turned you into a Roman after all.'

The two contestants were circling each other, getting their breath back. Consilius had his sword against Drenthe's ancient spear, held in both her hands like a pike. Serpicus looked appraisingly at the spear. It might perhaps still be strong, or it might be rotted through and shatter at the first impact. Against that, Consilius was bleeding heavily from a useless arm, whereas she was uninjured.

Drenthe jabbed with the spear low at Consilius' belly and he swung at it. His short sword struck the spear-tip a glancing blow. Serpicus watched intently as the spear shook under the impact, but held together. She repeated the movement, aiming lower at the Roman's groin. Consilius jumped back, arching at the waist. She slid her left hand along the spear so that it was held across her body like a staff and brought the sharp tip around to threaten his face. As soon as he raised his sword to counter it she stopped the movement, reversed it and swung the heavy butt around at his leg with all her strength. Consilius saw the movement and slashed frantically downwards. It was too late to stop her attack, but, as the handle of the spear smashed into his knee, the edge of his sword ran down the outside of her bicep and bit deep to the bone of her left forearm.

Consilius sank onto the ground in front of Drenthe, his face twisted with pain.

'Kill him!' yelled Decius.

If she thrust at Consilius with the spear he could not immediately retreat. However, she now had a wound of her own similar to the one she had given him earlier, and a one-handed thrust with a spear is easily deflected. She hesitated a moment, and then turned away from him. A couple of Consilius' soldiers started to jeer and then realized what she was doing. In a few steps she had retrieved her sword and was advancing again in a fighting crouch, with the ancient spear tucked under her wounded left arm and the sword ready for battle in her right.

'Throw the spear!' shouted Decius. She hesitated and looked at the spear as if the idea hadn't occurred to her. She looked across at Decius, nodding once as if acknowledging what he had said. Then she stood straight and dropped the spear on the ground. Consilius saw it and renewed his efforts to get to his feet. Drenthe stood in front of him and waited until he was upright. Then she held out her good arm until the point of her sword was aimed directly at his eyes.

'Hear me, Roman,' she said. 'You have invaded my lands, destroyed my village, killed my people. For that I will kill you, and I will think it a good bargain if I die with you. Can you say the same?'

'I don't need to, bitch,' hissed Consilius, leaning sideways so that almost all his weight was on his sound leg. Blood trickled down his arm. 'You're going to die, I'm not.'

Serpicus thought Drenthe had more to say but instead she let out a fierce yell and charged. Consilius stood up and roared back. In a moment the air was full of the sound of clashing metal and the flash of swords in the pale sunlight. Drenthe stood in front of Consilius and hacked at him without pattern, as if he were a thorn bush that had made her angry. It was an assault that had to succeed and could not slow down. If she left him a chance to attack then he would kill her because she made no attempt to defend herself. The blows fell on him like rocks falling down a cliff. It could not go on. With all her strength she swung at him, a jolting thrust that broke through his defence to cut a long furrow down his side. He grunted with pain and raised his sword for the next attack. It didn't come. She stood before him, her arms by her side, utterly drained. Consilius stood up and raised his sword. With a great effort she did the same, but the end of the sword trembled and dipped and ended up at waist height.

'Surrender, bitch?'

She looked up from under the veil of her hair. 'Only to your mother, and only after she's worn out every horse in your legion.'

Consilius smiled thinly. He lifted his sword high and stepped forward to bring it down on her head. Serpicus put a hand on his sword and gripped it tightly. Consilius was going to kill her unless she raised her exhausted arm to block it or else threw herself to one side to avoid it.

Or ignored his descending sword altogether, and attacked him.

She threw herself forward, every muscle in her body concentrated on the effort, and thrust at him with all her weight. His sword-arm came down hard on her, but by then her blade was under his breastplate and deep into him.

She left it there and staggered back against the fallen tree and watched him, her shoulders rising up and down with her breath. Serpicus realized he was holding his breath. Her strategy had worked, but he couldn't tell what the cost had been.

Consilius dropped onto one knee. His hands were around the hilt of the sword in his side as if to pull it out, but he made no movement. Blood spread across his tunic and stained the earth below him. He looked up into Drenthe's face.

'I'll wait for you in Hell, bitch,' he said.

'I look forward to it,' she replied.

He toppled over onto the ground and lay without moving.

Severus looked across the clearing. The Romans there were all standing, hands on their swords, waiting for Publius to give the order. Severus folded his arms and kicked absently at a clod of frozen earth.

'Everything all right?' he called.

The centurion looked at Severus for a long moment, then thrust his sword back in its scabbard.

'Yes. We will keep our agreement.'

Decius let out a cry and ran forward. Drenthe had

fallen sideways off the tree and was lying in the grass close to Consilius.

Before Serpicus reached her he could see that Consilius' last blow had found its mark. She had put him off his aim, but not enough. He hadn't split her skull as he'd intended, but the blade had struck her temple square on. The side of her head was a bloody mess. Serpicus knelt by her. He reached out and felt the wound as gently as he could with his fingertips. It felt like pulped fruit underneath the dark copper hair.

Decius sank to his knees and lifted her head gently onto his lap. She pushed the tears on his cheeks away with the back of her hand.

'You'll freeze to death,' she said. Her voice was hoarse. She looked up at Severus. 'Make the boy stand up, he'll be dead before I will.' The sound became a whisper and her hand fell slowly back to the ground.

Decius made an animal noise and crouched over her, his body shaking with silent tears.

Serpicus looked down at her still face and said nothing. Deep inside him, so deep and so long ago that he could only just hear it, a small boy was crying unrestrained tears.

Serpicus felt a large hand upon his shoulder. He turned to see Severus motioning him away from where Decius sat. They walked together to the side of the clearing. For a short while they watched the Romans on the other side of the clearing gathering their arms and disappearing back into the trees. Publius was the last to leave. As he reached the tree-line he paused. He turned around, stood to attention and saluted Severus with a slow respectful gesture. The centurion returned it, and Publius followed his men.

The silence was broken only by Decius' muted grief.

Galba stood beside Serpicus and looked around the clearing. 'Too many people have died here,' he said quietly. Serpicus nodded but didn't speak.

The lines in Severus' brow deepened. 'Now what will you do?' he asked.

Serpicus didn't reply immediately. He fingered the handle of his sword and looked out over the trees to the south. Then he looked at Severus with a decisive set to his face.

'We'll bury the dead. Then I'm going back to Rome.'

Severus nodded. 'Us too. We'll all travel together then. It'll be safer.' He hesitated. 'Then what?'

Serpicus looked to the sky again. 'I'm going to find that bastard Cato, and I'll kill him and see if that satisfies me, and if it isn't enough then I may just kill Blaesus as well.'

35

Severus raised both eyebrows. 'You'll have a job to do that, with the number of guards he goes around with. But if you manage it they'll probably declare a public holiday in your name.'

'You won't stop me?'

The centurion shrugged. 'Blaesus can take care of himself, and if you don't kill him then there are plenty of others who will try. You have as good reason as any.'

'And Cato?'

Severus frowned. 'Do what you want with him. I don't approve of assassins, or spies, or liars, or people who hurt the families of my friends. I never liked him even before I knew he was all those things.'

'I don't ask for your help. There's no need for you to be implicated. All I ask is that you don't try and prevent me.'

'None of us will.' He glanced across at Decius. 'What about the lad?'

'It's his choice.'

At that moment Decius laid Drenthe's head gently on the ground. He stood up, pushed something inside his shirt, and then faced them.

'I'm coming back to Rome with you,' he said, his face drawn with pain. The innocence of his face was gone. He had aged in a day.

'You don't have to,' said Serpicus.

'Yes I do. Cato and Blaesus killed her as much as Consilius. I want to be there when you kill them.'

Severus coughed and shook himself, then smiled. 'Looks like we'll have a good party then. Let's get going.'

Severus went off to arrange things. Serpicus stood still, looking into the forest. Galba reached out to put a hand on his shoulder and then moved away.

Decius spoke from behind him. 'You loved her too.' Serpicus said nothing. Decius came beside him, standing very close. 'She's dead. Why don't you care?'

Serpicus felt as if he was standing on the edge of a cliff on a moonless night. He'd lost his wife through Cato's malevolence and his own lack of faith, and he'd just watched the first woman he'd ever loved, who perhaps he still loved, die in front of him. Any normal person would surely be stricken with grief, but all he felt was a deep numbness, a cold polished space where the pain ought to be. It was as if the death that had followed his every step since his first meeting with Blaesus, that had killed almost everyone around him, had now entered his heart and set hard and cold, formed a dark lack inside him. Only one thing made sense. He knew what he had to do. He didn't know if Cato's death would make anything better; it didn't matter. The life he had loved was over. Only revenge was left. Everything else was meaningless.

And yet, as he stood staring silently and unseeing into the forest, he knew that in the dark, far below him, and out of sight at the bottom of the great cliff in front of him, a small boy remembered lying on his back to look up at the trees and wondering how it was that she was able to creep up on him and not be heard until she laughed to startle him, and knew that now all that was left of her to him was the memory.

Decius saw something in Serpicus' face and stopped asking questions. They stood together and gazed without seeing into the dark.

They were tired and the ground was hard, and so it took them the rest of the day to bury Brutus' and Drenthe's bodies. When it was done they stood back in a circle around the graves and there was silence for a while. Then Decius looked up at Serpicus with a face wet with tears.

'Please say something,' he whispered. 'They both deserve it.'

Serpicus looked down at the two mounds of earth.

'No man is so rich in friends that he can afford to lose two like these,' he said. 'They both died as they lived, freely choosing their own paths. It is too late now for us to tell them that we loved them, or to thank them for their company. It is too late to do anything but remember them, to keep their names fresh in our hearts, and to hope that we may meet them again one day.' He looked across the graves at Severus. 'They did not ask that we avenge them. Any debt we feel is our own, not theirs. Anything that is to be done is by our own choice and decision. They expect nothing of us, except that which we feel we owe. We will honour them, each in his own way. There is nothing more to say.'

The words sounded hollow to Serpicus, but Decius was right, they deserved more than silence. Everything Serpicus cared about was gone, dead or lost to him. Only finding Cato made sense, meant anything. Serpicus bent down and picked up his weapons and his pack. He started walking south without looking back.

36

To Aelius Sejanus, from his Servant:

I trust that your mission to Sicily has met with every success. I regret that I was not able to return in time to inform you of those matters that need to be drawn to your attention, notably the failure of General Marcus to prevent the loss of the camp at Gelbheim. I shall prepare a dossier for your return.

I regret to have to inform you of the death of Consilius, your nephew, who died fighting heroically against barbarian rebels in Germany. A great funeral games will be held to do suitable honour to his memory.

We have received confirmation of the death of the rebel leader Drenthe. She appears to have lingered for some days before succumbing to the wound I gave her. All obstacles are now cleared, as you ordered.

Rome awaits your return eagerly, as does your Servant.

The path back to Rome took them the way they had come. The men recognized where they were; it was the hill above Gelbheim where they had waited for Serpicus and Brutus to return on the day they arrived. Severus, who was leading the small column, raised a hand wearily.

'We'll camp here,' he said, looking around him for a suitable place on the grass to put his equipment, with the air of someone to whom the idea had just occurred. Serpicus and Decius exchanged glances, and waited for him to look up. When he did his face was innocent of guile, as if there was no significance to it.

'Thanks,' said Serpicus. Severus looked a little surprised and shrugged his shoulders.

Decius and Serpicus rode side by side down to where the village had been. Parts of it were still smouldering. As they approached a dog trotted out. It looked like the same dog that had greeted them the day they arrived. It heard the horses and hesitated, one paw off the ground, then decided to join them.

The Romans had burnt everything before they left. Their tracks were easy to follow, a brown rutted scar on the green turf running towards the setting sun.

They rode into the village. The Romans had burned it but they hadn't stayed to make sure it was destroyed. They looked around and found a little food, some usable clothes, even a few coins. The Romans had piled their own dead onto a pyre and burned them but there were the remains of Treveri bodies that no one had returned to claim still on the ground, their eyes gone to the crows. The survivors would wait in nearby villages and return once the Romans were gone. Until then, the crows had it to themselves.

Serpicus watched as Decius reached into his shirt and took something out. He opened his hand and showed Serpicus a blue amulet, the one Drenthe wore around her neck. Serpicus smiled as he recognized it. Decius got off the horse and walked to the centre of the smoking village. He knelt down and dug a hole with his hands, then dropped the amulet in and covered it again with the earth. He stood nearby for a minute, silently watching, then got back on his horse. The dog trotted up to the fresh earth, sniffed it, then took up position at Decius' horse's heels. The horse kicked out irritably and the dog fled with a yelp of pain.

'She would have liked it that something of her lies here,' said Serpicus, looking away from the young man's face.

They rode back and stopped at the top of the hill. Decius dismounted and stood on the edge where it overlooked the river, just where it rose to a slight peak before falling away to sweep down to the bend where the village had once stood. His head was raised so that his hair fell off his shoulders and straight down his back. As Serpicus got close to him he could see that Decius' eyes were closed and a slight smile lit up his face. Serpicus started to say something, but didn't get as far as speaking. He stood beside the young man, standing still and silent, waiting without knowing for what.

At last Decius took a deep breath and brought his head upright again. He looked out over the river valley.

'Do you remember how the boys used to come up here every day to practise throwing?'

Serpicus smiled. 'Yes. Sticks with dried balls of clay on one end to make them fly further.'

'And remember how sometimes you could persuade a girl to slip away from the camp fires and come up here with you? When you were so young you didn't know what to do with her, but just sat here holding hands and looking down at the fires burning in the village, at the dancing, at the light around your home, where your family was?'

'You started young,' Serpicus said. 'When I was that age I didn't like girls. I only started inviting them up here after I realized what they were for.'

Decius looked into the distance, narrowing his eyes slightly against the breeze. 'I was never that age here. By the time I was old enough to find out what girls were for, I was a hostage in Rome.' He paused and looked down at the blackened ruins of the village.

'Can you smell the roses?' he said.

Serpicus breathed in. The wind, and a faint smell of burning, nothing more.

'What roses?'

Decius gestured to where the fires set by the Romans had reached down to the riverside.

'The roses that used to grow here.'

They stood for a long time, looking down at the valley.

Serpicus remembered a night, a night like the one Decius described, not long before he left Gelbheim. He remembered dark hair in firelight and the clasp of slim fingers; wet grass on bare feet and warm lips on his, tentative but unafraid. He remembered looking into eyes so close that he could see the flecks of gold in them. He remembered how everyone knew the Romans were coming, perhaps tomorrow, and how there might not be a day after that for any of them. He remembered how nothing mattered except that she was next to him, the cool night air on their skin, nothing between them.

The memory was like a story that had been told to him by someone else; he felt numb, with no connection to it. But he was still able to smile; it was a good story. He didn't dwell on it long: the shadow of Cato was not far behind it. Perhaps there would be time for lingering on memories one day, but not yet.

He wondered if Antonia and his children were still alive. He felt as though he ought to know the answer, as if he should be able to sense their existence like warmth from a fire, but he had no idea at all. He wanted to feel in his heart that they were well, but there was nothing.

Serpicus became aware of someone calling his name, and looked around. Severus and his men had come half-way down the hill and were standing next to a clump of trees. Severus waved him across. High above the trees Serpicus could see a small dark shape hovering, suspended against the setting sun.

When Serpicus got close he saw the men standing by the trees in a half-circle, swords and spears in their hands. They were crouched and tense like men expecting attack. Severus waved them back and they moved warily away.

'What is it?'

Severus gestured to the centre of the trees. 'Thought you'd want to see this.' Serpicus took a step forward and

Severus put a hand on his arm. 'Here,' he said, holding out his sword.

Serpicus took the sword and walked cautiously into the circle of trees.

The bear lay stretched out on the ground. The off-white coat was stained dark red with its blood in a dozen places. Arrows stuck up from its sides and several others lay on the ground beside it. A deep cut showed the bone in its shoulder, and the jagged end of the shaft of a broken javelin protruded low in its chest. Serpicus could hear its breathing, rasping and bubbling in his throat. The bear wasn't dead yet, but it was dying.

Serpicus came closer, moving slowly and carefully. The only sign that the bear was alive was its stertorous breathing and the dry lids moving slowly across the dull eyes. Serpicus put out a hand and touched its huge head, then slid down to its neck. The white coat which looked smooth and soft was harsh and felt as if it had been oiled, but it was warm and he could feel the muscle underneath tremble under his fingers. It let out a deep groan. A slow thin trickle of blood seeped from its nose and pooled on the ground under the scarred muzzle. A single fly settled on it. Serpicus waved the insect away.

He sat up and reached for the sword Severus had given him. He knelt beside the bear and put his empty hand on its great flank. He felt the deep thump of its heart against his palm. He placed the point of the sword between the two ribs just below the heart.

'I'm sorry,' he whispered, and pushed suddenly with all his strength.

A single great sigh came from it, as if Serpicus had

481

lain his full weight onto its chest. Serpicus pulled the sword free. The bear's eyes were still open but there was a dull glaze over them. Serpicus stood up. 'I brought you here,' he said. 'I can't change that. But I owe you a life.' He looked at the blood on his sword and at the wounds on the bear's body. He felt a great pressure in his chest, as if death had a weight.

He breathed deep, easing the pressure. It wasn't over. One more was required to set the balance straight. Perhaps two. He looked up into the sky. It was too dark to see if the hawk was still there.

37

The journey south was by night, slogging and cursing through marshes and along sheep tracks. By day they rested the horses and did their best to plan the journey to avoid the legions who were marching to the war as well as the German tribes who were marching to meet them. By the time they reached the Hinterrhein Pass they were exhausted, filthy and saddle-sore, but were far enough out of the area of insurrection to be able to travel by day without it being automatically assumed that they were invaders or deserters. The men who had escaped the Roman attack on Gelbheim by taking to the river were waiting for them. They all had colds, but were otherwise unharmed. The weather was unusually warm and wet. They waited a day for the rain to lift and then slogged through the mud over the pass and down into Italy.

There was argument about whether to ride all the way south to Rome or to take ship at Genoa. Severus settled it. He had some questions to ask in Genoa.

The reunion with Graptus was short. The

harbour-master was sitting in a tavern on the dockside, where it soon became apparent he had been for some time. He was surprised and pleased to see them.

'I was told,' he said, 'by the Governor of Genoa himself, no less, that I was getting a new assistant. Normally of course the Governor wouldn't even know I existed, let alone take the trouble to find me an assistant to replace the perfectly adequate one I already had, so I knew something odd was going on straight away. But you learn not to ask too many questions if you make it to my age – in fact, that's how you make it to my age. I was told to carry on as if everything was normal, and that's what I'm good at. My usual assistant was sent away on holiday for a few weeks, and Cato appeared the next day. He didn't know much about boats, but he learnt the job in no time and I had nothing to complain about. Obviously he was waiting for someone to arrive but I had no idea who it was, or why. He'd been here just a couple of days when you lot turned up. I had no idea it was you that he was interested in until he told me he was leaving that night. Obviously I'd have warned you about him, but I never saw you after that.'

Serpicus remembered how Cato had arranged to join them as they were leaving Genoa. When Cato told Graptus he was leaving, they were already on the road north. He hadn't taken the chance that Graptus might tip them off.

Severus wasn't happy.

'I don't believe him.'

Serpicus found himself defending the harbour-master.

'He had nothing to gain by lying.'

'Apart from avoiding my sword in his guts and a long sleep in the harbour,' snorted Severus.

'Perhaps he was frightened.'

'He said he knew something was up. He should have told us anyway. That's what I'd have done.'

Galba looked thoughtful. 'Not everyone is as brave as you, Severus.'

The centurion opened his mouth and then closed it again. Even he could see that there was nothing to be done. Graptus may not have been a good friend, but he wasn't the enemy. The tide was turning and the ship was ready to leave. Serpicus bought the harbour-master a drink and wished him well, and they boarded the ship for Rome.

Several days of calm sailing later, the clear water around them became stained with the yellow mud swept down to the sea by the Tiber, and they stepped off the pier at Ostia.

Serpicus looked up the river towards Rome and the hills surrounding it. Rome was unchanged, and yet he knew nothing was the same for him. He, Decius and Galba went to Serpicus' house. The door was barred. Blaesus had obviously possessed it. Serpicus wanted to break the door down and take it back, but the others dissuaded him. The three of them went back to the tenement that Severus and his men were renting and hired a room for themselves. It was stuffy and dirty, but adequate. Serpicus wondered if it was not better from his point of view. His own house would have contained memories that would have confused the issue. He wanted to find Cato, but first he wanted to find his children.

Severus made him stay in the room. 'We'll wander

about,' the centurion said, 'see what we can uncover.' He looked sternly at all three of them. 'You lot stay put. No one knows us, but they'll be looking out for you. If word gets out that you're back then Blaesus will want his bear and you'll be in the shit. He'll kill you soon as look at you if he knows you've failed him.' Serpicus wanted to argue but couldn't; Severus was right. Even though they suspected that the bear was just an excuse to get to Drenthe, he didn't doubt that Blaesus wanted it.

The arrival in Rome brought fears crowding into Serpicus' mind, and confined to the room he found it worse. Up till then the numbness had filled him. Now it was as if the sight of the Seven Hills had unlocked his mind. Suddenly he was able to remember his children, not as the vague shadows they had been for the weeks of his journey, but alive and warm. He remembered how they felt in his arms, what their voices sounded like. For weeks they had seemed out of reach and he had been unable to even consider the possibility that they might be alive and that he might see them again. Now he was in Rome; if they were alive, then he would find them. If they were not, he would find the person who killed them. When Severus returned Serpicus interrogated him, made suggestions, accused him of not trying hard enough. The centurion kept his temper. He was asking questions anywhere he thought it was safe to do so. Blaesus was in Rome. A household slave had said that there were a woman and two children in Blaesus' house who never went out, but the description would have fitted almost anyone. There was no sign of Cato, but the slave knew who he was.

'He's no ordinary spy,' Severus said. 'He's Sejanus' best man, about the only person that bastard trusts.' He looked thoughtful. 'If he dies, a lot of good men will be avenged.'

That night in his dreams Serpicus saw Antonia's ghost, still beautiful but drawn and grey. She stood at the side of the bed and looked down at him as a nurse looks at a sick man. When he reached for her to tell her he was well, she shrank from him and vanished. He opened his eyes and saw nothing but darkness.

He lay awake for the rest of the night.

The next day Severus arrived with the news that it had been officially announced that the great soldier Consilius had died in Germany in an unspecified but undoubtedly heroic manner in the service of the Empire, and that there would be a games in his honour the following week.

'I'd like to be there,' growled Serpicus. 'Toast his demise.'

'Make sure he's really dead,' said Galba.

'There's more,' Severus said. 'Blaesus will be there, paying tribute to his valiant offspring.'

Serpicus' head snapped upwards. 'Blaesus?'

Severus nodded. 'And if he's there . . .'

'Cato will be too.'

Severus nodded. 'Perhaps.'

Serpicus thought hard. 'It wouldn't be difficult to get into the games, but we'd never get anywhere near Cato. There will be soldiers everywhere.'

Severus tapped a finger against the doorpost. 'There is one person who gets to stand right next to Blaesus.'

'Who?'

'The man who wins the chariot race.'

They talked most of the night. Blaesus and Cato were well protected everywhere they went. Serpicus suggested a dozen places where a man might get close to them, but Severus knocked down every possibility. Serpicus knew Severus spoke the truth. By the time the dawn was breaking Serpicus knew that he must either race and win, or spend the rest of his life lurking in alleyways hoping that Cato or Blaesus would wander past unguarded. That afternoon he went to see Sextus, his old employer.

Every night in the dark of his room, as he lay between sleep and wakefulness, Serpicus saw Antonia. She stood still, watching him. He tried not to speak, but every night he did, and then she was no longer there.

Three days before the games they were in a tavern near the Forum where Severus knew the owner. Serpicus was drinking his wine well watered. Galba was not so temperate, but was still being careful. Decius wasn't there. He said he'd drink for a year when Cato was dead and they were all safe, not before.

Severus arrived late. He'd stopped at the betting-shop to pick up a list of the men racing on the day of the games. The centurion put the much-used wax tablet on the table and yelled for a drink. Serpicus leant over and read the names.

' "Alraic" is me,' he said. 'Marinus, Pollo, Junius.' He tapped a finger on the table. 'Good drivers, but beatable.' He tilted the wax towards the candle. 'What does that word say?'

Galba put a finger beside another name lower down the list. 'Cassius? Which Cassius is that?'

Severus shrugged. 'No idea,' he said. He looked around. 'Hey, Burrus,' he shouted. A burly figure with thick eyebrows looked up from deep conversation with several disreputable-looking men.

'What?'

'The race in three days, the games for Consilius. Who's favourite?'

'Cassius,' said Burrus immediately. 'You might get someone to give you even money if you're lucky. I'll give you two to one on, seeing as it's you.'

Severus managed to look both thoughtful and dim at the same time. 'Which Cassius is that then?'

Burrus laughed and several of the men grinned with him. 'There's only one worth betting on. The man who won the games they held for that useless prick Claudius Appius.'

Severus leant forward. 'I saw Cassius win that race. Tall, thin, fancies himself, dresses well. Arrogant bugger, but a bloody good driver.' He looked at Serpicus' face. 'You know him?'

Serpicus nodded grimly, remembering a boy going under the wheels of his friend's chariot. 'Yes, I know him.'

Galba looked at him. 'There's history between the two of you. He's an evil bastard. You'll need someone there to watch your back.'

'He's got me,' said a voice behind them.

They turned around. Decius stood behind them with a serious face.

'What do you mean?' asked Serpicus. 'You aren't on the race list.'

Decius pointed to the tablet. 'Brutus. That's me. I thought it would do him honour.'

Galba shook his head. 'You've got to be . . .'

Serpicus put a hand on Galba's arm. 'You do Brutus great honour, and me. But you can't be in that race.'

Decius looked about to argue, then his face crumpled and he was a boy again. 'Why not?'

'Come with me.' Serpicus stood up, put an arm around his shoulders and led him outside. The streets were quiet. Serpicus sat on the low wall outside the tavern and motioned to Decius to sit beside him. Decius complied unwillingly.

'Why don't you want me there?' he asked. 'Don't you trust me?'

Serpicus chose his words carefully. 'Of course. I know that whatever happened, you'd be watching out for me.' He paused. 'But I remember two friends who used to race together, and I remember what happened to one of them.'

'So do I,' said Decius in a trembling voice. 'I'd know what to look out for. It wouldn't happen again, I swear it.'

'That's the point,' said Serpicus. 'I'd trust you to look out for me; I'm worried you'll be looking after me so well that you won't be looking out for yourself.'

'But if I don't do it then who will?'

Serpicus paused before answering. 'Give your place to Galba.'

'Galba? Why?'

Serpicus could tell that Decius already knew the answer.

'Because he knows all the tricks, and he's seen everything. He'll see what Cassius is up to and stop him, and leave me to get on with winning the race.'

Decius started to speak and then stopped. Serpicus put a hand on his shoulder.

'We've been through a lot together,' he said. 'You saved me on the Hinterrhein. Cato got the credit, but I know that if it wasn't for you I'd be at the bottom of that mountain. I trust you with my life, always will. I won't forget how you stepped forward for me this time either. But I need a cynical old hand like Galba for this job.' Decius looked at the ground and didn't reply. Serpicus leant forward. 'All right?'

Decius mumbled something he didn't catch.

'What?'

Decius looked up. 'You make sure that Galba looks after you properly, and that you beat Cassius, or you'll both answer to me.'

Serpicus laughed and pushed him so that he lost his balance and fell off the wall. Decius took Serpicus' outstretched hand and let him haul him back up again.

'Come on,' said Serpicus. 'I'll buy you a cup of lemon water.'

The night before the race they all met to make sure that there were no loose ends. They ate bread and olives and drank some well-watered wine, and they talked until late. Then Severus stood up, stretched and yawned.

'I'm going to stretch my legs before bed,' he said.

Galba stood up. 'I'll walk with you to the end of the street,' he said, grinning at Serpicus. 'There isn't enough wine in this piss he's giving us to put a man to sleep, I'll have to try fresh air and exercise.'

'If you aren't back very soon I'll send Decius to pull you out of the tavern,' Serpicus replied.

'I'll be back,' Galba said.

Severus opened the door and went out. Galba followed. Serpicus stepped out behind them to take a lungful of night air. The small warm room had left him hot and uncomfortable. He leant against a wall and watched Galba and Severus walk off up the street.

There was no moon but the sky was clear and the stars were clearly visible. He and Antonia had spent many nights looking up at them. For a moment time spun, and he was going to turn around, go back into his house and she would be there.

Then he heard a voice from the top of the street, familiar but unknown, the sound carrying to him clearly in the night air.

'Hello, old man. Remember me?'

Serpicus looked up the street. Galba and Severus were just indistinct shapes in the gloom. There were other shadows near them. Serpicus heard a dull thud, followed by what might have been a breathless cry. Then he heard Galba's urgent voice.

'Serpicus!'

As Serpicus sprinted up the street he could see through the gloom that someone was lying on the ground, and that several men were struggling fiercely nearby. He could hear muffled shouts and there was a brief cry of pain.

The nearest man was standing with a club upraised,

looking for an opportunity to strike. He had his back to Serpicus and Serpicus didn't know him. He kicked the man as hard as he could in the back of the knee. The man went down with a scream. Serpicus jumped over him and threw himself onto the other man, bearing him to the ground as he shouted Galba's name.

The reply came from nearby to his left. 'Serpicus, over here!' Galba sounded as if someone had him by the throat.

As the man under him fell to the ground Serpicus snatched a hank of the hair on the back of his head and smashed his face onto the cobbled street. The man let out a deep grunt of pain and lay still. Serpicus felt a hard blow across his shoulders, and he threw himself side-ways. His hand slapped down to stop the fall and he felt the unconscious man's club on the ground under his hand. He snatched it up and swung it across as his attacker followed up the first blow. The club hit the man's jaw. The impact snapped his head back like a boxer receiving an uppercut. Serpicus rolled away to avoid the man's tumbling weight and jumped up.

A big man was standing in front of him, one foot advanced, his arms outstretched. Serpicus glanced around to make sure that no one was behind him. It was too dark to see who was on his side.

'Galba?'

'Here.'

Serpicus could see three men hacking and kicking at each other as they rolled around on the ground. Galba was one of them, and seemed to be putting up a good fight. The big man was between them and Serpicus.

Serpicus called out again as he started to circle round.

'Severus?'

'Careful, the old bastard is at your feet,' said the big man with an unpleasant laugh. Serpicus glanced down. Severus was lying on the ground in front of him, unmoving.

'Why?' hissed Serpicus, looking up.

The big man laughed again. 'I'm sad you don't remember me.' He took a sideways step and moved into a patch of moonlight. Serpicus could see that one side of his head was almost smooth, and recognized him at once. It was the man called Josef who had led the attack on them after they left Genoa. The man who had lost an ear to Severus' sword.

'What do you want?' Serpicus said.

The man laughed again. 'Don't worry about me,' he said, gesturing at Severus. 'I've got what I want.' The big man stepped back and leant over the three struggling men. His fist slammed downwards and the struggling stopped abruptly. He stood up and looked at Serpicus.

'The old man took my ear,' he said. 'Now we're even.' He spat on the ground near Severus. Serpicus took a pace forward and the man raised a hand in warning.

'I was forbidden to kill you when we attacked you on the road,' he said. 'Now I can do as I wish. Do not cross me now.'

Serpicus hesitated. 'What do you mean, forbidden?' he asked.

The man laughed. 'You were to be allowed to escape. You and Cato only. The rest were to die.'

'Cato?'

The man nodded. 'Very cosy, just the two of you heading for Germany.' He turned to the other men nearby. 'Come on,' he said. 'We're done here.' He backed down the street, watching Serpicus. The two men got up, panting. One of them went immediately after Josef, the other launched a vicious kick at Galba on the ground before leaving as well.

Serpicus heard running footsteps behind him. He spun round, his arm upraised. Decius came to an abrupt halt in front of him.

'I brought your sword,' he said. 'What happened?' He looked around and saw Severus and Galba on the ground. 'Are they . . . ?'

'Of course I'm not,' said Galba hoarsely, pushing himself up slowly onto one elbow. 'Help me up.' Decius went to help Galba. Serpicus knelt by Severus. He put a hand on the centurion's shoulder and rolled him over.

The lined face was twisted with pain. A wood-handled knife protruded from his side and both his hands were wrapped round it.

'Pull it out.' Serpicus hesitated. 'Please. I can't.'

Serpicus took the handle in his hand and pulled it out as straight as he could in one motion. Severus gave a gasp of pain, then relaxed. Serpicus put a hand on the centurion's tunic and it was wet under his palm. He lifted his hand. It was dark with blood in the moonlight.

Severus lifted a hand and wrapped tense fingers around Serpicus' wrist.

'It's all right,' Serpicus said. 'We'll get you a doctor.'

Severus shook his head. 'Don't waste his time, or mine,' he said with difficulty. The grip on Serpicus' wrist tightened. 'You do what you talked about, and I don't mind dying.' His voice grew fainter. 'I'll be waiting for the bastards in Hell. You might like to tell them that before you kill them.'

The scarred fingers slackened and then released their hold. His head fell back and a long rasp of breath flowed slowly from him.

'Is he all right?' said Galba. Decius had got him to his feet and supported him as he limped over, holding his hand across his torso.

'He's gone,' said Serpicus.

Galba coughed and spat dark blood. 'The bastards jumped out of the shadows as we got to the corner. Severus pushed me out of the way and they got him. Then they came for me. If you hadn't come along I think I'd be lying there beside him.'

Decius was looking down at Severus. His voice shook as he said, 'Who were they?'

'The men who attacked us on the road from Genoa. Though I don't suppose they followed us all the way to Gelbheim and back. The person who sent them after us in the first place no doubt told them we were here.'

Galba coughed again and Decius staggered as he took his whole weight. Serpicus saw his tunic darkening under his palm.

'He's wounded, put him down.' He looked around. 'No, let's get him home, we'll have a look at him there.'

They carried Galba quickly back down the street. His breathing was hoarse and he didn't speak. They got into the house and laid him out on the bed. Serpicus pulled his friend's tunic aside carefully.

A deep wound under his ribs seeped blood.

Decius brought water and cloths, and they cleaned him up. They put a thick pad over the bleeding and bandaged around him as best they could.

Serpicus stood up and surveyed the result. He nodded with satisfaction. It was the best they could do. He took a step towards the door.

'Where are you going?' asked Decius.

Serpicus looked serious. 'I'm going to report that some poor bastard's been murdered in the street.'

38

The sun was rising by the time Serpicus got home. Galba was stretched out on his bed. The Thracian was conscious. His cheeks were pale, with a high spot of colour on each one. He was sweating, even though the house was cool. There was no sign of Decius, although he seemed to have done a reasonable job of swathing Galba in bandages before he left.

Galba opened his eyes as Serpicus came in and reached for his dagger. When he saw who it was he sank back on the pillow gratefully.

'Where is he?' asked Serpicus. 'I told him to stay here.'

Galba cleared his throat with difficulty, as if there was hardly any air in his lungs. 'No you didn't, I was there. I told him to go and do a job for me. He'll be back in a minute. Don't shout at him, it isn't his fault.'

The door rattled open and Decius came in, panting for breath. Serpicus stood up.

'Where the hell have you been? I told you to look after him.'

'I . . . I ran . . . all the way.' He couldn't speak for a moment. 'I did what I could, then went to fetch . . . something.'

'Did what you could? What if those bastards had come back looking for him?'

'I didn't . . . I don't . . .'

'I said it was all right,' muttered Galba. 'I told him to go.'

Decius nodded. Serpicus almost hit him.

'And since when have you done what he told you? Don't you see that . . .'

'Oh for fuck's sake leave him alone. There's no harm done.'

Serpicus opened his mouth, then shut it again. He cuffed Decius gently around the ear. 'Sorry,' he said. 'I don't want him to get what the old man got.'

'I know,' said Decius quietly. 'I miss him too.'

Galba was suddenly bent over with coughing. The two of them supported him while the fit snarled inside him. When he sank back the cloth held to his mouth was spotted with blood. Serpicus looked at it.

'That's that then,' he said and sat back on the bed. 'There's no way you can . . .'

Galba raised a hand and spoke breathlessly. 'If . . . suggesting that . . . won't be able to . . . race, don't . . . think it. I'll be there.'

Serpicus held up the stained cloth. 'There is blood in your lungs.'

Galba opened his mouth and put out his tongue, which had a deep cut on one side. 'Not lungs. Bloody well hurts though, I give you that.' Serpicus laughed despite

499

himself. Galba spat more blood into the cloth and looked up at Decius.

'Any luck?'

Decius pulled a small bottle from his tunic. Galba smiled and took it from him. 'The gods bless you for a fine person,' he said. He pulled the cork out and drank a good part of it straight off. Serpicus took it from his hand and put it to his nose. Galba laughed cautiously as Serpicus' head jerked back as if a sharp needle had gone up his nostril.

'That's awful!' said Serpicus with a shudder. 'What is it?'

Galba chuckled and took it back. 'I sent him to Ox's for some of the good stuff.'

'If that's the good stuff, what are the rest of us poor bastards drinking?'

'The gods only know, but it hasn't killed you yet.' Galba sank back on the bed with a smile, placing the bottle carefully within easy reach. 'Now, if you don't mind, it's been a long night, I have a race to go to soon, and I'd like to get some sleep so I can be at my best.' He closed his eyes and in moments was snoring.

Serpicus looked at the bottle suspiciously and then up at Decius.

'What on earth is in that?'

Decius shrugged. 'I don't know. He told me to go to Ox and ask him for some of what Antonius had when he fell off his chariot going round the last bend.'

'And that's what Ox gave you?'

'He laughed and gave me that bottle. He didn't say

500

what it was.' Decius looked at the floor. 'I wish the old man was here.'

Serpicus put a hand on his shoulder. 'The best way we can honour his memory is if we cut Cato's liver out and feed it to the dogs.'

Decius smiled grimly. 'He'd like that.'

Serpicus nodded. 'Then I think it's the least we can do.'

The race was scheduled for the middle of the afternoon. Galba woke in the morning complaining of a headache. His skin was dry and hot to the touch, and his dark eyes were deep in his face. The wound made it difficult for him to stand.

'You can't possibly race,' said Serpicus.

'I'm doing it,' said Galba. 'It's not open to negotiation.'

'You can't walk. You can hardly stand. How will you even get to the track?'

'Not your problem,' Galba said. 'I'll be there. You worry about yourself, leave me be.'

There was an obdurate note in his voice that Serpicus recognized.

'All right,' he said, but you'll stay here and rest until the last possible moment.'

'Can't,' Galba replied. 'I need to register to race.'

'I'll do it for you.'

'What if they notice you're not me?'

'They won't.'

'What if they do?'

'I'll say it was a mistake and send for you.'

'What about the horses? I have to take care of the horses.'

'I'll do it.'

'You'll do it wrong.'

'I'll do it better than you would have. Stop arguing and get some rest.'

'I need to check the chariot.'

'I'll do it. Properly.'

'What if you need me?'

'I won't.'

'But if you do?'

'Then Decius will come and fetch you. Or I'll find someone else. Or I'll write a notice asking for help in six different languages and I'll stick it on a column in the Forum. Stop worrying. Go and rest, or I'll punch you in the guts. I don't want to see you before the race.'

Galba gave up and went muttering back to bed. Decius placed food and water near him.

There was a knock on the door.

Serpicus picked up his sword and moved silently until he was standing behind the door. When he was ready he motioned Decius to open it. A slight breeze passed through the house and bright light flooded in onto Galba's bed.

'Hello, lads,' said a familiar voice. 'What's wrong with him?'

Serpicus came around the edge of the door silently and placed the point of the sword on the visitor's chest.

'Hello, Snake,' Decius said.

The Cretan slowly looked down at the sword and then up again at Decius.

'Came to see you,' he said, moving his head slightly towards the bed. 'Heard about Severus, and they told me that the fat man wasn't too well.'

Galba bridled. 'No one here of that description. You must mean some other fat man.'

Snake thought for a moment. 'No,' he said seriously, 'I meant you.'

Serpicus put the sword up. 'Come in.'

The Cretan entered cautiously, looking around as if there might be more men behind the door. When he was satisfied, he relaxed and sat down. He was wearing the waistcoat in which he carried his knives. Serpicus wondered if he ever took it off.

Decius handed the Cretan a drink and he accepted it gratefully. When it was finished he held out the cup for more.

'Good stuff,' he said.

'So,' Serpicus said. 'What brings you here?'

Snake swallowed half of the wine that Decius passed to him and glanced towards Galba. 'Thought I'd come and see if I could help.'

Serpicus raised an eyebrow. 'Can you drive a chariot?'

Snake smiled. 'To get to where I want to go, like anyone. Can I win a race? Afraid not.' He swallowed again. 'So, how did you escape the village?'

'Got behind the bear and ran like hell,' said Serpicus. 'How about you?'

'I saw you behind the bear as it went through the gate,' Snake replied. 'A big Roman jumped on me and by the time I'd got rid of him you were long gone. I followed the bear's trail as far as it went and then struck out south

503

for the mountains. I didn't have a horse, so I couldn't catch up with you. A shepherd on the way claimed that you had gone through the day before, although he might have been mistaken, or lying. I got back here and I've been waiting ever since. No one at the race track knew anything, and then yesterday I met someone in a tavern who said there had been a fight in this street. Every time I've been with you there has been a fight, so even though it was probably coincidence I thought I'd better come and have a look. And here you are.' He looked around at them. 'But I thought you were ahead of me.'

Decius shook his head. 'We were, but we went to the Teutoburg. Consilius caught us there and we lost Brutus and Drenthe.' He stopped talking and swallowed convulsively.

Snake looked at him keenly. 'When you say lost, you don't mean you just mislaid them, do you?'

Serpicus shook his head. 'Drenthe killed Consilius first, so it wasn't a totally wasted trip. And Brutus took a lot of Romans for company before he went.'

Snake tipped the rest of the wine into his mouth and swallowed. 'I'll miss the big man,' he said softly. 'And she was worth a dozen of Consilius.' He looked around as if hoping to see another jug of wine, then shrugged. He sat forward and clasped his hands. 'So,' he said, 'what's the plan?'

'What makes you think there's a plan?'

'There's always a plan. You have scores to settle. You've been travelling for days. I don't believe you've sat around and not thought about what to do. You'll need help, whatever it is. I'll do what I can.'

Serpicus looked serious. 'It will be dangerous.'

Snake smiled. 'So, completely unlike fighting a couple of Roman legions in Gelbheim then?'

Serpicus acknowledged his point. 'Put it another way then. You've done enough already. This is personal. I don't want to get any more people killed.'

Snake thought about that for a moment. 'Fair enough. But I'm an adult, I'll make my own choices. I want to help.'

'I don't know if . . .'

'Oh, for pity's sake, stop fucking around and tell him!'

Galba spoke so suddenly that Snake half rose out of his seat in surprise. He turned to look at the wounded man. Galba was propped up on one elbow. He indicated with a jerk of his head to Decius to stand by the doorway.

'It's actually quite simple,' Galba said in a conversational tone. 'We just have to win the race this afternoon.'

'Race?'

'Race. Hosted by Blaesus.'

'Ah, I see. And where Blaesus is . . .'

'. . . Cato won't be far away. Exactly.'

Snake nodded thoughtfully. 'I see. So you win the race, and then you go up to Blaesus' box, where he presents you with the victor's wreath?'

Galba smiled. 'Bright lad. We could use you.'

'I understand. Won't he recognize you before you get to him?'

Serpicus shook his head. 'I don't think so. He'll be too far away to see our faces and he'll have other things to think about anyway. We shave our heads, wear a cloth over our faces against the dust, use different names. By the time he realizes who we are, we'll be close enough to do what needs to be done.'

Snake looked dubious. 'He'll be surrounded by dozens of soldiers. I suppose there's no point asking what happens afterwards, once you've done it?'

Galba stroked his chin. 'I was planning on watching the bastard bleed to death slowly, myself. These two may have other plans.'

Snake grinned. 'No, I meant . . .'

'He knows what you mean,' said Serpicus. 'The plan doesn't go beyond getting us close to Blaesus and Cato. After that, we don't much care what happens.' He looked hard at Snake. 'Which is why we'll understand if you want no part of it.'

Snake looked back steadily. 'Have you news of your children?'

Serpicus shook his head. 'They are in Blaesus' house, we think.'

Galba grinned at Snake. 'Still want to be part of this?'

'If I can avoid committing suicide as you seem intent on doing, I will, but I'll take my chances.'

Galba and Serpicus glanced at each other, and both shrugged. Snake looked around to see what Decius thought, and received a sign of assent.

'Looks like you're in,' Galba said.

39

To Aelius Sejanus, from his Servant:

*I trust that the carrier of this message will meet your
returning mission and so be the first to welcome you
back to Rome. The whole city rejoices in your return.
Your welcome is arranged as the climax of the games to
honour Consilius. Notwithstanding the death of such a
great Roman, today is a great day.*

The last slaves were leaving the arena, the thin fabric of
their Mercury costumes heavily stained with sweat and
blood. The hot wind pulled at Serpicus' dry skin
and brought the familiar stink of fear and death to his
nostrils.

For a long time he had deliberately not looked up at
the Senator's box. Now he risked a glance.

Blaesus was sitting behind the low parapet, a golden
cup in one hand. His other hand was not visible but a
young slave was standing next to him, shading him from

the heat of the sun. It wasn't hard to imagine where the Senator's hand was. Serpicus looked up at Blaesus for a few moments. The Senator seemed to become uneasy and turned from the boy to look down at the track. Although he was much too far away to be recognized, Serpicus turned his face away and ran a hand over his freshly shaven scalp.

A fat man started yelling drunken abuse at him from the seats nearby. The crowd were restless. Someone in the stables had told Serpicus that there had been a lot of arrests the night before, that people were feeling insecure. Which didn't explain why the man was bawling insults at him.

To Serpicus' right Cassius stood tall in his golden chariot. A long red cloak hung from his shoulders, spreading across the back of the chariot and down almost to the hub of the wheels. He would take it off before the race began, but it made a fine show while he waited.

Long habit made Serpicus move his weight from one foot to the other to test the balance of the chariot. All seemed to be as it should. The men that he and Sextus had gathered to service and look after his equipment had done their job well. The horses were in fine condition. Serpicus looked to his left. Galba was leaning forward against the front edge of his chariot, his arm locked straight. From a distance it probably looked casual; Serpicus was close enough to see that the stiff arm was the only thing keeping him upright. His cheeks looked translucent, like a thin veil thrown over a pale stone, and oily sweat glistened on his forehead. Serpicus caught his eye.

508

'You look like hell,' he said, loud enough to be heard over the sound of the crowd. 'You can't race.'

'Try and stop me,' Galba said, his voice a rasp. He tried to smile, but Serpicus saw it become a grimace.

'You'll die.'

'I won't.'

Serpicus turned away so that he would not see the pain crossing his friend's face.

The three of them were the only remaining competitors. There had at one point been ten drivers. Some of the others had yoked their horses that morning, some checked their equipment, some even got as far as getting into their chariots. Then a message arrived that made them move away to read it, or someone approached them casually and indicated that they should lean over so that he could speak to them and not be overheard, or a woman came and smiled and took them to one side, or they were seen talking to a large man who had a brotherly arm wrapped around their shoulders. Within a short time of all of these events each of the other charioteers had withdrawn; one announced a hitherto unnoticed injury to one of his horses, another said unexpected mechanical problems, a third disappeared with an unforeseen family emergency. One man just disappeared. The odds were improving. Ox and his men could be most persuasive when they chose. Serpicus looked up at Ox in the stands and touched his forehead with a finger in salute.

The big man nodded acknowledgement. Decius sat beside him, scarved and anonymous in the crowded front row near the start of the race. Serpicus could see his pale strained face leaning over the edge. Snake sat on Ox's other side.

Serpicus looked up at the impassive men in rich linen clothes sitting in the best seats, surrounded by thin-faced Greek and Arab slaves with their slates and rolls of parchment. Shouting men surrounded them, gesturing towards the track and holding up hands full of coin, and the slaves were writing and taking the money as fast as they could. In theory a three-chariot race wasn't legal. Legal or not, business appeared to be brisk.

Serpicus realized that he hadn't placed his usual two sesterces on himself to win.

He leant across and put a hand on the edge of Galba's chariot. He could see drops of blood on the floor by his friend's feet and more staining the side of his tunic. They had bound the bandages tight and wrapped them thick around him. If they weren't enough then the wound must be bleeding freely.

'For the gods' sake,' Serpicus whispered, 'withdraw. You need a doctor. Leave him to me.'

Galba let out a wheezing chuckle. Serpicus thought he saw a shred of pink foam on his lips. Galba wiped it away with the back of his hand and looked across at Cassius with a leer. 'Beating that bastard will do me more good than any doctor ever could,' he said, his voice husked by pain. 'Besides, if I don't race then it's just the two of you left, and he's better than you are. He'll probably run you into the wall at the first bend if I'm not there to look after you.'

A piercing whistle came from the crowd nearby. Serpicus looked up and saw Decius signalling frantically. Ox was standing beside him, his hands folded and his face expressionless. Decius held up one arm and indicated to Serpicus to look at his hand. Serpicus could see that Decius was holding something. When Decius was sure Serpicus had seen it he threw it to him. Galba saw it too and lifted his arm as it spun through the air towards him, then groaned with the effort and leant against the side of the chariot. He stood, gasping for breath, his face contorted with pain. Serpicus caught the bottle. Galba held out a hand.

'I think that's for me,' he whispered. He sounded as if he was lying down with a large weight on his chest. Serpicus passed it across to him. Galba uncorked it and tipped over half of the contents into his mouth. Those nearest him in the crowd saw the bottle and roared encouragement. They liked drivers who drank, it made them reckless. Galba put the stopper back in and put the bottle in a fold of his tunic. The effect was immediate. Serpicus saw his face relax, as if he was coming out of a trance, and his back straightened. He stood up and let out a sigh. 'That's better,' he said, the pain gone from his voice. 'Those Egyptians really know what they're doing.' He saluted Decius in the stands, then looked deliberately sideways at Cassius, caught his eye and gave him a cheerful grin. Cassius met his glance for a moment, gave him a thin smile in return and then looked away.

Serpicus wondered if Cassius knew about the attack on Severus and Galba, perhaps even knew how deep the dagger had gone. Galba could be as brave and as strong as he liked; the wound was real and it was hurting him.

It took a strong man to guide two horses hauling a chariot at full gallop. No one could race properly with a wound like that. The bottle that Decius had thrown seemed to have put an end to Galba's pain for the moment, but it could not last long. And in the meantime Galba was standing with an amused smile and rocking gently from foot to foot, like a man standing outside a tavern who has had just enough to drink to leave him wondering whether to go home or go find another tavern.

Serpicus looked back up at the crowd. Decius had disappeared. He saw Ox, sitting now, his expression grim. Galba followed the line of Serpicus' gaze. The big man's face was at once filled with smiling optimism. He saluted Galba and made a clenched fist of encouragement. Galba gave him a relaxed wave and turned back to Serpicus.

'If they passed a law that said a chariot driver was only allowed to have one man in his supporters' club,' Galba said, slurring slightly, 'that's the man I'd choose.'

Serpicus gestured. 'What was in the bottle?'

Galba shook his head with a smile. 'Get your own. There's only enough for me.'

Several slaves ran past Serpicus on last-minute errands. The noise of the crowd was increasing as the start of the race approached. Last-minute odds were being shouted and latecomers were howled at to sit down. Serpicus looked up to see the race judge getting ready. The Senator was consulting with the Master of Games, and the judge was only waiting for him to nod before the race would start.

Galba looked past Serpicus at Cassius again.

'Hey, pig fucker! The last time we were all here you

killed a boy, just because he might have beaten you, remember? Well, I saw him in a dream last night, and he told me you would lose today and that he'd be standing beside you when it happens. Do you feel him near you?'

Cassius didn't turn his head but Serpicus was near enough to see the muscles tighten around his mouth. Cassius let a few moments pass and then he spoke to his horse's ears.

'I think I hear a drunk fat man talking, a drunk fat man already dead but too stupid to lie down.'

Galba's face was covered in a thin glaze of sweat as he leant against the rim of his chariot, his eyes unnaturally bright and fixed on Cassius' profile. The red stain on his tunic was now the size of a man's hand. Serpicus saw how he pulled the folds of the material, arranging it to ensure that Cassius would not see it.

'I'll outlive you, pig fucker, or die knowing you will be close behind me,' he said cheerfully.

Cassius still didn't look at him. 'In an hour or less,' he said evenly, 'perhaps even before the end of this race, you will be waiting on the banks of the Styx for Charon's boat.' Then he turned and gave Galba a look of chilling malice. 'And you will be waiting there for a long time, for I shall have taken the two coins from your eyes. I will use them to buy your mother for my ugliest privy-slave to have as his plaything, and when he grows bored of her I shall feed her to my dogs.' Serpicus didn't doubt that he meant it. Galba chuckled at the insult.

'As long as you are standing right beside me on the river-bank, I shan't mind how long we have to wait there,' he said.

513

The Master of Games leant forward importantly and made sure they were paying attention. He stepped back and Senator Blaesus stood up and walked forward. He gave a languid wave, which started with the chariot drivers and ended up in the crowd. Two of the drivers saluted back, while the other seemed to be having problems with his harness. The Senator paid it no heed. The crowd bayed their excitement and threw cushions and hunks of bread at each other. The Master of Games looked at the Senator and every eye in the Circus followed him. The Senator nodded, gave the crowd a final regal gesture and sat down. The Master of Games turned to the crowd.

'Citizens of Rome,' he declaimed. 'These games honour Consilius Sejanus. Let them begin.'

'Call that a fucking introduction?' yelled Galba, waving his arms like a demagogue. 'The man was a genuine Roman hero!' The excited cries of the crowd drowned him out. The Master of Games smiled indulgently down at the race track. Galba pounded his fist on the chariot rim with mock frustration. Serpicus put out an arm and then froze as Galba suddenly staggered and stopped shouting. Serpicus watched as Galba reached with awkward fingers inside his tunic and found Ox's bottle. He pushed the stopper off with a thumb and downed the remainder in one swallow. This time the drug took longer to work and he did not move so freely, but at least he could still stand.

Cassius saw it. He leant across. 'Don't worry, fat man. You will soon be with Consilius in Hades.'

'Only if you're there first,' growled Galba.

'Be calm,' Serpicus said urgently. 'He's just trying to upset you.'

'He doesn't have to try,' snarled Galba. 'His existence on this earth upsets me.'

The Master of Games leant forward again, received a signal from the Senator and looked back at the contestants.

'Ready?'

All three men raised their arms in the signal.

'Ready.'

The stadium became quiet. The Master of Games waited for a moment, enjoying the weight of every person's eyes upon him.

Then he signalled to the judge, and the judge opened his hand.

The silk rope strung taut between the statues of Hermes suddenly slackened, and then fell to the ground like a golden snake.

Although Serpicus was worried about Galba and distracted by Cassius' insults, long practice allowed a part of him to assess the coming race. In the near silence that hung between the release of the rope and the crowd's first scream, as every man inhaled, he looked up the course.

The arena track was the usual bow-shot out, bow-shot back in distance, a flat oval with each sharply curving end marked by stone cones. The outer edge of the oval was a stone wall, smooth and high, without obstructions. The danger, as always, lay at the two ends. Even if three chariots racing flat out could synchronize themselves to hit the corner line abreast and turn in exact formation all the way round – which was impossible – there was still not room for all of them. Someone was going to hit the wall, or smash a wheel on the stone markers, or get trapped in between. Serpicus raised his whip. He knew that normal tactics didn't apply; there weren't enough chariots in the race to hang back and rely on the other drivers to weed each other out, and then come through at the end. The man who was in front at the first marker would stand a good chance of winning the race. Anyone who knew anything about racing would see that, and all three of them knew about racing.

The rope hit the ground, and the horses reared as each driver laid his whip across their backs. Galba almost fell backwards as the chariot lurched forward, but closed his fingers on the reins at the last moment.

The sudden noise closed in around Serpicus, and as he automatically brought the whip down and twisted the reins around his fingers he felt his heart pound. He had not raced for two years, and everyone knew that only regular racing allowed a man to keep his competitive edge. Cassius had proved that he would kill a man if he had to in order to win, and was quite good enough to win without needing to. Serpicus couldn't allow that to happen. Only the winner would stand in front of Blaesus.

Serpicus didn't wait to see how Galba was doing. He forced the horses forward with a vicious crack of the whip over their backs. Within moments he was galloping at full tilt towards the first turn. The chariot bucked as it hit a hole in the track and as he reached out to steady himself he saw Cassius just behind him. Serpicus was on the inside; if he got to the turn first then he would come out of it in the lead. If he failed, Cassius would make him give way. It was simple. He brought the whip down again.

He could just see the nose of Cassius' horse from the corner of his eye. The chariot driver's rule of thumb; anything less than half a length isn't enough. Anything more than that is control.

He roared the horses on and they leapt forward with a squeal, pulling almost a length ahead. The noise of their hooves was drowned by the howling crowd but Serpicus felt their battering rhythm under his feet. He looked up. The corner raced towards him. Cassius was too far behind, he would have to drop back and allow Serpicus to turn first, keeping pace with him while hoping that he would turn too tightly and be forced to slow down. Serpicus pulled the right rein hard, swinging out into Cassius' path. A dense cloud of fine dry dust rose from his wheel. Then he pulled left and went into the corner. Serpicus felt the chariot skid on the corner but held his line. For an instant the inside wheel lifted off the track. Serpicus threw his weight to the side and the wheel smashed down again. Then he was round the turn and headlong down the back straight. He could see lines of faces lining the track, leaning forward, their mouths open, their words crushed together into one long scream.

He risked a glance backward. Cassius was right behind him, his face contorted into a leer. Galba was a full length behind Cassius but was still in touch.

The next turn was coming near. He could hear the pounding hooves of Cassius' team just behind him. He pulled slightly right again, forcing Cassius to hold back as before. While he was this far in front there was little Cassius could do to prevent him.

Then, just for an instant, he looked up, high into the crowd.

Time stopped.

The Senator's box had two new arrivals. They had their arms around each other.

Serpicus was surrounded by silence.

The screaming faces moved but seemed struck dumb; the hooves still pounded at the ground but he didn't hear them.

They were watching him.

He was too far away to see the expression on Cato's face, and yet he could see the colour of Antonia's eyes.

For the time it took him to see them he stopped urging the horses forward, and for three strides they faltered, and in that time Cassius was upon him.

The screams of the crowd as Cassius pulled level cut through Serpicus' reverie, jolting him into instinctive action. He cracked the whip over the horses' heads. The animals' ears went back and they dipped their heads, their mouths tossing flecks of foam back towards the driver. Cassius was almost level, but couldn't quite pull ahead. The turn was upon them. There was no chance of both chariots turning together, and nowhere for Serpicus to go. He held his line and waited for the shudder under his feet that would mean collision and the end. The sound of the crowd and the blood roaring in his head drowned everything else.

Then the sun was in his eyes, dazzling him. He was around the turn and out the other side, and he was still alive. Cassius had dropped back slightly to avoid the collision, and then whipped the horses as he was at the apex of the turn. The chariot reared up and came out of the corner on one wheel. It bounced down and shot forward again. The crowd screamed derision at Cassius for pulling out of the collision. He responded by a frenzy of blows to the horses, and they pulled almost level with Serpicus again.

Cassius raised his hand, and Serpicus looked at his face and knew what he was going to do. Cassius' wrist flexed and Serpicus remembered what happened to the young charioteer who lost his life in Serpicus' last race. The horses were pulling the wildly veering chariot flat out and Serpicus dared not let go of the reins. He could do nothing to prevent it. He braced himself against the chariot sides, wrapping the reins around the hand farthest from Cassius and waited; hoping he could catch the whip as it came down and pull Cassius off balance.

There was a sound like a flat hand slapping a polished wooden table. Above the screams of the crowd Serpicus heard Cassius cry out in pain. He risked another glance in his direction. Cassius was leaning over the side of his chariot, his right arm outstretched, blood dripping from his wrist. His hand was empty, his whip gone. Serpicus could see the leather thong trailing in the dust. For a moment Serpicus thought Cassius had dropped it, then he saw Galba and realized what had happened. As Cassius raised his arm to flick the greased leather forward to encircle Serpicus' wrist, Galba had wrapped his own whip around Cassius' arm. That was the slap Serpicus heard.

As Serpicus watched, Galba tossed the handle of the whip towards Cassius, where it fell amongst the hooves and wheels.

Cassius pulled frantically, but one end was firmly attached to his arm and the other was trapped around the axle of his chariot. He hauled at the reins to slow the horses down, but he was off balance and leaning to the right. His horses were well trained. Even though there was nowhere to go, they swung to the right as the reins commanded them, to where Galba's chariot was racing almost level with them. The wheel on Cassius' chariot touched the corner of Galba's and erupted in a shower of splinters. The chariot crashed down onto the track and then spun over like a thrown child's toy. Cassius' horses were knocked sideways and fell in a squealing froth, their hooves stabbing at the air. Over the howls of the crowd Serpicus heard one high-pitched scream and saw Cassius tumble forwards and disappear under a cloud of sand and dust. The crowd threw themselves forward to look over the edge and see what was happening.

Serpicus eased his horses to the right and suddenly he was almost at the corner. The horses pulled smoothly around the turn and he was heading back the opposite way. He slowed slightly and looked back across to the other side.

Cassius' horses were squealing in pain and terror, pulling panic-stricken against their traces. The chariot behind them was almost destroyed. Galba hadn't fared much better. He and his horses were wedged between Cassius' chariot and the low wall. One animal had a broken leg, the other was slumped on its knees on the ground. Galba was still just about standing, leant against the wall with one arm outstretched. The other hand was pressed to his side and he was bent over in pain. He waved Serpicus on. As Serpicus passed Galba he saw Cassius' crumpled body lying still in the centre of the track. The crowd was standing up nearby. Those who had bet on Cassius screamed abuse and cast about frantically for things to throw at him. Serpicus' supporters urged him on. He pulled the horses back to a canter and did another circuit.

As he passed the post at the end of the arena he saw the Master of Games and shouted up to him.

'Get some help for my friend.'

The Master of Games nodded. 'They are coming now.'

Decius jumped down from the seating area and ran past Serpicus' trotting horses towards the wrecked chariots at the other end. Other men made their slower way up the track carrying a stretcher and a box full of bandages.

Serpicus kept the horses moving and waved to the crowd as he passed. Some shouted to him to speed up, even though there was no one else to race. Serpicus paid no attention. He saluted Ox as he went past and did the remaining three circuits. As he crossed the finish line there was a glad roar from the crowd.

He jumped down off the chariot and ran to where the two chariots were still entangled and pressed against the wall. The crowd had largely lost interest in them. Some men who had bet against Serpicus stayed to shout unenthusiastic abuse as he passed; the rest talked about the next race. Decius was standing beside Galba, who was cursing loudly at one of the medical slaves trying to persuade him to climb down from the chariot.

'Tell them to look after the horses,' Galba said to Decius, his voice weak but insistent. His head dropped as he gasped for air and he gesticulated with the hand that wasn't pressed against his side in the centre of a large red stain.

'They are already,' said Serpicus. The slaves had managed to calm three of the horses down enough to disentangle them and lead them away. The fourth, the one caught between the wall and the two chariots, was dead. The Thracian looked down at Serpicus, his face agitated, eyes rolling.

'Tell them to look after the horses,' he said again.

'Don't worry,' Serpicus said gently. 'The horses are fine.' He held out a hand to help him down. Galba appeared to look at it and then looked away again. Serpicus moved a hand in front of Galba's face. His eyes didn't react.

The noise of the crowd suddenly became louder and more sibilant. Serpicus felt a tug on his tunic. Decius was pointing down the track. Serpicus turned and saw armed soldiers marching briskly towards them. He hesitated and then relaxed. There was nowhere to run to, no possibility of escape. He leant across to whisper to Galba.

'The soldiers are coming for me. Stay here with Decius.'

Galba started to say something and then his knees

buckled. Decius caught him as he fell off the chariot and let him slide slowly to the ground. Galba lay still with his eyes closed. Decius knelt beside him. Serpicus put a hand on Decius' shoulder and the young man looked up at him, his face pale with grief.

Serpicus turned to face the soldiers. There were ten of them, Praetorians, Sejanus' own bodyguard, led by a centurion. They stopped a few yards short of Serpicus' chariot. 'You two are to come with us.'

There was a drowning cough. Serpicus looked down. Galba was lying on the ground. The slave was working to staunch the blood that now flowed freely from his wound. It didn't look as though the slave was winning the race. Galba raised an admonitory finger to Serpicus.

'Mind you don't forget . . . about us little people, now you're going to be famous,' he croaked.

'I won't,' Serpicus said. Galba's hand dropped back to the ground.

The centurion beckoned to Serpicus to step forward. Six of the Praetorians formed a guard around him. The other four stood around the chariot. Serpicus put a hand on the centurion's arm, gestured at Galba and said, 'He should be with a doctor.'

The centurion glanced down at the wide circle of crimson blood that stained the sand around Galba.

'He's done for,' the centurion said. 'Hippocrates himself couldn't save him.'

The slave leant forward suddenly, paused, then lowered Galba's head gently to the ground. A bloody spume rimed his lips.

'He is dead,' the slave said quietly to Serpicus. 'The

wound was deep. There was nothing I could have done.'

Serpicus looked down at Galba's body. 'I know,' he said, and knelt down to brush the sand from his face and close Galba's eyes. 'Don't worry, old friend,' he whispered. 'Wherever you are now, keep watching. There'll be something to cheer about soon.'

The centurion laughed dismissively. 'If you aren't going to kiss him, then let's get going.'

The soldiers formed two ranks with Serpicus between them. A messenger came running down the stairs and across the sand to the centurion. 'Bring all of them.'

'Including the dead one?'

'All of them.'

The centurion looked down at Galba and shrugged. 'Bring him.'

'He's dead,' said Decius, standing in their way. 'You can't . . .'

The nearest soldier, a dark and scarred veteran, brought his closed fist up backhanded, snapping Decius' mouth shut and knocking him backwards onto the sand. A thin dark line of blood flowed from the corner of his mouth.

'All finished?' said the centurion. 'Good.'

The soldiers lifted Galba's body carefully off the ground and the little procession headed for the steps to the Senator's box.

'Careful, boys,' someone in the crowd shouted. 'He drove well.'

'He did,' shouted a deep voice that Serpicus recognized. 'He's done nothing wrong. Where are they taking him?' Ox never had trouble in getting people's attention.

A chorus of voices agreed with him. Serpicus looked around. The crowd was paying attention to them now. There was nothing else in the arena to watch except them, it might lead to something interesting, and some of them wanted the chance to cheer Serpicus when he received the winner's laurel wreath. Several voices called out to Serpicus and one man held up an over-flowing handful of money and tossed a coin to him with a shout of excitement. The centurion picked it up and handed it to Serpicus. 'I had a fistful of money on you at seven to one to win,' he said. 'They're likely going to get me to kill you, but if they don't then I'll buy you a drink myself when this is over.'

Serpicus looked to see how Decius was doing. The young man was walking up the steps with his head held high. Not bad for a youngster who's probably about to die, Serpicus thought.

They got to the top of the stairs and walked into Blaesus' box. Serpicus could hear footsteps behind him and excited voices. The crowd was following, eager to see what would happen, and the Captain of the Guard barked orders. The guards crossed their spears and held the crowd back.

The soldiers put Galba's stretcher on the ground. Blaesus was still in his chair. Cato appeared behind the Senator. He gestured to the centurion and Serpicus felt his arms grasped and pinned behind him. Cato moved to one side to come forward.

With the force of a blow, Serpicus saw Antonia, stand-ing in the shadow at the back of the box.

The soldiers behind Serpicus had his arms held so

tightly that he felt if he moved even slightly his shoulders would dislocate. Decius was in a similar grip, and his face was tense with the effort of not showing his pain.

The crowd pressed up against each other. Something was, it seemed, about to happen. They leant forward with interest.

Cato stood in front of them, his hair freshly pomaded and his clothes spotless and finely made. Not an ordinary spy at all. He looked nothing like the morose character who had stood on the dock at Genoa. Serpicus could smell the scented oils on the dark man's skin from where he stood. Serpicus looked at him and thought of Galba, Drenthe, Severus, Brutus, and all the others who had died or lost everything they had because of his intrigues. Serpicus' fists clenched.

In his right hand Cato held a scroll like a baton. He gestured with it and Antonia came forward from the shadows at the back of the box until she stood slightly behind him.

And then Serpicus saw more movement in the place where she had come from. Two slaves were standing in the shadows, and each was in charge of a small child. The slaves had them held tight and a hand over each child's mouth, but one of the children wriggled an arm free and reached towards him before the slave could pinion it again. The sight punched his heart. He made himself look away.

Antonia was as groomed as Cato was and there were gold threads twined into her hair. Seeing her alive filled Serpicus' chest and stopped his thoughts; all he could think was that he preferred her without colour on her face and in simple clothes, but she looked impossibly beautiful to him. Blaesus sat back in his chair and watched her, his thoughts written on his face. Serpicus wanted to look away but his head wouldn't move and his eyes refused to close. Cato saw it, and, with a malicious curl of his lips, held out a hand to her. She took it and came forward to stand beside him. Cato indicated that she should sit down. He nodded to the soldiers that they should release their prisoners. Then he stepped forward until he was only the length of Serpicus' arm away.

'So, Serpicus, you live still.' His voice was cultured and mocking.

'Yes,' Serpicus said, his voice harsh through the thick dust coating his throat. Cato reached out and turned his face to one side with a finger.

'You have my mark still, I see.'

Serpicus grimaced. 'I never travel without it. It helps me remember.'

Cato glanced at Antonia and then back at Serpicus with a slight smile. 'So,' he said slowly. 'What am I to do with you?'

'He won the race!' came a deep voice from the crowd nearby. Other voices agreed. 'Give him the wreath!' Serpicus didn't turn to look, he didn't need to. Ox was still on his side.

Cato looked amused. 'It seems that even criminals have their supporters. I suppose there will always be those who will bet on lost causes.'

Decius raised his head and spat bloodily on the ground at Cato's feet. 'Put us on trial!' he gasped hoarsely. 'If you say we are criminals, put us on trial, and listen while we tell the world about your crimes.' The nearest soldier put a hand on Decius' shoulder and held him still.

Cato's expression didn't change. He leant forward and tapped Decius on the chest with the scroll. 'You miss the point of the justice system,' he said cheerfully. 'It will be you on trial, and therefore it will be your crimes that will be discussed, not mine.'

Serpicus still couldn't take his eyes from Antonia. He told her once that it didn't matter what she had done, but it was a lie. It mattered. He cared too much. He had been jealous, the one thing he swore he would never be. He had doubted her, hurt her more than he thought he was capable of doing. But now, looking at her standing beside his enemy, dressed and made up so that she hardly looked like herself, he knew that he loved her and he knew that only loving her mattered. And he knew that something had changed between them, and he had lost her.

So Serpicus stared at what he had lost and didn't speak, and Cato smiled and played with him as bored children play with a captive animal, waiting with a shine in their eyes for the moment that the creature shows weakness and so invites the cruelty they intend.

Cato opened his mouth to speak again, and then lifted his head with a slight show of annoyance at a disturbance in the crowd around him. Decius turned to grin at Serpicus. 'Sounds like Ox has been having fun,' he whispered. Blood flecked his lips.

'What's happening there?' Cato gestured irritably to an officer nearby, who took four soldiers and pushed his way into the crowd.

Everyone in the crowd turned to see what was going on, including the guards watching. Serpicus saw Decius move sideways and then take a silent step past the soldier between him and Cato. Concealed in his hand was the sharp knife that every charioteer carried.

Cato was looking in the opposite direction and wouldn't have seen Decius coming. His fist gripped the knife tight and his body tensed. Cato was a dead man.

As Decius' hand drew back for the killing thrust his wrist was held. Decius turned, desperation on his face, to see Antonia close beside him. She didn't speak, but held his wrist fast. A fold of her dress hid both their hands. She stood pressed against him. Their eyes met and Serpicus saw him hesitate. To kill Cato Decius would have to kill her first. He glanced back at Serpicus, desperation in his face. 'No,' she whispered, and released him. The fabric of her dress fell to her side, and his hand was empty. The dagger was gone.

'Hey!' The guard realized with a start that Decius was no longer there. With his shoulders slumped Decius allowed himself to be pulled back and shoved towards Serpicus.

'Why did she stop me?' said Decius in a broken whisper.

'I don't know her any more,' Serpicus said softly. He watched with something like fascination as she leant forward to speak into Cato's ear. Cato listened, looking at Serpicus, and then smiled, in a way that made Serpicus know that he was the subject of her suggestion, and that whatever she was saying pleased Cato because it meant unpleasantness for him.

The disturbance in the crowd was getting closer. The Praetorians who had gone to see what the matter was were officiously escorting a man in the cloak of an Imperial courier back towards them. The noise of the crowd became louder, more excited. The message that the courier carried had, as such things somehow always are, been discovered and shared before it was even delivered.

Blaesus got up heavily from his chair and moved forward. He might be content to let Cato deal with the chariot race and the German criminals, but an Imperial courier was a matter for a senator.

Cato's eyes narrowed. He was still listening to Antonia but with less attention. He raised his arm in an automatic greeting to the courier.

Antonia turned away from Cato and towards Serpicus, and their eyes met. A breeze spread her hair out as if it was on a pillow and for the first time she smiled.

It was the same smile she gave him the day they were married, when her hand was in his, as they hung the two halves of an ivory amulet around each other's necks. Serpicus saw her face relax, and without seeing what had happened he knew what she had done.

Cato leant forward as if he were suddenly very tired. His left hand went to his side and his right reached out to the nearest soldier for support.

The soldiers finally managed to manhandle the courier through the crowd. The man shook himself as if covered in dust and held out a scroll emblazoned with the Imperial seal. Cato looked at it for a moment as if he had no idea what it was, and then dropped to one knee. A red stain appeared between the fingers of his left hand and blood flowed down the side of his tunic. The Captain of the Guard snapped an order and his men surrounded the Imperial messenger. A woman in the crowd screamed and the edge of the crowd moved as those in front tried to get away and those behind surged to see what was happening. Blaesus stepped forward and then recoiled as Cato put a blood-covered hand onto the ground to support himself. The Praetorian centurion saw the blood and jumped forward, drawing his sword. He ran up the three steps and knelt beside Cato. The dying man whispered something to him and then rolled slowly sideways onto the marble floor and lay still. Blood flowed slowly across the stone from beneath his body.

'No!'

Serpicus supposed he must have shouted, although the sound seemed to come from a long way off. He threw himself forward. His captors came after him but got in each other's way. Serpicus leant sideways to avoid a stabbing thrust from the nearest soldier and hammered with his fist on the man's forearm while wresting the sword from his deadened fingers.

The centurion jumped up and slashed at Serpicus. He pulled back, but not enough, and the edge opened a deep cut in his shoulder. Serpicus shouted with pain and lunged forward. The centurion reached out to seize Antonia by the arm and pulled her between Serpicus and himself. Serpicus hesitated, and in that moment she turned and stabbed at the centurion's face with the knife.

The centurion cried out and seized her wrist to pull the knife away. Blood poured down his cheek and neck.

He cursed and drove his sword deep into Antonia's side.

Several in the crowd cried out. She made no sound. The centurion pulled his sword free and she sank slowly to the ground. He stepped back and two of his men moved to stand between him and Serpicus.

Serpicus ignored them. He dropped the sword and knelt by Antonia. Her eyes were closed but as Serpicus' hands lifted her head he felt the faint pulse of life in her neck.

'Why?' he said.

'It had to be done,' she breathed.

'It should have been me.' Tears streamed down his face. She coughed once and a thin trickle of blood seeped from one corner of her mouth and ran across her cheek into her hair. She moved her head slightly from side to side. Serpicus wiped the blood from her face with his hand. 'Would you not have lived for me, for us?'

Her eyes opened. She reached up and touched his face with a finger that trembled as it traced a faint line on his cheek.

'Once I knew you doubted me, what was there left for me to live for?'

He tried to say something but couldn't speak. Her hand dropped from his face and she pressed her palm flat against his chest.

'I see you,' she said. She coughed, the sound rattling in her chest. 'I know you understand now, how it was for me. But you can only break a cup once.' Her hand fluttered against his skin. 'I know you loved me. I know that you believed in me, once. That is enough.' Her hand dropped away from him and her gaze held him with an intensity that contrasted with the fading whisper that was her voice, as if she was funnelling her last strength into her eyes. 'I never doubted you.'

Then her eyes closed and the pulse against his finger-tips died away.

Serpicus reached for the sword. The two soldiers standing between him and the centurion braced themselves. Behind them Serpicus could see the centurion striding to the back of the box, where he also saw the two small figures held by the slaves and he knew what the centurion intended. Cato's last order had been for revenge, revenge on his whole family. Serpicus saw the sword raised over them and opened his mouth to shout, knowing it was too late.

Something flashed in the sunlight and the centurion's arm halted at its highest point. A woman screamed, a single sound, loud and shrill. The centurion made a choking sound and staggered. His arm dropped to his side, and he fell slowly backwards.

A small bone-handled knife protruded from where his neck joined his shoulders.

Everything stopped moving.

Serpicus spun round, looking to see where the knife had come from. A legionary shouted and several soldiers ran forward. Snake's arm moved like his namesake and the legionary who had shouted fell backwards with a choking cry. A moment later the other two were also bleeding on the ground. The crowd shouted with alarm and fought to get away.

'Stop!' shouted Blaesus above the noise. The soldiers who were pushing their way past people to get to Snake hesitated and looked back, confusion on their faces. Ox grabbed Snake by the collar and shoved the Cretan behind him. He hissed an order to one of his men and in a moment Snake was nowhere to be seen.

The Imperial courier was standing alone, waiting. Blaesus stepped carefully around the bodies in front of him and held out a hand for the scroll. The messenger didn't move. Blaesus blinked with surprise then recovered his composure.

'I am Blaesus.'

The messenger looked at him for a few moments, then turned to the Captain of the Guard. He unrolled the scroll and showed it to the Captain. 'You recognize this seal?' The Captain nodded. The messenger began to read.

'The man Aelius Sejanus, who has been promoted and repeatedly honoured by the Emperor and appointed by Him as His Regent, acting for Him in all things, is hereby pronounced a traitor and an enemy to Rome. His treachery . . .'

The rest was lost under a gale of excitement and surprise, which spread the news around the arena like the dry sand that a breeze blows across the stone floor of a beach-front villa. The messenger waited calmly until he could be heard again and then continued.

'His treachery is the more vile because of the ingratitude it contains, as well as the offence it represents to the person of the Emperor and so to the people and city of Rome. His position is dissolved and his power ended in all its aspects, his lands and possessions are forfeit. His person is to be placed under immediate arrest, along with all those who have served him and whose names are attached, and held to await trial.'

Blaesus stiffened, caught between bluster and fear. Then the messenger made up his mind for him by directing the Captain to arrest him. The messenger waited, and then continued.

'The friends of Sejanus are the enemies of Rome. This is the word of Tiberius.'

The rest was confusion. Men shouted, cheered, cursed, circling each other in a storm of argument and fear.

At the centre of the storm a man sat on the ground with his wife's head upon his lap and his friends lying beside him. Two children held onto him as if he were a raft in a flood. The maelstrom circled above them and they heard none of it.

40

Serpicus stood near the top of a low hill outside the city walls. Smoke coiled upwards from three dying fires in front of him, emerging slowly from between the smouldering wood lying in the ashes, then reaching swiftly upwards into the early-morning sky as if it sensed its freedom.

He stared at the ashes for a long time, thinking of his friends. Antonia and Galba, gone. Brutus and Drenthe, gone.

Before the fires were lit Decius had stepped forward and put something between Galba's hands, lifting his stiff fingers and replacing them carefully on top of it. For a moment Serpicus hadn't known what it was, then he recognized Brutus' battered leather cap.

While the fires burned Decius and Snake waited a little way off, leaving Serpicus to his thoughts. As the smoke calmed they came to stand closer.

'What will you do now?' Snake asked. Serpicus took a deep slow breath. The dawn air was sharp and clear.

'Go back,' he said.

'Where to?'

'Gelbheim.'

'What will you do?'

'Help rebuild it.'

'I mean, how will you live?'

Serpicus took another breath and looked up at the paling sky. 'I don't know. I'll never catch another animal for the games again, that's for certain. He looked enquiringly at them. 'The business is yours, if you want it.'

Decius smiled. 'Thanks, but I've seen enough animals. I think I'll be having a word with your friend with the chariot.'

Serpicus looked surprised. 'You want to race?'

Decius nodded. 'I'd like to try again.'

Serpicus thought about it for a little while. 'You're good with horses. And you've seen what can happen, so you're going in with your eyes open. I won't try and persuade you out of it.' He raised an eyebrow at Snake. The Cretan shook his head.

'I'll be going home too. I've been in Rome too long. I want to see if the girls look as good as I remember.'

Serpicus reached out and they clasped hands firmly for a long moment. 'Good luck,' he said.

They stood in silence for a while. Then Decius spoke without looking at Serpicus.

'Where is Marcus?'

Serpicus' lips tightened. 'In Germany. Part of the permanent garrison.'

'Odd that he didn't go down with Sejanus and his cronies.'

Serpicus shrugged. 'He's a good soldier, the sort they can use. Nothing was proved against him. And garrison duty in Germany in peacetime isn't a promotion. More like exile, for an ambitious man.'

Decius hesitated. 'Do you think he knows about what happened to Consilius? People can be unreasonable about things like the death of a brother. He might want to talk to you about that one day.'

Serpicus shrugged. 'Then on that day no doubt we'll talk.'

'And if the conversation doesn't please him?'

Serpicus stared at the wisps of smoke that still seeped from the three piles of ashes in front of them. 'Then I'll have to pray that the gods give me the strength to bear the weight of his unhappiness somehow.'

In Rome everything was changing. Sejanus was dead, summarily executed and his body torn to pieces. Blaesus joined his nephew soon afterward, although he at least got a trial. Relatives of the dozens of men whose estates he had stolen came forward and denounced him. Their evidence didn't get them their inheritances back – the property of anyone condemned for treason is forfeit to the Emperor, and nobody wanted to be the one to tell Tiberius that he was holding their lands illegally – but they turned out in their thousands to see Blaesus spread on a wheel in the Forum and then strangled. It was rumoured that the executioner had been well paid not to hurry the job. If not recompense for their losses, his cries were at least some consolation.

When Blaesus' accounts were audited after his death it

was found that he had been buying up huge areas of land in northern Italy cheaply, aided by the unwillingness of Romans to live and work there if the area was under threat from invasion by German tribes. The revolt drove prices down even further. There were also payments to men who earned their living as assassins. It was never proved, but the sudden and violent deaths of three tribal chiefs, all of whom had been against the revolt, were assumed to be connected. Blaesus had taken out huge short-term loans, secured against his existing purchases and those to come. He couldn't afford to have anything but a full-scale rebellion, couldn't let the German tribes seem peaceful, not until he had bought all the land he wanted at rock-bottom prices. There were letters in his files that showed that the leaders of the Treveri tribe were a matter of particular concern.

Also in Blaesus' accounts were letters and bills from Cato, confirming his knowledge of the plan and participation in it. A percentage of the profits, which, had the plan succeeded, would have been enormous, were earmarked for him. It was clear that his position as head of intelligence-gathering made him indispensable for the plan's success. The full extent to which he misused his position never fully emerged.

As soon as Blaesus fell from power the German revolt collapsed. The Roman coin that funded it dried up and the tribes went home. Twenty years earlier Tiberius would have exacted a fearful price for their rebellion, but he was old and wanted only to be left alone. He sent another legion to the Rhine, took more hostages and accepted the oaths of loyalty from the tribes.

Even though his Regent was dead, the Emperor remained in Capri and the Senate governed Rome in his absence. Tiberius appointed no one man or group of men to represent him, but privately allowed each one to think they had his favour and then let them compete for his attention. This ensured that even the mildest accretion of power to any man or party meant that accusing letters went by fast ship to Capri. Tiberius didn't need Cato's secret agents any more to tell him who was growing powerful in Rome; the factions there were only too happy to do it for him.

The seasons were changing. Serpicus could feel winter still in the clear dew that pearled the grass and the cold earth underneath it, but there was a promise of spring in the way the sun fell on the river-meadow and in the flowers emerging along the banks.

Serpicus reached up and lifted the children off the tired horse. They didn't speak, but looked down at the valley as if gathering all their breath for a great shout of joy. Then his daughter turned, tilting her face up and squinting at him.

'Is this where we will live now?' she said doubtfully, as if it might still be snatched away.

He looked down at her. 'Yes.'

The child's face seemed to glow at him in the sharp light and she looked back at it again. Several young men appeared from a wicker shelter near the river and dived into the slow-moving water.

'Can we go down?'

He smiled, and the two children whooped and ran

headlong down the hill towards the village. He tugged gently on the rein and the horse grudgingly left off grazing and followed him in the children's wake.

The children reached the bottom of the hill and slowed down. There was no wall around the small group of houses, but even so the village looked bigger close up. They trotted uncertainly towards it, and then ran sideways towards the river.

As Serpicus approached the nearest house he saw a dog, a thin, sorrowful-looking creature, come out towards them from behind it. It stopped when it saw him and stood, one foot raised, sniffing the air. Then a familiar red-haired figure, not exactly fat but nowhere near thin either, appeared carrying fish from the river. He saw the children and called cheerfully to them. Serpicus couldn't hear what he said, but the children waved back to him. Then Hansi looked towards Serpicus. He stood a long time without moving, then raised his hand in salute.

Serpicus took a deep breath, pulling his shoulders back. There was a sweet smell in the air. A tangle of undergrowth now covered the soil scorched by the Roman fire, a green canopy spotted thickly with wild roses. The river idled calmly by and cattle browsed the dark grass at its edge.

As he breathed out slowly he heard the harsh *chukk-ah* of a hawk in the air high above him.

He raised his arm in reply to Hansi and walked towards the village.

THE END

Author's Note

Writers of historical novels are both helped and hindered by their subject. Any work of fiction that uses historical figures, events and locations faces the challenge of finessing fictional characters and stories into the immovable historical facts. Sometimes history lends the story a hand, and the writer seizes on these coincidences with a glad cry. More often, the writer must somehow write around the fact that the requirements of their story mean, for example, that two of their characters need to be in the same place at the same time, when history records that they could never actually have met, or that two places are five hundred miles apart and their wounded hero needs to travel between them in a day on foot. Much of the time, this sort of problem can be got around with a bit of judicious nudging of time and taking advantage of holes in the historical narrative. Sometimes this nudging and manoeuvring doesn't work. The writer can, I believe, take any liberties they choose in writing a story, but if the story does violence to history – particularly in a way that might lead a reader to have a false impression, or make it likely that they will accept something as a fact when it is not – then this should be acknowledged. Call me old-fashioned.

So, my confession runs as follows. Sejanus' fall and execution were actually in AD 31, not some ten years earlier as I suggest here. I have characterized the Treveri as unequivocally German, when in fact they were probably at least as much of Gaulish extraction. I suggest that their lands were about a week's winter march from the Alps, when they were in reality a good deal further away. I imply that the Teutoburg Forest was near the lands of the Treveri. The exact historical location of the forest is uncertain, but it was definitely several hundred miles north of where I place it in the story. Everything else is as accurate as I have been able to make it, and any mistakes or misapprehensions are mine alone.

Novels aren't history lessons, but with luck they might inspire one. If anyone wants to have a look at the marvellous books written by people much more learned and careful than me that went into my researching the background to *Hawk*, drop me an email (g.green@lancaster.ac.uk) and I'll send you a list.